Soon Forgotten
L.R. Benfield

To Val.

love.

Lena.

Prologue

She switched off the tape where her brother insisted he'd end up in a mental home and turned to the doctor expectantly, wondering if he'd grasped its importance - but then why should he.

'That recording was made seven months after his operation, doctor. That's how coherent he was.'

'Hmmm … I see what you mean. He did sound far more lucid then - but.'

She knew there would be a 'but' and crossed her arms and legs in irritation, guessing the excuse about to be given.

'You have to understand Mrs Bowers any damage to the brain will take time to settle down and heal. Unfortunately, it often deteriorates further whilst doing so … albeit slowly.'

This wasn't what she wanted to hear though and although she'd heard this excuse before she believed it was a copout ... but what did she know. Even his previous doctors had said - they weren't certain what the long term held.

Yet still she remained hopeful as the doctor looked through her brother's notes, praying this time there'd be some positive news, or at least what improvements might be expected.

It had been several months since she'd last visited her brother and although six years had passed since he'd initially entered this home; it was the first time she felt he'd made some obvious progress. Having suffered several bad setbacks, she'd given up any hope of him ever getting better and he deserved a break.

'A square peg in a round hole is what they told me, doctor... do you think there maybe chance of rehab now, given he's showing signs of improving?'

The doctor pondered on this for a while.

'Now how can I put this?' He ran his fingers threw his well-groomed hair and then turned towards her. 'If he had received rehabilitation at an earlier stage, he may have stood a good chance of improvement... but as it's been sometime since his initial operation I wouldn't hold much hope. You see as I've said before, the brain starts to settle down as it heals itself and stops at a certain level. The problem is, once this happens it's difficult to kick-start again, especially if left un-stimulated.'

The doctor placed his papers back in their file and turned again to face her, 'You have to remember Mrs Bowers your brother has become what we call institutionalised here and clearly feels safer amongst us. What would be the point of disrupting that?'

'Oh, I appreciate that, doctor, but it's annoying as my sister and I fought tooth and nail to get our brother the rehabilitation he deserved and from the very offset. They just kept insisting he wasn't good enough... they wouldn't even listen to us. I think everyone thought we were trouble makers ... made worse by his wife no doubt.'

Her eyes filled with tears as she thought of her poor brother. But pride wouldn't let her cry. She had prayed this doctor would be different but it seemed he was no different from the rest.

'The thing is doctor... I understand my brother's predicament, but I think he could still do so much better even now. With the right care I'm certain he could have some kind of near normal life - even if his wife doesn't think so.'

'Well, possibly ... and I do agree about his wife's lack of understanding ... being his next of kin that is, but' –

Holding up her hand in a gesture to stop him, she then said, 'the less said about her, the better,' she didn't want to go down that path again and quickly changed the subject. 'Having said all of that, doctor, there's no way my sister and I would want our brother moved at this present time. He has a lovely room and seems very well cared for. The only thing that's missing is help with improving his life skills... surely that's important.'

'This is a care home Mrs Bowers; we don't have those facilities or expertise.'

'Yes and as I said - a round peg in a square hole... my brother was only fifty five when he came here; it's a shameful waste of life. He was a good man; he just loved the wrong woman.'

The doctor nodded as if he understood. Yet what could he say, it was really up to his wife to be fighting his corner and as that had never happened before it wasn't going to now.

'Can I ask you a question doctor?' she said, not waiting for his answer. 'Do you believe there are evil people in this world or just those who've experienced terrible traumas, changing their perception on society?'

3

'As a psychiatrist that's a difficult one to answer, but I do know what a person is capable of when under excessive stress.'

'Have you ever read a book called, 'The people of the Lie' by M. Scott Peck?' she asked her face very serious.

'No, I can't say I have.'

'Well you really should, its brilliant. The book is based on the author's research as a psychiatrist into the existence of evil in people. Only he believes some are simply born that way, although sometimes passed from parent to child. He feels these people should be acknowledged as such and therefore treated appropriately and not just with pills and drugs.'

'Sounds very interesting Mrs Bowers, I must make a point of reading that book.' And he made a note on his pad. While her thoughts turned back to her brother and how he'd been treated over the years by his so called nearest and dearest. As she believed, his wife's actions over this time could only be viewed as evil. Or how else was her psychopathic behaviour to be explained.

Although some might prefer to call her a sociopath - a person who was far more personal, their lying even more convincing. And if it had been only for her actions leading up to her husband's demise and her ill treatment of him after, this was enough to convince her, her conclusions were right.

Concerned, she often wondered how it was that so many people like her sister-in-law ... psychopaths, crazies, call them what you like appeared to be living amongst us today. Hidden and yet functioning in a society that didn't realise or didn't seem to care - and with many holding top jobs too.

Their craving for money and power, completely inconceivable, as were their overly inflated egos. While their ability to feel empathy or any compassion at all appeared almost non –existent. How can this be?

Not wanting to keep the doctor from his needy patients, she then said her goodbyes; shaking his hand firmly and thanking him for his time. And even though she'd not received the news she'd wanted to hear, she was pleased nonetheless she'd managed to air her views - hoping this may trigger something off. But she doubted it very much.

Closing the heavy wooden doors behind her keen to be on her way she suddenly felt saddened by the dreadful hand life had dealt her poor brother. Yet pleased to be free again, free from the confines of her brother's prison and the dull heavy gloom of the home. She began to reflect over Sammy's sad existence as she commenced her journey homewards.

Pulling away slowly, she started to reminisce - remembering when her brothers' problems first started. And with the fresh autumn air from the open windows cleansing her senses, she found herself constantly mulling over the traumatic turn of events that led to her brother left abandoned in that place - his story, heart breaking.

Trying to come to terms with his terrible situation and the cruel way fate had handled his life. She quickly began to realise - her poor vulnerable brother would be living out the rest of his time in that home … a soon forgotten man.

Chapter 1 - The Accident.

Eyes like saucers, the flame-haired woman battled her way to the end of the platform in search of the man left lying on the ground. Her tall slim body ridged, a look of dread appeared on her face. While her tied back hair emphasised her pale gaunt features and staring eyes - too scared to make a sound it seemed.

Yet forcing her way through the tightly knit crowd now gathered around the unconscious man - a loud, piercing scream burst from her lips.

'Please, please, it's my husband,' she yelled, but no one seemed to hear her, still stunned by the scene in front of their eyes.

'I *need* to get to my husband,' she screamed this time, as the curious observers moved slowly to one side.

While the commuters still sat on the four fifty three train to Morden, oblivious to the drama, continued to wait in silence. No doubt wondering if they should leave the train. But having heard the screeching brakes and the ear-splitting screams, they surely must have realised - someone's life had just ended or someone's nightmare just begun.

In the meantime the dying man lay crushed against the wall bleeding profusely, his body lifeless, his face and head a mess. It would certainly be a miracle if he was still alive. And an eerie silence fell on the crowd as they waited with baited breath.

'Is he dead...Is he dead?' his wife kept repeating ... but no one dared answer − too frightened to make a noise maybe.

'An ambulance is on its way,' a policeman shouted from the back of the crowd, breaking the silence. 'It should be here soon.' but the minutes of waiting felt like hours in this disorderly setting.

'Are you the injured man's wife?' an attendant called over, approaching the woman with concern in his eyes.

'Yes, yes ... is he dead?' Her manner controlled and yet on the edge of panic.

'No ... he's still alive. Now you mustn't worry. They'll get him to the hospital as quickly as they can. They're sending a helicopter to airlift him to the Royal London. They are clearing the roads outside so they can land.'

'But why are they rushing, if he's as good as dead?'

'Well, we don't know that yet. That train may have hit him quite badly ms ... but I'm sure he'll be fine,' and he touched her shoulder gently. 'They will do all they can to help him.'

Placing her in the care of a sympathetic commuter, the attendant carried on with his job - trying to sort out this mayhem. While the station continued to fill with rush hour travellers, all pushing and shoving in selfish concern, looking for alternative routes home.

'Come on everyone, back away please,' an attendant shouted out. 'The paramedics will be here soon. Please leave the station or get on other trains.' And the Audio Address system repeated the same message.

Stood at the other end of the platform was the young driver of the train. He appeared badly shaken. The shock and bewilderment still left on his face.

'I couldn't believe it,' he groaned. 'He appeared from nowhere… he just got in the way. This was my first trip out on this shift as well. How on earth can I live with this?'

Clearly distraught, the attendant took him by the arm and led him off the platform, as a new driver got ready to move the train.

'Make way, make way,' a man bellowed from behind. 'The paramedics are here.' And the morbid onlookers immediately stepped aside.

On reaching their victim, they looked troubled though, 'He appears to have smashed his head quite badly,' the older medic said quietly to the other. 'And it looks like he's been thrown from one end of the platform and into this wall with quite some force.'

'His heart beat's still pretty strong though,' his partner replied as he felt the injured man's pulse. 'Let's get him out of here quickly.'

The paramedics took great care as they lifted him onto the stretcher. His body had taken a heavy blow and until he was checked out, they couldn't be sure just how serious the damage was.

'Excuse me, sir,' a concerned onlooker interrupted. 'I think that's his wife standing over there. She doesn't seem quite right… I think she maybe in shock,' and he pointed towards the woman with the bright coloured hair.

'Are you the injured man's wife?' the medic called out to her.

'Yes, yes… is he dead?'

'No, thankfully he's still alive. What's his name?'

'It's Sammy… Sammy Clayton… he was looking for mice.'

'Would you like to come with us to the hospital, Mrs Clayton?' ignoring her last comment. 'We can get you police assistance if you like?'

'No, no I need to get home for my daughter … I can get myself home.'

'I'm afraid we need to take your husband's details first … I'll let that police officer over there know who you are. He will come and help you and get you home safe,' and he pointed in his direction. 'Are you sure you're okay?'

'I'm fine ... just a bit shaken,' and she leant against the wall as if she might stumble.

Using his radio phone the medic connected to the policeman up ahead and passed him on the details.

Clearly not happy now with the way this woman looked, they had no option but to leave her for the police to sort out. Realising time was of the essence.

Pushing his way through the tightly packed platform, keen to get to the woman who'd now taken herself to one side, the officer looked worried. She had not approached her dying husband the whole time he lay on the floor alone and helpless and she seemed scared.

'I need to get home, I need to get home,' she shouted at the policeman as he came closer, appearing to panic in the claustrophobic atmosphere of the platform.

'That's okay, Mrs Clayton, calm down,' he said gently. 'Your husband's in good hands … but I'm afraid I need to take a statement. But let's get you to the hospital first … we have a car waiting outside.'

'No, no. I need to get home for my daughter; she'll be home from school soon,' and her hand began to tremble, while she fiddled with her hair.

Confused, he thought, and who could blame her. 'How old is your daughter Mrs Clayton? Can you not get a neighbour to look after her?'

'Oh dear no, she's only fourteen. She needs me. She'll be petrified if I'm not there.' Her voice almost inaudible she started to cry.

Raising his hand the policeman attempted to calm her down. She was clearly acting irrational - her husband the lesser of her concerns.

'Okay Mrs Clayton… that's alright,' he said, wiping the sweat from his brow. The air near the tunnel was suffocating. 'I'll take you home if that's what you want. Let's make a move now.

Fighting their way through the hordes of frenzied people now desperate to get home, they emerged from the dark and dingy station relieved to be free again, while the atmosphere outside took on a bright and sudden change. The light rapidly blinding both as their heads span back to a reality more in keeping with a normal day.

Appearing much calmer, the woman looked comforted by the fact she was on her way home to her daughter - safe in her little world. And not a mention of her husband or his welfare passed her lips.

In shock the policeman thought, understandable after all and a silence fell on them both as the car took them home in the heavy traffic that had started to build up. Looking out the car window, she stared at the passersby who still carried on with their busy lives - appearing to struggle to piece together the dramas of that day. But as it slowly began to sink in, she told the officer, how they'd been talking about mice that lived on the tracks of the railway lines. On reaching the station, her husband's curiosity got the better of him, making him stretch forward to look down the dark tunnel for the furry creatures they'd discussed earlier.

'That was when it happened,' she said. 'Whack, he was hit full force by the train as it came out of the tunnel.' She gave a muffled cry as if remembering the scene and then went silent again, deep in thought once more.

The policeman looked at the woman through his rear view mirror concerned by her ramblings. 'Looking for mice,' he mumbled, trying to comprehend. She must be in shock.

A lengthy silence remained between them for the rest of the journey. Until eventually they arrived at the woman's front drive where her demeanour changed yet again - her concern for her child foremost in her mind, like a lioness with her cub he thought.

'Do you have to come in with me?' she said in a tone more in keeping with a woman now in control, and eager to get out of the car.

'Do you not need my support, Mrs Clayton?'

'No. Not really. I would rather tell my daughter what happened on my own. She'll be home in a minute.' She looked at her watch; keen to get inside, it seemed.

'Okay, I can give you ten minutes … and then I'll have to take a statement I'm afraid.'

Walking her up to the gate, he noticed a panicked look appear in her eyes, although the trembling had subsided. And concerned for her welfare, he quickly changed his

11

mind. 'Look … would you prefer it if I came back in the morning Mrs Clayton?'

'Yes, yes, that would be good…. let me get myself together and sort my daughter out. You've given me the number of the hospital; I'll call them later to see if they need me… or if he's still alive.'

The policeman left perplexed as he made his way back to his car, but should he be concerned? After all, she had just witnessed a terrible incident.

Placing his seatbelt around him he noticed this now broken woman fumbling about for her keys, still eager to get inside. And a sense of compassion filled him as he watched her finally enter her home - to a life he guessed would never be the same, devoid of a husband who'd normally be there.

Hopefully he'll pull through the poor sod, although that seemed highly unlikely going by the look of him earlier. And he shook his head at the sad situation.

Starting up the engine of his car, he was glad he'd decided to leave her in peace. The neighbours were already curious of the marked car sitting outside. The twitching of their curtains obvious now as they tried to hide their inquisitiveness. It was best to give her some time to get adjusted. Her daughter will be home from school soon so she won't be alone for too long.

Deciding to call back first thing in the morning to get her statement, he made a note to himself in his note book, 28th May, man involved in a suspicious incident on the platform of Colliers Wood tube Station. Took wife home, will call back in morning for statement.

Satisfied with his decision the policeman drove away, thinking she was far better off around loved ones for now. No doubt she'll be making phone calls to family and friends and will surely have their support too. So he made his way back to the station...

Chapter 2 - Samuel Clayton's earlier years.

Samuel Clayton was a post war baby, born in the late Forties. One of three siblings, he was often thought of as his mother's pride and joy - the baby boy she'd always wanted.

Britain was at peace again and a feel good factor remained in the air. Life was a struggle but it felt great to be alive, as it so often did when people pulled together during difficult times.

An average family on the whole, they were not without their share of problems. But a family who were only too pleased to be united in a country now picking itself up from a war that had shattered the world.

South London had been Samuel's home throughout his childhood, only moving to Surrey in later life. Life had been a struggle, but his parents had always maintained, good family values with decent principles, so typical of those times.

Samuel, who soon became known as Sammy by family and friends, was a pleasant boy with dark brown curly hair and beautiful blue eyes which often held a sparkle. Eyes that had clearly made his mother's heart melt, even when she told him off.

He was like his mother in many ways, having her pleasant disposition as well as her looks. However, he could be an unusual child at times and definitely no angel, especially when led astray. But he never brought any trouble home that followed later.

Sammy was the second child, born between two sisters. Jill was the eldest by six years, a slim, sporty girl who always looked out for her little brother; fighting most of his battles when he was young.

His younger sister, Elaine, was five years his junior and appeared to have more in common with her brother, sharing in his fondness for animals. Consequently, over the years, many pets had been kept between them, much to Jill's disapproval - as Elaine particularly liked mice.

During Sammy's teenage years, in order to earn some extra money, he started breeding rabbits. It appeared to be a good idea at the time, until one day he ended up with more than twenty tiny babies and the family found this amusing.

Sammy had a favourite rabbit called Bruce, the proud buck who'd sired most of the litters. Bruce's little party trick when chased by the family dog was to leap in the air, while simultaneously peeing over him as he turned and flicked, in mid-air - reversing the tables on the dog instead. The family had thought this was funny but unfortunately the smell was not.

Sammy it seemed could be a strange lad at times but the sisters still loved their brother. But they often felt he wasn't the 'full ticket' although they could never put their finger on why. Yet having witnessed him on several occasions spending his pocket money on a pot of raspberry jam and a silver spoon, they sometimes felt they had good reason - especially as he would then proceed to climb the old Elm tree at the bottom of the garden to devour the whole pot of jam to himself – whilst using his shiny new spoon. And he wondered why he had spots.

Then on another occasion when their television broke down and a new one was brought into replace it, the family found him crying for the old one, adding further evidence to their concerns. But although a little odd at times, the sisters would often think - didn't most siblings feel this way about each other? He was obviously a sensitive lad.

Sammy's relationship with his parents had been a good one, although he particularly got on well with his father; an easy going man who always saw the lighter side of life. The only arguments between them, as Sammy got older was normally over football. His father always insisting his team, Chelsea was the much better one, tormenting Sammy on purpose – who was a Man United supporter. Amused, his father would then point out – that as a Londoner he should support a London team. It was always treated as light hearted banter and one that they'd shared for many years.

And as Sammy got older they also shared the odd game of snooker too, which was often followed by the odd pint or two. These were happy times it seemed and they developed a special bond.

Because of the huge age gaps between the three children, there was never any noticeable sibling rivalry, so no jealousies or grievances were ever felt as such. Well, not until the day Sammy met the 'girl of his dreams', Melissa. She was eight years his junior and he clearly thought she was 'the bee's knees' - God's gift to men.

She was a slim girl of medium height, attractive rather than good looking with very long straight blonde hair, which she always insisted was natural. She was also inclined to wear very short skirts as was the fashion at that time. But worn together with knee high boots and six inch heels; this would undoubtedly make men's heads turn.

It seemed it wasn't long before Sammy became infatuated with his new girlfriend, apparently flattered that a young girl like her, aged only sixteen at the time, would even consider dating him, he being so much older, and certainly not as confident. Yet their relationship appeared to flourish, even though it was proving difficult for the family to get to know her. And particularly for Elaine, as it appeared Melissa had taken an instant dislike to Sammy's younger sister, who at the time, was a pretty brunette. Being roughly the same age, perhaps she saw her as some sort of competition. Or maybe she just didn't like her but Elaine couldn't say she was bothered.

It was around this time Melissa had become completely obsessed with 'Abba'. She even told Sammy; she thought she looked like Agnetha, the blonde bombshell in the group, but Elaine said –'in her dreams.' Yet Sammy still thought she was gorgeous, and as they often say 'beauty is in the eye of the beholder.'

When Sammy had first left school, he started work as an apprentice for the local London Electricity Board and stayed with them for many years, until eventually promoted to management level.

He was a fairly fit man in those days as well, having joined a local rowing club. And often took part in competitions representing his firm, winning many medals on their behalf.

His round jolly face, now adorned by a neat and tidy beard, inevitably became his trademark. Often leading to comments regarding his likeness to the singer Tom Jones, who some thought was sexy.

His nervous laugh however, which had been with him most of his life, had become far more noticeable these days, as he tried to hide his awkwardness. And, although a shy man at times, he was never-the-less, warm, friendly and often child-like. A man who only appeared to want the love of a good woman, with the opportunity to do what society expected - marry, settle down, have his 2.3 children and live happily ever after and Sammy was the type of man who'd try his hardest to make this happen.

This made Sammy potentially a good catch for some nice young lady. But his insecurities often hindered his efforts to pull the right girl. It was therefore inevitable, after several upsetting split-up from Melissa, Sammy at the age of thirty decided to make her his wife. Even though the family still thought she was odd and a little self-obsessed. He idolized her and that's all that mattered.

Sammy's eldest sister, Jill, had already been married ten years. But the marriage hadn't been a happy one. With many problems she kept to herself, although she'd often confided in her brother. Still, she had two beautiful little girls that she adored and life went on regardless - as it so often did in those days.

A year after Sammy's wedding; Elaine was also married and was honoured by the presence of Melissa who turned up in a red skirt and jacket which didn't match - resembling a red coat from Butlins, that didn't do much for the photographs. She did however change for the evening celebrations that she appeared to enjoy immensely, toying with the men on the dance floor. But this clearly made

Sammy unhappy, as it seemed he now had a problem with her flirting. Yet still he appeared to accept this, 'after all', he said, 'she is my wife and I love her,' but the sisters knew he would need to keep her close, if he wanted their marriage to work.

Over this early period in their marriage, Melissa, it seemed had already started to alienate Sammy from his family and he inevitably drifted away from them. This was sad though, as he was still his mother's blue eyed boy. It was obvious she still felt protective, only Sammy had this vulnerability that clearly made her feel this way. The sisters always felt though, his instability had not been helped by the woman he'd married.

Melissa's controlling behaviour had started more or less from the very beginning with little things they thought at first were just misunderstandings – but later realised, were orchestrated, planned and schemed. A control freak some might call her. But because Sammy was obviously obsessed with her, she could manipulate him into her way of thinking without him actually realising. It appeared; he just couldn't see or want to see, anything bad in her.

Just like on their very first family Christmas together following Elaine's marriage, when they'd all agreed to meet up at their parent's flat in order to exchange gifts. It seemed Sammy at Melissa's suggestion, had given her the money to buy his family's presents that year and although a little mean at times, Sammy was always generous at Christmas.

But Melissa clearly resented him squandering money on his relatives, after all she was his family now and come Christmas day she told Sammy she'd forgotten to buy them.

She said, it had just slipped her mind. Even though she never went out to work and spent most of her time watching Television.

This left Sammy in a very embarrassing situation and had to rush out that morning to buy chocolates for everyone instead. Suggesting in the future, no gifts should be exchanged, which was probably what Melissa wanted.

Elaine should have realised there was something wrong when she arrived that morning with her husband Adam, as Melissa had pushed by them on the stairs without a word said.

'And a Merry Christmas to you too,' Elaine mumbled as Melissa slammed the door behind her, eager to leave. These were clearly signs of things to come she thought and looked at Adam in amazement.

Yet, although petty, this grieved the family, as they all knew Sammy only wanted to be a caring, loving husband as he clearly still idealized his wife. Even after her disappearance for several weeks with some guy she'd picked up from somewhere, shortly after their wedding. The family never knew the full story concerning this, they were never allowed to discuss it but they knew Sammy had been desperately unhappy.

It was only a couple of months after her return from where ever that Elaine, on one of her rare visits to see her brother had found him looking through a photograph album.

'That's a nice picture of Melissa,' Elaine said, looking over his shoulder and pointing at the photo in question. 'She looks so radiant there,' which was unusual for Melissa as she normally looked po-faced.

'shussssh.....' Sammy whispered, placing his finger up to his lips. 'That's when she went missing.'

Elaine couldn't believe her ears, shocked by her brother's naivety as he turned a blind eye to his wife's infidelity.

The sisters therefore felt, their brother's marriage never had a good start and hadn't been built on solid foundations. Yet they realised he still clearly loved her, so they were both prepared to give her a chance if only for Sammy's sake. But they knew the relationship was volatile.

Chapter 3 - Marriage Problems.

During this unsettled period within Sammy's marriage, the sisters were also busy dealing with their own marital problems plus the complexities of modern life. Consequently they didn't see an awful lot of their brother, which really suited them all. Although they guessed this particularly suited Melissa, as she could then carry on controlling Sammy with no interference from them.

Sammy's parents however, did get to see their son a little more, but the sisters knew this wasn't as much as they would have liked. They were clearly concerned for their son and troubled things were still not right within his marriage. Yet they would rarely tell the sisters of their findings, knowing Sammy wouldn't want it discussed. But this didn't stop his parents worrying, even though he didn't act like the doting son they surely would have liked. It seemed Sammy was far too concerned he'd upset Melissa by spending too much of his precious time with his own mum and dad.

Consequently, even when Jill's marriage broke up there was no real support from Sammy, which was a shame as they'd been particularly close at one time. But when by chance he did get to spend time with her, he was always eager to get back home, or Melissa would be phoning every five minutes to see where he was. So always looking at his watch, worried in case she'd get upset and perhaps run off again, Sammy toed the line. Eventually his visits to his sister became fewer and fewer; as they were just not worth the hassle.

Sometimes however, Melissa was quite happy offering advice to her sisters-in-laws, and was always able to explain in depth, what support and benefits were available. She appeared to be clued up on things like that and clearly knew most of the loop holes. Yet this alarmed the sisters, as it highlighted just how calculating she was, especially when it came to money and they were sure if anything should happen between her and their brother, she'd get every penny she could.

Over time it was inevitable the family would drift further apart, especially now Sammy was working all hours. In fact his life had become quite laborious it was said and although not normally a lover of hard work, Sammy was fond of the money - the overtime paying off his mortgage.

Enjoying this money on pleasurable activities though didn't seem an option sadly, only Melissa didn't like taking holidays. Well certainly not abroad as she didn't like the sun and the sisters guessed Sammy would have been disappointed, as he'd often travelled overseas before they were married. But as Melissa wouldn't even sit in the garden, telling everyone - the sun would ruin her skin and make her old before her time, holidays abroad were definitely off the list of to do's.

In fact, the sisters were also told, Melissa seldom ventured out of doors these days, but if and when she did, it was normally when dark or if the sun wasn't out. So their next door neighbours nicknamed her 'the princess of darkness,' especially as she'd run inside whenever she saw them coming.

It also appeared she didn't like socialising either, well not with her husband. And she certainly didn't like drinking alcohol; perhaps afraid it would age her or turn her into a raging alcoholic.

Sammy once said, she only ever enjoyed watching television and was completely obsessed with that. As it seemed - TV and films often mirrored a fantasy world within her head which she'd try to act out in real life.

It was also obvious Melissa didn't approve of Sammy's friends either these days and was often unfriendly towards them. So it was therefore inevitable Sammy would soon find himself a loner, which the sisters thought was sad, as he had always enjoyed company.

Nevertheless, he did have one good friend who'd stuck by him throughout his life. He first met Lawrence at the age of five and they become very close, often confiding in one another.

Over the years, he and Lawrence regularly met up for a drink and a chat but Melissa would never join them- not that they wanted her to as it was the only enjoyment Sammy had besides his football, which he played and later managed. Then of course there was his garden, which he loved and worked hard at to keep it looking good.

So perhaps his life wasn't that bad, as there are many people who live this way and maybe he was content with it and just happy to have his princess waiting at home.

In fact, maybe the family had got it wrong and Sammy had got it right, after all Jill was now separated from her husband and Elaine's marriage was also on the rocks. So hats off to Sammy whose marriage was still going strong, even though it was to the detriment of his own family.

****

It was when their mother died that the problems really started. She had suffered on and off for years with depression, headaches and not feeling quite right; consulting many doctors and even a psychiatrist. She was horrified the psychiatrist only wanted to talk about her sex life!

The family unfortunately had grown a little tired of their mother's medical problems and as the doctors couldn't find what was wrong with her, it was considered a case of 'cry wolf.'

Eventually, she was placed on what she called, her 'happy pills' and she started to enjoy her life again. It was great for the family to see her like this but alas it lasted just a short while. In fact, up until the day she was diagnosed with cancer. The family were devastated, each bearing the pangs of guilt for not taking her sickness seriously. And it was only after a fight of two years that the cancer won in the end as it so often did in those days.

Of course it was obvious their mother didn't want to die, as who really does. She said, she was concerned for her children and leaving them behind – worried because Jill was still split from her husband with two children to bring up - and Elaine, who'd just had a baby was now also on her own. Then there was Sammy who was married to Melissa and that was a concern on its own to their mother.

Before their mother died she'd asked her son to look out for his two sisters. 'They need a man they can turn to' she said, 'only dad wasn't up to it these days.' And although that was fine with Sammy, she hadn't passed this by Melissa, who wouldn't have stood for that. So needless to say, Sammy was nowhere to be seen as usual. Not that the girls really cared, but it would have been nice.

In fact there was no closeness between Sammy and his siblings anymore. Sammy even told Jill one day, 'We all have our own lives to live now and my priorities are to my wife.' But this was very sad as it was just another pull away from an already depleting family. Melissa was controlling his life and he seemed happy to let her.

Even while his mother spent her last few precious weeks in one of the local hospices, Sammy hardly visited. No doubt scared Melissa would run off if out of his sight for too long, overriding his concerns for his sick mother. It seemed Melissa had made sure she was the only important person in her husband's life and Sammy appeared to accept this. Yet the sisters were sure this would play on his mind at some stage, knowing how sensitive he was.

The sisters knew though, there was no way Melissa would leave her husband now. She had it far too good and things were far too easy. Sammy had now provided her with a lovely home in Banstead, Surrey and she still didn't have to work. And as there were no children at this stage, life must have been a doodle. In fact the sisters often wondered what she did all day. The family had been kept at a distance and life was surely sweet. No, she was going nowhere but their poor mother's heart must have been breaking as there was nothing she could do, Melissa already had full control.

Their mother's death felt very surreal for them all. After she went into the hospice they hadn't expected her to pass so quickly. Only, the big C was never really spoken of in those days always whispered about in corners, too awful to even mention.

Yet the wonderful, devoted care staff that worked there tried their hardest to keep their mother comfortable, using Morphine and the likes to deaden her pain. Until eventually she slipped into a coma for her last few days, when it quickly became apparent it would be far better if she passed away now. But it was still a huge shock when she did.

The family not having faced the death of someone so close before felt not only saddened but frightened by their loss. Sensing their unease it seemed, the elderly nun in charge, insisted they should say their last goodbyes to their loved one in person, believing it would help them, she said.

So tiptoeing hesitantly behind her, they followed the petite but determined nun in her flowing black gown, down into the basement. Scared at what they might find and yet not sure they had an option either.

Standing at the entrance of the cool stark room, too frightened to even move, the family again felt helpless. So the elderly nun with her strong determination and sheer sense of presence pushed them one by one towards the lifeless body, lying there alone. Each one now expected to say their last farewells, sealed with a loving kiss. An act they'd never dared dreamt of, too sad to even contemplate.

The cold, clammy skin of her forehead, tacky to the touch mortified them. This woman, who lay there in front of them, had once been a mother and a wife. Where had she gone? Where was her spirit? Where was her spark?

Her soul now departed left just an empty shell, lying there silently in peace. A wakeup call to their own mortality

27

perhaps; they said their sad goodbyes - except for Sammy of course. He was nowhere to be seen as usual.

Their mother's send-off was an extremely sad occasion, which had proved difficult for the family to handle, as she had been the strong one, there for them all. But it was their turn to be strong now, and they consoled them-selves with the fact she was no longer in pain, although they were all going to miss her, each in their own special way.

Before their mother died she'd asked to be cremated, which left them all with the decision as to where best place her ashes. But as their mother had been a florist for most of her life and Sammy had such a beautiful garden, it was easily agreed they would place her ashes there.

So to implement her wishes, a red Rose bush, her favourite flower, was planted just behind Sammy's house. Although Melissa preferred yellow and almost got her way.

Not long after their mother's sad passing, it quickly became apparent that Alf wasn't coping with life after mum and was finding it difficult living alone. After all, she had been the one who'd organised everything all through their married life. She had been his backbone and his mate, and he missed her very much.

Now almost a year after their mothers passing there seemed little change in their father and the family had to agree it was obvious he couldn't cope by himself; suffering with depression. This was a huge shock to them all, surprised by his reaction to the loss of his dear wife.

And this was when the problems got a little more complicated.

Chapter 4 - Daddy Dear.

Alf was an easy going man, who had this special endearing way about hm. But with his attitude to life being mainly light hearted, this could sometimes be annoying too – particularly for the family, as his childlike humour, wasn't always amusing.

Like many children of his time, Alf hadn't had a good start in life, his mother dying in child birth. Consequently, Alf soon found himself placed in a Children's Home - along with his older brother and two older sisters; their father unable to cope.

Needless to say, his time in this home hadn't been pleasant but at least he'd remained close to his siblings, giving him some sense of family. But blighted by occasional bed wetting, which often resulted in punishment dished out by the nuns in charge - Alf struggled with life in the orphanage. Particularly as the younger children were made to pray, morning, night and day - turning Alf into the atheist he'd inevitably became.

Once leaving the home, Alf and his brother joined the army, as most orphans did once coming of age - now ready to fight for their country. While his sisters went into domestic service instead, which was a usual for those day.

Sadly though, Alf lost his brother during the war, in an explosion on an oil tanker and he couldn't find his sisters ever again. Even after contacting the Salvation Army to help trace them.

So his sisters presumed dead and his father having died several years before, Alf was completely on his own.

Well that was until he met the beautiful Ella, his dear departed wife. She came from a very stable family and he slotted in quite comfortably between them all. He now had the family he'd always wanted and was happy with his lot.

Losing his wife when she was only sixty four devastated him. Faced with being on his own again was more than he could bear. Memories of loneliness and helplessness raised their ugly heads once more. Fear of old age alone seemed unfair. He was eight years older than his wife and he clearly felt cheated.

Lost in a world of desperation, Alf suffered a nervous breakdown. His children were more than surprised that their father, who'd always appeared self-sufficient, a man of the world, now couldn't cope anymore.

What was going on in their world? Things that were, were no more; people gone and people changing. They say life never stays the same. Live for now is what's important; enjoy it while we're here.

So Alf had now become a problem, which was proving difficult for his children to resolve at this present time - yet they knew he needed looking after. But as Elaine was only living in a small flat with her little boy, although in the process of looking for something bigger and Jill was living in a two bedroom council flat with her two young daughters, they were not in a position to take on that responsibility. Whereas Sammy, who lived in a three bedroom semi in Surrey, was clearly in much better position and was ready to take care of their father apparently.

It therefore seemed sensible that Sammy should ask him. But would he want to? The other problem being - how would the sisters react to that? After all it would mean him having to live with the wicked witch 'Cruella' and how would Alf handle that?

It all kicked off the day Alf went for Sunday lunch at his youngest daughter's place. He enjoyed his Sunday roasts and was looking forward to the juicy chicken she said she was cooking. Yet most of all, he was looking forward to the company, which he said he missed the most.

Sitting at the kitchen table, Alf fiddled with his knife and fork as Elaine began to dish up dinner. It was obvious he had something on his mind and clearing his throat he suddenly announced, 'Sammy's offered me a room at his place love... how do you feel about that?' Alf already knew her views regarding Melissa and looked nervous as he waited her reply.

'Well, it's up to you dad, if that's what you really want,' although, she was surprised he was even considering it. But realising how lonely her father had been since losing Mum, she didn't want to make things difficult.

'I know you and Jill don't like Melissa but she's not really that bad you know. She made me a lovely meat pie the other day.'

'Yes, I remember when she made them in the past for you and Mum and charged you for doing so!' Elaine was annoyed by his praise.

'Well I think she may have changed now love.'

31

'Look dad, you must do what you want. It's your life after all and I hope it all works out … but please don't try to convince me what a wonderful person she is when I know bloody different,' and she placed his dinner down hard on the table, already wishing she hadn't spoken out.

'No, no you're right,' he mumbled as he tucked into his dinner.

Elaine knew though, how desperate her father was. He didn't like living on his own or the responsibility that came with it. Her mother had always looked after things and Elaine knew he wanted looking after now.

Trying to understand her father's predicament, she tried to be sympathetic but she had to wonder if this had been orchestrated by Melissa in some way to get Alf under her control, just like Sammy. After all, she didn't normally do anything for nothing. And considering Sammy was under her spell more than ever these days, this didn't make Elaine happy.

Alf enjoyed himself at his daughters and seemed reluctant to go back to his empty flat and didn't leave till fairly late. Elaine couldn't wait to ring her sister to tell her the unexpected news.

'He's only talking about moving in with them!' she said, raising her voice as if by some miracle it may change things. 'I can't believe it, Jill. Especially after the way they'd treated him and mum in the past... Sammy never had any time for them!'

'Yes I know … I spoke to dad myself yesterday and he told me what he was thinking,' Jill too, sounded alarmed. 'You do know it will mean him selling his flat as well?'

'Oh, great, then there's no turning back. What did you say to that?'

'I went mad ... I told him off, said he was being bloody stupid and it would all end in tears. After all, Elaine, he knows what they're like, especially her.'

'Well, hopefully he'll listen to you.'

But realising how lonely their father had been since losing mum, Elaine guessed what was about to happen. Especially as she knew Alf wouldn't want to upset Sammy by going against his wishes, and so she didn't hold much hope of their father changing his mind.

Alf went ahead with his plans as they guessed he would, much to his daughters' disapproval and he quickly placed his property on the market only too pleased to get rid of the responsibility that came with it. Promising to split the proceeds between them all, he probably thought this would act as a sweetener. But, Elaine didn't trust Melissa, who she felt would be after the lot, as sadly - greed often drives a wedge between families, especially in times of needs. So the sisters decided to keep a close eye on him, or at least as close as would be allowed. After all he was their father and they were concerned for his welfare, still suspicious of Melissa's motives.

The plan was for Alf to be given his own compact room at the back of the house, which overlooked the garden. Here he was expected to stay for most of the day, which would still give them some privacy, although he was still allowed to come down for his meals but to return to his room after, left to watch television all on his own without any company - so not much had changed for poor old Alf.

It had only been a week into his stay when Jill received a strange phone call from her father, which completely confused her, 'I'm sitting here with Melissa, love, having a nice cup of tea and a lovely piece of cake.'

Jill was just about to say 'how nice that was' when the phone went suddenly dead. Jill was perplexed; particularly as there was no answer when she tried to call back and wondered if it was Melissa who'd got him to call. Perhaps she was playing mind games?

London had been Alf's home for most of his life and it wasn't surprising when he told his daughters, he wasn't happy living in the countryside of Surrey. He felt miles away from anywhere and one, he said. It seemed poor old Alf, was still disgruntled; or was he actually still depressed? Had he truly gotten over his breakdown and the loss of his dear wife? Yet one thing was certain, he definitely wasn't happy living with his son or his daughter-in-law, as they were quickly finding out.

Time had slipped by fast, as it so often does when people lead busy lives and Elaine suddenly realised she hadn't spoken to her father for some time, as Alf was always in his room when she rang him. Melissa usually told her, 'he was too tired to come to the phone.'

Concerned, Elaine called her sister to see if she'd heard.

'No. When I ring, Melissa always answers, she normally tells me, he's already tucked up in bed. Only by the time I get home from work and I've sorted out the girls it's already well past eight!'

'I know, same here … but this is all very worrying; I don't like not hearing from dad.'

'Well hopefully we'll see him at Aunty Floe's funeral this coming Friday,' reminding her sister of the up and coming event.

'Yes, I'm sure dad wouldn't want to miss that, he'd always been fond of Aunty ... although who knows if Sammy intends to take him. You know what he's like.'

'Well I've heard he does,' although Jill didn't sound too convinced.

What a place to meet up though. But at least they'd get to see their dad and finally find out if he's actually settled in.

The sisters met up at their cousin's house before the actual funeral, where they intended to follow the hearse to the chapel. Here they could share their tears of love, regrets or concerns, depending on their thoughts of course. But it seemed the family were depleting day by day, albeit distant family this time and they were sure their father would feel the inevitability of it all. A generation disappearing before his very eyes, only to find himself at the top of the list - how sad must that be?

But then, was he even going to make it to the funeral?

To the sisters' surprise, Alf did arrive and on time, linked arm in arm with their brother as they watched them walk slowly together, along the pretty pathway that lead up to the chapel. The sisters joined them there. Here they could see clearly the sadness in their father's eyes, a distant look devoid of feeling. But it was a funeral after all, what did they expect?

'Hi, Dad, how are you?' Elaine said, planting a big kiss hard on his cheek while trying to sound cheery.

'I'm fine, love,' he replied robot fashion as Sammy stood closely beside him, as if standing guard. And Elaine had to wonder, was Sammy worried he might run off, or say something out of turn? Alf definitely didn't look comfortable and she wondered if he was already under their spell?

Melissa on the other hand was nowhere to be seen as usual, so no respects were paid by her. Sammy told his sisters; 'Melissa didn't like funerals,' but who does?

The sister weren't really surprised by her absence though, but had to wonder if Melissa's non attendance was really due to her reluctance to mix with them.

During the church service, the sisters watched their father from the opposite pew; it was as if he was glued to Sammy. But lost in their little individual worlds, as the vicar gave his sermon, Elaine noticed Sammy constantly checking his watch, anxious to get home no doubt, their time up already.

'Why are they sitting so close together?' Jill whispered to her sister, peering in their direction 'It's like dad's a prisoner. It's very odd.'

'Yes it does look strange,' she replied, looking towards her brother too. 'I think perhaps we should both pay dad a visit and soon ... we need to see what's happening there...' and Jill agreed.

After the service had finished, Sammy was keen to leave and didn't stay for the usual celebratory or commiserating drinks - depending on your view. Sammy had obviously spent far too much time away from Melissa; it was time to get home. So leaving fairly swiftly the sisters promised their father, they'd visit him early next week.

Ringing first to make sure it was suitable with Alf's keepers, the sisters made plans for their visit.

Much to their surprise they were made very welcome. Melissa actually looked pleased to see them both.

But with visiting kept strictly to Alf's room, it was up the stairs they went with cups of tea and cake in hand. On entering his room though, Alf didn't appear happy, although pleased enough to see his daughter's. Yet he didn't say an awful lot. The sisters got the impression he was holding things back, perhaps frightened to express how he truly felt. Maybe thinking, he'd made his bed he must lie in it, especially after the girls had tried to warn him.

'So how's it going dad?' Jill asked as she looked around his room, which all looked neat and tidy; everything spick and span.

'Oh I'm okay,' he said, sounding slightly shaky, 'but I think she keeps taking my socks.'

'What do you mean dad?' Jill replied.

'Well they keep disappearing love ... I haven't got any socks to wear.'

'Perhaps Melissa's washing them for you,' Elaine butted in, trying to make some sense of this strange conversation.

'No, she's not,' he insisted, 'and my feet get cold during the night.'

Elaine looked at Jill perplexed. Perhaps he was losing his mind, after all why would Melissa take his socks?

'I'm frightened of that dog you know,' Alf continued, unaware of the concerned looks on his daughters faces.

'But you like dogs Dad?' Elaine said.

It seemed Sammy had recently acquired a young Staffordshire terrier, which he was still training up. But he was usually very good with dogs and would certainly not allow one to be aggressive, he loved them too much.

The sisters were surprised though that Melissa had allowed Sammy to have a dog, as they knew she didn't like them. She would have found them far too messy and something that would take Sammy's attention away from her for sure.

Yet Alf was also fond of dogs, just like his son and wasn't normally afraid of them, so where was this coming from? What on earth was going on?

'It keeps going for my bare feet when I come down the stairs to go to the toilet in the middle of the night.' Alf sounded upset.

'Give it a little kick then dad,' Jill encouraged, 'so it keeps well away from you.'

'It's a shame you have to go down the stairs to go to the loo anyway,' Elaine interjected. But she knew this was a problem in Sammy's house.

'Only I nearly fell down the stairs the other night when the dog went for my feet…he waits for me at the bottom of the stairs!' Alf looked upset.

Alf was clearly distraught but what could the sisters do, and they looked at each other both baffled. He was certainly not happy living there but they wondered if he was trying to find an excuse to get away? But what were his options? The sisters were speechless.

It had been more than two months since Alf had moved in with his son and his property had only recently gone under offer. Alf was pleased, he said, keen for the sale to go through still and happy to be rid of the responsibility.

It just so happened, Elaine was also in the middle of selling her flat and was in the process of buying a small house. She was relying on the money her father had promised them, to help decorate and furnish it and was keeping a keen eye on the sales; hoping they'd coincide.

'It's good about the flat being sold at last Dad. It'll be good if they go through together. Shall I give you a ring in the week to see how the sale's progressing?' Elaine hoped he was being updated, only she often wondered if Sammy actually kept him informed, given he'd taken over proceedings. 'Perhaps when I call next, some progress may have been made.'

'Yes, love, that would be good,' but his mind was elsewhere now.

'Come on Dad, eat your chocolates up. We brought you your favourites,' Jill was trying to distract him.

'No, love, take them with you. They'll only disappear.'

'Don't be silly, Dad' Jill insisted. 'Keep them for in the week.'

But Alf only smiled, as if he knew better.

The sisters looked at each other confused but what could they say. And unable to cheer him up they decided to leave - promising to call back and visit him soon.

Feeling now as though they'd outstayed their welcome anyway, the sisters couldn't wait to leave, as a strange and unhealthy atmosphere, hung around the house.

Still concerned for their father though, the sisters tried to visit more often but this wasn't always possible. Busy lives, children and work often got in the way. Yet when they did get to visit, they'd always find him in a similar frame of mind. Normally confined to his room and still complaining of things going missing, and sometimes being locked in, which worried the sisters immensely. Although it did cross their minds, he may be making things up, in order to get away. Whatever the reasons though, things clearly weren't right.

Chapter 5 - Overdose.

Three months had now passed and the situation with Alf still didn't seem any better. Even though the sisters were ringing regularly and visiting as much as they could, he still didn't appear any happier. And on top of everything the sale of his flat was taking longer to complete than expected.

On one particular evening, when Elaine had promised to call her father, the phone just rang and rang. She tried several times that evening but there was still no answer. Strange she thought. Where would they be at this time? They were normally at home by the latest six thirty – if they ever ventured out. Dad a prisoner in his room and Sammy and his wife a picture of domestic bliss in the kitchen... the thought made her laugh. Oh, well, perhaps they've gone somewhere nice, and she promptly forgot all about them.

That was until she received an unexpected call, later that evening from Melissa.

'Hi, Elaine … have you been trying to get hold of us?' she sounded a little too chirpy.

'Yes, I have actually,' but how did she know and why the interest anyway?

'Only we had to pop out, 'she said, not elaborating any further and Elaine shrugged her shoulders nonplussed.

'Anyway, Alf's tucked up in bed now. He was very tired when we got home. He said he'll call you back tomorrow evening.'

Elaine felt uneasy, as Melissa sounded smug. Although she managed to shake that feeling off, after all, this was Melissa she was talking to; she always made her feel like that.

'Okay, no problem,' she said, still perplexed by her call, now wondering why she'd rung and not Sammy - only Melissa didn't normally go out of her way to talk to her.

Expecting her to put the phone down, Melissa's conversation then carried on for a good thirty minutes or more, mainly talking rubbish. In fact Elaine couldn't get her off the phone, which was very unusual. She talked about the strangest subjects too, porno being the main one. She clearly liked that topic and wanted to talk about a film she'd watched only the other day, explaining just how noisy they can be at times - as if Elaine was interested. Finally placing the phone down, Elaine shook her head, wondering what on earth the call had really been about.

Baffled still, Elaine tried to forget their weird conversation and carried on with the ironing she'd originally planned to do. But on reflection, she found the call almost disconcerting.

At work the following day, Elaine received another unexpected call.

'Hi Elaine, its Sammy … I'm ringing from the hospital… I'm really sorry … but … I'm afraid dad has taken an overdose.'

'What! When,' she said her mind in turmoil, not sure she'd heard him right.

'We found him yesterday afternoon. We didn't tell you because we didn't want to frighten you. Anyway he's in Reigate Hospital at the moment and appears to be fine. But they want to keep him in to keep an eye on him. They said if you want to visit, it will be alright to go this evening. I've already told Jill.'

Elaine was shocked and wasn't sure how to respond. Sammy sounded nervous and she understood that but not once had he offered an explanation as to why and how it happened and she thought perhaps he felt guilty. Elaine wasn't happy, left speechless by this terrible news.

Ringing her sister later, Elaine became extremely angry, as she thought more clearly about the situation.

'That bitch kept me talking about crap for ages last night, and all the while she knew Dad was in hospital critically ill? She is one controlling cow I tell you... how dare she... I just knew there was something wrong.' Elaine was furious.

'Yes I agree, it's just unbelievable ... I wonder why she didn't tell you what happened?'

Keen to offload, Elaine found herself shouting down the phone, 'It's pretty obvious, she was hoping they didn't need to ... but because the hospital wanted to keep him in under observation, I guess they had no option. Yet that doesn't excuse why that she rang me last night and made out Dad was tucked safely up in bed and then went on for ages about porn! That's warped ... she must be sick in the head to do that... I wonder if Sammy even knew she rang. This really stinks, sis.'

'I know, Elaine. None of it makes sense ... but I'm planning to visit Dad later tonight; so let's see what he has to say.' Jill too seemed exasperated.

****

43

Alf didn't say much to either of his daughters on their visits, embarrassed by his actions maybe. Yet he clearly felt relieved to be free again - relaxed and peaceful once more. Not wanting to push him for answers though, in case he got upset, they didn't learn much from their visits.

A few days later, Alf was eventually moved to a psychiatric ward for further observation and therapy work and Elaine went to visit him there. The grey clinical unit stripped of any atmosphere and warmth, filled Elaine with dread, not realising she'd get to know this unit very well in the future.

Elaine was delighted however, when she spotted her father coming out of one of the rooms, wearing a smile the likes she hadn't seen in a long while. In fact she was surprised to see him looking so good. He'd clearly picked up since she last saw him; in fact it was the best she'd seen him look in ages.

'I can't go back to live with them, love,' Alf immediately blurted out, keen to get things off his chest it seemed.

'What do you mean, Dad?'

'It's because of them, I can't stand it. She keeps taking money from my pockets and she feeds me different food from Sam. He gets steak and I get sausages. She hides things too… she's very odd, I don't like her.' Desperate to confide in his daughter now, he ranted on and on wanting to off load his problems.

Elaine grabbed his hand. 'Oh, Dad, why didn't you tell us before?'

'I didn't like to, love. I knew I'd made a big mistake.'

'You'll have to go back there though Dad, but only for a little while, until we sort things out that is… at least we know what's going on now.'

Alf felt a lot better already, she could tell. He'd clearly unburdened himself - his pent up feelings of desperation having spilt out at last. He looked relieved.

Leaving the hospital, Elaine reflected over their conversation ... surely not, she thought … but was it really a surprise? Or had this all been part of Dad's breakdown, after all he had been pretty cut up about Mum.

Hoping to make some sense of it all, Elaine tried to rationalise this strange situation, trying to find an excuse for her father's sad confession. But it proved very difficult.

Once home Elaine rang her sister straight away and told her about her visit and what their father had said.

'But I saw him myself yesterday. He never said a word to me,' Jill sounded miffed.

'Well, I'm not making it up sis.'

'No, I'm sure you're not.'

'Maybe he was frightened to tell you because you told him off for going to live with them in the first place Jill.'

And she agreed.

Visiting her father the following day, Alf told Jill the same story; pleased to off load again.

'But why did you do it dad?' she asked as she slipped her hand in his.

'I didn't want to be a burden love.' And Jill wondered what on earth had been said to make him feel that way - there could only be one person responsible.

Alf was discharged a few days later and went back to stay at Sammy's, albeit reluctantly. But Alf was a different

45

man now, and told his daughters he wasn't going to stand for anymore nonsense. He was feeling so much stronger.

It was only a couple of days later; Jill received a frenzied phone call from her father.

'I'm on my way round, love. I've told them to sod off. I'm not eating the crap she feeds me anymore, not when Sammy gets the best.'

Jill couldn't believe her ears.

'Anyway, Sammy told me not to speak to his wife like that and he wants me to leave … so I am, I've packed my case and I'll be there shortly. I'm catching a bus.'

Jill was surprised by her father's sudden bravado and thought he sounded almost triumphant. She placed the phone down amused by his tale, although wondering how she'd find him when he arrived at the door. He seemed in control. But he was still very fragile.

Elaine, who happened to be at her sisters when Alf rang the front door bell, was also amused by the story. Jill ran to answer the door, still not sure what to expect and she opened the door with caution, only to find her father grinning from ear to ear, with his suitcase in hand.

Relieved to see him looking so happy, Jill gave him a hug, placing a kiss on his cheek. Alf explained his lucky escape and how much he hated Melissa. All their suspicions regarding her were now confirmed it seemed and this alone felt good. They had not been imagining these things after all, and nor were they losing the plot. They should trust their gut feelings from now on.

With Elaine moving into her new house a couple of weeks later, giving her the extra room for her father, it all worked out well in the end. Alf staying at Jill's until her place was ready.

It was strange the day the family went to Sammy's house to pick up the rest of Alf's things though, only when they got there, they found Sammy very upset indeed. It just so happened the day Alf had left; the dog had mysteriously died too.

Sammy looked up from the album as Melissa showed them into the lounge, his eyes still puffy from the tears he'd clearly shed.

Pouring over pictures of the dog in the album, Sammy eyes were red. Elaine felt sorry for her brother and his loss. Even though he hadn't shown his own father that much compassion in all the time he'd lived with them or before come to that. But that was probably down to Melissa.

'He died the very same day dad left you know… they said it was poisoning,' he said.

They guessed by Sammy's tone he thought their dad had poisoned him and probably out of spite. But the sisters knew he wouldn't do anything like that, he loved animals too much. If it was going to be anybody, it would probably be Melissa, although Sammy would never believe that. No it was her chance to be rid of the dog and blame someone else for doing it and their father was the obvious target - distancing him further from them.

'What a shame.' Jill said, clearly not interested in Sammy's loss. She was more concerned about collecting her father's things, and wanted to get on with the job. Melissa however, stayed out of the way, not wanting to get involved it seemed - leaving them to take what they wanted - which wasn't very much.

Having collected the bulk of Alf's things, they then got ready to leave, happy not to step foot in Sammy's house again. But Elaine's heart went out to her brother as he sat all alone in the lounge, sure in her mind, he was a lost soul - still in love and obsessed with a woman who called herself his wife. So who was going to set him free?

Elaine's new boyfriend, Mark, who had come along for moral support, had only met her brother once before. He said he couldn't believe how Sammy was behaving over a bloody dog.

'But if Sammy thought Dad had murdered the dog, that would explain it, wouldn't it?' Elaine tried to defend her brother but she found it very hard.

'I'm not so sure about that ... I just think, his not all there, ... think about it ... his father's just moved out of his house after recently taking an overdose and all he's upset about is the dog. It just doesn't make sense.'

'No, you're right, it doesn't,' and embarrassed by his actions, she still wanted to defend him. 'But can you really blame him Mark, having lived with her for all those years; she's enough to send anyone round the bend.'

'Yes, you're certainly right there,' and although not having met Melissa before today, he appeared to have sussed her out already and he opened the door eager to leave.

Job completed and ready to go, on the way out Alf passed Sammy a cheque; after all, he was still his son. At first Sammy looked puzzled but soon realised it was his share of the money from the sale of his father's flat, which incidentally came through at the same time their father had taken his overdose, which of course made Elaine suspicious.

'I didn't expect that, dad,' Sammy said softly.

'Well, it's what Mum would have wanted and it's only fair.'

'Thanks, Dad,' he whispered, and it was as though he was Alf's little boy once again.

Leaving with tears in his eyes, his conscience clear, no doubt, Alf closed the door gently behind him, now free from Melissa's clutches and his son's weird obsession with her.

And sadly, they never heard from Sammy again, after that. Well not for a very long time.

Chapter 6 - The Rift.

Life picked up for Alf once he was back on his old stomping ground, returning to his normal jolly self with ease.

Living with his daughter now, Alf had a great room at the back of the house, over-looking large playing fields. Here he could watch at his leisure some of the local cricket teams' play their friendly matches - a popular pastime within his wife's family, one that he had shared.

Happy to be living amongst familiar surroundings again, Alf bought himself a little car, which now enabled him to get around. He seemed to be far more contented these days and this pleased his daughters no end. No more depression and no more blues, these were things of the past.

In fact life seemed far more settled and it showed, even though Alf didn't particularly get on with his grandson, who was only three years old at this time. But this didn't prove a problem; it was just like having two children to bring up. Yet everyone slotted into their roles quite nicely, Alf helping his daughter as much as she helped him, so life was pretty sweet all round.

This made Elaine wonder if the whole episode with Sammy and their father was just a mistake, or a stupid misunderstanding. After all, Alf was very low at the time and she didn't like to think unkindly of her brother.

Alf rarely spoke about his time at Sammy's home though, although on the odd occasion he did confess privately about a few antics pulled on him there. But Elaine suspected he held a lot back, perhaps because of Sammy - after all he was his son.

Elaine was sure there was far more to tell and could only imagine what secrets there actually were. Yet not wanting to dwell on these stories, she felt it was best to move on.

There was one story however; which had made Alf very angry and shared it with his daughter. It seemed one day, Melissa had suggested, Alf should do some gardening in order to help his son out. Passing him an old pair of Sammy's trousers, she demanded he changed them there and then, in case he got his dirty. It was while he worked in the garden and his own trousers were left in the lounge, it seemed Melissa emptied out his pockets and took all his money. Something she did to Sammy when they were first wed but that got hushed up too.

Needless to say, Elaine wasn't sure what to believe and thought, it was probably best to forget these unpleasant stories. After all, what could she do? It was all in the past now. Her father was much happier and life was too short for grievances, there seemed no point in digging up dirt, only she wasn't really sure what happened. And she preferred to give her brother the benefit of the doubt, taking into account her father's mental state at the time.

Well, that was, until the day she heard from a friend who knew Sammy's next door neighbour. The neighbours, apparently not having seen Alf around for some time, asked

Melissa, how he was doing, concerned for him it seemed...
only to be told - Alf was dead.

Elaine was incensed when she heard this, and furious
with Melissa. This was the final nail in the coffin and she
decided - she didn't want anything more to do with either of
them again. She'd made plenty of excuses for their strange,
bizarre actions and enough was enough. Melissa was
wicked as far as she was concerned.

However, Elaine decided she needed to make sure her
brother knew exactly what his wife had been saying. She
felt it should be spelt out to him once and for all. She knew
that love was blind but someone had to put him straight.

Unable to speak to Sammy alone these days, always
heavily guarded by Melissa, Elaine decided to send him a
letter. Although she knew it would be a waste of time
posting it to the house, suspecting Melissa would destroy it
before it got to him - only this had happened many times
before, in the past, when cards and invitations were sent of
which Sammy had no knowledge of.

So Elaine decided to send the letter to Sammy's best
friend Lawrence who could then pass it on to him when
they next met. This she felt was the only way to make sure
he definitely received it. He would then finally know what
his wife had been up to, although she guessed he probably
already knew.

It read...

Dear Sammy,

I'm so sorry it has come to this but it's time you knew
the truth about your wife.

Dad has told me about the appalling way you both
treated him while staying at your house, which

consequently had led to him trying to take his life. I can only hope you are both ashamed of yourselves as I cannot imagine what mum would be thinking, as I'm sure she wouldn't be happy.

More importantly though, how can you live with yourself knowing how cruel you and your wife have been, especially Melissa by what I've heard. Do either of you have any remorse? It certainly doesn't seem so.

Your wife's behaviour has been nothing but disgusting, her lying even worse. Are you aware that she is now telling your friends and next door neighbours that Dad has actually died? This is disgraceful and unforgivable. If she can lie about things like this she can lie about almost anything, which we now know she does.

Mum would be so upset with you, as I am too, although I also feel sorry for you, as you are the one having to put up with her and her lies.

I only hope that you never have any children of your own, as life does have a tendency to repeat itself as you are no doubt aware. And what goes around will eventually come back around ... its karma. Maybe then you'll understand what Dad has had to go through.

Dad is very happy now, no thanks to you two. And I can only hope life treats you better than you have treated your own father.

I therefore have no wish to see either of you again, so please don't try to get in touch.

I can only but wish you good luck for the future as I'm sure you are going to need it.

Elaine.

Jill wrote something similar - sharing in her sisters' sentiments, while also expressing her disappointment with regards to their father.

Shortly before writing the letter Elaine heard rumours that Melissa maybe pregnant and had hoped her reference to children would be more poignant. However, when she asked Lawrence if the rumours were true, he had denied them. Whether he knew and was told to keep it a secret, Elaine didn't know.

The sisters were still surprised though when they finally received confirmation of the expectant baby. As they had been led to believe, Melissa had difficulties conceiving, having been trying for some time. But they guessed their brother would be delighted.

When Elaine worked out the dates later though, she realised, Melissa must have conceived when Alf had been living there. At least he had brought them luck.

The sisters never heard back from their brother regarding their letters, although they hadn't really expected to. And with no contact anymore, life carried on regardless, which was probably best all round. But was it really the best for Sammy?

Melissa had a baby girl four months later who they decided to call Kelly. By all accounts Sammy was over the moon. Alf however remained unaware of his new born grandchild; still happy living with his daughter, it appeared. Yet Elaine was sure her father still thought about his son and was no doubt, upset by the outcome, only Sammy was rarely discussed anymore.

Years went by without a mention of Sammy amongst the family, well not to Elaine. Although she'd heard he was still living in the same area, as friends still saw him about.

Kelly was growing up fast it seemed, the spit of her mother - with curly blonde hair and very pale skin. Unfortunately they discovered quite early that she suffered with epilepsy, a condition often triggered by stress. Being a shy girl, the sisters heard she didn't like mixing with other children. Especially at school and would run away and hide, telling them to leave her alone.

Sammy took his role as a father very seriously though and was very proud of his daughter it appeared. Although, according to Lawrence, Melissa had taken full control as usual. She didn't need or want any interference from her husband or anyone else, come to that, especially on matters concerning her child.

Lawrence also told them, that mother and daughter were now inseparable. And they often disappeared for long periods of time up to their bedrooms where they giggled whispered and conspired and Sammy wasn't part of that world. In fact, Sammy told Lawrence, he often wondered if his wife's relationship with their daughter was a healthy one. Still, she knew no different and while Sammy was around, Kelly was at least well provided for. But mental damage, if it existed, could he stop that?

A year later, Elaine decided to move to Singapore to be with her now newlywed husband Mark. Tessa, Jill's youngest daughter, would be looking after Alf during her absence, given they got on so well. Tessa was an air stewardess and her shifts enabled her to spend more time with her granddad, particularly during the day, giving him the company he sometimes craved. Although it was said, they often fought like an old married couple, but it was always in good fun and they'd normally make up by hooking little fingers.

A year or so on, out of the blue, Jill told her sister over the phone that Sammy had made contact with Alf again. This surprised Elaine and she thought perhaps his conscience had got the better of him; especially now Alf was much older. Or maybe he just wanted to make amends. And given Sammy was a proud father these days, perhaps he just wanted to share this with his own.

But Elaine suspected, Sammy never brought his daughter to visit her granddad, as she was sure Melissa wouldn't allow it. That's if she even knew Sammy had made contact again.

It was on Elaine's next visit home with her son Joe; Tessa admitted to her Aunty, that Sammy had been to the house the previous week to visit Alf. Alf had told Tessa; he would have preferred to have kept it a secret though, not knowing how his daughter would react. But as it happened, Elaine was pleased, as her gripe was really with Melissa not Sammy; she'd always felt sorry for her brother. As she realised, as did her sister, he was just a weak man who couldn't or wouldn't see the bad in his wife, especially now she was the mother of his daughter.

'He was acting rather weird Aunty' Tessa said quietly so Alf couldn't hear. 'He didn't stop complaining about his aches and pains. He was very restless and wouldn't sit down for more than five minutes, up and down, up and down all the time he was'.

'That's odd,' Elaine said now amused. 'Still perhaps he felt uneasy being here; only I'm sure Melissa didn't know he was.'

But Elaine didn't really know her brother anymore and as she poured herself a cup of freshly brewed tea she became lost in her thoughts of him once more.

'Well, possibly Aunty, but he kept going on and on about having the same symptoms as Nan. I think he believes he's now got cancer,' and Tessa laughed, raising her eyes in jest. The family all knew he was a hypochondriac and Elaine laughed too.

'There is actually a name for that condition you know; I believe its called Carcinophobia … apparently it's a fear of cancer,' and smiling to herself she wondered what on earth had become of her brother.

Tessa laughed again. 'Impressive Aunty … still perhaps Uncle Sammy does have good reason to moan and groan. Look what he's had to put up with all these years,' and chuckling to herself, she went upstairs to her bedroom with cup of tea in hand.

Elaine decided to join her father who was relaxing in the lounge. The tea Tessa had fetched him earlier, still sat at his side.

Sitting down beside him, Elaine sensed his unease. 'I hear Sammy's been to visit you, Dad?' she said, not waiting for his answer. 'That's really nice for you both. I'm so glad you've made it up.'

Alf looked surprised and nearly spilt the tea he'd placed to his lips.

'Are you?' he said. 'I wasn't too sure how you'd feel,' he put his cup down carefully.

'No, Dad, I quite understand.'

Alf passed her a photo that he kept in his pocket.

'Is this Sam's little girl?' she asked, starring at the photo she now held in her hand, which unfortunately looked like Melissa's double.

'Yes, love. They call her Kelly.'

'I know Dad. I do have my spy's,' she laughed. 'However Dad,' she continued, 'I don't mind Sammy coming to visit you here but I really don't want to see Melissa in this house… ever!'

'No, love, of course not,' he said, now sounding more like a scolded child rather than her father, and she handed him back the photo, which he placed back in his top pocket.

Chapter 7 - Alf's death.

It was shortly after this reveal that Elaine and her son went to visit a friend who lived fairly near her brother. This friend often mentioned, when she saw Sammy and his wife about, although she pointed out this was rarely together these days.

After a glass of wine or two over lunch, Elaine started to reminisce. And feeling sentimental, she mentioned to her friend that Sammy and her father were now reunited.

'I feel as though I would like to go and see him; tell him I don't mind him visiting Dad. After all, Alf isn't getting any younger; he is eighty one now.'

'Why don't you then?' her friend said egging her on. 'Life's too short, after all.'

'Yes you're right, but I don't want to talk to her. I don't want her thinking I've forgiven her.'

'Well Elaine, if it makes YOU feel better, I'd go,'

'Anyway, why shouldn't I? He came to my house uninvited. Why shouldn't I go and knock on his door?'

Elaine also had the devil may care in her that day, which may have been caused by the drink. So, with a little bravado and her son in tow for support, she made her way round to Sammy's house. On her way there though, Elaine felt a sense of sorrow as memories came flooding back - some good but mostly bad and she started to wonder if she was doing the right thing. After all what if Melissa should answer the door? She didn't want any trouble.

Her heart in her mouth now, she knocked gently on their door, still not sure if she was opening a can of worms or not. Eventually, the door slowly opened and Elaine wanted to run. She had come to see her brother with peace in her heart but who knew with this pair?

The door fully opened, there stood before her, larger than life, a face which had once been so familiar to her, a little older, a little greyer maybe but still sporting that very same beard that seemed to cover more of his face these days.

At first Elaine wasn't sure he was happy to see her, after all, he didn't really know why she was there, so she spoke first.

'Hello Sammy. Long-time no see. …how are you?' She tried to sound casual. 'This is Joe. Do you remember him?' She pushed her son forward.

Joe stared curiously at his uncle who he'd not seen in a long time, perhaps trying to work out why this man had caused such stirrings within the family.

'My, he's grown since I saw him last,' Sammy said, followed by his usual laugh.

'Yes, he's nearly nine.' Elaine felt a little awkward now and tried to explain her visit.

'Look, Sam, I've only come to say I'm really pleased you and dad have made it up - so please don't feel you need to sneak around in future.'

'Why don't you come in Elaine?' he said, holding back the door.

Elaine wasn't expecting that, 'Are you sure?' and now assuming the coast was clear she agreed, although she wouldn't stay long she said.

Taking her through to the lounge, Elaine noticed the place had hardly changed at all, which made her feel uncomfortable - like stepping back in time. Offering to make her tea, Elaine declined but then spent the next half hour catching up on old times and all the years they'd missed out on together. But mainly they laughed about the good old days and things they'd got up to as children, while Joe sat close by, quietly listening, visibly amused by their tales.

Elaine enjoyed their chat and thought how lovely it was, to be with the brother she'd been denied the company of for so many years. She had missed him more than she thought.

However, Sammy never mentioned Melissa or his daughter the whole time they talked. Except to say Kelly was very shy, although Elaine could tell he was proud. Then suddenly she heard it, a movement from behind. Elaine couldn't look. She guessed who it was but wasn't sure how to react - or how Melissa would respond to her being there. She didn't want to be her friend but she certainly didn't want confrontations.

'I thought it was your voice,' she growled.

Unnerved, Elaine chose not to answer and didn't even bother to turn around but the voice carried on regardless, 'If I had answered the door, I would have shut it straight in your face,' she groaned.

Well, Elaine certainly knew where she stood, which was fine with her and to her surprise, she responded very calmly.

'Well it's a good job you didn't then.'

But this put Sammy in a very difficult spot, having kept quiet up to now.

Turning to face her old arch enemy, thinking it best she should, Elaine was surprised to find her standing directly behind her, carrying a bird in a silver coloured cage, her face extremely menacing.

Surprised - she wondered what on earth she was doing. This woman was definitely nuts.

'How or why do you put up with her Sam?' she said turning to face her brother again. 'She has never liked me and I really don't know why.'

'She's my wife Elaine and I love her.'

What could she say to that, and taking hold of her son's hand she made her way quickly to the door - eager to leave.

'Well, I'd better go then Sam. All I can say is good luck and I'm sorry.'

Closing the door behind her, Elaine caught sight of a little girl running up the stairs, her pretty blonde hair bouncing in ringlets around her tiny shoulders. So that was Kelly, she thought. It was such a shame, as what chance did she have with Melissa in control.

On the way back to her friend's house, Elaine thought about their altercation and her inexcusable attack, and became very angry. How dare she interrupt their conversation and confront her like that, especially in front of her son. For all Melissa knew she could have been there with some sad news about their father, especially as he was getting on. Still, that was typical of Melissa she wouldn't care less about that.

It was soon after, Alf did sadly pass away. It was around the Christmas period too, which was very upsetting for the family. It seemed her father became depressed again and his doctor made the terrible mistake of placing him in a psychiatric ward in one of the nearby London hospitals - for a respite period only, he said. But here he rapidly declined, his care apparently abominable, and he shouldn't have even been there

It was thought perhaps Alf had been initially admitted because his doctor believed he might try to take his life again, given he'd done so before - thanks to Melissa. Which meant the family also had her to thank for this doctors decision as she was the one who'd initially drove him to taking an overdose.

It took them a fight and a half to get their father removed from that ward, having watched him deteriorate quickly. God knows what they were giving him as his deterioration had probably been caused by these drugs, making him hopelessly despondent and weak, which made it more difficult to move him. But often covered in cuts and bruises from the many falls he had on this ward, they knew they had to move him and quick.

Thankfully, Alf was finally placed in a very nice Care Home, looked after full time.

The Owner of this new home was alarmed by the strength of the drugs having been prescribed for Alf and believed they hadn't been necessary. Normally only ever used on harden criminals in order to calm them down she said. Consequently, having only lived there a short time, Alf passed away from a heart attack, which the Home felt had been brought on by these drugs, although they had no means of proving this. Still at least their father had been happy again, if only for a short while.

Coincidently a few days before Alf's passing Elaine had a dream that really upset her. In the dream she had seen her father in his new home, looking extremely happy. Laughing and joking with his new friends as they sat in the lounge area together. When she suddenly noticed her mother sat beside him. She told Elaine – she'd come to take her father to bed, which even in her dream seemed strange. And as Elaine watched them walk slowly away together, arm in arm, she began to understand its significance which of course upset her – was her father to pass away soon?

Consequently when Elaine finally received the news she'd been expecting, just a few days later, she wasn't totally shocked. Instead, she took great comfort in the thought that he was once again with her mother, his dear departed wife.

By all accounts, Sammy was distraught by the news of his father and sadly through some silly mix up, not of his doing, he missed his funeral by minutes, no doubt adding to his stress.

It seemed, Jill, who was still in touch with her brother since their father's hospital problems, had according to Melissa, given them the incorrect address of the crematorium to be used that day. But could it possibly have been Melissa who had passed on the wrong details on purpose? It was the sort of thing she was capable of, and the sort of thing she'd do. Still whoever was responsible; it clearly upset Sammy.

Unaccompanied by his wife as usual, he did however make it back for drinks at Elaine's, in order to show his respects. Although this wasn't to be for long, for when Elaine approached her brother to ask him how he was, he ran from the room quickly, muttering 'Please don't speak to me Elaine.'

Elaine was confused. Was he so upset about their father's death that he couldn't talk, or was it – he just didn't want to talk to her?

Mark, her husband who was over from Singapore for Alf's send off, told Elaine later, he thought she'd told him to sod off, especially after everything that happened previously and he thought she was in her rights to do so. He hadn't realised he'd just run out because she dared to talk to him. But Elaine guessed he'd probably been given strict instructions that under any circumstances were he to talk to her.

Years went by after the death of their father without any contact between Elaine and her brother, although Jill had managed to bridge that gap, unbeknown to her sister. It appeared Jill felt Sammy's daughter was missing out on his side of the family and she wanted to make amends.

So occasionally, it seemed, Jill would visit her brother with her husband Jeff. However, Jeff confessed later, he always felt the atmosphere in their house was more than a little strange and especially the unusual mother and daughter relationship that was still going on. And Jill had to agree.

This rekindled relationship between Jill and her brother was kept quiet from Elaine for some time, even though Jill admitted to her husband she'd felt awkward about this, particularly as her feelings regarding Melissa were the same. But Jill clearly felt her brother needed her support and wanted to stay in touch - no doubt feeling protective again. As Sammy had told Jill, he'd started to feel isolated from his own wife and daughter; still excluded from their strange relationship.

A year or so later Elaine moved back to the U.K and moved into a pretty house in the very same area as her brother. This didn't prove a problem though, for on the odd occasion when she did bump into him, they'd just ignore each other. But this was really sad as this was all because of one controlling woman with ideas of her own.

It was soon after her move back; Elaine was driving around the same area with her mother-in-law, who happened to be staying with her at the time. Stopping at nearby traffic lights, there waiting to cross the road in front of them, were two young women both wearing denim jeans. One also wore a cap with a large broad peak that partially hid her face. While the other woman, looked masculine, with dark red, short cropped hair and baggy clothing, which didn't suit at all.

Her mother-in-law, who was clearly amused by these women, pointed them out to Elaine as they started to cross the road, cuddling one another as they went – suggesting they were lesbians.

Elaine, who hadn't taken much notice up till then, peeped under the cap of the slimmer of the women and immediately recognised Melissa and guessed the other person was Kelly. Elaine was left speechless, although she wanted to laugh. As what were the chances of seeing them together? But more to the point, what did this behaviour indicate?

Elaine never said a word to her mother-in-law though; it was too complicated to explain - she never having met her brother or his family before. But as Elaine had already heard rumours about Melissa and her daughter, from friends who lived nearby – who'd spotted them in the area acting like this before, she wasn't shocked. Although she hadn't actually seen it for her-self and it did look strange.

As time went by, Jill and Sammy still remained in contact, although they only normally met at Christmas and birthdays. But when they did, Jill had to admit, the atmosphere in the house was no better. In fact it seemed to be worse, as Sammy was now spending most of his time downstairs, while Melissa and her daughter stayed upstairs, living in some kind of fantasy world according to Sammy.

On Jill's visits, Melissa and her daughter would often join them, all sitting in the lounge together. Yet the whispering and giggling still continued as if they had a something to hide. Jill was annoyed and very upset for her brother as she thought their behaviour rude. It was as if they had a secret that couldn't be shared, which was very embarrassing for Sammy. He was definitely being shut out and Jill sensed his discomfort, as he was clearly struggling with the unhealthy situation there. Consequently, he started suffering with depression and Jill was concerned.

Elaine on the other hand, who was still unaware of the secret meetings, had always felt Sammy had brought on most of his problems and was more concerned about her mothers' ashes, scattered around the rose bush, which hopefully still stood in Sammy's back garden. As she often felt how sad it was she had nowhere to pay her respects.

Until an acquaintance who just happened to be a Clairvoyant, that knew nothing of Elaine's family or her thoughts, told her during a reading, 'Your mother is aware of your concerns and wants you to know it is not important to go to a particular place to lay down flowers in order to show your respects. It's the thoughts that count and your mother will be aware of those.'

This comforted Elaine in more ways than one, as she had no desire to ever enter Sammy's house or garden again, although, she often wondered what her mother would be making of it all. As Elaine felt sure she was the only one who would really know the truth.

Chapter 8 - The Depression.

Depression can sit heavily on the mind when pangs of guilt and darkness play havoc with one's sub conscience. As sleep deprivation and recriminations are also symptoms of this illness.

Poor Sammy, it seemed he now believed he was to suffer the same fate as his dear mother. Convinced this was his destiny, his feelings of despair constantly dragged him down. And always comparing his health problems to hers, Sammy grew steadily worse.

Losing one's grip on reality can hit us all at one time or another but most of us have supportive families, loved ones and friends to help us through it. In Sammy's dark world, there appeared to be no one. It seemed things were out of his control and having distanced himself from the people that truly cared, what was he to do?

It appeared his wife had now grown tired of her husband's problems; even though it was obvious to most she was the main cause of them, having clearly lost interest in him some time ago. Although it was always in question she ever was. So not being helped by his nearest and dearest only added to his ever increasing sense of despair.

Losing his long standing job with the LEB during a period of serious cut backs a few years earlier had probably not helped Sammy either. Even though he'd taken on a part time job in the local aquarium shop, which he'd said he enjoyed - having kept tropical fish himself for many years before. His knowledge and enthusiasm on the subject was remarkable.

Yet his sense of worthlessness still prevailed it seemed and his depression got steadily worse, leaving him with feelings of inadequacy, his confidence long gone.

It appeared, Melissa had also recently taken on a part time job and they were rarely spending time together. Well, certainly not alone, as Melissa always left the house with Kelly whenever she went to school. Apparently Melissa told Sammy, 'this new job was very important,' only she had to switch on the computers, ready for the staff when they came into work." A friend had recommended this job to her, she said, but no one had heard of such employment.

Yet Sammy still believed her, even though he never knew who or where her employers were and he certainly never thought to ask. All of which, clearly caused him further stress, as he was always left on his own.

In fact Jill said, Sammy had found himself, alone more than ever these days, which wasn't helping his depression. Particularly after being dragged into an argument between Melissa and her mother – with him inevitably becoming the enemy, while mother and daughter quickly made up. This had then resulted in Sammy being further alienated and excluded from any future trips to his mother-in-law - on the pretext they now weren't talking.

Apparently Sammy wasn't too upset about this though, as he didn't really care for his mother-in-law, although he'd always been fond of her husband. Sadly, he'd passed away a few years earlier.

When Sammy told his sister about this so called argument, Jill felt sure this had been planned to ostracise Sammy from everyone, only Sammy had suspected as much himself and had indicated so to his sister. Which made Jill wonder if perhaps his depression had been brought on by the realisation of her games?

Even Sammy's best friend Lawrence had been told to keep away – having arrived earlier than his allotted time for a get together on Sammy's birthday. It seemed Melissa, who normally kept Kelly out of the way on his visits, went potty when Lawrence accidently bumped into her at the door - accusing him of 'chatting her up' and corrupting her in some way.

Lawrence was outraged he said, and told her she was mad. And he never saw his friend again after that. Melissa said, his visits were far to upsetting and unfortunately, Sammy was too weak to speak out.

Jill couldn't believe what was happening to her brother, things had really got quite bad. Well it certainly seemed that way. Or could it possibly be Melissa who was suffering; having to cope with the problems of a mentally sick man that she now claimed he was?

The eight year age gap between Melissa and Sammy also appeared to be a topic of conversation these days according to Lawrence, as she now delighted in telling everyone that people thought she looked like Sammy's daughter. And sadly, Sammy would only agree, feeding into her-self obsession and his obvious low-self-esteem.

Melissa appeared to go out of her way to upset Sammy these days, pulling all sorts of little stunts that even Jill couldn't comprehend and Lawrence had thought the same, apparently. He once told Jill, 'On the odd occasion, when they did venture out in the car together, Melissa would sit in the back as if she were a passenger and Sammy the taxi driver. Only Melissa said "she felt sick sitting in the front and felt better in the back," which is contrary to informed opinions.'

Now that his daughter was growing up fast and becoming a young lady, it appeared she too was being kept at a distance. Depriving Sammy of the love and contact he so desperately needed, which of course upset him further. And Jill often wondered if Melissa thought he may steal her love away. Or perhaps she just didn't want to share her? But this didn't make any sense. Although Sammy told his sister it was best he complied as she might call him a pervert, only no one would put that past her, with her warped and wicked mind.

One evening, much to Jill's surprise, Melissa, acting very much out of character, phoned her unexpectedly. She wanted to discuss Sammy's problems she said. Her mother told her, "Jill should be made aware of just how ill and depressed her brother was," and she asked Jill if she would come to visit him later that week.

Alarmed by the news, Jill promised she would, but wondered why Melissa had phoned her from a call box instead of from home - a practice she employed thereafter. And she wondered, was this to keep her calls a secret from Sammy?

Worried for her brother, Jill decided she would try to keep a closer eye on him, only on her last visit he'd appeared sullen and withdrawn and she wondered how she'd find him this time. As no one knew what was causing this strange state of affairs and it had gone on far too long for her liking.

As promised, Jill visited her brother the very next day and was surprised to see how quickly he'd deteriorated from her last visit. Alarmed by this further decline, Jill tried to reassure her brother that all was fine and that there was nothing for him to worry about - trying to offer some comfort. But Sammy told her, he was still extremely anxious, although he never explained why. He did however, make reference to the fact he found it very uncomfortable whenever he tried to urinate and Jill wondered what was causing this. She knew he'd already taken prescribed medication for an infection but it seemed it hadn't cleared up. The doctors told him it was nothing to worry about, but Sammy clearly thought it was.

Her brother's situation continued to trouble Jill and she decided to confide in her sister who still had no idea she was even in touch with Sammy. Elaine had lost contact with her brother after their last encounter at their father's funeral and had had no wish to communicate further.

Listening to Jill's story, Elaine too became alarmed, although peeved that all this had been kept from her and for a long time too.

'I don't like the sounds of all this Jill … I mean how would you know if he wasn't being slowly poisoned, only this could be causing his strange discomfort… after all it's pretty obvious she doesn't want him around by what you've told me. And if the doctors have no reason to look for poisoning, why would they. Let's face it Jill, look what happened to the dog.'

Jill didn't answer but nodded in agreement, her face pale and long.

'I wouldn't mind betting Sammy suspects her anyway and that's why he's acting so strange.' Elaine was convinced of her analysis.

Jill looked thoughtful. 'I know what you're saying makes sense, sis, but surely not,' she said. 'Although I must agree there's definitely something else playing on his mind but he won't discuss it with me.'

'Well, it's up to him, Jill; you can't force him. Look, if he wants to talk to me at anytime, please tell him I'm always here. I only live up the road … I mean … I don't want to see him suffering. If he wants to keep it a secret from Melissa that's fine with me, tell him we can always meet in the park.'

'I will do, sis, and from now on I'm going to keep an even closer eye on what's happening there, that's if I can of course.'

'Well, for some reason, you seem to be the only one allowed anywhere near him. I mean, you were even summoned there out of the blue. Are you sure you're not being used as a witness to something more sinister? Only I'm sure something's going down.'

Jill looked horrified. 'Don't say things like that, Elaine.'

'Well, I certainly feel someone should be reporting this to the police … so they have it all on file,' and Elaine really meant it, but of course she never did, even though she still considered Melissa very dangerous.

Ironically, it was only a few days earlier Elaine had been cleaning out her study and had come across some old photographs of her and Sammy together. But barely recognising the children in front of her, Elaine thought how sad it had been – only since those photo's both she and Jill had been through some difficult marriage problems. So hats off to Sammy whose marriage to Melissa had stood the test of time; perhaps she had misjudged her after all - but how wrong had she been. It seemed her initial feelings were right.

It was shortly after this unexpected reveal; Jill found Sammy's situation had grown even worse. It seemed every time she went to visit him he was more and more depressed. The atmosphere in the house always filled with a morbid kind of dread and she couldn't wait to leave.

It also appeared Sammy was now living permanently downstairs, sleeping on a mattress in the lounge. Never bothering to venture upstairs anymore, he paced up and down day and night because he couldn't sleep, while the incessant whispering between mother and daughter still carried on - upsetting him even further.

So poor Sammy, what chance did have with no one to give him comfort, as all his friends had disappeared driven away by his wife? The only contact he had left was with his sister Jill.

A couple of weeks later, Jill received another call from Melissa.

'Is it Sammy?' she asked, startled by yet another unexpected call. 'Is he okay?'

'That's why I'm phoning Jill ... he keeps asking for you now. He said he needs to see you. He just can't seem to sleep. Do you think you could come and visit him again tomorrow?'

'Well, I do have to go to work, but if it's really important … I could call in sick I suppose and then come along in the morning.'

'Oh thanks Jill I appreciate that. He'll be so pleased.'

Jill put the phone down baffled once more, wondering what was going on this time. Something was afoot, she was sure. But she had to play the game as she knew if she didn't the contact with her brother would immediately be stopped? Then who would be there for Sammy. No she had to keep the peace and not question.

Not able to sleep that night, worrying about Sammy, Jill wondered why he was so desperate to see her. Concerned how she'd find him she realised now she had to get to the route of his problems. Something was making him ill and it had to be sorted.

The next day Jill knocked on her brother's front door, wondering what she'd encounter this time. Melissa sounded so desperate on the phone she wasn't sure she was prepared for the drama she guessed would follow.

'Hello Jill. I'm so glad you could make it,' Melissa gushed as she opened the door.

Jill's face fell at the sight that stood in front of her, as Melissa hair was now bright red.

'Oh …you've changed your hair colour,' she said stating the obvious, shocked at its vividness, while thinking was this really appropriate to do right now?

'Yes, I thought I could do with a change. I think it's rather nice don't you,' she said, touching her hair for effect. 'I've always fancied being a redhead.'

Bewildered, Jill asked after her brother as she made her way into the house.

'He's actually not too bad today. In fact he's back in his bedroom. Go straight up if you like. We've decided he should really be in a proper bed seeing he's not sleeping too well downstairs. I've decided to share with Kelly from now on … so I don't disturb him that is,' and she gave an awkward laugh.

Jill was confused, she'd thought her visit was a matter of life and death and wondered what on earth Melissa was up to? This woman was definitely mad. Still, she was here now and she made her way up the stairs, keen to see her brother.

Entering Sammy's dark and gloomy room, Jill made her way to his bedside, feeling again that terrible presence of dread.

'Hello Sam, are you okay?' she whispered gently. But Sammy didn't answer.

Unable to see him properly in the dimly lit room, Jill went to the window.

'Let's open these, Sammy. It'll do you good to let some light in' and she pulled the curtains open, lighting up the room.

She noticed immediately the look of surprise on her brothers' pale drained face, as he rubbed the sleep from his eyes.

'Hello Jill, what you doing here … I wasn't expecting to see you?' He sounded as if he'd just woken up.

'I've come because Melissa said you were asking for me Sam… she said you couldn't sleep?'

Sammy didn't answer, but the look on his face said it all. Melissa had been lying again, but why this time, she thought?

Sammy looked terrible, the troubles of the world on his shoulders although he was clearly pleased to see his sister and immediately picked up. The colour returning to his cheeks, as they carried on talking.

Just as Sammy began to relax, he started to tell Jill something in private, when Melissa popped her head round the door. If looks could kill, Jill was certain Melissa would have dropped down dead, there and then; as the look on Sammy's face was pure hate.

'I think that's enough for now.' Melissa said. 'We don't want you wearing yourself out and getting upset again … do we Sam?' and she glared at her husband distastefully.

Sammy never said a word, but looked at Jill instead. He seemed so annoyed. Jill was confused; she'd only been with him ten minutes, so why the interruption she thought.

Dragging Jill out of the room on the pretext of showing her something she'd recently bought, Melissa took her into the spare bedroom. It seemed she too wanted to confide in Jill and lowered her voice to a whisper.

'Did you know he's been acting very strange just lately Jill … well, for quite some time actually?'.

'No?' she replied cautiously, although interested in the story she felt was about to follow. 'Steve … you know him … he was Sammy's old friend from work - they often went fishing together.'

'No, never heard of him.'

'Yes you have. Well, he stopped me the other day when I was walking along the street … he told me he'd found Sammy wandering around near the main road; he said he appeared to be lost. Anyway when Steve spotted him, Sammy looked dazed and very unhappy and didn't know where he was. You can check it all out with Steve if you like, I've got his number.'

Jill was intrigued but she didn't know what to say and definitely didn't want this man's number.

'Only it was Steve who was with Sammy when he had his first fit in the back of the works van all those years ago. He thinks Sammy's never been the same since.'

'Oh, I didn't know Sammy had a fit; poor thing. Well let's hope we can get him better and back to work soon.' Jill wanted to bring the conversation back to normal.

'Oh no, he won't be going back to work. He's lost that job. They don't want him back at the Aquarian shop anymore.'

More lies, Jill thought. After all why would he lose his job? She would pass that one by Lawrence later. See if he knew if it was true or not.

Jill attempted to get back to her brother's room but Melissa pulled her into the bathroom this time. It appeared she hadn't finished with her yet and didn't want her to leave, still talking constant drivel, none of which made any sense.

'Look Jill, these are the products I use to colour my hair, they're the same make that I use when I want to go blonde,' and she picked up a bright coloured packet, while rambling on about all sorts of stupid nonsense, mainly concerning hair, appearing to be stalling for time.

So, she was finally admitting she wasn't a natural blonde; Jill was amused by her confession. Being a blonde herself these days she knew when someone was dying their hair and had always guessed she'd been lying.

Confused and agitated now, Jill desperately wanted to leave although she wondered why Melissa was trying desperately to detain her. It was obvious she had some sort of plan in mind and started to tell her a story concerning Lawrence, Sammy's best friend, explaining how she felt his relationship with Sammy was strange. She even admitted she'd stopped him from visiting Sammy, saying she thought he upset him. Although Jill guessed it was probably her he upset. She then said, 'Sammy had come home one evening after meeting Lawrence with his trousers all ripped and torn, and blood on his backside… It was best he kept away.'

Jill didn't know what to say, after all, what was she implying? Was she suggesting Lawrence had attacked Sammy or that perhaps he was gay?

Thinking now that Melissa was completely balmy; Jill ignored her remarks but quickly realised, these accusations towards him were perhaps an attempt to convince her that Lawrence should be kept from the house. Perhaps also hoping, Jill would stop confiding in him, even hinting; this may be why Sammy was depressed.

Having heard enough of Melissa's rubbish, Jill was just about to make her excuse to leave when a knock was heard at the door.

'Ah, that must be Sammy's psychiatrist,' Melissa announced. 'He sees him quite regularly these days. He's been helping Sammy with his high anxiety and panic attacks,' she said, running down the stairs to let him in.

Jill realised then, this caller was probably the reason she was being held back. Melissa had wanted her to see him calling for some reason. Although Jill had never heard of a psychiatrist giving home visits before and why hadn't Melissa ever mentioned him?

Saying goodbye to her brother quickly, Jill promised she'd call again soon, still wondering why she'd been summoned there so urgently that day. It certainly wasn't because Sammy had asked to see her. And still annoyed that she'd missed her opportunity to talk in private with her brother, she hoped next time she would.

On the way out Melissa introduced Jill to the doctor and mentioned again how frequent his calls to Sammy were. The man nodded in response as Jill eyed him keenly, thinking his dishevelled appearance was not in keeping with a man of his profession, but what did she know.

Thanking Jill for coming, Melissa quickly passed her Steve's number, insisting she should call him regarding the strange incident in the street. Jill placed the note in her pocket.

Closing the door gently behind her, she watched them make their way towards the staircase - a feeling in the pit of her stomach that something wasn't right. She only hoped it was a figment of her imagination.

At home later, Jill couldn't wait to tell her sister about her earlier visit, hoping she could shed some light on the strange goings on in her brother's life.

Chapter 9 - Sinister suspicions.

Elaine picked up the phone and listened to her sisters rambling.

'It certainly sounds as if something's going down, sis. I would definitely say you're being used to witness, Sammy's poor state of mind, which is clearly being made to look as if he has serious mental issues.' And Elaine suspected another attempted suicide might possibly occur, just like her fathers.

'So why does she want me involved?' Jill asked.

'Well I suppose, if something should happen, they'll put this down to his depression, which of course you will be able to verify, having just witnessed a psychiatrist coming to visit him, and often according to Melissa.' Elaine felt sure this was the plot and became extremely concerned for her brother.

'No... you don't really think that, do you?' Jill was clearly puzzled and still not convinced about her sisters summary; although she did admit, something certainly was amiss, it seemed, she just couldn't accept how wicked Melissa could be though.

'Well, I don't trust her, and nothing would surprise me with that woman; in fact I really do think I should report this to the police now.'

'They'd think you were mad if you did.'

'Exactly, and that's what's alarming, as it's not me that's bloody mad, but I know who is and it's not Sammy.'

****

Lawrence, who was still unable to get near his dear friend, was normally kept updated by Jill and still concerned about Melissa's spouting's she rang him that evening to give him the latest news. Wanting some answers, she asked Lawrence, if he knew who this Steve guy was that Sammy had supposedly gone fishing with.

'Yes, I know him … Steven Brown. He's no friend of Sammy's. He fell out with him years ago... I believe it was over some private work they were doing together. Apparently Steve tried to rip him off and I understand Sammy's not spoken to him since.'

'That's strange; Melissa said he was a good friend,' but she should have known it was a lie. 'Did you know that Sammy had a fit at work, Larry?'

'That's the first I've heard of it.'

Jill then told Lawrence about the rest of her visit and Sammy losing his job, although omitting the accusations concerning the ripped trousers.

No doubt concerned for his friend, Lawrence sounded troubled and promised he'd look into it.

Still shocked by the news of Sammy and wanting to help, Lawrence called in at the Aquarium shop to see his boss John he said later – he wanted to ask specifically if he'd lost his job.

'No mate, of course he hasn't. He's a good worker here; we appreciate his knowledge and expertise. I told his wife; as soon as he's better he's welcome back here anytime.'

'He seemed fairly genuine,' Lawrence told Jill when he rang her later, 'In fact he seemed a charming man. He told me, Sammy had a job whenever he was ready to go back.'

Jill didn't know what to say. She'd guessed this had been another lie and Melissa only wanted to upset Sammy.

'You know he really enjoys that job Jill, he would be truly gutted if he thought he'd lost it.'

'Yes I'm sure he would.'

'Anyway … because I wasn't happy about Melissa telling lies, I've left my number with him, just in case he ever wants to find out more about Sammy.'

'Good idea. Well I suppose there's nothing else we can do now Larry. Let's just hope Sammy pulls himself together.'

The next day Jill decided to phone this so called friend of her brothers, out of curiosity more than anything else. Although she had no idea what she was going to say. The phone rang for quite a while and Jill was just about to put the phone down when someone answered.

'Hi, is that Steve?' she asked embarrassed at having phoned now, still not sure what to say.

'Yes, this is he. Can I help you?' a deep rich voice bellowed down the phone.

'Yes, I'm Sammy's sister, Jill?'

'Oh hi, I've heard a lot about you.'

Jill wondered what he'd heard. 'Melissa said you found Sammy wandering about lost and confused the other day?' She had no idea where she was going with this though.

'Yeah, that's right: I was worried about him. That's why I mentioned it to Mel, only I bumped into her at

Sainsbury's only the other day. I was with my wife at the time and thought I ought to tell her.'

A little discrepancy there Jill thought, Melissa didn't say they'd met at Sainsbury's, and why was he keen to mention his wife, she was curious.

'So ... how was he when you approached him?' she asked. 'Was he okay?' She still felt stupid at having called.

'Well he was acting kinder strange ...but then he has been ever since he had that attack in the work's van and that was a while ago.'

'What sort of attack was that?'

'A panic attack I suppose. I understand he's seeing a doctor about it now... well so Mel said, they think he may be suffering with high anxiety or something like that?'

'Yes, I believe so,' and not really having any other questions to ask, an awkward silence fell between them. So thanking him for his concerns she quickly said her goodbyes.

'Don't forget; if there's anything else I can help you with, please don't hesitate to get in touch. Sammy was a dear friend.'

Odd, Jill thought, why was he still insisting they were such good friends? She hadn't even heard of him before. And why did Melissa insist she should ring him? After all, he'd said himself; Sammy was consulting a doctor now, what else was there to do.

On Jill's next visit to see her brother, a week or so later, she found him much improved.

'My, Sammy... you're looking so much better,' she said, relieved, now watching him sat at the kitchen table, out of his pit at last and drinking a mug of steaming hot tea. Jill was pleased that Sammy appeared back to his normal self but the atmosphere in the house felt no better, especially with Melissa hovering around.

'Look at him, Jill,' Melissa nagged, as she eyed him with distaste. 'He's got to pull himself together, don't you think so Jill. Only he's looking more and more like my father every day – you wouldn't think he was my husband. Would you?'

Jill looked at Melissa in disbelief. Shouldn't she just be thankful he was up and about and feeling that much better? She was unbelievable Jill thought.

'Yeah,' Sammy remarked, half-joking, 'Everyone thinks she's my daughter these days,' and he raised his eyes in jest.

'Well, you should be doing something about it then… don't you think so Jill? I mean, I do look like his daughter… don't I?'

Jill was speechless and looked on in amazement.

'Okay Mel, don't go on. Yes, I probably do look like your father but you keep going on and on, wearing me down,' and he pushed his thumb hard on the kitchen table, showing her exactly what he meant.

'She keeps doing this to me all the time, pick, pick, pick, especially about Larry. She keeps going on and on about him, she really doesn't want me to see him again!'

Having made Sammy lose he's cool - mission accomplished; Melissa quickly ran up the stairs in order to join her daughter, 'to help her with her homework', she said.

'So, Kelly's at home?' Jill said surprised, although still baffled by Melissa's performance.

'Yeah, she's got this week off school,' and he quickly changed the subject, suggesting they went out into the garden.

'It's such a nice day; we can get some fresh air.' He sounded very weary.

'Good idea Sam, let's do that.' Jill knew Melissa wouldn't follow them out there, which would leave them free to talk. She felt sure Sammy wanted to confide in her and out of earshot of others.

It was early May, and the garden was starting to look lovely. Jill was impressed, although it wasn't as well maintained as it usually was, owing to Sammy's illness she guessed.

Taking in the beauty surrounding them, Jill noticed the pretty pond which sat close by, now full of gliding carp, in a myriad of vibrant colours. Fascinated, she watched them bob their little heads above the flowing waters as they sang their soundless songs. This was clearly Sammy's little haven where he could escape from all his troubles, far different from the dull, heavy, atmosphere inside the house. She then noticed the pretty rose bush that still stood at the back of the house its flowers in tones of deep, blood red now in full bloom. And this made her think of her mother, wondering what she would make of it all.

'The garden looks beautiful Sammy. You must work hard to keep it looking so good.'

'Yes, I do Jill,' he said, sounding very tired. 'It's just a shame Melissa doesn't appreciate it. In fact she won't even come and sit outside. I brought her a canopy to keep the sun off her as well … but she isn't interested. Cost me a fortune too.'

God, she doesn't know how lucky she is, Jill thought. I would love a garden like this.

'So how are you really feeling now, Sammy?' she said, grabbing his hand. 'You're looking so much better.'

'Yes I do feel better Jill but I still have some problems I need to sort out.'

Jill remained silent as she wondered what they were; although she had a good idea.

'Firstly I need to sort myself out, only I must get back on track – and secondly, I have to sort out my marriage.'

What, did he mean by that, Jill didn't like to ask? It was obvious from his manner he didn't want it discussed. Loyal to the end and still in love, she guessed.

With Sammy not wanting to elaborate on his marriage problems, Jill wondered if Melissa wanted to leave him. Perhaps there was someone else, only this could be the reason why he'd been so depressed and would also explain why Melissa was dressing so much younger and even changing her hair colour.

Still struggling with what he wanted to say, a lengthy silence fell between them. It was obvious he couldn't express his true feelings and sensing his awkwardness, Jill changed the subject not wanting to upset him further.

'So how's Kelly doing, Sammy … only I don't see her very much these days?' thinking it safer to talk about his daughter.

'I wouldn't know. I don't see much of her either Jill.'

Jill felt so sorry for her brother. What had he done to deserve this? After all he had provided well for his family and even doted on them both. She couldn't understand it; there seemed no justice in the world as both she and Elaine had struggled in the past without the support of a husband. Melissa was an ungrateful cow. She'd never had to work and the work she did at present was questionable; it just didn't seem fair.

'I don't understand, Sammy, what do you mean? Of course you must see her.'

'Jill, see that window up there,' and he pointed towards a window at the top of the house. 'That's where they spend all their time together, normally in a different room from me and watching bloody television as usual. She's still obsessed with films and always seems to live in some kind of fantasy world and she's encouraging Kelly too. I just don't know what to do. I can't even separate them.'

'Oh, Sammy, that's terrible... can't you have a word with Kelly?'

'Don't be daft; Melissa won't even leave me alone with her. In fact I never get to spend any quality time or any time at all with either of them.'

'But what does Kelly say?'

'Kelly even blanks me sometimes and won't speak to me for days. It's absurd... I mean she's off school today and that's the only reason why Melissa's here. I don't usually see her during the day. She normally goes out when Kelly's at school.'

'I don't know what to say, Sammy. Perhaps Kelly's just at that funny age where kids don't want to talk to their parents. Although I must admit it doesn't seem right.' But Jill knew nothing appeared to be right, when Melissa was involved. And Jill wondered why Sammy put up with it, wife or not?

Jill could tell Sammy had a lot more on his mind than he dared to say. He should really talk to someone else, as she lived so far away. She couldn't just pop in every day; she had to go to work. Furthermore she was going abroad with her husband in a few days and for almost three weeks. If only he would talk to sis.

Remembering their conversation, Jill mentioned Elaine's suggestion, hoping this might help. 'You could meet in the park if you like Sammy … and you don't have to tell Melissa if you don't want to.'

Sammy thought for a while and sounding regretful, replied, 'I know Elaine and I used to get on … but I'm afraid Melissa wouldn't like it.'

So she still had him under the thumb, even now. Oh well, at least she'd put the offer forward. The main problem was it seemed, he'd been controlled for so long it had clearly become the norm, he knew no different now. And she wondered if he'd ever escape her clutches.

Jill hugged her brother close as she struggled to say her goodbyes, promising to come back to see him straight after her holidays. But tears had sprung to Sammy's eyes as he hugged his sister back and Jill knew then things were still not right, even though he appeared more positive.

Glad he was at last out of that morbid state though, and in a much better place in his mind, Jill hoped whatever had caused it was over with now. Although when Melissa was involved, it was never that simple, as they were all about to find out.

Chapter 10 – The birthday

It was the 29th May, 1998, the day after Elaine's birthday and a day she knew she wouldn't forget in a hurry. Already middle aged, she still found her birthdays a good excuse for a celebratory drink or two, and this one was to be no different.

Not a bad looking woman for her age she thought, having kept a decent figure, and a young dress sense. She wore her hair long and blonde these days, determined to find out if they did have more fun.

Sheila a very dear friend, whose birthday was a few days earlier had travelled that morning from Southampton in order to celebrate together. Elaine had known Sheila from her younger days, when they worked together in a well known London department store, at the ripe old age of sixteen. They often reminisced about those days and their past expediencies - talking fondly of times gone by. And Sheila also spoke fondly of Sammy too.

She was surprised at the way his life had turned out, as she remembered him as a 'fun guy', who liked a good time, she said. However she didn't really know Melissa but had witnessed her performance at Elaine's first wedding, and had formed her own opinion of her, which she admitted, wasn't particularly nice. But as both women had been through their own marriage problems they understood only too well, things were never as they seemed

As Elaine's husband, Mark was still working abroad at this time; it was difficult for him to join her for her birthday. So Elaine thought a fun night out with a few close friends would be a brilliant idea instead. A bite to eat, a few exotic cocktails and an enjoyable dance at Chicago's, could be just what the doctor would order. Even if it was the day after her birthday, Friday was always a much better night out anyway.

In the meantime the two friends spent most of the day catching up on old times; laughing about all the silly antics they got up to as young girls. While joking about their more recent exploits too.

Sheila had been an attractive girl in her youth and had carried those looks into womanhood. A vibrant character, whose life it appeared, had been one drama after another, which never seemed to get her down. And being a pretty good story teller too, conversations normally ended in hoots of girlish laughter.

The story telling however was suddenly interrupted when the phone rang in the lounge. Expecting it to be a friend calling about the evening's arrangements Elaine ran to answer it. She was surprised though when she heard a voice she hadn't heard in a long time - a familiar voice which she couldn't quite place at first.

'Hello, Elaine ... it's me... Larry.'

'Larry?' She repeated. Then she remembered - Sammy's best friend Lawrence. What did he want she wondered?

It's funny how the mind works quickly in just a few seconds, putting two and two together and coming up with eight. As all sorts of thoughts ran through her mind, imagining the worst of course and she wondered why he'd called.

Was there a problem? He didn't normally ring to wish her a happy birthday and he sounded so strange, almost upset. Was it to do with Sammy? After all, things hadn't been right she knew.

Hoping there was nothing seriously wrong and it was just a catch up call, Elaine replied calmly. 'Oh … hello Larry, how are you?' and she held her breathe while she waited his reply.

'It's Sammy, Elaine … I'm afraid I have some bad news.'

Oh no, I knew it she thought, still suspecting the worst.

'There's been a bad incident … Sammy was hit by a train,' and emotions getting the better of him, he blurted out, 'I'm sorry Elaine; he's dead… it happened yesterday.'

Elaine placed her hand over her mouth as she heard him say those words and even though she'd been expecting something like this, it was still a huge shock when she did.

'Oh my God Larry … I'm so sorry, I know how close you two were.'

'I know, Elaine. I just can't believe it.'

'But what did you mean by an incident Larry? Did he jump?' Elaine needed to know the truth.

'I'm not sure. They said he was looking for something on the tracks. But I think he may have, although they didn't say that … it just doesn't make any sense. Apparently Melissa's said it was all on camera so the family will know it had nothing to do with her.'

Elaine couldn't believe what she was hearing, typical of her to think like that, which was enough to make her suspicious.

'I would have called Jill ... but of course she's still on holiday,' and at this point she heard him sob. Unable to carry on, his wife Jackie took over the call – 'Sorry Elaine he's very upset.'

'I quite understand Jackie. It's a shock for me too, but I must admit I'm not completely surprised. I was half expecting something... but not this.'

Elaine was stunned, although she wasn't sure how to feel. After all she hadn't had any communication with her brother in years. In fact he'd cut her dead several times and turned down her offer to talk. How on earth should she feel?

'I know it's terrible.' Jackie agreed. 'Larry and I just cannot believe it. It's all so sad.'

Still shocked by the news, Elaine explained how she hadn't spoken to Sammy in ages. 'Although I always knew what was going on and how depressed he'd become lately only Jill always kept me up dated. I personally blame Melissa for this; I'm sure she's got something to do with it!'

At this point Lawrence came back on the phone. Keen to speak about his friend again.

'I hadn't seen Sammy for sometime either, Elaine. Melissa banned me from the house ... she said I upset him too much.'

'That woman's mad, I tell you,' and Lawrence agreed.

'I was told they were on their way to buy some clothes,' Lawrence continued, 'they'd decided to catch a bus to

Wimbledon. Only Melissa wouldn't let him drive apparently, given he was still on medication. It seems on route they realised the M&S they were heading for didn't carry clothing so they got off the bus to catch a train.'

'But there are loads of M&S branches much closer that do carry clothing... so why go there?'

'What was he doing on the Tube anyway Elaine? He hadn't been on one in over twenty years!'

Up to this point, Elaine didn't realise he'd been talking about the underground and was even more perplexed.

'He never saw the train coming, apparently,' Larry said, carrying on with his story.

'What do you mean, he never saw it coming. You can feel the wind from the tunnel as it approaches the station?'

Lawrence went quite and then replied, 'you know you're right ... I think I'll check that out myself. Make a few enquiries ... because it does sound rather suspicious.'

'I tell you that woman's responsible for this in some way. I told Jill I wasn't happy with what was going on there.' Elaine was convinced something untoward had happened.

Lawrence, who sounded more contained now, was determined to finish off his story. 'Anyway, after the accident they airlifted him to White Chapel Hospital.'

'So it was definitely an accident then?'

'Well I think that's what they're saying... it had something to do with mice. Apparently they'd been talking about them on the bus. When they reached the station Sammy was looking on the lines for them and that's when it happened.'

'Are you sure? Who told you that?'

'Sammy's boss, John... Melissa must have rung him to tell him the news and as I'd left my telephone number with him the other day when I called in to ask about Sammy's job, I suppose he thought he should ring me... although I'm not sure if Melissa asked him to; he didn't say.'

'Yes, I heard all about his job and her lies. But why would she ring his boss before ringing the family... mind you Jill is away on holiday and she only really speaks to her. I'm sorry Larry I need to get my head around this and of course I need to ring Jill … she'll be very upset.' And she promised she'd call him back with any further news.

Well, happy birthday, she thought to herself as she placed the phone down, the feeling of merriment long gone and impossible to recapture. And a heavy gloom descended on the house that only minutes before had been filled with fun and laughter.

Sheila walked into the lounge having heard part of the conversation -clearly concerned for her friend whose face looked drained and pale now.

'Are you okay?' Sheila asked, placing her arm around her.

'Not really.' But even though she was shocked, she still couldn't cry. Not even as she explained the terrible news to Sheila, as there was far too much going on in her mind to be upset at this moment. She was sure there'd been a crime committed somewhere along the line and she wasn't happy.

'I must call Jill … tell her what's happened,' Elaine said not relishing the task. 'Jill will be home in a few days, so she shouldn't need to change her ticket...after all, what's the point - although it will certainly ruin the rest of her holiday.'

'Do you think it might be best if we cancel tonight?' Sheila asked, clearly concerned for her friend still.

Elaine thought a while and then replied, 'No, I think it should still go ahead … yes, let's celebrate … celebrate his great escape from her,' and she laughed in exasperation.

Elaine managed to track her sister down after only a few short phone calls, and needless to say, she was devastated by the news. Being the closest to him she must have felt the loss more deeply, no doubt wondering if she could have done more for him. Although what more could she possibly have done? And she mentioned as much to her sister.

'It's far too late to be wondering what and why, Jill. At least he's at peace now.' And she reluctantly agreed.

There were only a few more phone calls required after that, informing his nieces and a few mutual friends. Only Sammy didn't have a big family or many friends. Melissa made sure of that.

The evening out wasn't much of a success either, unsurprisingly, although the girls did manage a few large drinks when toasting to her brother and including his great escape from the witch. Yet pointing out it needn't have been so drastic.

'Well at least she can't get to him anymore, poor sod,' Elaine said, as they raised their glasses again. And although strange to be out celebrating at this particularly time, it was only a small group of friends and Elaine felt happier amongst them.

'What a birthday! … and one I won't forget in a hurry,' she said looking at Sheila who sat at her side. In fact, she'd thought about that a lot, as it was rather strange it happened on her birthday. It couldn't have been planned any better, if

97

indeed it was. But knowing how Melissa hated her, she wouldn't put that past her at all.

Elaine went to bed late that night with her mind working overtime and still wondering if Melissa was guilty of causing her brother's death. But more importantly, was she going to get away with it.

But surely if she was responsible, the police would find out. Or was it up to her to make her thoughts and feelings known? She only wished she'd gone to the police when she had her first suspicions. Although, was there any point - they wouldn't have believed her. And anyway it didn't really matter now; she couldn't save her brother, he was already dead!

Chapter 11 – The enquiry

The police officer arrived at 8 am the following morning keen to take down the statement from the injured man's wife. By rights he should have insisted he took it the evening before but concerned for the woman's wellbeing and believing she was in shock, he made the decision to leave it till now.

Knocking on her door, he wondered how he'd find her. Would she have come to terms with what had happened yet?

Answering the door fresh faced, she invited him into the house, her voice still hoarse from her screams of the previous day, she said.

Showing the officer into the lounge, Melissa seated herself at the large mahogany table placed at one end of the room, and waited for him to join her.

The room with its oversized green printed sofa and matching curtains still remained closed, making the room dingy and dark; the atmosphere heavy and gloomy. Brushing aside unsettled feelings, the officer sat down beside her, poised with pen in hand.

'Right, Mrs Clayton. Can you tell me exactly what happened from the moment you left your home yesterday? You said something about shopping and looking for mice?'

'Mice… No. What do you mean?' Melissa looked astonished.

Her attitude had changed yet again he thought. And confused by this woman who appeared so composed now, he wondered what happened to the distraught looking woman from yesterday.

He then noticed a young girl standing nervously in the doorway and guessed she was the daughter, her face bewildered and scared. A tall girl, who looked much older than her fourteen years, worried for her father and mother, no doubt.

Hesitant to come forward, she remained in the hallway. It was only after a sign from her mother that she eventually disappeared, leaving them free to talk.

'Have you rung the hospital yet, Mrs Clayton?' he asked, realising she hadn't mentioned her husband yet. 'How is Mr Clayton today?'

'Yes, I rang earlier this morning... he's still in a coma and barely alive. They don't hold much hope of him pulling through now.'

He thought her reply sounded cold and uncaring and he gave her a quizzical look. 'Oh that's a shame Mrs Clayton. Let's hope they've got that wrong... now let's start from the beginning,' he said, still baffled by her tone.

Settling herself down, Melissa began what seemed like a well prepared story.

'Well ...Sammy had been suffering with depression these last few months, a form of high anxiety we were told. Only he'd been under the doctor for some time you see. He's suffered on and off with this for year,' and casually added, 'his sister Jill will vouch for that,' and the policeman made a note on his pad, while she carried on her story.

'He was starting to feel a lot better of late but he'd lost a lot of weight over this period. Anyway, he didn't have any trousers that fitted properly, so we were on our way to buy him a new pair.' She paused at this point, pushing her hair from her face while pulling a tissue from her pocket.

'Okay, Mrs Clayton, let's take it slowly, I understand how you must feel.'

But Melissa carried on un-wavered. 'Anyway, he wanted to go by car…but I wouldn't let him as he was still on medication.' She then dabbed her eyes with the tissue, muttering, 'If only I had.'

'Are you sure you're okay, Mrs Clayton, or would you like to stop for a while?'

'No, no … I'm fine' she insisted and instantly composed herself, as she then proceeded to tell him how they'd caught the bus to Wimbledon in the hope of buying the trousers. Until she realised the store they were heading for didn't carry clothing.

'So, we got off the bus at Colliers Wood, to catch the tube which would take us to Tooting … only we both know Tooting Broadway very well, only Sammy lived there when we first got married,' and she smiled as if remembering something nice.

The policeman carried on making notes, but thought the story strange as there were many Marks and Spencer's much nearer to their home that did carry clothing. So why pick Wimbledon he wondered? Oh well, an easy mistake. At least she was concerned about him driving.

'So what happened next?' he asked.

'Well, we got what we wanted in British Home stores and we were on our way back home… but when we were on the platform, Sammy realised he'd dropped his ticket. After searching everywhere he believed it must have fallen on the tracks. It was while bending over to look for it that it suddenly happened. The train just appeared from nowhere. It was awful!'

'So, what happened about the mice?'

'What mice?'

The policeman realised he was getting nowhere with this line of questioning and decided to change tactics.

'So, it was an accident then?'

'Yes, most definitely'

The policeman hadn't told her he'd already viewed the CCTV footage of the incident the evening before and was baffled by what he'd seen.

'It appears you were hanging around on the platform for some time, Mrs Clayton. Why didn't you get on the first train that came along?'

Melissa looked surprised and immediately turned defensive.

'Well he couldn't find his ticket and if we'd carried on we would've received a fine - wouldn't we?'

The policeman didn't answer but made more notes, while Melissa carried on with her story.

'I was also very worried about my daughter at this time and wanted to get home quickly, only Kelly was due back from school. I was keen for him to find the lost ticket, as I was starting to feel shaky.'

Melissa looked upset by the policeman's questions but he was annoyed and not happy with her explanations as they didn't make any sense. After all, she told him initially; they were looking for bloody mice!

'So, although on medication and not fit to drive you let him approach the edge of the platform looking for a lost ticket, even though there are yellow lines placed there for everyone's safety?'

'Well I didn't push him, if that's what you're inferring.'

'No, Mrs Clayton, it shows that on the camera footage quite clearly. You were nowhere near him at the time, and, considering he wasn't a well man I'm surprised you left him unsupervised.'

'Well my hair was blowing about with the wind from the tunnel when the train approached the station... I left him at that point and went to the bench to tie it back.' She sounded quite irate now.

The policeman then wondered - if she knew the train was coming, why didn't her husband?

'Okay, Mrs Clayton I will leave it at that for now. I expect you need to visit Mr Clayton ... don't you?'

'Yes, I'm waiting for my mother to arrive; we're going together to the hospital,' she looked at her watch. 'She should be here any minute.

Unsure what to make of her statement, the policeman decided to leave it for now but he felt more perturbed than ever. Although for sure, he knew she hadn't pushed him.

The following morning, Jill's eldest daughter Caron, who'd already been told of her uncle's sad death via her Aunty, had discovered to her surprise, he was actually still alive. Having rung Whitechapel hospital to find out the details of his passing, she had found her enquiry met with much confusion.

103

'No? ... Mr Clayton's not dead!' the nurse on reception replied. 'However he is in a coma and the next few days will be the most critical ... but we have great hopes for his recovery. I'm sorry; who did you say you were?' The nurse was clearly confused, after all why would anyone think a patient was dead when they certainly weren't.

'I'm Mr Clayton's niece, Mrs Caron Ball. And that's great news about my uncle; although I was told only yesterday he was hit by a train and had died!'

'Who told you that?'

'Well, my aunt, Mr Clayton's sister, who was told by my uncle's best friend, who'd been told by my uncle's boss. Who I assume was told by my uncle's wife.' Realising this all sounded ridiculous Caron tried to make light of it all. 'Oh well, at least we know he's still with us ... that is definitely good news,' and she then proceeded to take down the name of the intensive care unit her uncle was on and the visiting times.

Later that morning Elaine received a call from Caron with this unexpected news.

'What! You're joking,' Elaine was mortified, although of course pleased with the outcome. 'But Larry was told he was dead. This is ridiculous!'

'Well, he is in a coma, Aunty, but stable they said and definitely still alive, although he is in intensive care. I've rung mum already and told her. She'll be home in a couple of days and said she'd go straight there to see him.'

'Well I'm picking Mark up from the airport later today; I might go with him to visit Sammy. If I bump into Melissa, she'll have to lump it. Sammy is more important now.

Thanks for letting me know Caron. I'd better let Lawrence know too. I'm sure he'll be pleased, although shocked of course.'

'By the way, Aunty, I also called the Metropolitan police to find out exactly what happened on the underground. But they said only his wife was privy to that information, although they assured me there was nothing untoward.'

Elaine wasn't so sure about that though, but she didn't pass comment, this wasn't the time for that. So Caron gave her Aunty the hospital details and said her goodbyes, promising to ring her if she heard any further news, clearly happy to have helped.

Elaine put the phone down completely confused, wondering how anyone could have made such a mistake. It all seemed bloody ridiculous.

Picking up the phone again, Elaine dialled Larry's number and told him the surprising news.

Baffled, for sure, Lawrence was finding it hard to comprehend, 'I don't bloody believe it!' he said, venting his anger.

'I know Larry; I can't understand it either. I mean how can anyone say someone has died when they haven't? Although that same person had done so before, when neighbour's had asked about Dad.'

'Yes, it beggars belief … but that is what John told me Elaine. I'm not making it up.'

'Oh, I don't doubt it, Larry. I just think its wishful thinking on her part.'

'I'd better go see him straightaway then. Thanks for letting me know Elaine.' And they promised to keep in touch.

Elaine met her husband at Heathrow airport later that afternoon and took the train straight to London and the tube onto Whitechapel and the hospital.

Elaine wasn't sure how she'd find her brother but she was glad she had her husband's support. She only hoped she didn't bump into Melissa, she didn't need confrontations.

On reaching Sammy's ward, they approached his bed with trepidation, feeling now they shouldn't be there, especially as they knew Melissa wouldn't approve. But Elaine needed to see her brother; after all it could be her last chance. And out of respect for Sammy and their parents, she put her grievances to one side. She needed to be strong for her brother.

Taking a deep breath Elaine pushed back the long blue Plastic curtain from around her brother's bed with caution, only to be greeted by a warm and friendly young male nurse who said he'd been with Sammy since he first came on the ward. Who appeared to be making notes of all of Sammy's visitors, which immediately made her suspicious, wondering why he was.

Shocked by Sammy's lifeless body, Elaine grabbed her husband's hand. He looked so weak and frail laying there - his complexion pale and drained. The bandages wrapped around his badly damaged head a similar colour. And with his beard now stripped away, he no longer resembled the brother she'd once known and this made her feel uneasy. Yet the rhythm of his heartbeat echoed steadily around the room.

Too scared to make a noise, Sammy remained oblivious they were even there. While also unaware of the strange array of tubes and wires attached to his body. And this reminded her of the film she'd once watched of an alien undergoing experimental surgery and she felt for her brother.

The nurse smiled at Elaine reassuringly. His blonde curly hair now sat like a golden hallo around his head.

Afraid to speak too loudly still, she whispered to the nurse as she introduced herself.

'How's he doing?' she asked.

'He's doing very well actually. They operated on him yesterday, taking away the lower right lobe of his brain. The bandages are hiding most of the damage. But it's all looking good.'

'What about physically' Mark asked, eyeing Sammy sympathetically.

'His body has taken quite a blow, but he's a tough guy and has only come away with a few broken ribs. Although there's a lot of internal bruising, but that should heal quite quickly.'

'So how will he be when he comes out of the coma, if he does?' Elaine asked.

'We don't know for sure… the brain can be difficult to diagnose at times as it responds differently with each and every person. This particular part of the brain should only affect his personality - but it could take him a while to recall. The short term memory is normally the most affected but we can only wait and see.'

'Has his wife been up to see him yet?' Mark dared ask.

Elaine gave him a dirty look; she'd wanted to keep well away from that subject.

Keen to reply at first, the nurse hesitated, it seemed he wasn't sure if he should ask or not. 'Is she okay?' he finally said. 'I mean … has she had any psychological problems?'

Mark hid a smile as he looked at Elaine. But she didn't say a word. She'd promised herself she wouldn't.

'Well, we do have our doubts let's say,' Mark said, realising the nurse had no doubt sussed her out.

'Only she doesn't seem to comprehend what's being said, especially regarding her husband's condition. But I suppose she has had a terrible shock… anyway, I've made a note in my book.'

'What about his daughter?' Mark asked, clearly wanting to push this as far as he could.

'Well … the mother didn't want her to see him at first … but I thought she was old enough and insisted. I thought it would help her psychologically you see. However, the mother became very agitated, even though the daughter was fine with it all. The grandmother on the other hand got hysterical and flung herself across his bed. I had to ask her to leave in the end.'

Elaine looked at Mark in amazement, shocked by her actions, considering they'd supposedly fallen out.

Still unable to communicate with Sammy and not wanting to intrude any longer, they thanked the nurse for his time and made tracks back to the airport to pick up the car, pleased they'd made the journey, although all very sad.

Chapter 12 - Feedback

Lawrence rang Elaine later that evening to report on his visit earlier that day. He too had been given the same information concerning Sammy's present state. Much to his surprise, however, he said he'd bumped into Melissa.

'Never ... what did you say to her?'

'Well, I had hoped I wouldn't see her. After all, the last time we met, she had a right go at me, and just for talking to Kelly. Banning me from ever seeing my friend again'

'Well, I said she was mad... so what happened?' Elaine was keen to hear the whole story.

'I asked her why she was telling everyone Sammy was dead.'

'And?'

'She said, he was as good as and it was just a matter of her telling them when to turn off his life support machine. She actually said "she was waiting for Jill to get back from her holidays before letting them do so".'

'But that's nonsense.'

'I know and I told her so ... I also told her it was more than likely Sammy would pull through; but I don't think it sunk in.'

'No, because she bloody doesn't want him to,' Elaine was furious.

But then Lawrence sounded sheepish, 'You know, I actually felt sorry for her; she looked so scared and pathetic. She was there with Kelly and her mother, so I suggested we went for a coffee. I thought what a sensible girl Kelly was; so well adjusted, considering.'

'Well, that's not right is it if she's just nearly lost her father. Shouldn't she be upset?'

'Yes, I suppose so.'

On reflection though Elaine thought perhaps she was being unfair; after all, the whole event must have been traumatic. Yet there were still too many things that didn't add up, which didn't make her happy. But what could she do?

So Elaine decided to wait till Jill got back to see what she thought.

Once home, Jill went straight to the hospital, only to find Sammy in much the same state - still in a coma but stable.

Jill, who was staying at her daughter's overnight, just happened to live in the same area as Melissa and so she decided to pay her a visit the next day. She wanted to ask her, face to face what actually happened on that day- prepared to go into battle for her brother once again, just as she did when they were children.

Having decided not to take anymore of Melissa's nonsense, Jill knocked firmly on her door, wanting a full explanation. But when the door sprung back, there stood before her a short dark haired, dumpy woman with large bulging eyes, which threw her completely.

'Who are you?' the woman asked abruptly as she eyed Jill up and down.

'I'm Sammy's sister... who are you more to the point?'

By this time, Melissa had come to the door.

'Oh, come in Jill. I'm glad you're back. Have you been up to see him yet? Doesn't he look awful?' Jill didn't answer, annoyed by her uncaring tone, given her husband's poor state.

Standing in the hallway, Jill could tell Melissa was already comfortable without her husband there. Probably what she wanted all along she thought.

The strange woman with the bulging eyes, who turned out to be Melissa's mother had obviously noticed the tension between the two women and quickly disappeared to the lounge, leaving them free to talk.

'Doesn't he look a state Jill? He isn't very good at all you know,' and not waiting for Jill's answers, Melissa rambled on. 'I'm afraid they don't hold much hope. It's only a matter of time,' and clearly not wanting her mother or her daughter to hear she checked the lounge door was shut, before she carried on. 'He'll be lucky if he lasts the night you know.'

'That isn't true, Melissa,' Jill said at last, having heard enough of her twaddle – now exasperated by this woman who stood there boldly lying. 'They're expecting him to come out of his coma pretty soon.'

'Well, I hope he's okay and not depressed like he was before. Or an invalid come to that; I just couldn't cope with it all. My mother said I should have left him years ago!'

Jill was incensed.

'Well, I have no idea what your mother means,' she said raising her voice. 'You've done quite nicely for yourself madam, marrying my brother and I really don't think you have anything to complain about at all!'

Jill looked angry and Melissa quickly backed down 'No, no, you're quite right; I didn't mean anything like that. My mother's completely wrong.'

Melissa then changed the subject, not wanting to upset her further and said all excited, 'Did you know they airlifted him to Whitechapel hospital Jill? He's always wanted to ride in a helicopter.'

Jill couldn't believe her ears, 'I don't think he wanted it quite like that Melissa!' And not wanting to listen to anymore of her nonsense, Jill asked her outright, what happened on that day.

Melissa then told her the story of the lost ticket and how Sammy was accidentally hit by the train, which further confused Jill, as she'd only heard the story, involving mice.

Not sure what to believe, Jill left the house speechless, vowing she'd get to the bottom of it all. Convinced more than ever that Melissa was completely round the twist.

Hearing this new story about the lost ticket from Jill later, Elaine also became confused, and twiddling with the wire attached to her phone she reflected over Melissa's ramblings.

'That's weird. I wonder why she's changed her story. I bet she told Sammy's boss about the mice without even thinking, he being the first to know. But why change it and why did she ring him anyway?'

'I really don't know sis,'

But this left Elaine even more suspicious, not trusting Melissa or any of her motives anymore and she considered all the facts carefully. 'I would still like to know why, out of all the Marks and Spencer's in the area, she chose to go to the one that didn't carry what she wanted. I definitely think it was planned to get him on the underground. After all, Larry said he hadn't been on a Tube in over twenty years.'

Jill nodded in agreement, 'What a mess', she said.

'Anyway,' Elaine continued, 'why, if you were concerned about your husband's state of mind and the effects of his medication, would you leave him standing on the edge of a platform looking for whatever? I mean you wouldn't let a toddler wander around unsupervised. That would be a criminal act. So what's the difference when she knew he wasn't in a stable state of mind?'

'I see what you mean.'

'After all, we knew she was aware of the effects of his medication, as she admitted that, when she wouldn't let him drive. So this doesn't make any sense.'

'Well the important thing now is getting Sammy better. We must do what we can to help him,' Jill said.

And Elaine agreed, although she still found it hard to understand this strange state of affairs. She could only hope by concentrating on their brother's health and well being, eventually the truth would come out.

The next day, Lawrence sent the sisters a copy of a letter which was written by Sammy's doctor, specifically for Melissa, explaining in full their brother's present condition and their expectations for his future. The doctor had provided this to help Melissa understand the situation, only she was still refusing to accept his possible recovery. Still telling everyone he was going to die. It read:

Notes of Meeting Consultant Mr. David Leverrick.

Royal London Hospital 3rd June, 1998.

Sammy is NOT in a 'wake up' state. This will take a long time. He is (and has always been) in a 'comatose' state.

. Over the past week there has been a slow improvement (healing process) in his condition – still a long way to go.

. His breathing tube (which goes down past the vocal chords to the lungs) is starting to make his throat, mouth etc sore. They will replace the tube by making a tracheotomy (surgical incision) in the throat to insert a tube directly into the throat. This may (and most probably will) involve a minor operation.

. They are slowly taking him off sedation and are doing tests to find out his awareness of pain. So far his eye lids flicker to 'lots' of pain. The next stage is for him to react, more (example, by moving his left hand over to his right hand when pain is inflicted to the right hand).

. The operation entailed the REMOVAL of the front lobe on the right side of the brain – due to severe physical damage as a result of the accident. There is also residual injury to the rest of the brain, which was caused by the head being forced one way (violently) and then the other way. The brain injury is described as DEFUSED and SEVERE but tests show that the brain is recovering.

. However there is/will be long lasting permanent damage to the brain which leads to the following prognosis:

1.   Sammy may die (this is now considered unlikely, after 6 days and the positive signs of recovery).

2.   Sammy on a 'worst outcome' may never recover and will stay as he is.

On a 'best outcome' Sammy will never be the same person as before (due to that part of his brain being removed.) There will inevitably be some form of 'disability' – not the sort which leaves you in a wheelchair (paraplegia) but some form of mental (speech, thinking) change, which may also be behavioural.

Regarding his physical injuries, the hospital are not bothered (worried) as they are so minor compared to his head injuries. For the record they are:

. Fractured rib

. Disrupted Pancreas

. Bruised, swollen duodenum (this was caused by the force that damaged the pancreas)

. Some problems with his feeding for example He is being fed through a tube (mouth) but his stomach is not absorbing the food. They are giving him drugs for the bowel. If no success they will feed him via a vein in his neck.

Lawrence placed a footnote at the bottom of the letter, explaining to the sisters that the above maybe of use to them. And he promised to keep them up dated if in receipt of any further news, given he was in contact with Melissa again.

Chapter 13 – High dependency

Over the next few days, Sammy remained in a coma induced state, although no longer at risk of dying and a nurse no longer stationed at his bedside. With more evidence of movement in his body and an obvious awareness in his mind this suggested it was only a matter of days or even hours before Sammy would regain consciousness.

Certain now he'd soon be coming round, the professionals decided it would probably be in their brother's best interests to move him to a hospital much closer to his home. This in turn should make it much easier for his friends and family to visit more regularly, which hopefully would help his recovery.

His wife it seemed had already made it perfectly clear she couldn't travel into London every day, only her dislike of hospitals was far too daunting she had said. And this made her visits, already few and far between.

The hospital authorities therefore hoped a move much closer to home would improve the situation. Which pleased Elaine, given she lived very near to the hospital under consideration.

With one month now passed since Sammy's terrible accident, it was at last agreed to move him to Reigate Hospital. Which was clearly good news for them all – enabling those that wanted to visit, to do so more regularly.

Keen to see him at his new abode, Elaine went to visit him on his first day there, now placed on the high dependency ward with a room to him-self.

Unaware that Sammy was already out of his coma though, Elaine went along unprepared. She hadn't expected this to happen so soon, particularly just after his move. And hearing of this news on arrival, she started to panic, concerned by his possible response to her. After all, would he want her there? Would he remember who she was? Would he be upset by her presence? Or worse still, would he be afraid of upsetting Melissa by talking to her again? Or would he even remember the conflict between them all? And believing this was probably all irrelevant now, she still had to consider the outcome.

Elaine then realised, she hadn't a clue what to say to her brother on his first day awake. No one had prepared her or given any advice. And these questions, though simple, went round and round in her mind, as the last thing she wanted was to upset him further.

'Oh well, I'm here now,' she mumbled as she entered his room quietly, 'let's just see how he responds.' So crossing her fingers that all would be fine, she prepared herself for his rebirth back into this life.

Elaine had already been warned that they couldn't predict exactly how he'd be at first, mentally or physically when out of his coma. So acting cautiously she forearmed herself by expecting the worst, realising he may have to start all over again, just like a tiny baby - learning new skills for the very first time. And Elaine was happy to help him, if she was allowed to do so.

Helping her brother wasn't a problem for Elaine as she was no longer working and had the time. She also thought it would be good to be doing something worthwhile. Especially as she knew it would be what her mum and dad would have wanted - although perhaps not someone else a little closer to Sammy's heart.

Elaine, who considered herself a spiritual person, had already been sending him distant healing. In fact, since the day she'd learnt of her brother's close escape from death and had marvelled at his recovery so far. Yet, not sure if this had helped or not, it gave her comfort to feel she was doing all she could.

His wife however said, she preferred not to be around him at this present time, telling everyone 'it was far too upsetting to see him like this,' and she kept her visits brief, if she should make an appearance.

Now inside his room Elaine held her breathe, afraid she might startle him, only to find him lying in a cot-like bed, which was she guessed was for his safety. At first Sammy didn't appear to notice her stood there and continued to stare into space, while Elaine gazed down at the man she barely recognised now, with tears in her eyes.

Now cleanly shaven except for a tiny moustache, instructions dished out by his wife apparently, looked strange. While his clear blue sparkly eyes appeared enormous against the pale drained complexion of his lily white skin. And with the dreadful scare now exposed, which ran down the whole of one side of his head, Elaine thought how lucky he had been.

Pulling at the nappy that he now had to wear, which seemed to entrap him below, Elaine watched her brother with a heavy heart as she prepared herself to speak.

'Hello Sammy' she said softly, touching his arm gently and hoping he wouldn't jump.

Sammy turned his head slowly towards her and a glimmer of recognition shone in his eyes. And Elaine hoped it wouldn't fade, as he started to put the pieces of his life back together, slowly, bit by bit.

Still holding her breathe she waited his response but Sammy didn't flinch, so Elaine spoke again; 'Do you know who I am, Sammy?'

But he carried on staring, so Elaine took his hand and held it in hers and a smile touched his lips. Remaining like this for a while, Elaine felt privileged to be there. Pleased to be with him at this special time and she tried to explain who she was.

'Do you remember me Sammy, its Elaine?' she said again.

At first he didn't answer and then slowly he repeated her name.

Surely this was a good sign, just the fact he could speak, let alone whisper her name. Although it didn't sound like Sammy anymore, his throat still sore from the tubes that were helping him to feed but more importantly to breathe.

Elaine had already been told, his long term memory would be better than his short and so she sat down beside him and started to talk of old times. Things they did as children. After all these were really the only memories she shared with her brother.

Elaine was also aware the earlier she started this process of recall and stimulating his mind, the better it would be for Sammy. So she set to work, only too pleased to be helping.

Feeling happy with her accomplishments, Elaine vowed to help as much as she could and promised she would visit again the next day. Pleased with her offer to help it seemed the nurses asked if she'd bring along some family photographs or something that might help jog his memory and Elaine said she would.

It appeared the doctors had hoped this process of recall would help catapult his memories back to present times, until eventually his brain reached some kind of norm.

Elaine was of course happy to oblige and tried to visit her brother most days after that, if only for a short while. And each day Sammy would say and do something new, while his body was busy repairing itself. She could see already he was so much stronger.

Jill too visited as much as she could, but her work often limited her time. So the sisters tried to alternate their visits, in order to ensure he had someone with him most days. While it seemed, Melissa on the other hand appeared only briefly in the morning after dropping Kelly off at school, which wasn't very far from the hospital - and that was if at all. And this apparently, became less and less frequent as she still insisted, 'seeing her husband in this state was far too upsetting,' - her loathing of hospitals, still not helping.

However, when she was pushed into visiting, which did sometimes happen, she made sure it was only for a short while. During which time, her lack of interest and apathy towards her husband meant there was little chance of her trying to communicate. And if she ever found him sleeping, she would never think to wake him, and would leave after no time at all.

'He doesn't know who I am, anyway,' she'd tell everyone. 'He doesn't even know my name.' But she didn't even try to talk to him the sisters were told. And as time went by, Sammy would close his eyes whenever he spotted her coming, pretending to be asleep it seemed. The nurses told the sisters he obviously had no wish to speak with her.

But this was very sad as Elaine was sure there could have been great benefit by him talking to his wife, his nearest and dearest, after all they'd shared so many memories. And Elaine was sure he would have loved to see his daughter. Yet she never came to visit apparently, which was a shame, as she might have helped in his recovery, although they guessed Melissa wouldn't allow it. Only the sisters just couldn't accept his daughter didn't want to see him and wondered if she was too scared to ask.

The whole situation was sad, although this reluctance to visit had suited the sisters, even though it was a little unfair on their brother. But they liked the fact it was highly unlikely they'd ever bump into her.

Still trying to help Sammy as much as they could, Elaine brought him in a lovely picture of their mum and dad, in a pretty ornate frame that she placed at his bedside. Sammy looked delighted and clearly remembered who they were, which of course pleased the sisters. It was only upsetting, when Sammy once asked Elaine, where and how they were now, that she actually got upset. Holding back the tears, she tried to explain they were both in heaven and looking out for him from up there.

He seemed to like that explanation but it made her very sad, as it was like having to tell him for the very first time that both their parents had died.

Jill also experienced something similar after tucking him into bed one late afternoon and saying goodnight. As Sammy suddenly grabbed her arm and pulled her towards him, whispering, 'say goodnight to mum and dad when you tuck them into bed tonight … and tell them that I love them and miss them very much.'

This of course upset Jill, shocked by his unexpected words. And Jill being Jill fled from the ward, unable to hold back the tears - as nurses looked on bewildered.

These were sad and happy times, as they watched their brother slowly remembering his life again.

Chapter 14 - Progress

Albeit slowly, Sammy continued to improve each and every day, but sadly none of these improvements appeared to be noticed by his wife - as her visits still remained short and infrequent. Which clearly started to prove a problem for the nurses on his ward, as not only did Sammy need help with learning new skills, he also required many basic essentials (amongst other things) that the hospital just didn't provide. And given his stay was expected to be lengthy; this needed sorting out.

Needless to say Melissa believed these problems were no longer hers, and had to be called in several times to be told her responsibilities.

Frustrated by Melissa and the lack of interest shown, the staff carried on as best they could, while she continued to ignore their requests, making life difficult for Sammy.

Yet for some strange reason, still she would get away with this. No doubt under the pretext she was still in shock.

Much to the sisters surprise though, after many requests for photographs, a couple of small photos did eventually appear which seemed to be, Melissa's great contribution towards helping with his memory problems.

Soon after, there also appeared another small photo of Sammy and Melissa on their wedding day that was placed on the wall along with a small picture of Kelly as a young child. Although they were so far away from his bed, the sisters guessed he could barely see them. And given they were all old photos, the sisters wondered why there wasn't a recent one insight? They could only assume, Melissa didn't want him remembering his more recent times.

Trying to keep Sammy occupied during this period of healing hadn't been easy for the sisters either, as they didn't have a clue what to talk about. So Elaine brought him in a large fantasy poster to place on his wall, to use as a stimulus.

This poster enabled Sammy to look for the various pictures hidden within its main composition as he lay in his prison like bed. This also gave them something to focus on, while they encouraged Sammy to talk, having already exhausted his older memories. Elaine not being part of his life for many years, they often found themselves restricted when trying to discuss his more recent times.

It also became obvious that Sammy wasn't happy talking about his home life. Or Melissa, come to that. So conversations became even more limited - only on the odd occasion, when she was accidently mentioned, Sammy became visibly distant. So not wanting to upset him further, Melissa was hardly ever mentioned anymore. Which was ridiculous given they wanted to help him with his more recent memories.

Yet not knowing how Melissa had treated him in the past, although they had a good idea, they thought it best to leave well alone. While still continuing to help with his more distant memories, they suspected his recent ones were slowly disappearing for good. Perhaps what Melissa wanted?

******

Over this early period in Sammy's recovery, the sisters noticed his terminologies and facial expressions were very different from how they remembered them. It was as if he'd taken on a different persona, which the doctors said could happen. It was only when Elaine asked him - if he liked the poster on the wall that she realised who he now resembled. No longer looking like his mother, Sammy had become what seemed a reincarnation of their father. Those sparkly blue eyes, expressions and sayings, and many terminologies, were all of his.

There was an all knowing air about him, an uncanny resemblance that she'd never noticed before. And if Elaine hadn't known better, she was sure her father had taken his place, perhaps why she felt so close to him.

It was only when Jill revealed her thoughts to be the same that Elaine had to wonder. As Elaine hadn't told her sister about her feelings, thinking them too bizarre.

Elaine was delighted though when she thought Melissa maybe thinking the same. Perhaps wondering, if Alf had come back to haunt her. But Elaine knew this was highly unlikely, as Melissa never spent enough time with her husband to even notice any likeness, which was a shame

Over the following weeks Sammy continued to improve, physically and mentally, although he still had a long way to go. Yet he was definitely talking and responding much better, which was now making their visits more interesting.

Sammy had also started to feed himself, which was far better for him having only been fed fluids through a tube for some time, and had lost a lot of weight.

In fact it wasn't long after, that all the tubes attached to his body were finally removed. But learning to eat his food properly again was proving very difficult and also very messy, even with the nurses and his sisters help.

Still visiting their brother regularly, the sisters had hoped they'd soon gain access to his more recent memories and perhaps discover what actually happened on that fateful day, although they were sure, Melissa wouldn't approve of that.

In the meantime, in order to help Sammy further, they'd often sit and talk together about stories from his past and would even mention famous people, hoping he'd remember more. And sometimes they'd talk about interesting places, the Queen and the royal family, pointing out birthdays and of course his favourite football team. While they would even encourage him to finish off well known sayings, which impressed Elaine who often struggled herself, and she marvelled at his brilliant progress.

It seemed his memories were slowly and surely beginning to return and the sisters thought this was wonderful. Although he still wouldn't mention or remember his wife, or his daughter come to that and even when occasionally prompted. Making the sisters wonder if his memories of them would soon disappear for good.

And if by chance the accident did get mentioned, a prolonged silence would prevail, and it therefore became apparent; he no longer wanted reminding. So not to upset him further, they'd push him no more. After all, it should have been Melissa helping with this, she being the main person involved. But they knew that wouldn't happen.

Melissa's continued absence had certainly made things easier for the sisters to step in and help. But this was also

126

particularly sad, as it seemed Sammy hardly had any other visitors. Well, except for his friend Lawrence and his wife Jackie of course, but this was only occasionally, due to work and family commitments.

Still visitors or not, Sammy was doing exceptionally well. The sisters were pleased and promised they'd continue supporting him. He was their main priority now.

It had been just over two months since Sammy's move to Reigate hospital and he could now sit in a chair unaided, amongst other things. However, the hospitals main problem at this present time was Sammy's obsession with his penis and the wires attached to his catheter. Only having rediscovered his manhood again, Sammy wouldn't leave it alone. And appearing to have no shame anymore, always pulling it this way and that, he would show it to whoever came near him. He clearly didn't realise this wasn't acceptable.

The sisters had been warned there maybe changes in their brother's behaviour but they hadn't expected this and at times didn't know where to look. Mortified for their brother and his decency, the sisters would scold him like a little child, demanding he left it alone.

The nurses were brilliant with Sammy over this difficult and embarrassing period, and still managed to get him up and out of bed most days, trying to get him moving. It therefore wasn't long before he was able to take a few wobbly steps when aided, which was marvellous at this early stage, given their initial doubts.

So Elaine made it her purpose at every visit to help him walk a little further, until he could do it on his own.

****

Sammy was doing extremely well it seemed, although no one was actually telling them, yet everyone involved in his progress were clearly very pleased – except Melissa of course, who still seemed unable to accept these improvements. It therefore wasn't a surprise to know, this eventually started to take its toll on Elaine, even though initially the strong one. Only she'd been finding it difficult of late, dealing with the emotional side of her brother's sad predicament - Melissa's attitude over this period had been more than upsetting. She actually felt she'd reached that point where she just couldn't take anymore.

Particularly as it was pretty obvious to most, that Melissa had more or less abandoned her husband. But no one in the hospital seemed to acknowledge this. Even though it was evident Melissa showed no desire to be anywhere near him, let alone help him get better - although she would never admit that.

No ... it was pretty clear Melissa had already given up on Sammy. Yet she showed no desire to give up anything else, it seemed. Things like his pension or property she would feel were her God given right.

So no doubt having to keep up appearances she continued to play her little games with whoever she needed to do so, while telling them all whatever they needed or wanted to hear. Always making up excuses as to why she didn't visit and why she refused to let her daughter near, and this all became unbearable to the sisters, and particularly Elaine.

Especially as Melissa was unable to even accept her husband was getting better. As it appeared she was now telling everyone he was going to remain a cabbage for the rest of his life; never to walk or to talk again. How could she possibly say these things? How could she be so unkind?

Elaine tried to understand Melissa's situation but it was very hard to fathom. Although it was suggested she maybe eliciting sympathy by telling these lies, exaggerating the seriousness of her husband's condition in order to gain pity but she didn't think that was the case. Still, at least she was now admitting her husband was alive, that was an improvement.

Yet sometimes on Elaine's visits, she'd often find her brother distracted, lost in another world it seemed. And she'd ask herself how it was he'd ended up like this. Where was the wife he once loved so much? Why wasn't she here? Life was so cruel at times - and saddened by her brother's situation and his wife's lack of concern, Elaine felt extremely low, particularly as she'd recently heard rumours, Melissa was having an affair.

Worried for her brother and his life going forward, Elaine decided to call in on Citizens Advice to see if they could help. But when waiting in the reception area of their busy office; Elaine began to question why she was even there. After all was it a crime to abandon your husband? And so many people had affairs.

It was shortly after, Elaine found herself sat opposite an elderly looking woman, with grey thinning hair scraped back in a bun. And with beige avant-garde glasses, perched neatly on the end of her nose, Elaine wondered yet again what on earth she was doing there.

And it was while trying to explain her brother's situation to this seemingly detached, expressionless woman; she suddenly felt a strange mixture of emotions welling up inside her. With the pent up feelings of the last month or so, coming to a boiling point, Elaine felt the heavy tears filling her eyes, now ready to spill over. As the uncaring look on the woman's face when she tried to tell her story was far too much to bear and so the flood gates opened up. Elaine had never cried over her brother's terrible situation and unable to control her tears, she let them flow freely.

Clearly unsure how to react to this emotional display, the elderly woman rushed off to get help, and returned within just minutes with tissues in hand. Elaine then realised the importance of having allowed herself to cry, even though it was extremely embarrassing.

Eventually calming down she apologised to the woman for her lack of self control. While quickly learning, the only course of action left open to her was to apply to the Guardianship Office for jurisdiction over her brother.

This wasn't what Elaine had in mind though, as she didn't need or want any complicated battles. So the woman also advised her to make contact with the social workers attached to Sammy's case, who were based at Reigate Hospital. Now this seemed a much better course of action. And Elaine hoped that once they knew the truth about their brother's predicament, they would help.

Elaine learnt a little later that there had been a social worker assigned to Sammy's case from the very beginning - there mainly to look after his interests, while constantly assessing his progress it seemed. Although the sisters had to wonder why they hadn't made contact with them.

Still at least there was someone else they could talk to who could hopefully help and advice them, which made them feel more positive. As sadly the rest of the family had grown tired of the constant chatter regarding Sammy's problems and had let their feelings be known - and who could really blame them. And unable to turn to them for support these days, this had left the sisters feeling very much alone.

Although there had always been Lawrence, who did understand their situation and their brother's predicament but being a busy working man, it wasn't always possible to contact him. Plus, they realised, he often found it difficult accepting his friend's situation. So they hoped social services would be the answer to their problems. And after talking it over, the sisters agreed, they would make an appointment, once they'd listed all their concerns.

Sammy in the meantime was still making great progress, even without the help of his wife. His sisters were extremely pleased, although they would still worry about his future, as they just couldn't imagine him ever going home. After all, to date, Melissa hadn't shown him any compassion at all, so what would be the point and they could only console themselves with the fact this was probably the last thing she wanted. And they tried to stay positive.

But tired of his wife's attitude, the sisters wondered why it was only they who could see how uncaring she was. There was no doubt in their minds she was playing games and playing them very well. So they thought perhaps, going through the Guardianship Office might be the right course of action after all. So they applied for the appropriate papers just in case.

Chapter 15 – The recovery

Sammy had made a miraculous recovery over all, no doubt cheating death. In fact he'd improved so much over these last few months his doctor decided to move him to the Neurological Ward, in the same hospital. Here he could recover amongst other patients, in a far more normal setting.

The sisters were pleased with this decision, although they were still happy to continue with their visits, as this clearly suggested they were helping. Melissa however, still kept her distance, keeping her visits to a minimum. Telling everyone how affected she was still by the trauma of that day.

In fact comments from other patients on his new ward got back to the sisters regarding her strange and infrequent visits. Pointing out that when she arrived, she'd sweep her way through the ward, upsetting Sammy in the process and then leaving after no time at all. The patients thought this was strange, as she would never say a word to her husband while there.

On the sisters' first visit to his new ward, they discovered to their amazement, the nursing staff had started to call their brother by his formal name Samuel, and they knew he didn't like this. Even spelling it out in bold black pen and placing it above his bed. The sisters were not amused and wondered why Melissa hadn't told them he preferred the name Sammy. Perhaps she thought this would confuse him, as who knew Melissa's motives. Needless to say Jill put them straight.

Angry by Melissa's antic, the sisters refused to even acknowledge her these days and she was therefore hardly mentioned. Her actions of late were not only annoying but upsetting too; God knows how Sammy must have felt. And so they decided - they wanted only to concentrate on their brother, they needed to get him better. They had to ignore her.

Trying to find new things to stimulate Sammy though was becoming an even harder problem, as they were running out of ideas. So Elaine brought a small cassette player into the ward, in order to try and help him, having been told music could form an essential part of his therapy. It seemed music from the past often proved a good way of prompting past memories.

But Elaine didn't even know what type of music her brother liked these days. Or what he'd listened to over the years. Although she remembered as teenagers he especially liked the Rolling Stones and Aretha Franklin, amongst a few others.

She also recollected Sammy liked a song called 'Sitting on the Dock of the Bay' by Otis Redding as he often played it in his room. Unfortunately, Elaine didn't have a copy of any of these artists or any other favourites from his past.

So Elaine decided to play him some soft soothing music from her own collection just to see his reaction. It was while Sammy lay quietly in his bed, his eyes tightly closed and no longer obsessed with nappies and wires, Elaine turned on the little music player.

Suddenly, the soft soothing sounds, from the beautiful voice of Andrea Bocelli singing 'Con Te Partiro' gently vibrated around them, wrapping them both in a wonderful embrace. With tears in her eyes now, she watched her brother slowly opening his, wearing a look that said - he thought he'd died, and gone to heaven. Elaine looked down at her brother and smiled, still lost in the emotions of this lovely song and Sammy smiled back.

Elaine reached for her brother's hand as he quietly whispered, 'how beautiful'. He surely still appreciated the sounds of good music and this gift still remained in his grasp.

Pleased this exercise had proved successful; the sisters still found it difficult to come up with new ways of helping him, only, to date no one had advised them on this process. Whether Melissa had been told and hadn't passed it on, the sisters didn't know but she certainly hadn't spoken to them on the subject.

Fed up with drawing pictures and playing simple games; the sisters were also fed up with the so called professionals now. Not one doctor or psychiatrist had even bothered to discuss their brother's case with them and even the nurses were limited to what they could say – still considered unethical. In fact, it seemed they weren't allowed to discuss Sammy's case with anyone, other than his wife, she being his next of kin. Which was difficult considering she was hardly ever there.

The only help or communication on offer to the sisters was a tatty red book that remained at Sammy's bed side. Here, they or his carers could leave little messages, comments or requests, which didn't prove much use to the sisters, or Sammy they guessed. They could only think it was there for Melissa in order to get her involved.

Yet even after countless messages left in the book for her, to bring in some more up to date photos, it appeared she'd just ignore them. Given they were never forthcoming. So Elaine decided it was time to take matters into her own hands. And armed with a camera, Elaine set off to her brother's house to shoot whatever she thought he'd recognise, while avoiding Melissa in the process.

Feeling like a Russian spy in a James Bond movie Elaine took some pictures of Sammy's lovely home, his car, which sat in the driveway and anything of interest. She also tried to take a photo of his beautiful back garden and particularly the rose bush where their mother's ashes still hopefully lay. But this sadly proved impossible, even though Elaine knew the people who backed onto his garden. The heavy foliage and large wooden shed blocked the view; making it impossible to photograph. Nonetheless pleased with her efforts, Elaine couldn't wait to share what she had with her brother.

'Look Sammy,' she said pointing at the photo in her hand, 'do you recognise this?'

'Yes,' he said his eyes lighting up, 'that's my house.' Now excited, he looked eagerly at the others, pointing out this and that, while even announcing the name of his street. But then he saw his car. Thrilled to bits, he pawed at the photo of an old grey Rover which had once been his pride and joy, still where he left it on that fateful day.

Sammy appeared overjoyed with these significant reflections of his previous life and a sense of reality touched Elaine as she watched him remembering all again. Which then made her wonder if his short term memory was really as bad as they said.

It was great he could now recall so much more But Elaine often wondered why Sammy still couldn't remember his wife or her name. It seemed very strange, as he could remember everyone else's. And when she sometimes reminded him, his wife's name was Melissa; Sammy would nod, as if reflecting, and then raise his eyebrows as if surprised.

Elaine was over the moon with these unprompted reactions to the photographs though. She was also grateful this would give them something else to talk about on her future visits, hoping they would stimulate his mind further.

But why Melissa hadn't done this herself, Elaine didn't know, as it was obvious it had helped him immensely. And under normal circumstances, she was certain, with Melissa help, he could achieve so much more. Yet even after all these new reveals, he told Elaine, he still couldn't remember his wife, or daughter, which was strange considering what else he recalled.

Still it was brilliant these photographs had helped to release some of his more recent memories, but who should they tell? It seemed there was still no one to turn to. Perhaps they should consider social services after all.

Pondering on this problem, Sammy carried on looking at the photographs, no doubt remembering more of his life, when he suddenly became agitated. It seemed he'd now realised he no longer had his door keys, but more importantly the keys to his precious car and kept asking where they were.

'Have I lost them?' he said, clearly upset now, perhaps remembering how important they'd been.

'Melissa, has your keys, Sammy, She's looking after them for you. You mustn't worry yourself; you'll get them back when you're better. Remember to ask her for them when she next see's you.'

But Elaine knew, Melissa wouldn't care less about explaining to Sammy or hurting him with her explanation, although she doubted she'd even offer one. In fact, Elaine guessed she wouldn't even look at her husband, let alone talk about keys or cars.

Still, Sammy appeared happy with her suggestion and settled back down as he looked at the photos again.

With all these new and exciting developments occurring, the sisters felt they should really be sharing this with at least one professional. But they still didn't know who they were.

'Surely this should all be down on record,' Jill moaned over the phone the following evening. 'All this progress is being missed and wasted. It's almost as if no one wants to know. It just doesn't seem right.'

And the sisters realised, if the only information that those in charge were receiving, was from one source only, other than the staff, this could be a problem, only who knew what Melissa was telling them. As they knew she had no idea how her husband was progressing, and didn't want to either? Yet shouldn't those who were making decisions on their brother's life, be checking this out?

Concerned now that Melissa could be giving out incorrect or damaging information, they also discovered Sammy had recently been given a professional assessment on his present capabilities, which they hadn't even been told about. Discovering he hadn't done well, the sisters were angry; as they were sure he could do better and were certain they could have helped - giving them important information on his mental state. As this test apparently would have provided access to a rehabilitation centre nearby, which they knew could have helped him immensely.

This therefore upset the sisters as they couldn't understand why he hadn't done better, having witnessed the opposite, and still couldn't believe they hadn't been asked what they may have accomplished. Or had they been only prepared to accept Melissa's lies regarding her husband's useless state, as it certainly seemed that way.

Perhaps it was now time to meet with Sammy's social worker, who still hadn't bothered to contact them. Surely they were aware of their involvement. After all, didn't they wonder who was visiting him most days? Or maybe they didn't care.

Unhappy by the lack of communication - given how much time they'd spent with their brother, the sisters decided to make their appointment, wondering why the nursing staff hadn't suggested this also. Still, if guide lines had to be followed, this could explain it, as they knew these nurses were not allowed to get involved.

So perhaps social services didn't even know of their existence? As why would Melissa tell them? She was in control as usual. And the sisters made their appointment for later that week.

Chapter 16 - Update.

The sisters met up on Sammy's ward, before they went along together to Social Services. Their temporary offices were laid out in the hospital car park - a dull and strictly functional structure, which didn't look very inviting.

Knocking on the cold metal door that rattled on contact, Elaine still wasn't sure what she was going to say. Although convinced more than ever, something needed to be said and soon.

The door eventually swung open and they were quickly invited into their surprisingly spacious offices. Here they soon found themselves, sat opposite a plump, yet fairly attractive middle aged lady, with shoulder length shinny auburn hair, cut in a bob. And although her face was kindly, her clothes were dishevelled and unkempt. Just like the paperwork spread across her desk.

Eyeing the sisters suspiciously, she rearranged her skirt as she waited for them to begin. Flustered by the purpose of their visit though, the sisters nervously introduced themselves, still unsure why they were there, as the purpose wasn't to cause trouble, well certainly not for Sammy.

Perplexed by their visit it seemed, the social worker replied in a more formal tone. 'I'm Sue Webster; I'm in charge of your brother's case. What can I do for you both today?'

Relieved the meeting had now started, Elaine replied. 'We're here because we're concerned about our brother, Sammy, and the fact we've had no contact at all regarding his progress.'

'Well that's understandable,' she said dismissively, 'as it's his wife we would talk to about Samuel.'

'Really?' Jill remarked. 'That doesn't make much sense.'

'No it doesn't,' Elaine quickly added   '... and it's actually ridiculous considering his wife has had no input whatsoever in helping in his recovery,' and she paused waiting for her reply.

But Sue didn't respond, so Elaine carried on.

'In fact she's been a hindrance most of the time... and it's been a bloody miracle that we've had some great results with our brother. However, we now feel we should be passing this information on.'

Sue still showed no signs of comprehension though and Elaine felt she was wasting her time and looked at Jill for backup who nodded in response.

'The thing is,' Elaine continued, 'we understand they want to dismiss him as a hopeless case and not give him the rehabilitation he deserves... and I can only think this is because the information you've been getting is coming from one source only, that being his wife and she wouldn't know anyway.' Elaine paused again, waiting for Sue.

But Sue still remained silent and Elaine became increasingly annoyed, thinking - who do these people think they are? Surely they're here to help and support us too; only it certainly didn't appear that way. And showing signs of losing her cool, Jill interjected.

'So, who exactly are you getting your information from?' Jill asked, a little more calmly.

'The doctors and psychiatrists, and of course, the nursing staff,' Sue said a tad too cool.

'Well, I hope it's not just his wife,' Jill said, probably sharper than intended, only it seemed this woman's attitude was starting to irritate her too. 'The thing is we know the doctors make him nervous because the nurses have told us this. It's the white coat syndrome apparently. So that means they're not getting a true and fair picture when they're assessing Sammy. Especially if his wife is with him, as she makes him worse - which seems quite deliberate I might add.'

Sue Webster started making notes. So Jill carried on, still keen to put her views across.

'And we know the nurses are not allowed to comment on their patient's progress or any family problems. So I don't see how you can be asking their opinions, or does that rule just apply to us?' and she looked at Elaine, who also nodded.

'So that really only leaves us to speak up for Sammy, as I doubt his wife ever does,' Elaine said taking over. 'After all we've been involved in his recovery from the very get-go, and we do know what progress has been made ... and yet no one has bothered to ask us. And this I find astonishing, particularly as our interactions with Sammy could be of great importance - especially when everyone else is deciding his fate.'

Elaine paused at this point, not happy with the vacant look still on Sue's face, but continued nonetheless.

'If Mrs Clayton had managed to spend some time with her husband, as most caring wives would have, you and everyone else would now know just how well he was doing. As I guess, you are asking her?'

'Although we can only imagine what she might be telling you,' Jill quickly added, sarcasm in her voice this time, 'only I've heard some of her comments and things like cabbage and brain dead come to mind.'

Sue remained silent, still reluctant to answer it seemed.

Exasperated by this woman's non comment strategy, Elaine couldn't hold back any longer, 'So? If you're not asking her, who the bloody hell are you asking?' Elaine demanded. And laughing to herself she answered her own question, 'no one by the sounds of it.'

'Fair enough, point taken' Sue said at last. 'Perhaps we can organise something in order that this information does get passed on, although I'll have to speak to the doctors first.'

The sisters weren't particularly happy by her weak response and the more than obvious lack of support but given they'd been getting nowhere before, her suggestion was better than nothing. Maybe there'll be some assistance and continuity now.

'Of course you realise Mrs Clayton is the only one privy to information on Samuel, being his next of kin. So, why don't you discuss this with her?' Sue looked puzzled as she chewed on the end of her pen.

Elaine then felt embarrassed, and confessed she hadn't spoken to Melissa in years and didn't really want to now. Jill jumped in quickly though, explaining there'd always been difficulties in the past between them all. Although pointing out – she had been party to the goings on in her brother's life, particularly before his accident. Confirming there'd been many problems in their marriage, especially at that time.

'Only Mrs Clayton is a very difficult woman. ... difficult in the sense, you would never know if she was telling the truth or not,' Jill added.

'Yes, I did sense a little problem there, but I put that down to shock. She has had quite an ordeal you know,' and she sounded dismissive again.

'And so have we!' Elaine added.

'Yes ... but she was there at the time of the accident... and he is her husband after all. It must have been a terrible shock.'

Elaine looked at Jill in disbelief wondering what yarns Melissa had been spinning; only she was more than fine, the last time Jill spoke to her. And Elaine wondered if she'd been acting the drama queen again?

Sue Webster now looked troubled by the situation and suggested perhaps a meeting should be called to get them all together and clear the air. 'Any questions that needed answered could be asked there and then.'

Elaine wasn't particularly happy with this though and doubted Melissa would even take part. But for Sammy's sake she decided she'd go along with Sue's plan.

Still wanting to tell her more about Melissa's antics, the sisters realised it was in Sammy's best interests if they concentrated on his future care. After all, his health was priority now – title tattle as Sue clearly saw it, wasn't helping.

Leaving Sue's office down hearted the sisters were not sure if they'd achieved anything concrete but waited with interest for confirmation of Sue's suggested meeting.

Eventually it came with a date set for two weeks' time. Elaine was flabbergasted Melissa had agreed.

The only other positive that came from their meeting, if you can call it that, was another tiny book that appeared the following day, placed at Sammy's bedside. On the front of this book was a message that read: 'Visitors, please make a note of any significant improvements or any notable response experienced during your visit.' Each page was divided into sections - the date, the name of visitor and their relationship to the patient, plus a space for any comments.

'Well, I suppose they're trying,' Jill said begrudgingly. 'But it's not really the same as having a one to one chat with a doctor.'

Elaine on the other hand found it a downright insult and said, 'Surely they can do better than this, a chat now and again wouldn't hurt.' Elaine was angry at the unsatisfactory response to efforts made by people who were trying to help a patient in their care.

Needless to say nothing much was ever entered in the book, as to explain a situation or a reaction to a certain conversation or even a past memory in just a few words was almost impossible. And ironically, as Melissa never sat at her husband's beside long enough, they guessed she never knew the book was even there. In fact Elaine had to wonder if anyone ever looked at it anyway.

It was well over three months now since Sammy's accident and although Jill had been the one who'd kept in touch with

Lawrence, Elaine decided to call him herself. It had been sometime since they'd spoken.

As it was Lawrence who'd told her about her brother's accident and the original story concerning the mice, she wondered if he'd heard the latest version.

'Apparently, he'd actually lost his ticket and was looking for it on the railway lines,' she said, explaining to a now confused Lawrence 'Jill got that straight from the horse's mouth.'

'Well I never! That's not what I was told.... John said he was looking for mice after discussing them on the bus earlier.'

'I still don't understand why Melissa rang that John in the first place Larry. After all, why would she tell him about the accident before letting you or his family know?'

Lawrence didn't answer still baffled himself it seemed.

'It's funny you know Elaine I went to the tube station myself the other day. I wanted to see where it actually happened, see if Sammy would have known the train was coming from that tunnel. And you know what; there's no way he wouldn't!'

'So, do you think he jumped?'

'I wouldn't be surprised... I just don't understand why.' Lawrence sounded deflated, perhaps missing his good friend.

'Have you heard anything more from Melissa?' Elaine said fishing for info.

'Yes,' he said, hesitantly. He clearly didn't want to pass on any information that may cause further trouble. 'You know I said I felt a bit sorry for her when I spotted her at the hospital that day?'

'Yeah?'

'Only she looked so lost and helpless. Well ... I thought I should really offer to help her ... you know with paper work and that sort of thing? Only I'm sure Sammy would want me to.'

'Yes I'm sure he would Larry,' she said, keen to hear the story about to follow.

'Anyway,' he continued, 'she didn't want my help as it happens. Apparently she's got this bloke Steve helping at the moment. You know, that old work friend of Sammy's - the one he fell out with years ago. I just don't know when they supposedly got back in touch. I certainly hadn't heard about it.'

'Well I've never even heard of him Lawrence, but that's understandable I suppose,' and Elaine wondered if that was all this guy was helping her out with.

'Apparently, he's been wonderful ... her words,' he added. 'He's been helping her come to terms with everything it seems, looking after all her official stuff and that ... while supporting her through this difficult time. In fact, he's also been sorting out her finances too ... she calls him 'her rock.'

'I bet she does... you sure his name's not Paul Burrell?'

Elaine wanted to say much more regarding her suspicions, but Lawrence wasn't the type of person who appreciated sarcasm, and ignored her innuendos.

'Did you know she's sold Sammy's car too ... and to that guy Steve,' Lawrence added. 'He wanted it for his wife supposedly ... but Sammy really loved that car Elaine. It was his pride and joy,' and Lawrence sounded upset.

'No!' Elaine said, shocked. She'd only just taken a photo of it the other day. 'I know he won't be able to use the car again Larry, but that's not the point. She didn't have to sell it so quickly. It's like she's given up on him already. Blimey Lawrence … it's only been a few months!'

'She's laying down a new driveway as well,' Larry continued, 'and putting a new roof on the side garage.'

'No! Why would she do that if she's sold his car ... and she doesn't even drive herself! I think she just wants to spend his money.'

'Well apparently, she said she's going to be looking after that Steve's brand new Merc in her newly roofed garage. He told her he hasn't got enough room in his own and she wants to do him a favour given how good he's been to her.'

I bet he has, Elaine thought, and a good excuse if someone notices his car there too often. "Oh I'm just looking after it," she'd say. Elaine felt sick; she couldn't even answer and thought, Melissa could have at least waited a while. But no, she was playing a game and playing it very well, with an answer for everything as usual.

Not wanting to talk about Melissa any longer, in case she lost it completely, Elaine explained how well Sammy was now doing and how exciting it was he could remember so much more.

'It's strange though, he can never remember his wife. Or the accident, come to that,' she said, putting Lawrence straight. 'But that's probably because he doesn't want to, eh?'

Lawrence forced a laugh. Although he sounded surprised that Sammy was doing well and admitted he'd been told otherwise and she guessed who by. But pleased to hear of his friend's progress he said, he promised to visit him soon. No doubt wondering why Melissa had told him Sammy was no better.

Chapter 17 – Puzzle pieces

Over the next following few days, Elaine kept receiving yet even more intriguing information concerning her sister-in-law. Even though she didn't want to know about her misdemeanours – as it normally wound her up. But friends of friends kept calling her, dishing all the dirt. Until eventually all the pieces began fitting together, piece by piece - just like a great big jigsaw puzzle, which was starting to make a very clear picture.

Even Elaine's friend, who lived in the house that backed onto Sammy's garden, had decided to ring her one day. She said she had some news about her brother that maybe of interest, which involved the old man who lived next door to her, who Sammy knew well, apparently. Although she did say, she didn't know if the information was of any consequence but repeated the story nonetheless.

'My neighbour said – "He'd only just heard about Sammy's accident," her friend said, 'so he asked me if I knew how he was doing and if I'd heard anything more - only he appeared very concerned. In fact he seemed upset and felt he should tell me something that was playing on his mind. He said "he'd known Sammy for many years, as he was the manager of his grandson's football club and they often met up for a coffee and a chat while his grandson played football" The last time they spoke, Sammy was very low and the old man said "I'd never seen him like that before." Worried for him he asked Sammy what was wrong, and he replied "He had a lot of problems at home that needing sort out". In fact his exact words were, "he was in a loveless marriage and the child wasn't his".'

'No, you're joking!' Elaine was shocked, although it didn't really surprise her. But she did wonder if Melissa had told Sammy this just to keep him away from Kelly - legally cut the strings so to speak, wanting full control as usual. 'What a cow! No wonder Sammy was depressed. However, I'm not so sure that's completely true, Melissa does have a tendency to lie. Did your neighbour tell you who the father was?'

Her friend, clearly unsure if she should divulge anymore, decided to finish off what she'd started. 'All I was told ... it was the man who built the pond.'

Elaine was none the wiser though, as she'd no idea who built her brother's pond. Kelly was now fourteen, so it was a long time ago. Although as Elaine thought back, it was at the same time her father had been living there. Perhaps he'd known she was having an affair and had been too scared to say. In case he upset Sammy. So making his life hell in the process, maybe this was why he took the overdose.

Convinced of her analysis, Elaine's mind drifted further back, to the time when she'd received that strange and unexpected phone call from Melissa, many years before. When all she wanted to talk about was porno films, even though, unbeknown to Elaine - her father was in hospital fighting for his life. Had Melissa been setting up her alibi, just in case Alf survived and happened to mention he'd heard her having sex in the bedroom next to his - and with someone other than his son?

Now that did make sense to her. Explaining why, Melissa had insisted that porno films were so noisy. And a valid reason why her father tried to take his life, as he never did explain exactly - perhaps knowing how devastated his son would be.

It was the middle of September, and almost four months after Sammy's accident. At this time of year Elaine's gardener, Martin, normally called around to cut back the beautiful wisteria that surrounded the front of her house. Coincidently, Martin was the son of her brother's next door neighbour and had lived there for the last twenty years. Martin therefore knew her brother and Melissa very well.

Arriving at Elaine's house soon after her friends phone call, Martin seemed genuinely concerned when he enquired sympathetically after her brother, keen to know of his progress. Although occasionally letting slip a few sarcastic comments, normally regarding Melissa and Elaine suspected he knew a little more than he was letting on.

Nevertheless, Elaine brought Martin up to date, explaining just how well Sammy was now doing. Martin looked surprised.

'Really... I understood he was a cabbage and couldn't do anything for himself. … supposedly bed bound and never to talk again.'

'I can guess who told you that. I can assure you he's not like that at all. In fact he's getting better every day.'

Martin looked at her suspiciously. He didn't seem to know who was telling the truth. Perhaps he thought she was being overly optimistic given Sammy was hit by a train.

Elaine also mentioned just how uncaring his wife had been over this difficult period, rarely ever visiting and being particularly unkind. Yet Martin didn't look surprised by that.

Still curious, Elaine asked him if he'd seen Melissa about.

'Yes, I have actually … in fact I've seen more of her in the last week or two than I have in the whole time I've lived there,' then he laughed and Elaine looked at him quizzically.

'What do you mean?'

Martin didn't reply but smiled as he carried on working, so Elaine continued to goad him.

'Are the rumours I've heard true then… she's got some bloke in tow?'

Martin remained silent but eventually admitted; he didn't want to be called a trouble maker as he knew the guy in question well.

'It's some bloke called Steve I hear; she calls him her rock,' she continued to bait him; wanting to know the gory details.

And probably believing Elaine already knew what was going on; Martin no doubt decided, it wouldn't hurt to confirm a few details.

'Steve's not a bad bloke you know but I must admit I had to ask him what on earth he was doing with 'the princess of darkness? And he told me "she's not that bad really"... So don't ask me what's happening; I can't stand the woman.'

'So it is an affair then?'

'Well, let's put it this way; I can't see what goes on behind closed doors can I ... but we do see him leaving very early in the mornings. And he always leaves his work van parked around the corner.'

'But I hear he's married. What does his wife think of that?'

'I don't know. It's none of my business. Anyway he's just given me a job to do for her. In fact it's her front drive as it goes ... so I don't want to cause any trouble.'

'Can you tell me how long it's been going on, then?' Elaine said, persistent for answers; she didn't want to give up now.

'You need to talk to my mum really. Sammy used to talk to her all the time; he was always popping in for a chat.'

'Really' Elaine said surprised. 'Do you think she'd mind if I gave her a call and perhaps pop round?'

'I shouldn't think so,' but he didn't sound too sure. Was there someone else too afraid to speak out about the witch she wondered?

Elaine rang her sister later that evening to give her the latest news on Melissa while also filling her in on her plans to visit Sammy's neighbour; hoping she would join her.

'Of course I will,' Jill said, more than happy to do so, although she wasn't impressed with the news about Kelly and said she thought it could be people trying to cause trouble. But Elaine didn't believe that, as they had no reason to lie and it all made perfect sense to her.

'But she looks like Sammy,' Jill protested.

'No she doesn't... when she was a kid she was the spit of Melissa and nothing like Sammy.'

'Well, she looks like him now.'

'You mean she's big and stocky and her hair's a reddish brown … and even that's been dyed so you wouldn't know what colour it really is. And why has she cut it so short? She looks like a bloke.'

'Oh, I just don't know,' Jill said, clearly not sure what to think.

'Maybe that's why Sammy was so depressed,' Elaine continued, 'as I'm sure Melissa would have rubbed his nose in that little lie, if of course it was.'

'Emm I see what you mean.'

'And knowing her, she probably thought it was a good way of keeping Sammy away from Kelly, as we know she didn't want them close for some reason.'

'Yes, possibly…so do you know who this guy is that built the pond?'

'No I don't. But do you think it could be that John? His business is to do with pond equipment, although I'm not sure he actually builds them? I mean it could be the reason she rang him first regarding the accident.'

'But Sammy worked for him.'

'Yeah, but did Sammy know about it then?'

The sisters decided this was getting too confusing and was really of no relevance to Sammy's current situation. Or was it though? Still, at the end of the day, it served no purpose to speculate, Sammy had more important problems that needed sorting out.

'Oh and by the way … that Steve guy you were told to ring, he's the one she's having an affair with by all accounts. Mark more or less confirmed that'

'The cow!'

'She apparently told Larry, she calls him her 'rock' and said he's been helping her out big time.'

'I bet he has!' Jill was clearly annoyed. 'Well, I've got his phone number now. I've a good mind to ring his wife and tell her what he's been up to!'

'Well, it also gives Melissa a motive for trying to get rid of Sammy, especially if the affair has been going on for some time. Because I'm sure she took him on the Tube on purpose. As she knew how depressed he was... only Lawrence told me there was no way he wouldn't have known that train was coming!'

Elaine rambled on as though unravelling a murder mystery. Not even giving Jill the opportunity to comment - lost in her analysis of the crime she thought it was.

'After all Jill, we both knew Melissa didn't want him, that was obvious to everyone, and she probably had plans to leave him anyway. But the greedy cow, had no doubt decided, she didn't want to give anything else up either. No, she wanted everything. So, controlling and scheming as usual, she made her plans and acted on them. The only trouble was from her point of view, he didn't actually die.'

More than certain this was the case; Elaine promised her sister she would call the police the following day. Nobody so far had actually made a formal complaint and this needed sorting.

As promised, Elaine dialled 999, not knowing where to start, and oh boy, did she get the run around. Initially being put through to central services, she then went on to a main police station, which then led to the local police. Here she was finally connected to the Metropolitan Police where her

155

niece had ended up several months before, after she discovered her uncle was alive.

Considering she'd been trying to report a prompted suicide, or maybe probable manslaughter, Elaine was concerned that no one seemed interested in her call. Although someone at the other end of the phone right now appeared sympathetic, and clearly wanted to help this overly distressed woman, she no doubt sounded like.

'I want to report a suspicious incident that happened on the 28th May this year at Colliers Wood tube station,' she said at last.

'What do you mean by suspicious madam?'

'Well, I don't think things are actually as they appear. I have information that makes me suspect there was foul play.' Oh dear, I sound just like someone off the movies. Where do I begin with this? It all seems so ridiculous now.

'I see,' he said.

'Only I think there maybe ulterior motives as to why they were on that station in the first place,' she said now wanting to fully explain.

'Who are you in relation to the man in question?' the officer asked politely.

'I'm his sister,' and thought now - for goodness sake, just let me tell my story.

'Well, madam, we do have the incident on camera, but you're not really privy to that information - that's only for his next of kin I'm afraid... but let me have a look at the camera footage anyway. Let's see if I can tell you something that will put your mind at rest.'

'Thank you, thank you,' she said, hoping this caring man might be able to help, although she didn't feel that optimistic, as they were really going over old ground. She'd already heard they hadn't considered it suspicious.

Ten minutes later the policeman returned, 'Sorry to have kept you, madam... I'm afraid all I can say is, his wife was nowhere near him at the time. But what she might have said to him beforehand - we will never know. Although I will say, they did let three trains go by that all went to their destination.'

Elaine was confused but thanked the policeman for his help, believing he had implied her brother had actually jumped? Otherwise why would he even mention what she may have said to him?

Ringing her sister later, Elaine repeated her conversation with the policeman, and mentioned the trains they missed. 'Melissa must have been waiting for him to jump sis, otherwise why let those trains go by.

'Emm ... possibly.' Jill sounded confused.

'It also explains why she may have changed her story about looking for mice. Only, why else would they be hanging around, unless she said he still couldn't find the lost ticket.' It all made sense now.

'So, what do you think she said to him to make him jump, Elaine?'

'Perhaps she told Sammy she was going to leave him... after all you thought she was having an affair - and probably with that guy she calls her rock. I bet she taunted Sammy by telling him all about it, provoking him in some way.'

'Still, there's nothing we can do about that, Elaine. She didn't push him, after all.'

'No she didn't, but she bloody well as good as, knowing his mental state, which she caused in the first place… but try explaining that to the judge!'

Jill was clearly baffled, still not knowing what to believe. 'So why did she want it to appear like an accident then?' Jill questioned.

'I suppose if it looked like an accident and he died - if Sammy had life insurance there'd be a big pay out.

'If he had any, although knowing Sammy, I'm sure he probably did.'

'And if he didn't die … I suppose she may be able to claim compensation, if it was considered an accident. But I suppose if it was proved he tried to commit suicide that maybe a different story; she might not be entitled to anything. Although I don't think that was part of her plan, she just wanted him out of the way I reckon.'

Jill shook her head, 'I don't know sis. It all sounds unbelievable.'

'Well I hope I've got it wrong Jill, only I'm trying to be rational, or do you think I'm losing the plot?' Elaine was exasperated but she was more than sure her summary of events were correct and it made her very angry, as her brother didn't deserve any of this.

'I know, it is difficult… but I am inclined to agree with you.' Jill finally admitted, 'It's just terrible to think it possible.'

'No, you're right Jill… but even if we gave her the benefit of the doubt, this still doesn't excuse the way she's treating him now.'

Frustrated, the sisters both agreed, either way this whole scenario was extremely upsetting and far too complex to contemplate. Yet what could they do anyway. So their minds no clearer, they made their arrangements to visit Mrs Nolan the following day, hoping she might help.

Chapter 18 - Connecting the dots.

Still very concerned about their brother, the sisters knocked on Mrs Nolan's door hoping she could shed some light on Sammy's problems.

At first she had seemed reluctant to meet them and they wondered if she thought, they were trying to cause trouble. But wanting to help her friend if she could, she said, she agreed to meet.

Welcoming the sisters into her home, which all looked warm and cosy she offered them both tea. Declining her offer, they sat themselves down on the large blue sofa in the lounge, while she explained, Sammy often popped in for a drink and chat, normally to discuss his problems. She told them, 'he'd been extremely preoccupied of late and very anxious regarding something that was happening within his marriage - although she didn't know what that was,' she said.

The sisters however got the impression she knew more than she cared to let on, as she stressed several times their conversations had been in strict confidence and she wouldn't break that. She did however express her concerns about his depression, which was definitely getting worse, indicating it had likely been caused by Melissa in some way.

Mrs Nolan then told them, 'Melissa actually came in with Sammy one afternoon; checking on what he was saying, I guess. Only it was very unusual for her to make an appearance.' She then remembered Melissa brought up an earlier incident when Sammy had come home after visiting a friend - with his trousers all ripped and torn. 'Melissa apparently believed Sammy had been raped, as there was blood on the backside of his trousers.' At which point Jill nodded, clearly remembering the conversation she'd had with Melissa before Sammy's accident.

'Anyway, Sammy told Melissa not to be so ridiculous, and turned to me and said, "She only thinks I'm gay!" His life was a mess it seemed; I don't think he could cope anymore.'

Mrs Nolan looked down at her hands, wondering no doubt if she should tell them more. Deciding to carry on, she told them about another day, when she'd been walking past their house at the time she knew Kelly would be home from school but Sammy still at work.

'His car wasn't on the driveway,' she said, 'so I knew he wasn't home just yet. But I suddenly heard a voice shouting from inside, which I instantly recognised as Melissa's. She screamed out several times, "I thought you loved me, not him". Now my guess is as good as yours who she was screaming at, but I'm sure it was Kelly.'

Mrs Nolan then went quiet, leaving them to work it out for themselves, which made Elaine wonder if Kelly may have spoken to her father, without her mother's permission. Or perhaps even shown him some affection? Or could there have been another man involved. Who knows? But it was all rather strange.

'It seemed there was a very unhealthy atmosphere in that house for all and sundry,' Mrs Nolan stated. 'God

161

knows how poor Kelly has managed. I even spotted her not long after the accident slinging bags of rubbish away. She had so many; she had to climb over to the house on the other side to put some in their bin. Now, I've no idea what was in the rubbish, but I know Kelly was very embarrassed when she saw me.'

'I bet I know what was in the rubbish! Jill said. 'She couldn't wait to get rid of Sammy's stuff,' and Mrs Nolan raised her eyebrows as if to say, who knows.

'I understand Melissa may have a boyfriend, Mrs Nolan?' Elaine asked directly, wondering if this nice woman would now spill the beans.

'Well, I wouldn't like to say really, but we do see a man leaving very early in the mornings at times,' which confirmed Martin's statement. 'Also, we often hear a male-voice coming through the walls; in fact we've heard a lot of singing and laughter lately, as if they were celebrating.'

'I bet they are!' the sisters said together, their imaginations getting the better of them 'The bitch!' Jill said.

They realised now, there was no point in asking how long this affair had been going on as this lovely lady was obviously trying to be discreet.

'So, how is Sammy doing? Mrs Nolan asked ... 'Melissa tells me he's just a vegetable and will never walk or talk again. She said he doesn't even recognise her. But that's a result, eh?' and Mrs Nolan laughed.

The sisters smiled knowingly and explained it was only wishful thinking on her behalf.

'In fact he's doing really well,' Elaine said. 'We're so pleased with his progress. In fact if it's okay with you, we thought perhaps we could bring him here for a quick visit. Only we will start taking him out and about soon. We've already cleared it with the hospital. It'll give him the stimulation he so desperately needs.'

'Yes that's fine with me... It would be nice to see him again,' but Mrs Nolan looked puzzled, probably still imagining him in a vegetative state. The image Melissa had unkindly implanted in her mind.

Apologising for the inconvenience caused, Mrs Nolan's warm friendly smile reassured them both that it hadn't been a problem. It was then they realised why their brother had befriended this kindly woman, who'd always been prepared to listen to his troubles.

Promising to call soon to arrange Sammy's visit, they thanked her again for her time and left.

Jill was not amused by the stories unfolding and was certainly fed up with Melissa still not visiting her husband, and particularly annoyed with her spreading untruths about his health. Frustrated and angry, after staying overnight at her daughters, who lived close by, Jill decided to pay her sister-in-law an unexpected visit the very next day.

'Do you actually care about your husband? Jill demanded as she stood on Melissa's doorstep, having caught her unawares it seemed. 'I mean do you really love him ... and if so, do you actually intend to do ANYTHING for him?'

Melissa didn't answer but stared.

Annoyed... hands on hips, Jill bombarded her with more and more questions, raising her voice at the fraught looking woman who still called herself Sammy's wife.

Melissa flicked her long red hair off her shoulders, refusing to answer though. And Jill looked her up and down, while thinking, who the hell, did she think she was? Her clothes were far too young and looked like a stick thin bimbo on the pull. Who was she trying to fool?

Lost for words it seemed, Melissa continued to stare, which annoyed Jill even more. She obviously hadn't been prepared for this onslaught and looked astonished by it all.

So Jill repeated again, 'Do you love him Melissa?'

Eventually she spoke and calmly said, 'Jill ... of course I love him. He is my husband after all and there really are no problems ... in fact I have everything in hand. I'm actually going to see him tomorrow, so please don't worry yourself.'

Jill was not amused. She sounded so patronising; she wanted to knock her out. 'Well, I'm telling you Melissa, if you don't care about him, I do, and it's about time you started doing things for him. He is your husband after all ... so act like he is for goodness sakes!'

Melissa didn't answer though but started looking anxious and Jill got the impression she wanted her to leave, explaining, she had to go out soon to pick Kelly up from school.

'She's fourteen. Does she really need you to do that?' And feeling as though she'd been dismissed, Jill suddenly realised she hadn't been invited into the house this time and wondered if there was more to this agitation than wanting to pick up her daughter. This left her in a fit of rage, especially when she noticed an LEB van parked up just along the road. She guessed immediately whose van it was and why Melissa wanted her gone. Jill was furious. Yet what could she say or do? Melissa was clearly enjoying

164

herself, while poor Sammy was the one still suffering. Not happy, Jill left, hoping at the least Melissa might start helping.

In the meantime, Sammy continued to improve each and every day, enjoying it seemed the pleasant company and kindly words of all the pretty nurses around him. Only it appeared Sammy had now developed a soft spot for one or two of nurses working there and Elaine would often find him flirting, even in his present state of health. Yet they appeared to find this amusing as he clearly still had his old cheeky charm.

However, should Elaine dare to ask him by way of a joke, if one of them was his girlfriend? Sammy would reply, indignantly ... 'I'm a married man!'

But this didn't make any sense to Elaine as he still didn't talk about his wife and therefore guessed he was probably afraid to do so. It seemed she still had control even now, a conditioning of many years no doubt.

As Sammy steadily improved, he had become more than capable of performing many daily tasks. Things like - washing and dressing him-self and taking him-self to the toilet, were all now part of his routine. As were cleaning his teeth and tidying up his bed, always keen to make a good impression on all the pretty nurses and would follow them around in his eagerness to please. But they didn't seem to mind, always amused by his humour and great sense of fun.

The sisters were pleased with their brother's progress and recaptured high spirits. And often when playing noughts and crosses, which he usually won on merit, they'd find themselves laughing happily together. But if they brought him in the newspaper to discuss world events, he didn't always find that funny, which was understandable. It was obvious he was doing much better. But still to their amazement, not one single doctor came anywhere near and this continued to concern them.

It was also evident that his wife was still rarely visiting; as the nursing staff would often complained to them – only his toiletries and clean clothing were constantly running out and they needed her to replace them. But unable to track her down most of the time, they found this not only irritating but also uncaring. Yet for some strange reason social services didn't think this was strange. God knows what excuses she was giving them. If indeed she did.

Melissa however, did make the odd appearance apparently but the sisters guessed it was to keep up the charade, only her visits were never long enough to make an impression on Sammy it seemed. In fact, he couldn't connect with her at all these days according to the nurses, and clearly found it harder as time went by.

Elaine even started to wonder if people thought she was Sammy's wife, as she was the one mostly visiting. So Elaine made sure everyone knew she was his sister. After all she didn't want people thinking Melissa was actually doing her duty as a supposedly caring spouse.

Four months had passed and Sammy was walking so much better, although still unsteady at times. So whenever the sisters went to visit they'd try to help him further by walking him around the hospital grounds, although always arm in arm to support him. And sometimes on their travels they'd pass a pretty nurse, who Sammy often recognised, and would give her a wink and a cheeky smile. He still had that same cheeky charm.

Wanting to help their brother improve even more, the sisters decided it was about time they took him out for a drive around the local area. Clearing it with the nursing staff again, who thought it was a good idea. Given his wife hadn't been anywhere near him lately, they guessed it wouldn't be a problem.

Over this period of healing, the nurses on his ward had been fantastic with Sammy, always caring for him and his needs. It seemed they were only too pleased that others were trying to help him, knowing there were difficulties in the family. But clearly not able to comment on their patient's situation or to become involved in any family matters as they could lose their jobs, they had to keep their distance. Yet it was obvious they were certainly fond of Sammy.

The physiotherapists at the hospital were also exceptional with Sammy. Investing a vast amount of time and energy in trying to get his co-ordination corrected, which in turn had clearly helped sort out his balance, particularly when trying to walk.

The sisters only criticism with the hospital at this time was the lack of communication from the doctors and consultants. And this made them think - had Melissa been restricting them in some way? After all she was his next of kin? She had control as usual.

The nurses who were unable to express their true opinions would occasionally confide in the sisters though; particularly if they wanted to moan about Melissa, although this only happened in secret and out of earshot of others.

But they knew she was a problem and it was fairly obvious the nurses had become attached to Sammy and his fun loving ways. They'd certainly grown a soft spot in their hearts for him and it showed.

Amazingly though, after all this time and after all of his improvements, Sammy still wouldn't mention his wife, and not even to the nurses. It was therefore evident to the sisters his memory was selective rather than faulty, as Sammy still turned moody whenever she was mentioned.

The sisters were sure he was trying to block her out and this continued to greatly concerned them not knowing why this was.

So not to annoy him further she was hardly ever mentioned at all these days, which was probably just as well. Although wasn't this what she wanted?

Chapter 19 – The meeting

The day before the arranged meeting with Melissa and social services, Elaine had a small operation on her shoulder. Not wanting to miss out on Melissa's performance though of the' poor injured wife', she was determined to still join them. Particularly as Sue Webster had organised it to iron out their differences, so she said.

As far as the sisters were concerned though, the main purpose of the meeting was to put together a programme to ensure their brother received the rehabilitation he deserved. Although they weren't looking forward to meeting Melissa again, especially Elaine, yet she wouldn't have missed this for anything.

Arriving in plenty of time, the sisters met first on Sammy's ward and from there went together to Sue's office, bracing themselves for the unpredictable - as they were never quite sure what to expect when Melissa was involved.

Sue looked up as the sisters entered the office, the loud bang of the heavy metal door closing behind them making her jump. The sisters could feel her unease, and wondered why she was in fact. She seemed so anxious

Melissa was already waiting in an adjoining room, according to Sue, well ensconced in her lair they guessed. No doubt having primed Sue to be sympathetic to her needs.

Sue definitely wasn't herself, although Sue had once let slip in an earlier meeting – this wasn't the right job for her. "People's problems could sometimes be very draining", she said and the sisters understood that.

Elaine too was also feeling uncomfortable about this meeting, as she hadn't seen Melissa in over ten years and guessed it wouldn't be straightforward.

Sorting herself out now and gathering her things together, the sisters followed Sue to the adjoining room where Melissa sat quietly waiting - rehearsing her stories most probably.

Keeping her head down as they entered, they could see Melissa hadn't changed much at all even after all these years, except for her hair of course. Elaine couldn't get over its brightness, particularly up against her pale gaunt face, which on closer inspection, showed very few lines. And the sisters had to wonder if all those years of keeping out of the sun had actually paid off.

Her thoughts now interrupted, Melissa slowly looked up from her trance like state. Her eyes unblinking, she undoubtedly expected the worst. But the sisters ignored her obvious discomfort and sat down on the allocated chairs close by, so they formed a semi-circle facing Sue.

After exchanging a few small pleasantries and pretending to be nice, Sue started off the meeting by giving them a brief account of Sammy's progress.

The sisters listened intently, as she explained what the hospital had planned for their brother over the following few months, and even beyond. The sisters were delighted with this as they hadn't been given any information on Sammy before and were pleased this was finally being shared. Melissa though, looked disinterested at the doctor's suggestions, repeated by Sue and didn't even comment, except to say, 'It was all if's and but',' and Sue could only agree.

'Now, Melissa,' Sue said looking directly at her, 'would you like to tell us how you've been coping over this period - with your husband being so poorly I mean? It's been almost four months. It must still be very difficult.' Sue fidgeted with her blouse, opening the top button as if she were hot.

Elaine felt extra awkward - why was Sue feeding her these lines? It's Sammy that's suffering, not her, and it's mainly due to her that he's in this state. Surely they've got this wrong somewhere along the line. And already disheartened, Elaine realised the games about to be played.

Melissa sat straight backed, as she thought on Sue's question. Cocking her head to one side she pushed her bright red hair away from her shoulders as she prepared her reply.

'Well ... I am getting much stronger,' she said, pausing for effect. 'In fact, I think I may be coming to terms with it all, at last.' She stopped again and turned to one side, an uncomfortable look on her face now. 'And I have to admit I'm no longer listening for his car coming up the driveway when he's normally due home from work.'

No because you've bloody sold it, Elaine thought and at this point Melissa got a hanky from her handbag, dabbing her eyes before she continued.

'This has been a very difficult time for me and Kelly,' she said with more emotion. 'It's all been so upsetting... still, I'm not crying quite so much these days and I can now

171

see a future in front of me - a light at the end of the tunnel. In fact, I believe this has made me a much stronger person.' Melissa looked down at her outstretched hands as if looking for answers, her face now hidden from theirs.

'Oh, you poor thing, it must be very difficult for you,' Sue said offering more sympathy than necessary. 'Would it help if you had counselling?'

'Oh dear no, I don't need that!'

Elaine looked at Jill, who knew exactly what she was thinking. Surely this woman wasn't being sucked in by her lies.... after all, who the hell was she kidding? Where does poor Sammy come into all this?'

'Now, I understand you've sold Sammy's car,' Sue questioned as she looked towards the sisters who'd mentioned this earlier. 'Would you like to explain why?'

Sue raised her pen ready to take notes, her face already confirming she knew there'd be a perfectly good explanation and this made the sisters angry.

What were they doing witnessing this sickening performance. They were clearly all part of Melissa's game and this apparently gullible woman appeared to believe every word she uttered?

Melissa continued on with what they felt was an obvious act, confident in the fact she'd taken in at least one woman in this room. 'Well the car was just sitting outside doing nothing,' she said. 'And because I can't drive, I thought it was better to sell it. I didn't get much for it though, it was very old and what I did get I didn't spend on myself.'

What could the sisters say to that? But Sue made more notes, no doubt confident in its authenticity.

'In fact, I've put the money towards doing up the front drive, because that's what Sammy had planned … before the accident that is and I wanted to carry out his wishes.'

What a load of rubbish, the sisters thought, Sammy had been too depressed to be planning things like front driveways and he'd certainly never mentioned it before in any of his conversations with Jill, but what could they say?

'Steven, an old friend of my husbands,' she continued. 'He's been helping to sort all this out. He's been very good to me.' Her face was now a picture of pure innocence.

No mention of him being her 'rock' then, the sisters thought and the fact that he and Sammy had fallen out years ago, which made them question why they had anyway. Because if the rumours were true and it was this guy that Melissa was having an affair with, they had to wonder when the romance first started. With him being an old friend - and an ex one at that, it obviously made the sisters suspicious.

Elaine was livid. But what could she do or say? She still couldn't prove anything different.

After her star performance, Sue then put forward, Sammy's doctor's recommendations, regarding his care. Suggesting he should stay on in his present ward for now. To which Melissa agreed without question. Yet not once were the sisters asked what they thought. In fact not an acknowledgment went their way. It seemed they were irrelevant as usual, after all Melissa was his next of kin and she had the final say. And they noted, rehabilitations wasn't even being suggested.

Devious to the end though, the sisters realised, whatever was decided, Melissa would make sure it didn't affect her or her life in any shape or form, even though she agreed with all their proposals. She had control as usual.

Once Sue had finished her final summary on Sammy's health prospects, she then asked the sisters if they had any questions - given there'd been little communication with Melissa in the past.

'Yes, actually I do,' Elaine quickly piped up; after all, she could play this game too - just put me on that stage.

'They keep asking on the ward for more up to date photographs and sadly, most of mine are old ones … do you think you could possibly bring some in Melissa. And perhaps some of Kelly,' she added, smiling sweetly.

Clearly not happy with Elaine's involvement, Melissa's face said it all – now wearing a look that said, who was this interfering woman who sat in front of me now? Who did she think she was? A look that spoke a thousand words and yet not one actually uttered.

'Oh don't worry about that,' she said flicking her hair to one side. 'I've got that sorted already. In fact, I've got it all in hand... I'm putting together my own book of photographs.'

Elaine wasn't trying to score points and was more than happy with Melissa's new suggestion, particularly if it helped Sammy. As long as he got what he needed that was all that mattered.

'Well, I think Sammy should be back on the ward by now,' Sue said, now sounding much happier, although the sisters wonder where Sammy had been. 'His home visit earlier must have been exhausting.' Sue dropped the bombshell with no explanation.

Surprised by this announcement, the sisters realised, they'd been kept out of the loop yet again, having not been told of their plans or what it was even about.

'Shall we all go and see him together then?' Jill suggested, keen to get Melissa involved, and clearly determined she should join them. She was fed up with all this business about her not liking hospitals she told Elaine, and for sure it was getting quite tiring.

'It was time she actually visited her husband and talked to him for a change', she whispered to Elaine as Melissa walked ahead.

Not having any option now - as Melissa still needed to be seen playing her part in front of Sue, she reluctantly agreed. And so they made their way to Sammy's ward just like old friends.

However, as Elaine went to leave, Sue stopped her at the door, relieved for some reason it appeared.

'I'm sorry Mrs Bowers if I seemed a little nervous during that meeting but Melissa told me you were bound to cause trouble. In fact, she said that's what you did whenever she was involved. And that's why she's so frightened of you.'

'What! ... I don't believe it ... so she was stirring things up and telling you lies before we even got here. Whatever is the matter with the woman?   Please, Sue, don't believe everything that woman tells you.' And flummoxed by her outrageous comments and lies, Elaine ran off to catch up with her sister. Leaving Sue to decide who was telling the truth.

Keen to know what Melissa had been up to, Jill had already started to ask her questions, trying to find out what her plans were for the future it seemed.

'So, what have you been up to lately Melissa?' Jill said probing already and probably wondering what lies she'd conjure up.

'I'm modelling actually,' she announced straight faced. 'I'm doing very well, in fact.'

'That's nice. What are you modelling?' Jill looked her up and down in amazement.

'Actually it's underwear. It pays very well.'

Elaine, who'd quickly caught up, had heard her replies and stared too astonished, although keeping her distance and her mouth firmly shut. She couldn't believe what she was hearing and thought - who did this woman think she was? Who the hell was she kidding?

'That's interesting,' Jill said her face now as straight as Melissa's. 'So where do you go to do that?'

'Up in London… I was in Ann Summers one day just looking around and this man came up to me and asked if I would like to model for them.'

Elaine wanted to laugh. She had worked for many years for a catalogue company and part of her job was selecting models and she was certain Melissa wouldn't be one of the chosen. Although they may have thought she was a man in drag, only that had been mentioned before to Elaine, which certainly made sense.

'In fact life is treating me very well,' Melissa continued, swishing her hair off her shoulders.

The sisters were gobsmacked, having only just heard her Oscar winning performance in front of Sue, and they couldn't believe their ears.

When suddenly, she lifted up her flimsy top, only too keen to show them both her newly pierced belly button, while announcing, 'Sammy would never let me have one of these before.' And with her jeans slung low on her skinny hips, she pranced herself before them as if she were a model.

So she still fancied herself ... Elaine was astounded, Melissa hadn't changed at all. And looking at Jill, Elaine guessed exactly what she was thinking, dumfounded by her actions too.

But this was really pathetic and childish, wasn't it time she grew up, after all, her husband was still recovering from major surgery having nearly lost his life. Yet all she could do was brag about her-self. That's if any of it was true of course, which Elaine strongly doubted.

'Yes, life is very good and I'm living it to the full,' she gushed. 'In fact I'm going for gold.'

The sisters weren't sure what she meant by that, but continued to listen anyway, pretending to go along with her fantasies and lies. Realising it was important that they all remained friends, if only to get the best for their brother. But, oh boy did they think this woman was nuts. Although clever enough and cute enough to keep all this rubbish from Sue or anyone else of importance they guessed.

Making their way to Sammy's ward, the sisters were surprised when they bumped into him waiting by the lifts. Sitting in a wheel chair, he looked none too pleased when he spotted them coming towards him. And Elaine had to wonder if he was concerned at seeing the three of them together, as this may have been confusing, considering their past history. Or perhaps there was something else on his mind altogether?

Melissa then explained, they'd taken Sammy home briefly that morning, to see if she could cope with him there. The sisters were surprised they were even considering this though, particularly as Melissa had shown little interest in her husband. And Elaine had to wonder why Sue hadn't mentioned this visit home before today. It was obvious Sue thought this was none of their business, even though they'd played a big part in Sammy's life to date. But why was he now in a wheelchair, left waiting by the lift?

According to Melissa, while Sammy was at home she thought he'd taken a sip from the bleach bottle that she'd left on the kitchen worktop- mistaking it for something else, she guessed. Although, there were no tell-tale signs of a sore throat or burnt lips it seemed.

Melissa also said, she thought he may have put something in his mouth and possibly swallowed it. So the hospital, now thinking he might have caused himself some harm, decided to take x-rays. But thankfully they apparently found nothing and hence why he was waiting there now - ready to go back to his ward.

Sammy looked worried though, concerned by all the attention it seemed, and clearly didn't understand why these x-rays needed taking and kept asking 'why?' He was clearly agitated and Elaine got the feeling there something else on Sammy's mind but what was he covering up this time? Or did he know nothing had entered his mouth and it was just a pack of lies made up by Melissa to make sure this little experiment to send him home wasn't going to work.

Yet, if that was the case, this certainly pleased the sisters, as Sammy going home was the last thing they wanted. Thinking Melissa may finish off what they felt she might have started.

Sammy was already on the ward by the time they got there, sitting in his chair by the window, a smile on his face now. The sisters were relieved by this brighter mood and thought perhaps he may be thinking – at least they were all good friends at last. Which they were in away - well 'make believe' ones anyway but he didn't know that. And perhaps he thought, Melissa wouldn't stop him seeing his sisters again.

Which was good, if that was the case, only Sammy needed his sisters' support more than ever these days, as he certainly wasn't getting it from his wife. Although she had said she was prepared to help him with the photographs – one step in the right direction.

His dinner served up earlier, was placed to one side and being Friday fish and chips was on the menu. But after Sammy's previous ordeal he didn't appear very hungry and it sat there untouched. Well that was until Melissa started grabbing it, declaring to Jill how wonderful it tasted.

'Why don't you try some ... go on,' she prompted, waving a large piece of Cod between her fingers and directly under Jill's nose.

Jill looked disgusted; this was Sammy's dinner after all. And Elaine wondered what had happened to the - 'she didn't like hospitals, and how she'd found them too upsetting'. This woman was unbelievable, as it certainly didn't put her off her food.

Elaine looked at Jill in amazement, but neither said a word; they needed to keep the peace for Sammy.

'It's Jeff's birthday next month Jill, isn't it?' Melissa said out of the blue.

'Yes, that's right. My, you've got a good memory. Fancy you remembering my husband's birthday.' Jill looked perplexed.

But Elaine wondered why she would even mention this?

'Yes, I remember most people's birthdays; always have done,' she said, a smile on her face resembling a smirk.

Elaine knew exactly what she meant by that, referring to her birthday she suspected. But would anyone believe her, she doubted it very much? It seemed Melissa was playing mind games again.

Not wanting to waste any more of her precious time with them, no doubt, Melissa left soon after. And although confused by the whole event and angry by her blatant lies, the sisters could now at least relax. While Sammy's face said it all, clearly pleased she'd disappeared. He was certainly more aware than anyone thought.

Chapter 20 – Dirty tricks

A few days after their meeting with Sue, Jill went back to see her brother - only to find him sat by his bedside back in that faraway place yet again. Oblivious to her presence; he starred out the window towards another world it seemed.

His mind elsewhere, Jill wondered what he was thinking. She had no idea what had caused this change of mood and there was nothing she could say or do to distract him. But then she saw it, sat on his bed side table, just as she had promised. Flicking through its pages, Jill became extremely angry. Her thoughts all over the place she waited for her sister.

Elaine made her way through the ward she'd now become familiar with, keen to see her brother. Since their last meeting, she too was keen to know if there'd been any changes, or any new developments.

Approaching Sammy's bed, Elaine could see her sister standing by her brother's side and looking none too pleased.

'What's ever up, sis?' she asked, taking off her jackct. 'Phew!' she groaned. She always found the wards too hot.

'She's brought that book in … you know the one she promised us,' and Jill gestured towards it with her eyes as it sat on Sammy's table. The expressions on her face suggesting trouble.

'Oh … that's good, isn't it? At least she's managed to do that for him, something positive at last?' Yet why the long face she thought?

'Have a look at the picture on the very first page… is that her brother-in-law she's got her arm around?' Jill spoke quietly, clearly not wanting to alert her brother.

But Sammy remained distant, still looking out the window. He seemed unaware of this present intrigue. Or was he?

Elaine grabbed the book and opened it with caution as if a trap lay in store. Not sure what dirty tricks were to be uncovered.

'No … that's not her brother-in-law, he's tall and slim. No I bet that's the boyfriend, 'her rock,' or 'cock', whatever you want to call him!'

'Fat bastard!' Jill replied and Elaine nodded in agreement.

Guessing Sammy had probably seen the book earlier, when Melissa first brought it in, keen to show him her new conquest, the new man in her life - the man Sammy had supposedly fallen out with all those years ago, Elaine couldn't comprehend the nastiness. But soon realised, Melissa wouldn't have been able to resist rubbing his nose in that little foray and at his sisters' request for photos too. She probably found that funny. And going by the expression on Sammy's face now, he surely knew her game. Yet as always he would never say.

Still avoiding eye contact in case he gave the game away, they assumed. They continued to keep their comments low, not knowing for certain if Sammy was aware of this present dilemma.

'I found him like this when I came in' Jill said, 'I wouldn't be surprised if it's this that's upset him,' and she pointed at the book.

'Well, of course it has Jill, that's pretty obvious and she knew it would too. After all how would you feel if your husband was standing there, cuddling another woman right in front of your eyes? Especially with someone you were no longer friends with.'

'Yes,' Jill said, 'it's incredible … and she's in the garden too … she won't normally step foot out there.'

'She's taking the piss out of us all. You want pictures, now you've got them!' Elaine was angry. 'I wouldn't mind, but she hasn't even put any other relevant photos in the bloody book and after asking for photos of Kelly too,' she said while flicking through the rest of the pages, of which only a few were filled. 'I mean there's nothing in here we can talk to Sammy about. After all we can't talk about this bloke, can we?' and she pointed to the photo in disgust. 'Although I bet, she would like us to.'

The rest of the pictures seemed pretty innocuous and insignificant overall. Nothing that would substantiate any particular part of Sammy's life, and therefore of no consequence. Except for this one picture, which as far as the sisters were concerned was only there to upset Sammy and cause him further harm. And it looked as though it had worked.

Elaine considered telling Sue Webster what their sister-in-law had done. But decided all Melissa needed to say was the photo was of an old friend or even a family member and thought it might jog his memory, and Sue would be none the wiser. No, she always had an answer for everything; she would have calculated it well.

Unhappy about the photo but unsure what to do, Jill looked over at the album and whispered to Elaine, 'As Sammy doesn't seem himself,' she said, 'why don't we lose it? After all we don't want it upsetting him again, do we?'

Grasping her meaning, Elaine slipped the photo out of the book. 'Oh dear, look, it's accidentally fallen out,' and she placed it in her handbag, her brother none the wiser.

'She's unbelievable that woman. She's trying to drive him insane!' Jill was visibly angry.

'Well, it seems she definitely doesn't want to see him get any better, that's for sure.' Elaine placed her hand gently on Sammy's shoulder but he still didn't respond.

Later that afternoon on the same visit, the sisters were told by one the nurses that Sammy had been for further assessments earlier that morning and at one of the better rehabilitation centres in the area too. Unfortunately, Melissa had gone with him yet again and as her effect on Sammy was usually problematic, having witnessed this themselves, his assessment didn't go well, especially after being shown the new book of photo's that Melissa had kindly put together they guessed. It was therefore no wonder he didn't pass the tests and yet again why hadn't they been informed? Surely their comments regarding his progress would have helped. They were certain, with the right encouragement he'd have responded far better.

The sisters had planned to take Sammy out that afternoon to see how he coped with the outside world. But in view of his present mood they felt this should wait till later and took him for a walk around the hospital grounds instead, although at first he seemed reluctant.

Popping into one of the coffee shops on site, here they drank their teas with a nice piece of cake. But as Sammy's preference to eat while standing up, always anxious to be on the move, this made the situation embarrassing. As it seemed, this continuous movement showed an anxiety, which often meant he wanted to get back to his bed. So they didn't stay very long.

The next day, Sammy was back to his normal jolly self. So the sisters felt it would be safe to venture further afield, agreeing it with the nurses first of course.

Driving around the local area, Sammy was visibly excited, especially when he started to recognise places he'd been to in the past. Even remembering some well enough to direct Elaine at times. And would point out quite happily when he thought she was lost or took the wrong turning, plus making comments when he believed he was near his house.

The sisters were impressed, amazed by his knowledge and new found memories. Particularly as he even once dared to criticise Elaine's driving, to which some had been hung for less before. And had even passed comment when a driver cut them up, which was really amazing considering his supposed mental state.

This had to mean his new awareness suggested the damage to his brain may not be as bad as the doctors first thought. They could only conclude from this exercise there was certainly more hope than they were originally led to believe.

Of course the sisters didn't expect he would ever drive again, but they now felt confident he could at least achieve some kind of near normal life, if given the chance. And they were certain these things were still in his grasp.

Over the following few weeks, the sisters took Sammy out as often as they could; hoping to lift his spirits, which in turn would hopefully help him recover. The nurses it seemed, were only too happy for the sisters to do this, as it gave them and their brother the respite they all needed, if only for an hour or two.

Keen to keep Sammy in this better mood, the sisters would often take him to one of the garden centres nearby, as he always appeared to enjoy this. Especially when they strolled around the Aquarian area, arm in arm, as this probably felt like another world to him – a world within a world where they could lose themselves together.

Here they would watch the running waters of the Lily ponds, with elegant figurines that carried pots and jugs above their heads and shoulders. And as jars and buckets filled with water, frothing, bubbling and spilling over - whirling, gurgling sounds echoed all around them, as if it were a magical place.

Sammy was in his element and as hundreds of bobbing heads glided up to greet them, he smiled with excitement. As a mass of Koi Carp, resplendent in bright colours came up to say hello. Their eyes in shock and their mouths agape, the shiny slippery creatures clearly waited to be fed.

Sammy was always happy when he came here to visit. As he could still name most of the fish they kept there. After all this had been his job before his so called accident, which always impressed Elaine, as she couldn't even pronounce the names.

Overjoyed by his accomplishments and pleased with his progress thus far, the sisters scratched their heads for other places to take him, often running out of ideas. So just for a change, Elaine would sometimes take him back to her place, although at times this could prove difficult, as he would never want to leave. But he never wanted to drink from the bleach bottle either, which always amused the sisters.

Also Sammy had now reached a stage where he thought that pleading with his sisters was a good idea, especially when he didn't get his way. And he'd often ask if he could go back to theirs to stay a while, which didn't prove a problem at first. But this constant request to visit and let him stay, later upset the sisters, as they knew this wasn't possible and certainly not an option. But what could they tell him? After all they didn't want to hurt his feelings.

Yet even if it were possible, their complicated lives, busy schedules, lives within lives, would almost make it impossible. While getting custody of their brother would surely prove a problem also - involving a fight in the Courts no doubt. Even though they were certain Melissa didn't want him. As they guessed she wouldn't want anyone else to have him either.

On one particular day Elaine was desperate for somewhere different to take her brother and decided to visit his former boss, John, at his old place of work. Thinking this would be a good opportunity to see how he coped and responded, they walked into the Aquarian shop, arm in arm, as if they were customers. John at first didn't seem to notice them, busy with his work. But after a few minutes, he looked over again and on recognising Sammy appeared visibly shocked - speechless and confused no doubt. After all he'd initially been told Sammy was dead, and since then most probably a cabbage, with no hope of getting better. That's if he was even aware Sammy was still alive, only the look on his face indicated otherwise. Perhaps he thought, Sammy had risen from the dead.

Still if he knew Melissa well, which the sisters suspected he might, he should have guessed it was a lie, although something someone wouldn't normally lie about.

Saying their awkward hellos, Sammy looked overly attentive when he spoke to John and was acting very different in front of him. Elaine couldn't work it out at first but it certainly seemed as if Sammy wanted to impress him. In fact it was as though he was attending an interview, shaking his hand firming, while standing straight and to attention, his hands down by his side. Maybe in Sammy's mind he'd wanted to keep his job, as he even thought to enquire after his business - appearing more than capable of many social graces.

After chatting with John for five minutes or so, Elaine felt a strange awkwardness developing between the men, which she didn't quite understand. And she thought perhaps it was time to get back to the hospital.

Saying their goodbyes, John promised he'd visit Sammy soon, given he knew now how well he was doing, but of course he never did. Yet Elaine wasn't surprised by that, just a little sad for her brother.

Sometimes when driving close to Sammy's house, he would often ask his sisters if he could go and visit his home, always well aware they were near. Although he never once mentioned he wanted to see his wife, or his daughter come to that. It seemed he just needed to see his house and most probably his lovely garden. His home was clearly important to him and a link to a life that had once been his. But more importantly, Elaine was sure he wanted to see his pride and joy still sitting on the driveway just where he'd left it on that fateful day. The day Melissa had persuaded him to take the bus.

The sisters were more than happy to take him there of course, as they realised it may help with his memory recall. But guessing Melissa wouldn't want them there they had no option but to make their excuses - knowing she'd make it obvious they weren't welcome.

So, not wanting to upset Sammy, the sisters would lie, telling him they needed to get him back to the hospital, either for his dinner or to see a doctor. And Sammy would happily believe them, accepting their weak excuses. After all, they guessed, he thought they were his guardian angels, who else could he trust?

As time went by, Sammy had become far more talkative and became even more persistent about visiting his home. The sisters were exasperated with his pleading, tired of making excuses for Melissa's non help.

'I know Melissa keeps saying she's going to take him home for a visit … but when?' Jill said, as they sat one day together in Elaine's kitchen, while Sammy looked at photographs of Joe, her son in an album.

'Well maybe it's because she doesn't drive that she's not been able to do it.' Elaine said, clearly deciding to give Melissa the benefit of the doubt for a change.

'I'll ring her then, see if she wants us to help her.' Jill too was trying to be sympathetic, although she found this difficult at times, given that contact with Melissa usually made her angry.

So with reluctance, Jill dialled her number, exchanging pleasantries between gritted teeth.

'I'm at Elaine's just now and we've got Sammy with us at the moment. He's okay … but he keeps asking us to take him home. It seems he wants to come and visit. Anyway we were wondering if it was possible to bring him there now. We wouldn't stay long.'

'Oh dear, no… that's really not convenient at the moment. Kelly and I are just about to go out.'

'Look Melissa, I know it's very difficult for you because you don't drive but we could always help by bringing him there another day.' Already Jill's patience was running out, still unable to accept her uncaring ways.

'Really, Jill, please don't worry your-self, I've got it all under control. In fact I have it all in hand. When my sister comes to visit me next, we're going to pick Sammy up in her car.'

So what could Jill say - this woman needed a slap. Not once was she thinking of Sammy's needs, or what he wanted now.

Jill put the phone down unable to speak. Not sure what to tell Sammy this time, the excuses were running out.

Chapter 21 - Hospital Care

The hospital these days had become more like Sammy's home than his own. While the nurses who looked after him more like his family, as they probably gave him more attention than his wife or daughter had ever done. So it wasn't much of a surprise that Sammy was still fond of a few of them working there.

In fact the sisters would still catch him flirting with a nurse or two and normally the prettier ones on the ward, to which they would tease him and make him laugh. And he still followed them around eagerly as they preformed their daily tasks. Yet they never appeared to mind at all. They told the sisters, 'Sammy was a kind and soft hearted man, who just wanted some fun and a little attention,' and this made the sisters wonder, if this was the new Sammy. Or had he always been this way?

Sitting with Sammy one afternoon, Elaine noticed he was taking a special interest in one nurse in particular.

'She seems a very nice young lady, Sammy. Is she your new girlfriend?' she teased, not expecting him to answer.

But the smile on his face soon faded. 'Noooo ...!' he said again, 'I'm a married man!' And when the nurse in question happened to look his way, he turned the other way. Shy she guessed, or guilty, Elaine couldn't believe it, he was still bloody loyal!' It was just a shame it wasn't reciprocated.

The large cardboard box that now sat at Sammy's bedside, which acted as his wardrobe, was full of Sammy's clothing. And even though no longer wearing nappies, he still needed lots of clean clothes, as he still had occasional accidents, especially when he'd tried to feed himself, only he always got in such a mess. But as the hospital only did essential washing on the premises, such as soiled bedding and towels; patient's daily clothing were expected to be done at home.

Annoyed by the lack of clothes often left in Sammy's box, the nurses had to insist, Melissa kept up with her husband's washing. Only the nurses often moaned to the sisters that he was frequently running out of things to wear.

But as Melissa undoubtedly knew this, the sisters guessed, she just didn't care and shocked at the thought of doing more she exploded one day, apparently telling the nurses, 'It's not my problem ... I haven't got time for all of that!' And she quickly popped out to the local shops and returned with a large parcel. The nurses told the sisters, 'she looked very smug, and told them "here, I've bought you a big box of washing powder. That should last a while. I suggest you do his washing," and she pushed the box into one of the nurse's hands, and quickly made her getaway.'

The nurses were not amused by Melissa's antics they told the sisters, but as usual there were never any comebacks. And they never thought to ask the sisters to help which was probably just as well; particularly as the powers that be had never considered anything else to be their business and this wouldn't have been well received. Anyway Melissa should be doing his washing; she was his wife after all, what else did she do?

So still running out of clothing, the nurses had no option but to do the washing themselves.

Realising just how disgusting their brother's clothes had become and how tatty he was looking, the sisters decided to sort through the box for them-selves - to see what they could salvage.

'A tramp wouldn't wear these, sis,' Elaine said as she held up a pair of badly stained joggers.

'I think Melissa must have got these from the charity shop...' Jill replied, digging further into the box, 'Although, I think they belong in the bin,' and she scrunched up her nose at the state of it all.

'More likely Kelly's cast offs,' Elaine complained, as she too rummaged deeper. And pulling out by the tips of her fingers - what resembled a bright red crumpled jumper; she slung it back down in disgust.

Elaine was not amused. This was humiliating, how could she treat her husband this way. Yet still social service didn't believe it was necessary to do anything about this, even though he looked more like a clown these days, rather than someone's husband.

No the sisters were not happy as they needed him looking smarter in order to take him out. But with his trousers always worn at half-mast and most of his jumpers thread bare, the sisters despaired. And although they realised he'd lost a lot of weight over this period and clearly needed new clothes that fitted, they knew this could be expensive. But thought, surely Melissa could provide a little better. As they knew his pension was more than adequate to cover some clothing.

Fed up with Melissa and the thought of more confrontations, the sisters decided - rather than extra hassle with their sister-in-law they'd club together to buy a few new things. After all they didn't want him looking like a tramp anymore, particularly when going out.

On top of this, he didn't appear to have any toiletries left either and he didn't possess a pair of slippers. Melissa insisted they'd all been stolen, accusing the hospital staff of taking them. She certainly didn't feel she should replace them. Even though, she was living quite comfortably on his money and whatever other benefits she got.

Infuriated by her antics and their brother's shabby appearance, Jill told her sister - she needed to tell her exactly how she felt, even though she guessed it would be a waste of time. As trying to get Melissa to except her responsibilities was virtually impossible, although it was worth another try.

Later that day, Jill knocked hard on Melissa's front door ready to give her piece of her mind yet again, while Elaine waited in the car not wanting to antagonise further. After all they wanted results for Sammy.

'Oh ... hi Jill!' Melissa gushed, looking rather flustered by her presence. She clearly hadn't expected her sister-in-law to be stood on her doorstep today.

'Melissa, do you love my brother?' she asked, wadding in full pelt and forgetting all the niceties this time.

'Of course I do,' she stuttered, 'we've been married for twenty five years this coming Monday. Of course I do,' she repeated as if that explained it all.

'Well, if you do, will you please show it for God's sake's and take care of your husband as you should do. His clothes are like rags and are simply disgusting. And his toiletries have all run out … I mean do you actually care?'

Melissa looked shocked by Jill's questions and didn't seem able to answer, which set Jill off again in a rampage of further accusations, expressing her true feelings with regards to Sammy's obvious neglect. She needed this out in the open now and dealt with once and for all. But whether she was listening was anyone's guess.

'Don't worry, Jill,' Melissa said calmly, which infuriated her further. 'I'm actually going out today to get him some new things; I've got it all under control. In fact I'm going out any minute,' and she looked anxiously at her watch.

Keen to get Jill off the doorstep, it seemed, Melissa whittled on, clearly thinking she'd put an end to her sister-in-law's attack. But Jill wanted things sorted and wouldn't budge. She hadn't noticed the man's jacket hanging on the banister just inside, but Melissa obviously thought she had.

'Look, I've even brought Sammy's winter coat down,' she said, pointing to the brown jacket hanging behind her. 'I'm going to take it in for him later. Now it's getting colder, he'll probably need it.'

Still angry, Jill was taken momentarily aback by what seemed a thoughtful gesture, which threw her for a while.

'Look, Melissa, I just want you to do your duty as his wife. He keeps pleading with us to bring him here to see you. Can you not even do that for him?'

'I've told you Jill … I've got it all arranged with my sister, but she's not very well at the moment. In fact she's got meningitis and won't be able to come just yet … but I will do it, don't worry.'

Twiddling with her hair, Melissa seemed extra nervous.

'I'm sorry Jill, but I really must get going, I'm meeting Kelly soon.'

Dismissed again, Jill wanted to punch her lights out, but what would that achieve? If anything, it would only provoke her further and make matters worse.

Her patience at an end, Jill returned to the car where Elaine was quietly waiting, when Jill spotted an LEB van trying to park up ahead.

'Don't drive away just yet Elaine. I think this van in front, maybe her bloke, turning up.'

'No! ... What a result!' The thought of them being caught out clearly appealed to her sense of humour. And knowing he'd have to pass them on route to the house, they waited.

'Is he coming yet?' Elaine asked, scared to look herself.

'Yes, he's coming right now.'

'Is it him then, the man in the photo?' she whispered.

'I think so, the fat bastard!' and she watched him come closer.

Amused, Elaine peeped at the now passing man who seemed unaware of their presence. But as they watched him walk up to their brother's house and his front door as though it were a regular occurrence, the sisters were soon seething.

'Yeah, that's him Jill, that's the guy in the photo, I can't believe it.

'Well I think we should wait and see if they come back out together? Then we can open the window and say 'hi' as they pass us. That should get them thinking - caught in the act.' And Jill laughed in frustration.

Waiting a good fifteen minutes or more, Melissa and her rock still hadn't appeared. Jill was furious. 'I thought she was in a bloody hurry as well!'

'Yeah, because he was about to turn up … they're probably at it right now. She wasn't going anywhere; she just wanted you out of the way.'

'Unless she knows we're still sitting here of course and she's too scared to come out.' Jill reasoned.

'Well, that would be even funnier, especially if Kelly was really waiting for her to turn up and couldn't because of us.' And Elaine laughed.

The sisters decided there was no point in hanging around any longer, after all what would it really accomplish. But they still wondered how Melissa was getting away with this? She surely had the cheek of the devil.

'So what did she actually say to you at the door?' Elaine asked, as she started to drive away, still looking in the rear view mirror to see if they appeared.

'She basically said she had it all in hand and not to worry. She intends to take him home for a visit once her sister gets over meningitis.'

'Meningitis!' Elaine said surprised. 'Well, it's going to be a long time before she gets over that. That's really serious, sis. Mind you, it's probably a lie. She knows if it's something like that she can keep putting it off under the excuse she's still not well.'

'Or who knows, perhaps she'll be telling us next, her sisters dead,' and Jill laughed herself this time.

'Yeah, that wouldn't surprise me; after all she's said it before, several times.'

'Although she must think of Sammy sometimes,' Jill said thoughtfully, 'only she had a jacket of his hanging on the banister … she said she was going to take it in for him later because it was getting cold.'

'Oh, you silly cow, Jill …you should have taken it. I bet that was her bloke's jacket. She must have thought you saw it.'

'No…do you really think so?'

'I think we should hold her to it and make sure she brings it in for Sammy next time she visits. After all, he will need a heavier jacket soon, especially during the winter months when we both take him out,' and Elaine smiled at Jill, mischievously.

'Yes it's getting much colder now.' And driving away, they giggled like silly school girls. Although still not happy with the situation as what had they achieved?

Sure enough, after a couple of persistent phone calls from Jill regarding the brown jacket, it eventually appeared on the ward, although four sizes too big for poor Sammy, and bigger than he'd ever been. They also knew Sammy would never have been seen dead in a jacket of this style, with its grey poodle like fur collar and brown synthetic base. But the sisters had to laugh at the thought of Melissa's boyfriend losing his winter coat.

Cheesed off with it all, the sisters decided it was now time Sue Walker was brought up to date regarding Melissa's latest antics and especially the terrible way she was still treating her husband. But they also wanted to tell her about the boyfriend. Having seen him for themselves they thought she may be interested.

'Well, did you actually see him put the key in the front door?' Sue asked, as she eyed the two women suspiciously, probably now thinking they were there to cause trouble.

'Well, not actually opening the door,' Elaine replied honestly. 'We couldn't see that far, only we were sitting outside in the car a few doors down.'

Sue shook her head. 'There's nothing we can do really. She's entitled to live her life as she wants, and, if she has a boyfriend, that's not against the law. With regards to the other stuff, his clothing and care I will look into that and have a little word.'

The sisters left again disappointed, 'She seems to be getting away with everything sis; it's unbelievable. 'We should have just bloody lied about the key? After all, that's what she does all the time,' Elaine was annoyed.

'I wonder if that would have made any difference though … only I'm sure Melissa would've made some excuse or other for him having a key. Anyway we're not like that, sis; we were brought up to tell the truth.'

But the sisters felt like giving up now, as nothing they did or said seemed to make any difference. When all they wanted to do was help their brother.

Chapter 22 - The Visits.

Not prepared to give up on their brother, like others appeared to have already. The sisters decided it was time to pay another visit on Sammy's next door neighbour – she had told them they were welcome anytime. And as Sammy had done so well of late, they felt this meeting might help him further.

Sammy looked delighted when they told him where they were going, the smile on his face proving this. So dressing him up as smartly as they could with the miss mash of clothing from his old cardboard box, the sisters took him to see his dear friend, Mrs Nolan.

Pulling up directly outside her home, Elaine noticed Sammy looking over at the house next door, the one he'd lived in for over twenty years. But he never said a word. He seemed more interested in visiting his friend and appeared unaware that his car wasn't there. And this pleased the sisters no end, as no explanations were needed and no lies any longer required.

Elaine got out of the car first and knocked on Mrs Nolan's door, who answered it straight away.

'Is it okay to bring Sammy in, Mrs Nolan?' Elaine asked. 'Only he's sitting in the car at the moment and he'd love to see you.'

'Yes, of course … but don't you need some help?'

'No, that's okay?'

'Are you sure … don't you need us to help carry him in?'

'No, don't be silly. Sammy can walk by himself, quite easily. He's really looking forward to chatting with you.'

Mrs Nolan looked surprised. 'Really … we understood he was in a wheelchair and couldn't walk … let alone talk.'

Oh, my God, she was still under the impression he was wheelchair bound, and a cabbage no doubt. This must be the lies Melissa had fed her, guessing this was where she got her information from. Although she thought she had put her straight.

'No, Sammy is doing very well, Mrs Nolan, I thought you knew that. You'll be surprised when you see him,' and she went off to fetch him.

Sammy walked slowly and a little unsteadily into the house, but with the biggest smile on his face, his sisters hadn't seen in a long time.

Mrs Nolan looked pleased to see him too and gave him a kiss on the cheek. While her husband on hearing them arrive, came in from the garden followed by Martin who'd been helping him outside.

Surprised to see Sammy looking so well, they said, both under the same impression as Mrs Nolan, they shook his hand and stood there chatting, although, only small talk. They had known each other a long time and this was great for Sammy.

Knowing how much he loved his garden, Martin suggested they went outside to look at the flowers, telling him that from there, he could see his own garden next door. And going by the expression on Sammy's face he was obviously happy to do so and followed them outside.

201

Without Sammy in ear shot, the sisters brought Mrs Nolan quickly up to date, telling her all about Melissa's latest antics.

Mrs Nolan didn't seem surprised by their stories at all but didn't comment; although she did say she hadn't seen much of her lately. Melissa as usual, had kept out of her way and Mrs Nolan said, she preferred it that way. But she did confirm, she'd noticed the gentleman caller was still hanging around and was seen leaving early most mornings. In fact, Melissa had told her a few days earlier, the guy in question was helping Kelly with her computer and Elaine wondered if this was yet another excuse for him always being there. That's if she ever needed one of course.

The three men eventually returned from the garden, laughing and joking like old times - just as Mrs Nolan poured the tea. The cosy sitting room which had once been familiar to Sammy, with its blue velvet drapes and squidgy armchairs, appeared to make him relax. After all, this was the place where Sammy once told this sweet kind lady all of his troubles; his confidante and friend. And Sammy looked happy to be part of this lovely family again.

'So what did you think of the garden Sam?' Martin asked, passing him his tea.

'Yeah, it's really nice; you've done a good job there,' he said, taking the tea, his hands shaking slightly.

'Did he manage to see his own garden?' Elaine asked, directing her question at Martin.

'Yes, you could, couldn't you, Sam? We both had a peep over the fence. It was looking very nice....wasn't it Sammy?' Clearly aware how much his garden meant to him, Martin was obviously trying to reassure him, especially after all the hard work he'd put in over the years.

Sammy smiled and nodded eagerly, pleased with what he'd seen and achieved, no doubt. But more importantly, Elaine guessed pleased that his garden was just as he'd left it, with the rose bush still at the back of the house now in full bloom. Making its last appearance as winter drew near.

Holding onto his cup and saucer, tightly, Sammy's hands still shook with excitement, although he never spilt a drop; again on his best behaviour. And while appearing to enjoy his visit, Sammy spoke slowly and clearly to his friends, albeit a little muddled at times. The sisters were pleased with what he'd achieved and realised this was yet another significant step in their brother's brilliant recovery.

Not wanting to outstay their welcome though, they made their excuses to leave having been there over an hour already.

As they were leaving, Mrs Nolan promised to keep them posted on what was happening next door. She also promised they would try to visit Sammy too, especially now they knew how well he was doing. But of course they never did. Worried perhaps they might get caught up in one of Melissa's dramas, and who could blame them for that.

Saying their goodbyes on the doorstep, the sisters noticed the lights were on next door.

'They're in, Jill,' Elaine said discreetly, not wanting to draw Sammy's attention to the fact.

'Why don't you knock and say hello then?' Mrs Nolan suggested, a mischievous smile on her face.

'Do you think we should Elaine?' Jill said more cautiously.

'Why not? He owns the bloody property. Why shouldn't he? It shouldn't even be debated?'

'Well, I agree with you, why shouldn't he?' Mrs Nolan added. 'You could tell her - you called in because you were next door and thought it rude not to.'

Jill didn't seem convinced though, but clearly outnumbered as even Sammy looked excited now – having obviously cottoned on to their plan.

'Oh, come on then, lets' see what she has to say about us turning up,' Jill said hesitantly, quickly giving in. 'Only it looks like Sammy's up for it as well,' and a wide smile appeared on his face, keen to see his home again. Although he still hadn't noticed his car was missing. Well, at least he never said.

So like an army going into battle, Sammy and his sisters marched up the driveway, arm in arm, with Sammy in the middle. Knocking firmly on the front door, the performance that followed was good enough for Melissa's second Oscar, as she welcomed them into the house, just like old friends.

'Come in; come in, what a surprise! … It's lovely to see you,' she gushed.

The sisters were dumbstruck, as going by her facial expressions they would not have known she was anything other than overjoyed to see them.

My God, Elaine thought, what's happening here? They weren't expecting a reception like this. Oh well, make the most of it. This is for Sammy after all.

Melissa showed them into the lounge, where Kelly hung around in the background, looking extremely nervous, which was really rather sad as she didn't even acknowledge her father, reluctant to go near. She was no doubt embarrassed, and wore a smile that looked strange and twisted and eventually slipped out of the room. This left the sisters wondering what lies she'd been told. But even so, surely she loved her father?

Melissa had been in the middle of cooking dinner when they'd knocked, and a shepherds' pie she'd just prepared, big enough for more than two, was now cooling on the kitchen counter. Sammy eyed the pie keenly. His excitement at being home was obvious. And having already looked around the rooms downstairs, he was clearly pleased to be amongst familiar surroundings. After all, this had been his home once, for over twenty years and the reassurance that all was well, just as it should be, undoubtedly brought peace to his troubled mind.

This long awaited brief visit home had at last made him contented it appeared; happy to see that all was as he had left it. Well except for the missing car that is – the new driveway and the garage roof. But he never said a word about them.

Realising the atmosphere had now become awkward; Elaine began to feel uneasy and wanted to leave this uncomfortable situation. Well away from this woman who still called herself Sammy's wife.

'Come on Sammy, we've got to go now. They're about to have their dinner. Yours will be waiting for you back at the hospital.'

Elaine had a strange feeling there was someone else upstairs, perhaps working on Kelly's computer and she wanted to leave quickly.

Sammy didn't protest either; still happy with what he'd seen no doubt and satisfied with his visit. Although the family he'd once been part of for so many years, now looked contented in their own little world. A life they'd already built for them-selves and a life Sammy was no longer part of - yet none the wiser they hoped.

So with everyone playing their little games, they said their goodbyes, pretending all was well in their worlds, which wasn't really fair on Sammy.

Pleased to be free again, free from the suffocating atmosphere in that house, they made their way back to the hospital, returning just in time for Sammy's dinner.

Laughing and joking about their mission accomplished, Sammy now seemed happy to be back in the confines of the hospital, safe on his ward again, away from that house they guessed. And the sisters hoped, he wouldn't ask to go there anymore.

The next day the sisters returned to the hospital keen to know how Sammy was doing after his visits of the previous day. After all these new developments had been a big step forward for him.

Sammy appeared fine when entering his ward but the reception they received from the nursing staff was more than a little starchy, informing them both in no uncertain terms that they mustn't take Sammy back to his home again, not without his wife's permission.'

'What do you mean?' Elaine exclaimed. 'His wife was more than happy to see us.'

'Not according to her. She's complained about you both. She said she was completely shocked to see you all stood on her doorstep and doesn't want you to ever do that again.'

'She's a bloody good actress then if she reckons she was shocked.' Jill said, still wearing her surprised look.

'Well, she does have a point,' the nurse said a tad too serious, 'especially if she'd come here to visit him and he wasn't in his bed … she might have thought the worse.'

'So, what does that mean, we can't take him out anymore?' Elaine was worried; she didn't want her brother to suffer because of this.

'No, not at all, but please don't take him back there. It will only cause trouble.'

Unbelievable, the sisters thought. This just wasn't fair.

'But she made out we were so welcome,' Jill grumbled to her sister later.

Elaine shrugged her shoulders, unsurprised by Melissa actions, and wondered if this may have been because Melissa's boyfriend was probably staying there. She couldn't have them just turning up whenever they fancied, could she - that would be too embarrassing. After all how many excuses could she come up with for her rock or cock always being around?

'I don't know why she didn't take Sammy home in the first place,' Jill grumbled, 'then we wouldn't have bothered ourselves and we wouldn't have had all this upset.'

'Oh well, Jill, we tried. What more could we do?'

The nurses were of course sympathetic, the sisters could tell, but it was more than their jobs were worth to be seen taking sides or even expressing an opinion, only this was considered unethical. But Elaine believed this ruling was stupid, particularly if something wasn't right. Still this was typical; our laws always appeared to protect the guilty.

Having spent a huge amount of time with Sammy though, the nurses had obviously grown fond of him and had clearly come to understand the situation, which must have made it difficult, knowing how little his wife really cared. Yet somehow, this didn't seem to make any difference to how social services and the powers that be appeared to view the situation. And the sisters wondered how that could be.

Chapter 23 - The confrontation

The sisters continued to take their brother out as often as they could, although they never dared to go near his house again. And each day he carried on improving, never failing to astound them with his unexpected reactions and clever remarks.

Sadly though, not one professional had come anywhere near to give them an update or a progress report. So it wasn't surprising that no one was ever told of Sammy's amazing achievements and no one appeared to care.

Except for the little book that was still sat at Sammy's beside which now contained random comments the likes that read - he brushed his teeth today- he took himself to the toilet. Simple daily tasks that he performed on a regular basis, nothing that would amaze the doctors and make them sit up and think - there was more to this patient than they realised. Not that the sisters thought they ever read the book.

Yet how could they write down in brief, the response to a history they'd shared together for so many years? To explain how his brain was responding cach and every day, when answering questions that only they knew the answers, was virtually impossible.

But this shouldn't have been down to them anyway; this should have been Melissa's journey, revealing a history they'd shared together for so many years … over twenty five in fact, well so she liked to tell them. Then maybe the doctors would sit up and listen, believing at last in his progress. Which was an insult in its self, as they were sure Melissa still didn't realise the book was even there.

Still helping their brother regardless - one crisp winter's afternoon when walking around the hospital grounds, arm in arm with Sammy, who was now wearing his newly acquired jacket that didn't suit him at all. Elaine noticed just how unsteady he was on his feet, particularly when walking outside. Thinking it was his balance; she tried to encourage Sammy by negotiating the stairs, believing it would help him and give him the practice and exercise he so desperately needed.

Keeping a keen eye on where he placed his feet, they walked up the stairs slowly together. When it dawned on Elaine, just how large the black trainers on his feet appeared to be. She hadn't noticed this before, given Melissa bought them for him some time ago.

Once back on the ward, Sammy slipped the trainers off with ease, while Elaine quickly checked the shoe size not trusting anything Melissa did anymore. Noticing the figure 12 embossed on the sole underneath, she thought this rather large for Sammy. But not knowing his shoe size she rang her sister later to check.

'To my knowledge, Sammy's only a size 8 - four sizes smaller.' Jill confirmed.

'You're joking, what's she trying to do to him? I mean … bloody hell, did she want him to have another accident? He could have easily fallen over.'

'Yes it's unbelievable.' Jill too sounded shocked.

'Surely she knows how unsteady he is on his feet. Or did she think this was funny? That woman's bloody mad, I tell you; I wonder what her excuse will be this time!'

Elaine had also heard recently, Melissa had been asking where the winter Jacket was kept, the one that was four sizes too big for Sammy. The sisters thought she was probably trying to retrieve it for her boyfriend, given it had turned icy cold these last few days and they found this amusing. However the nurses appeared concerned by her enquiry and thought she might accuse them of stealing again. So acting cautiously they advised the sisters to own up.

'No problem,' Elaine said. 'Just tell her I'm keeping it safe at home, so it doesn't get lost, after all, it's normally me that takes him out.'

Elaine found the situation funny; although the shoes were definitely not, because if Sammy had actually fallen, she could have caused him serious harm

Jill decided to phone her sister-in-law the following day to give her a piece of her mind but found herself speaking to Julie, her sister instead, who'd, answered the phone in her absence.

'I'm sorry Melissa's not home at the moment.'

Not put off, Jill explained to Julie the incident of the shoes and took the opportunity to vent her feelings regarding Melissa's obvious neglect.

Realising then she must be over her illness, Jill enquired after Julie's health.

'I'm fine,' she replied, curtly, 'but I haven't been ill?'

'Well, that's funny, because Melissa said you had meningitis.'

'No!' she said clearly alarmed.

'I'm sorry but that's what she told me.'

'I can assure you I' m fine. The thing is… I'm sorry to say, but my sister does have a tendency to lie.'

So her family all knew she was a liar and it was only now they were admitting to it.

'Well, could you pass on the message about the trainers and tell her we are not amused?' And Julie said she would.

Not a word was heard back from Melissa, but a new pair of white trainers magically appeared a couple of days later, with a very large figure 8 written on the inside of the sole, in bold black pen so everyone could see. She was obviously being funny but the sisters were not amused.

Still taking their brother out on regularly trips, even though it was icy on the roads now, the sisters promised faithfully, they still wouldn't go near his home. And funny enough Sammy never asked again. He appeared contented with his brief glimpse of his former life, a life he'd once shared with others, those who no longer cared it seemed. And they thought perhaps, he was glad he was no longer part of it, as who knew what he'd put up with in the past.

After yet another trip out to the garden centre, which Sammy still enjoyed, Elaine dropped him back on his ward and then went straight home. Five minutes after returning, Elaine received a call from Jill.

'I've just heard from Melissa.' Jill said, excited. 'She's actually taken him home at last.'

'Has she? When did that happen?' No one at the hospital had mentioned he'd already been out today. If she'd known, she might not have bothered herself.

'She rang me just now in fact. She's actually got Sammy with her this very minute.'

'Are you sure Jill? How do you know he's actually there?'

'She put him on the phone and he spoke to me.'

'Are you certain it was him ... because I've only just got home from the hospital after taking him back there. She must have walked in as I walked out for her to get him there so quickly. What did he say to you?'

'Well he was actually beside her when she rang me. They were in the garden looking at the fish pond, she said. Anyway, Sammy got so excited he pissed his pants, her words not mine, and she needed to go and change him.'

'Well, that's a lie for a start. He doesn't do that anymore.' Elaine was angry as she knew Melissa delighted in belittling him.

'Anyway,' Jill said eager to finish her story 'she asked if I wanted a quick word with Sammy and that's when she put him on the phone. He said, "Hello Jill, how are you?" but then Melissa took the phone back before I could answer.'

'It was definitely him speaking then?'

'It was his voice.'

'I'm sorry Jill, it's not that I don't believe you but I'm going to ring the hospital to see if he's there... I'll ring you straight back.'

Elaine was sure this was another of Melissa's tricks and dialled the hospital keen to find out.

'Hi, it's Elaine Bowers here. Can you tell me if Sammy Clayton is still on the ward please?'

'Yes, he's in his bed. He's been there since you brought him back this afternoon.' The nurse sounded confused by Elaine's enquiry.

'It's just that my sister seems to think Sammy's with his wife at the moment.'

'No... but she did call in this morning with her sister. They took him out for a little while... I think they just went outside in the grounds, only she wasn't gone long. But she's not been in since.'

'Thank you,' she replied.

Elaine rang her sister back to tell her the news, relieved he was in the hospital still, 'He was safely tucked up in his bed when I rang sis,' and she then explained what the nurse had told her. 'Maybe while she had him outside she managed to tape him on her phone and got him to say "hello", by simply pretending you were on the other end. Either that or she got the boyfriend to make out he was Sammy.'

'The cow! She must think I'm bloody stupid!'

'She thinks everybody's stupid Jill, except her ... I really don't know what to say. I'm just glad he's safe in the hospital and not out with her.'

'I give up sis. This is all so she didn't have to take him home after promising she would.'

'Well, she's come unstuck this time. She probably didn't realise how much time we spend with Sammy, and she obviously wasn't counting on me being with him this afternoon, that's for sure.'

'I don't like having the piss taken out of me Elaine. I think it's time for another visit!'

Jill, being true to her word, made arrangements to see Melissa on the pretext of picking up some more of Sammy's clothing. That's if they hadn't all been chucked out yet.

'She said, she had a smart pair of shoes for Sammy, so I thought we could go and collect them. And then we can have a proper word,' Jill suggested.

It seemed Jill was determined to sort this out, once and for all, 'no one makes a fool of me,' she said and Elaine knew she meant business. And although not keen on confrontations herself, she knew this was long overdue.

Marching into battle the sisters went together in full solidarity, ready to face the enemy so to speak. Jill pretended to be pleasant at first when she asked for the extra clothing, which threw Melissa for a while it seemed, as Elaine looked on, happy to remain in the background.

Requesting the smart shoes also, Melissa went off to fetch them and disappeared upstairs, her air of smug superiority infuriating them further. Elaine could tell Jill was determined to sort her out.

Melissa, returned with the shoes a few minutes later, unaware of the animosity the sisters were harbouring, although Jill did look visibly angry.

Unable to hold back any longer, Jill snatched the shoes from her hands. 'In future madam, don't bloody take the piss out of me!'

'What do you mean?' Melissa said, shocked.

215

'You know what I mean. You and your bloody boyfriend ringing me up trying to make out he was Sammy.' Jill spat out her words with venom.

'I don't know what you mean. What boyfriend?' she protested with the conviction she normally saved for other people.

'Don't bloody give me that. We know exactly what's been going on. Trying to make out Sammy was here!'

'I don't know what you're talking about.'

The tension in the room was mounting and Jill looked ready to strike. But Melissa, who'd clearly been caught unawares, looked nervous and seemed unable to handle this precarious situation. As the hatred the sister had for this woman, and with good reason, was fairly plain to see. Although according to Melissa she had done nothing wrong, her actions were clearly excusable and she was the innocent party as usual.

Frustrated, Jill placed the shoes in her bag with the clothing, pointing out that they'd cottoned on to her games.

'You've done very nicely out of our brother so far madam. It's about time you showed some appreciation.' Jill was so angry.

Melissa showed no signs of comprehension though. Not a look of remorse or reflection crossed her face, just the look of sheer contempt that seemed a permanent fixture these days.

Trapped like an animal in a cage, not sure where to go, her instincts only to survive, Melissa turned her attentions on Elaine who had kept quite up to now.

'As for you' she hissed, 'you wouldn't even be allowed in this house if Sammy were here.'

Elaine, who had managed to keep her cool up to now, had heard enough. If Melissa was as innocent as she professed, shouldn't she be appreciative of the support she'd given her husband, instead of insulting her like this? So far she'd kept her distance, but no more.

Melissa made her way hastily into the kitchen no doubt realising she'd pushed too far and Elaine followed quickly behind her. Caught in a corner, Elaine confronted her face to face and lifted up her fists to show she meant business.

'I beg your pardon...' Elaine growled. 'No, he wouldn't let me in the house, because you wouldn't bloody let him! You evil, controlling cow!'

Elaine had no intention of hitting Melissa but she certainly wanted to scare her and guessed she'd done that. She was surprised however, at just how elated she felt at showing this pathetic woman some of her own medicine and that alone felt good.

'Come on, Jill. Let's get out of this place before I do something I'll regret!' And keen to get away, they left in a hurry, without looking back.

'You know what, Jill? ..... I really enjoyed that. Can we go back and do it again?' and still laughing, they left the pathetic scene, shoes and clothes in hand.

That evening, walking her dogs, Elaine saw a shooting star. Smiling to herself, she thought of mum and dad, certain they were up there looking down, giving their approval of the earlier conflict. Sure they would be saying, 'Well done girl you should have done that sooner'.

Elaine was pleased they'd finally confronted Melissa and was surprised at just how satisfied she still felt. It had clearly been the right thing to do and she hoped this would be the end of all her dirty tricks.

Without any doubt though, Elaine knew Melissa would report this and she didn't disappoint. As on her very next visit to the hospital angry remarks were made by the staff regarding the conflict.

Melisa had phoned them and Sue, they said, and told them Elaine had threatened her and was too scared to go out unaccompanied now.

'But I'm not the one that's scary; she's the scary one!' Elaine said defending herself, although still promising to keep her distance. She didn't want to go anywhere near the woman anyway.

Sammy had been on the same ward now for nearly seven months and Christmas was approaching fast. Yet still nothing had been mentioned regarding his care going forward. Well, not with them anyway, they were still out of the loop as usual.

And even though it was obvious to most that their brother would benefit from rehabilitation, this still didn't appear on offer. Although they were sure Melissa hadn't helped with regards to this either, as it seemed every time Sammy went for further assessments she went with, making him nervous by ridiculing him as usual.

The sisters knew this was true for a fact, as they'd witnessed her in action themselves, always openly moaning in front of him as if he wasn't there - or wouldn't understand.

'Look, he doesn't even recognise me. He doesn't know my name … or who I am. He can't remember anything.

He's stupid.' Melissa was always belittling him - surely not the words of someone who cared? And they noticed at the mere mention of Melissa's name these days, Sammy would go quiet.

Knowing Sammy couldn't stay in hospital indefinitely though, the sisters worried about his future. Only Sammy not only had his wife to contend with, but the local health authorities too it seemed - now battling over his funding, they'd been told - each one expecting the other to pay.

It appeared the sisters were the only ones fighting Sammy's corner at the moment and they wondered if anyone else really cared about his fate. So Elaine decided, with a little encouragement from the nurses, that a formal complaint should be made.

Writing her letter as she saw things to be, she covered all relevant points and copied it onto the departments connected to her brother's case, hoping it would eventually reach the right person. She needed things to start moving now. Sammy was doing well but they needed professional help to carry this forward.

But little did she know what stirrings her letter would cause.

Chapter 24 - Help

Elaine waited eagerly for a response to her letter, hoping she may have at last alerted the right people to her brother's terrible predicament. Whilst also hoping to make them all aware of his wife's obvious insensitivity and appalling neglect. Pointing out - although Sammy was improving, this wasn't down to his wife in any shape or form.

Not having done anything like this before, Elaine spelt it out in layman's terms, after all she wasn't trying to win awards for writing; she just wanted to make sure those in control of Sammy's fate, knew exactly what was happening to a patient in their care. And she made it perfectly clear, sending Sammy home shouldn't be an option. Although she guessed that was probably unlikely as she was certain Melissa wouldn't be agreeable to that and kept her fingers crossed that was the case.

This situation with her brother had gone on far too long; it should have been sorted out and discussed by now. And along with the unusual and unhealthy relationship that still appeared to exist between mother and daughter, only more rumours had got back to the sisters regarding their strange and public displays. How could they not be worried?

It wasn't too long after Elaine's forwarded correspondence; a meeting was finally arranged between Sue and the sisters, wanting to discuss the letter and the problems raised.

Sat in her small office, Sue fiddled with her notes as the sisters waited her full attention, keen to get on with the meeting. Sue appeared down hearted though, which didn't surprise the sisters as Elaine's letter hadn't been exactly complimentary towards her. Only she'd accused her and social services of being neglectful in their handling of Sammy's case. And she may have also mentioned, Sue might have felt intimidated by Melissa in some way.

Elaine felt sorry for Sue though as she clearly felt her efforts hadn't been appreciated by them. Nevertheless, if she was doing all she could, as she claimed she was, it just wasn't good enough!

In fact the sisters had always thought, if it wasn't for their input, Sammy would not be receiving any stimulus at all, or any family care or affection come to that. Maybe if they were to stop helping; it would become apparent to everyone that Melissa was doing nothing. Surely then they'd be aware of his terrible situation and would finally make her accountable.

But how could they just stop helping their brother ... it wasn't possible. Yet in order for them to carry on supporting him, they needed to know if there were any professionals who actually cared, as it wasn't apparent to date. And sadly Sue was the only one they could turn to.

No, they needed to know now, what their future plans were for Sammy going forward, as nothing had been decided on, as far as they knew. Also they had to make sure these decision makers realised – Melissa hadn't the best interests of her husband at heart and they must be made aware of her lies.

Sue finally looked up from her notes ready to make a start, clearly scornful of the letter, even though she probably knew most of these facts were true. And this made Elaine wonder why she still had pity for Melissa. Had she convinced them all she was still the one suffering, milking it to the full as usual?

'It's been very difficult for me too, ladies', Sue confessed eventually. 'There are lines I cannot cross and rules I must follow. Of course I can see that Mrs Clayton has a problem, but you must appreciate she has had a shocking experience.'

Here we go again, Elaine thought. More excuses for Melissa. Let's all feel sorry for her; let's forget about poor Sammy. And the sisters looked at each other in shared disbelief.

'Well it certainly seems you're not interested in the tricks she's been pulling. Let alone the lack of help and care,' Elaine sounded weary. She already felt depleted and awaited Sue's reply curiously, yet there seemed none coming.

'Sue, can you tell us exactly what you've got planned for our brother?' Jill quickly interrupted, keeping the subject on Sammy.

Sue looked edgy, obviously uncomfortable with this meeting. Probably thinking - whatever she said sounded unfair to the sisters, who clearly considered her opinions to be biased.

Fiddling with her papers as if looking for answers, she finally looked up to face their stares. 'Well, we're hoping to find a suitable home where he can get the rehabilitation he needs, although I'm afraid that's not easy to find in this area. Also, we're still trying to sort out the funding. With all the cut backs, it's just taking time.'

Elaine was surprised and wondered how it was that in this time of spend, spend, spend, started up by Tony Blair's government, backed by Gordon Brown's no more boom and bust, that funding should even be an issue today. The country was doing well, they'd been told.

'Well, my brother has paid his taxes all his life' Elaine replied indignantly. 'He's entitled to be looked after!'

Sue kept quiet.

'Would they have to sell their house?' Jill enquired, 'Only I wonder how Melissa would deal with that ... if they needed to collect the money that is?'

'No it shouldn't come to that, not while Kelly's at school,' she said, almost with certainty. 'But in the meantime, we must carry on looking after Sammy as best we can and I'm very sorry ladies if you're frustrated by it all. It must be very difficult for the both of you.'

At last, a bit of recognition for the upsets they too had endured. And Elaine smiled a smile that said it all. 'It's a bit too late mate.'

'By the way ... what about the daughter? What do you intend to do about that matter?' Elaine asked.

Sue looked up from her notes again, the look on her face emphatic, as she stared directly at Elaine, 'You cannot save everyone, Mrs Bowers,' a statement she'd never forget.

Flabbergasted, Elaine looked at Jill in amazement. Is this how social services carry on? No wonder so many children fall through the net. Too much paper work, too much bureaucracy, too much PC; it's no wonder society is falling apart and cases like baby P go undetected.

Unbeknown to Sue, a friend of the sisters had already made a complaint to a certain care line regarding her concerns for Kelly. Only to be treated with contempt and thought of as a nosey neighbour, an interfering busybody, not as someone who might care. And her concerns were dismissed immediately. It really made the sisters wonder, what these so called services actually do. It seemed society and its systems had become very uncaring and jobs in the public sector were just jobs, more worried about their pay and pensions she suspected. It was obvious that the system was letting everyone down.

'So what about the shoes?' Elaine asked, not wanting to give up just yet.

'Mrs Clayton said she got them bigger so they were easier for him to get on and off.' Sue replied smugly.

'What, four sizes bigger!' Jill remarked.

'And what about our unexpected visit to the house? How dare she complain about that? It is his house, after all.' Elaine was incensed by the ban, thinking it unbelievable.

'She told me she was shocked when she saw him at the door. After all, she hadn't seen him out of the hospital in a long time.' But Sue didn't sound too convinced herself by this excuse and kept her eyes fixed on her notes.

'Yeah, I bet she was,' Jill replied.

'The thing is...,' Sue continued, 'she told me she wanted to organise the visit herself so she could surprise him by baking a cake.' Sue sounded almost defensive.

'Oh sod off' Elaine muttered, and laughing with annoyance as she looked at her sister to back her up. 'What rubbish!'

Sue stood up. They could see she wasn't impressed by her own replies and walked over to the open window, hot and bothered now. Sue had told the sisters earlier and in private that she'd recently put in an application for a transfer to another hospital. 'A change of area might do me good,' she'd said. The restrictions on what she could and could not do or say were bringing her down it seemed and the sisters could see as she looked out the window, she clearly wasn't happy. But like so many people with high mortgages, bills and financial commitments they find themselves tied to their jobs, too scared to leave. And Elaine thought how sad that was.

'So let's get this straight' Jill interrupted, 'she doesn't want us bringing Sammy to visit her, but she still won't visit him. Well, not for more than five minutes – so what exactly does she want … oh, yeah, her husband out of the way by the sounds of it,' and she sounded exasperated, particularly by Sue's lack of understanding, as was Elaine.

'Well, it takes time to get over something like this.' Sue replied, returning to her chair, trying to sound sympathetic now.

'So, why doesn't she have the bloody counselling then if she's still not right? It's been over six months for god's sake.' Elaine was peeved that this woman appeared more than a little biased still.

'We can't make her take it,' Sue said.

'Well, you seem to think we're lying,' Elaine replied. 'So perhaps you should offer it to us instead. You must think we need it. After all, we're in shock too; we were initially told our brother was dead!'

The sisters felt they were wasting their time, but they needed Sue to know exactly how they were feeling and what they knew had been happening to Sammy by his so called caring wife. Or should that be - not happening.

'We understand she maybe considering having Sammy at home,' Elaine said, fishing for information, having heard rumours.

But Sue remained non-committal.

'Well if she is saying this,' Elaine continued, neighbours have already told us, she has no intention of doing so and is only saying she will - thank goodness,' and Elaine looked worried at the thought.

'And apparently,' Jill added, 'Melissa's told her neighbours; she only comes to visit Sammy when she's pushed to do so. Nice and caring I must say.'

'Yeah, and when he does eventually go into a home, she's told them – "she has no intentions of visiting him there." I mean are these the words of someone who really cares?' Elaine was angry as she stressed her point.

'Well, I don't really know about that, Mrs Bowers. I mean that's all hearsay,' she mumbled, placing her papers away in the draw.

'And by the way, we still haven't heard from any one of Sammy's doctors. It would be nice if at some stage we could discuss his progress, only we mentioned this to you before and you said you would arrange it.'

'I have tried.'

Elaine was relentless. 'It seems at this moment, the doctor's are only hearing what Melissa wishes to tell them and what, would she know anyway.'

226

Sue looked at the sisters, a quizzical expression on her face, and they were sure she was thinking - why were they really here. Was it only to cause problems for their sister-in-law? She'd been through such a difficult time as well.

'I did try to organise a meeting with one particular doctor,' Sue replied, although reluctantly, 'but legally they're only required to talk to Mrs Clayton. I'm afraid; it's up to her to keep you informed.'

'You know that's ridiculous and it's not going to happen. After all it's not in her interest to do so… she likes the fact she's in control.' Elaine was exasperated.

Sue didn't reply and Elaine got the feeling there was more to this than she was letting on - were the doctors hiding something?

Jill too looked agitated, annoyed no doubt by Sue's replies always in defence of Melissa and was now clearly angry by the lack of support they'd been given. 'What about his clothes then? Have you actually asked her about them … or even seen the state of them?' Jill asked.

'Well, not really,' Sue admitted.

And the sisters had to wonder if Sue had actually made any contact with their brother at all, the person whose life she held in her hands.

'Well I suggest you do Sue,' Jill said, raising her voice. 'You'll see they're not fit for purpose! In fact they're disgusting!'

Sue looked embarrassed. 'I promise I'll have a word with her again. I know she said something about things going missing.'

Elaine hid a smile, wondering if she was referring to her boyfriend's jacket. She was still convinced it was his.

'Yes, we've heard her use that excuse before. But none of the things we've ever brought him have ever gone missing.' Jill sounded exhausted.

'I will definitely follow that up then.'

Jill was on a roll and obviously happy to continue her attack. 'Could you also ask her, while you're at it … why she doesn't talk to her husband when she does manage the occasional appearance? Only we've been told, she just sits there and stares at him… and if he's asleep she doesn't even bother to wake him.'

The sisters knew though, Sammy often closed his eyes pretending to be asleep if he didn't want to talk to anyone. But, this repeated action with Melissa, baffled them.

'Really?' Sue said sounding quite bored now, keen to wrap things up it seemed. 'Is there anything else you would like to discuss?'

'Yes there is actually.' Jill said determined to tell all, 'Did you know she wants to get Sammy a crash helmet because he keeps falling out of bed? Well that's what she's told her neighbours.'

'Yeah,' Elaine said taking over the story, 'and when he did fall out of bed one day, the nurses couldn't even get hold of her to report it. Apparently she'd changed her telephone number weeks before and hadn't even bothered to inform them and they had to call Jill instead… I find that incredible.'

But Sue just smiled her useless smile while the sisters shrugged their shoulders in response. After all what could they say to this woman to convince her Melissa was evil?

228

Still desperate to dish all the dirt though, especially while they had the chance - Elaine remembered the latest piece of news which had made her very angry.

'We've also recently found out Melissa had been given a list of volunteer workers, who were prepared to come in on a regular basis to talk to Sammy'.

Elaine heard about this from the nursing staff as they couldn't understand why it hadn't been implemented; as Sammy had missed out again.

'This would have helped greatly with his speech and memory recall. Only this sort of interaction with other people is just what he needs. In fact, Melissa should be helping him with this too and not just us!' Elaine was still annoyed.

Sue looked sheepish. She'd clearly been aware of this list but hadn't mentioned it to the sisters. And embarrassed no doubt, she admitted Melissa didn't even bother to get back to her. Consequently Sammy missed his opportunity... and the sisters wondered how many others there'd been?

'So what about the man in the photograph' Jill asked, knowing Elaine mentioned him in her letter. 'If he's a friend or a family member, as I guess she must be saying, why doesn't he come to visit?'

Sue didn't answer. What could she say?

With nothing more to be said, the sisters left Sue's office still none the wiser. Her answers had been uninformative and useless as usual and they were unhappy with what they'd achieved. But at least they had managed to air their views and who knows, Sue might start thinking of Sammy for a change, although they doubted that very much.

Yet if this meeting had only pointed out Melissa's mental instability; surely this could help their brother's cause, if only by raising alarms. Therefore, if no action is then taken to protect Sammy, or his daughter, come to that, even after their warnings, surely any wrong doings that might follow would be down to social services. And if their hands are tied as they say they are, is it not then the fault of their superiors, or the hospital's bureaucracy. Or even the government in control at the time?

Elaine thought long and hard on their dilemma, knowing the blame must stop somewhere. But having considered all they had discussed in this meeting; she still didn't know who would be responsible if things went terribly wrong, as no one seemed accountable.

'Sis, do you think it's us? Are we the ones in the wrong? I mean, are we so involved in our brother's problems that we can't see the wood for the trees?'

'Don't be silly Elaine…. although I must admit I am beginning to wonder myself.'

Disillusioned yet again by the lack of help available to them, the only route left open now was to go through the Guardianship Office as was suggested by Citizens Advice, months ago, which they had already implemented.

Ironically it was soon after; the sisters received some official looking paper work from the G.O office for them to fill in, although they were still not convinced this was the right route to take. But with no other option on offer, they filled in the forms as best they could. Stating their case and the reasons why they felt their brother's best interests were not being served - particularly by his wife, the person who had jurisdiction over him.

230

They also sent a copy of Elaine's letter of complaint which had previously been sent to Sue Webster and all concerned, hoping this would bring them up to date, while also making them aware of their brother's precarious situation at present. They also recommended that an independent panel of people should preside over any decision making required on Sammy's behalf. Perhaps, someone like his best friend Lawrence could take control as Elaine certainly didn't want that responsibility. After all she didn't want a certain person thinking she was after her brother's money.

Jill also went through the same procedure, confirming her sisters' statement, hoping to give her brother a stronger case.

Chapter 25 - Changes

Later that week, still down hearted about her brother's situation, Elaine noticed an article in one of the daily tabloids, which made her instantly think - perhaps they weren't as alone in their dilemma as they first thought. She had felt so isolated and distanced while trying to find a solution to Sammy's problems and this had given her some hope.

Elaine read the article out to her sister while commiserating over coffee the following day.

The article was called – SAVED BY THE POWER OF LOVE.

WHEN MATTHEW SUFFERED HORRIFIC BRAIN INJURIES IN A FALL, DOCTORS TOLD HIS PARENTS HE WOULD BE A VEGETABLE FOR LIFE. THEY REFUSED TO ACCEPT IT … AND THEIR DEVOTION BROUGHT TRULY INSPIRING RESULTS. :

The Doctor's words were cruel, I almost gasped out loud. 'Your son will be a cabbage for the rest of his life.' My husband Keith and I sat and stared at him. We couldn't believe what we were hearing…………..

EXTRACTED FROM A BOOK CALLED 'SHATTERED,' BY MAVIS MARSH.

The article went on to explain, that although Matthew had been written off by the doctors, his parents fought to get him the best care available. They devoted themselves to teaching him to eat and walk again. In spite of receiving no support or explanation from those in charge, they found out about other cases where great progress had been made. Acting on this information, had enabled Mathew to recover sufficiently to live at home and lead a relatively normal life. A family's support and devotion can work wonders.

'What do you think?' Elaine said, looking over the top of the paper at Jill. 'It's very similar to Sammy's situation, although Sammy does appear far better physically than this poor lad.'

'Yes, I see what you mean,' Jill pondered.

'I know we've done a lot already for Sammy but just think how much better he'd be if Melissa had played her part, especially as she has the power to push things along, being his next of kin that is. It's just isn't fair.'

Lost for words, Jill finally nodded, saddened no doubt at the difference between loving parents who cared and a wife who appeared to want rid - while clearly pretending otherwise.

'It just goes to show, Elaine, what you would do for someone if you truly loved them.'

'Yes I agree,' she said.

The following week Jill watched a television documentary on people who worked on the railways. To her amazement one of the staff interviewed was a man called Chris Tagget. She was sure, from the details given; he was the person who'd driven the train that knocked her poor brother from one end of the platform to the other.

"It was awful" he said, tears in his eyes. "I've not been able to drive a train since ... I will never get over this. I think people who do this sort of thing are selfish. They don't realise the effect it has on other people's lives. I doubt I'll ever drive a train again … I'll have to work in the office if I want to keep my job."

Jill was upset by the programme and immediately rang her sister.

'Well, don't you see Jill that means he jumped? After all, that's what he's implying. If it was an accident, he wouldn't expect him to think about the effect it had on others?'

'Yes I see your point.'

'Although I don't know why he thinks these people are selfish, they're obviously just desperate. People who fall to these lows are normally at their wits end and not thinking rationally. It's an irrational act after all,' Elaine was thoughtful. 'The last thing on their mind would be how their actions would affect others.' She wasn't happy. 'I mean if he wants to blame someone, blame the person who drove him to it!'

But of course she understood how the driver must have felt. She was only defending her brother who was obviously confused at the time, which was probably caused in the first place, by the person who pretended to care.

In the meantime, Sammy continued to improve, never ceasing to amaze them with his good humour and wit. His progress was amazing – although evident to everyone except his wife of course and perhaps even the professionals.

The sisters were very pleased with the nursing staff who they felt had done a brilliant job with Sammy. And he appeared to appreciate this too, only he seemed very close to some of them now - and clearly them to him. After all he'd been on the ward for a while and obviously felt comfortable with them.

In fact one afternoon, whilst lying in his bed, one of the nurses' told the sisters – Sammy had found himself listening to the radio playing in the cubicle next to his. Realising he was following a football match between Manchester United and Fulham, he became very excited. Not only that his team was winning but because he was able to follow the game. According to the nurse, 'this particular awareness had marked yet another significant step in Sammy's brilliant recovery.'

After this incident, when the sisters popped in, they often found him bantering with the other men on the war, still cheering on his team. Telling them, how Man U had slaughtered Fulham in that match, and this would normally end in hoots of mannish laughter. It seemed he had now become this sweet, kind, funny man that everyone appeared to love. How could anyone be unkind to him? If the operation had changed him, it had changed him into this lovely man, and who could complain about that.

Although, he wasn't always so sweet, for when the sisters dared to ask him too many questions, he often became agitated and once or twice had told them, in no uncertain terms, to 'sod off', which amused the sisters slightly. And they'd quickly point out, this wasn't a nice thing to say, to which Sammy would immediately apologise, upset he'd done wrong. It was like having to teach a child all over again. But he learnt very quickly.

Now that he appeared to be interested in so many other things – Sammy's world had opened up. So Elaine brought him in a small television in the hope of stimulating his mind further.

On one occasion, however, a visitor complained that his television was on too loud. Elaine of course apologised but Sammy having overheard the complaint, looked upset, obviously realising he'd caused some tension. Of course this wasn't a problem but it proved to Elaine just how aware her brother had become. But did anyone else even know this?

Yet sometimes, they'd still find Sammy starring out the window, mournful and preoccupied again - oblivious to who was there. And when the sisters asked 'what was wrong,' he'd often tell them - he felt as if his head was spinning, making him giddy and sick. He was clearly still not right.

But the sisters knew this might be a problem for rest of his life. After all he had been through major surgery but hoped for his sake when his body got stronger this would pass.

As Sammy continued to improve, over time he became extremely talkative but sadly with this came the pleading, persistently asking to be taken home to theirs. Although this time, he didn't just mean for a visit, he actually meant for good.

Upset by this constant request of his, the sisters would make their excuses and take him for a walk around the hospital grounds instead, even though it was cold outside. But sometimes Elaine relented and she'd take him back to hers, just for a short visit, hoping to placate him.

The first time she took him back, he was met by her two very excited cocker spaniels. Sammy was overjoyed at first but in their eagerness to meet and greet him; they wagged their tails so hard against his legs he soon complained it hurt and quickly became less interested, even though fond of dogs.

It seemed in Sammy's mind the main purpose of his visit was to lie down on his sisters' couch and go to sleep. And he managed this quite easily, ignoring the dogs in the process, even though they'd try to join him.

Sammy on another visit took himself upstairs to one of the bedrooms and promptly climbed onto the bed, which was all very amusing. However on another occasion, he actually got inside the bed and buried himself under the covers refusing to come out - the bed becoming his safe zone. He obviously wanted to remain at his sisters, probably feeling safer with her. But of course this caused a problem, as she couldn't get him out.

'Come on, Sam, you've got to get up. I've got to take you back to the hospital,' not happy by his defiance.

'No, I want to stay here. I want to live with you. …go on Elaine, let me stay,' he pleaded.

'But you can't Sammy. You've got to go back.' But he wouldn't budge and Elaine started to panic, still unable to move him.

'Come on Sammy, you must get up,' she said firmer this time. 'If you don't get up I won't be able to take you out again - they won't let me next time and you don't want that, do you?'

Sammy never said a word but buried deeper.

'Anyway, Sam, they'll have your tea ready shortly and it'll be waiting for you there.'

Sammy thought on this and eventually got out of the bed, which of course pleased Elaine, as it showed Sammy actually understood her reasoning. He'd clearly worked it out for himself. Yet, whether it was the thought of food or not, she really didn't know. But she did know, it was too difficult now to let him come back for a visit, and even more difficult trying to explain why he couldn't stay; only she didn't want him thinking he wasn't wanted.

Overall Sammy's improvements had been remarkable, considering his initial injuries. Yet the sisters were still convinced he could improve even more, if the opportunity was given. And for this reason they worried for his future. The main problem being, they were still up against Melissa and who knew what plans she had in store.

Around this time the sisters had heard rumours that Melissa was threatening to have Sammy home again. And they could only hope these rumours were just that. As they were sure, this wouldn't be good for Sammy.

However, a short while after hearing this, to their amazement, they discovered Sammy was going on another one day visit home - to see if Melissa could cope this time.

Sammy appeared very upset by the news when the sisters went to visit him, asking them constantly if they'd be there too. As it seemed he was worried she wouldn't know what to do with him. And they could only surmise he was frightened for some reason, not helped by the fact, Melissa hadn't even bothered to come into explain the visit. Or any other professional in charge come to that – it was as if they thought he was brain dead.

The visit home went well by all accounts and Sammy appeared to perk up, or perhaps he was just relieved to be back again, unharmed. The sisters were also relieved by their brother's happy return and they could only hope this had all been part of Melissa's game of playing the loving wife. As it was clear she needed to be seen doing the right things in front of certain people and was going along with procedures. And they kept their fingers crossed this was the case, only they believed going home would be the worst thing for their brother.

However, they knew if Melissa really wanted this to happen, it would. And it would then be out of their hands, which left them feeling very frustrated. Leaving them wondering yet again - who'd be held responsible if this all went terribly wrong.

As Sue would soon be leaving Reigate hospital, having received her transfer letter, a meeting was arranged to introduce the sisters to the new social worker taking over their brother's case.

Janet Armstrong was a young woman, with dark short curly hair. Her mannish style clothing and no nonsense approach made her appear much harder than Sue, her counterpart, although that wasn't hard to do. And if selected to intimidate the sisters in some way, this wasn't going to work.

Pleased with this change at first, the sisters soon discovered Janet appeared no better than Sue. Clearly of the same ilk and trained in the same way - don't cross any lines – and don't think for your self - the powers that be know best. And this made them realise they shouldn't count on her to get better help for their brother.

At first, Janet made the normal sort of promises, offering to assist and advice them but they soon became frustrated by the whole event, with nothing achieved as usual. And although she was more outspoken than Sue, underneath it all, it seemed she was no different - Janet just said it with a smirk on her face.

Genuine or not, the sisters felt they should point out exactly what Melissa had been up to over Sammy's time in hospital. Put her in the picture so to speak; make her aware of the tricks she'd been pulling, in case she didn't realise – as who knew if she'd fall for her lies.

But even if she wasn't taken in by Melissa, at the end of the day they were all dictated to by people above them. They had no real say. So what was the point? Although, Janet had confirmed - she'd follow up enquires into rehabilitation at Claygate, which was a really good rehab centre in their local area and this pleased the sisters greatly.

So left again with just a little bit of hope, they tried to stay positive, wondering if this new women could really help their brother.

Chapter 26 - Advice

With all the various upsets occurring over the last six months or so, it was inevitable they'd start to take their toile on the sisters, even though they'd been more than satisfied with their brother's progress. The fights with Melissa and the complicated web she spun had started to drain them both.

In fact the whole episode had begun to put a strain on the wider family in general, and especially on Elaine's marriage. Particularly as her husband Mark was facing his own difficulties at work and had clearly felt neglected. He told Elaine, she only appeared to be concerned about her brother. 'Too wrapped up in his problems,' he said. 'Her support seemed only available for Sammy,' which of course wasn't true but it probably, looked that way at the time.

On reflection, Elaine realised she should have stood behind her husband more but she'd always thought he was big enough to look after himself. He could fight his own battles, not like poor Sammy.

So in order to give them some quality time together and perhaps save their marriage they decided to take a short break away. So just before Christmas they took a cruise to the Canary Islands, stopping in Morocco and Madeira on route.

During the cruise Elaine and her husband made friends with a very charming and charismatic couple who sat at their dining table each evening. Elaine got on particularly well with the husband, Frank, who had recently injured his arm. He explained to Elaine how he was being treated by a craniologist and how it was helping to heal it, he didn't stop singing their praises. He, like Elaine, was very spiritual and was interested in holistic matters - believing in the spirit world and strange synchronicities - things like chance meetings, information being passed on at the right time, books falling into your lap just when you needed them (not literally of course) and mysterious and unusual coincidences. And they'd often sit and chat about these things, discussing the many books they'd read on this matter. But never once did either of them mention the problems they were facing at home, after all they were on holiday and they didn't need reminding.

During the trip, the two couples often went along together to watch the colourful shows preformed on board. One evening, Mary, Frank's wife, decided to confide in Elaine, while watching a lively version of the Blue bell girl's, parading before them on stage - their vibrant flamboyant costumes were amazing. When out of the blue, Mary leaned over and said, 'My mother's just recently moved into a care home and I'm very worried about her.'

'Why? Is she not being cared for properly?' she asked, wondering why she'd brought this up now, she could hardly hear her over the music.

'No, she actually gets good care… but it's my brother; I think he's trying to take control. Only he's getting her to do things that she really shouldn't … like signing important stuff, which I know she wouldn't do willingly. And sometimes she tells me she's afraid of him. I just don't know what to do for the best.'

'Oh dear, that's terrible.'

'The problem is, he arranged this care home and it's very close to his house but miles away from ours, making it difficult for me and Frank to travel there too often. This means, I don't get to see my mother enough to check she's alright.'

'Oh, that's a shame.' But Elaine understood all too clearly just how wicked families can be at times, especially when the whiff of money's in the air. And she thought how strange it was that Mary should tell her these problems, when considering her own.

'Yes it is and it's difficult to know what to do for the best,' Mary said.

'Well that's really weird, because I'm facing something similar myself at the moment,' Elaine said, deciding to share. 'Only it's my brother who needs protecting. He's in a hospital at the moment and his wife hasn't been treating him too kindly. We - my sister and I, don't know what to do for the best either. It's like we're hitting our heads against a brick wall all the time.'

Mary, who was clearly sympathetic, thought perhaps she could help her new dear friend and tried to advise her.

'I actually tape my mother's conversations when I go to visit her these days, just in case I should ever need proof of what's been going on. You should do the same. It may prove important … for you and your brother.'

Elaine thought about this seriously during the voyage and felt this would also prove just how well Sammy was communicating. Proving he wasn't the cabbage that

Melissa liked to make him out to be. Yes, this was a good idea. And she decided to purchase a small, discreet tape recorder as soon as she got back.

Elaine never saw the couple again after that trip and thought it rather strange that Mary had decided to confide in her the story of her mother, just when she too needed help... the wonders of synchronicities'.

Back from their holidays, Elaine couldn't wait to see her brother, keen to give him his Christmas present, which was a blue woolly hat and matching scarf that would keep him warm on their trips out together - only the weather man promised snow.

On that visit, Sammy appeared in good form. And she was told by the nursing staff he'd taken part in several Christmas festivities held on the ward that week and he'd enjoyed them immensely. Unfortunately, there were still rumours on the ward about Sammy going home, which didn't please Elaine or her brother it appeared, even though he'd been fine with his brief visit home a few weeks ago.

Wanting to spend some one to one time with Sammy, Elaine took him to a different cafeteria on the hospital grounds. Given it was a little further away she thought it would give him the exercise she knew he desperately needed and some time to talk out of earshot of others.

The whole time they spent together though, Sammy did nothing but complain, making it quite clear he wasn't happy about going home and so the pleading started up again – now wanting to go back to hers, which wasn't only upsetting but annoying. As not once did he say why he didn't want to go home - or anything derogatory about his wife.

Elaine wondered, if this could be the conditioning of so many years embedded in his sub conscious mind, unable to say how he truly felt. As over the last six months, Melissa had proved to her, exactly what she was like and yet Sammy would still defend her, using his non commenting strategy as usual if questioned.

But if by chance, he should pass an uncomplimentary remark in his wife's direction, he would quickly retract it, which made her wonder if he even noticed her lack of commitment to him. Although as time passed by, it was clearly evident he did.

So Elaine decided to have one more last attempt at trying to convince Janet Armstrong, his new social worker - that it wouldn't be a good idea to send him back to Melissa, and would explain, how he was constantly pleading to her, not to let them do so. But guessing Melissa may have told Janet the sisters were making things up, after all Sammy didn't even talk to her, so why would he talk to them, Elaine guessed it would be yet another a waste of time. But it was worth another try.

'He was actually pleading with me, Janet. He definitely doesn't want to go back home!' she said, sounding frustrated. But now aware of the disinterested look on Janet's face, Elaine knew for sure this conversation was going nowhere.

Janet starred over the top of her glasses, perched on the end of her nose, as she looked up from her paperwork, 'Well, he may be a little concerned about the unknown,' she said, 'which is only understandable. After all he's been on his ward a long time, cared for and protected. He's probably scared to leave.'

'But surely you wouldn't class his wife and home as the unknown?'

'Yes, that's true, but Mrs Clayton has expressed a need to show us that she loves him, she feels she has neglected him for some time now.'

Elaine was dumbfounded. 'Why doesn't she come to visit him then?'

'Well that's because she really doesn't like hospitals and she finds it difficult to see her husband in this state... she said she wanted to remember him as he was.'

'Yeah I've heard all that before and anyway who does like hospitals? And if she doesn't like to see him here like this, how will she cope with him at home?' Elaine was fed up with her excuses and wondered what Melissa was really up to now. 'Anyway, if you truly love someone, you forget all your dislikes.'

'Well, exactly. That's what she's trying to say... she does love him and wants to prove it to everyone. She told me, she hasn't been a proper wife to him these last seven months and wants to make it up to him now.'

'You're joking!'

'No ... that's why she wants him home ... she feels she's been pushed into a corner and has no option.' Janet dropped the bombshell with a smile on her face and Elaine was not amused.

'That's terrible!' she screeched. 'So that's why she's having him home ... nothing to do with helping him get better or it being in his best interest. Believe me, I would agree with this if she was a normal person, but we all know she's not.'

'He is her husband,' Janet reminded her.

'Well, I want to know who's going to be held responsible if this all goes wrong.'

But Janet shrugged her shoulders. 'There's nothing we can do. It's out of our hands really. If she wants to have him home, we can't stop her.'

'Great!'

'If it's any consolation ... Mrs Clayton did say his sisters could come to visit.'

'No thanks, I don't want any part of this.'

Not happy, Elaine slammed the office door behind her as she left - thanking her for her non help

That evening Elaine wrote yet another letter of complaint. She also rang Lawrence, requesting him to do the same – asking him to express his concerns regarding Melissa's mental state and instability.

'He needs proper care, proper rehabilitation Larry. They promised originally he would get that!'

'It certainly would be better if he did, I agree. ...' Lawrence sounded surprised by this unexpected outcome. 'And I must say, with regards to Sammy going home ... I was always under the impression Melissa didn't want him there.'

'Me to ... do you think she's decided to take him home so she mucks up his chances of rehab? I mean she doesn't really want him to get better, that's obvious - it wouldn't suit her plans. It's just ... he was pleading with me Larry; he definitely doesn't want to go back there to her! He sounded so scared.'

Lawrence remained silent and Elaine felt sure he thought she was making things up - only Sammy never spoke to Lawrence that much, so how was it he spoke to her?

Elaine tried hard to convince Lawrence this move home definitely wasn't going to be beneficial for Sammy and explained - as social services appeared to view them as trouble makers; they needed someone outside the family to express their concerns too. Melissa had made sure, all Sammy's friends had been kept away over the years, and he was their only hope.

Lawrence still seemed reluctant to get involved though, still sympathetic towards Melissa for some reason, even after all she'd done, and Elaine thought he should have known better. Nonetheless he promised Elaine, he'd send a letter of concern and said, if he was sent home, he'd keep a watchful eye.

Great! The whole time spent helping Sammy get better was soon to be destroyed. Elaine was exasperated.

The next day Elaine went off to buy the tape recorder as planned. This could be her last chance to record her brother and collect some evidence on his present mental state. If he was still pleading like he'd been the day before, it would surely be an interesting listen.

Elaine arranged to meet Jill on Sammy's ward that same afternoon. Her mother-in-law, who was visiting, joined them. And feeling like some kind of secret agent, Elaine hid the small recorder in her handbag, ready to complete her mission, while still trying to be bright and cheery for Sammy. Today was going to prove difficult for one and all but particularly for Sammy if he was in the same mood as the day before.

As it happened snow had fallen that morning and the day was crisp and bright. The trees and their branches, now covered in what appeared a sprinkling of white powder, resembled one of Elaine's Christmas cards still sat on her mantel piece at home.

Ironically, with Christmas just gone and a brand new year beginning, a feeling of merriment remained in the air. People were feeling positive and so was Elaine even with this present problem at hand, still sure they could solve it.

Pleased to see her brother, she slung her arms around him hoping to cheer him up. But Sammy looked none too happy and hardly acknowledged her presence - or her mother-in-law's. Jill hadn't arrived yet.

'What's a matter with him?' Elaine asked a passing nurse, as she nodded in Sammy's direction.

'He's been told he's going home for good tomorrow,' she whispered.

Elaine was stunned. She wasn't expecting this to happen quite so quickly, especially after what she'd told Janet yesterday. They should at least be looking into her queries.

Sammy turned slowly to face her and Elaine tried hard to hide her feelings. Although it was obvious to see how Sammy felt as it showed on his face.

'I don't feel very well, Elaine,' Sammy said. 'I feel sick and my head keeps spinning,' and he placed his hands up to his forehead as if trying to stop the whirling.

'Did you know Sammy's feeling sick?' Elaine called out to another nurse.

'Yes, he told us earlier,' and she whispered also, not wanting to upset him either she guessed, 'He was fine this morning, laughing and joking about the snow he was. After we told him he'd be going home tomorrow, his mood suddenly changed and he began to feel ill.'

'Say no more.' Elaine wasn't happy and worried for her brother, she tried to console him, almost forgetting to switch on the tape. Thank God she'd purchased it that morning; otherwise she may never have had the opportunity to talk with him like this again, and record it.

Jill walked in five minutes later having heard the news from the nurse on reception. Stunned too by the suddenness of their decision, she looked at Elaine and her mother-in-law, bewildered. 'Can you believe it?' she whispered, as she gave her brother a hug.

'I know it's not good,' she said, as she moved the recorder in her handbag closer to her brother. Sammy remained silent though worried by what might lie in store. They could see he wasn't able to relax but soon the pleading started.

The sisters tried to reassure him that all would be fine, hoping to calm him down, while the tape began recording. Proving just how coherent he was at the time and how adamant he was about not going home. But little did they know how upsetting this tape would be in the future, a sad reminder of how things were and could have been?

Chapter 27 - The Recording.

The following conversation was transcribed from the tape.

Elaine: What's the matter with you Sam?

Sam: I'm not very well, love.

Elaine: Do you think you have flu?

Sam: I want to come back with you love.

Mother-in-law: He wants you to look after him

Elaine: Do you want us to look after you Sam?

Sam: Yes, I don't feel well.

Elaine: But you're going home tomorrow Sam your wife will look after you there.

Sam; I want to come home with you tomorrow.

Elaine: What about Melissa though?

Sam: Melissa doesn't care. She doesn't know what I'm doing. I need to be with one of you two.

Elaine: But she wants you to go home to her tomorrow.

Sam: Take me back with you tomorrow. Make sure she knows what's going on. In the last hour I've come over so rough..

Elaine: The nurses are here to help you Sam if you don't feel well.

Sam: No, no, no I want you two and Caron.

Elaine: Caron? (She was surprised that he remembered his niece's name)

Sam: If you could have me just for a few days to get me right. I've suddenly come down the last few hours, come down rough.

Elaine: You've been told you're going home that's why?

Sam: Yeah that's right, because I'm going home.

Elaine: So you're not happy about it?

Sam: Well, I'd sooner go home to one of your places.

Jill: I suppose you've been here for such a long time it's a surprise for you.

Sam: No. I need one of your flats for a day or two just to get me right.

Elaine: But you'll be able to do that in your own house.

Sam: If that's necessary but I haven't arranged that. I'd rather be with you two.

(They move to another room Jill holds on to him because he is groggy.)

Sam: I've got to get out of this place, I don't feel right.

Elaine to Jill: He's changed, there's panic in his voice.

Sam: I really am rough. I want to be with you and Elaine.

Elaine; Won't Melissa be worried about you.

Sam: Well today would be a start. I could be in one of your homes, somewhere where I can sleep tonight.

Jill: Do you want to lie down Sam

Sam: Yeah. I've got to go to bed so I can sleep well.

Elaine: So you do that at your place.

Sam: Could one of you two help me out? Melissa doesn't know what it's about.

Elaine: So you don't want to go home?

Sam: No not yet.

(Sam gets into bed. Jill tucks him in)

252

Elaine: Are you ok?

Sam: I really do need you, honestly.

Elaine: You'd better tell the nurses that you're not well.

(Elaine tells the nurse again that Sam's not been well f or the last couple of hours)

Elaine: He feels terrible.

Sam: Just you and Elaine (he looks at Jill) get your heads together, give me a few days and I will be alright.

Elaine: Don't worry, Sam; it will be alright, honestly.

Sam: I really do need your help; really do need your help. Need your help badly.

(Sammy gets out of bed and starts to wander, gets confused and looks for his sisters)

Elaine: I'm here Sammy, I'm here.

Sam: I'll come back to your place Jill or Elaine's eh?

Elaine: Not today, love.

Jill: Tomorrow… You'll be going to your place in Howard Avenue.

Sam: No, that's empty.

Jill: No. Melissa's there.

Sam: That's right. It's got Melissa, but with you two today.

Jill: That's right, we're here... have you seen Melissa?

Sam: No. She doesn't know what I'm like.

Elaine: What do you mean? She comes to see you, Sam?

Sam: She doesn't know that I'm like this.

Elaine: She does know you're like this.

Sam: No, she doesn't. I'm sorry girls I'm like this. I feel so bad.

Elaine: Do you not want to go home?

Sam: No, I want to go to your places. I'm sorry about this.

Elaine: Are you worried?

Sam: I am

Jill: What are you worried about?

Sam: It's the way I feel, it's the way I feel.

Jill: Are you worried because you want to be with the people you're used to?

Sam: Yeah, I really don't know why I'm like this, but I really do need you two. I'm so bad, so bad, it's the way I feel, so groggy. I need your help, Elaine.

Elaine: Well, we're here for you, aren't we?

Sam: I don't know. I feel good with you two. Can I have your flats and that?

Elaine: My mother-in-law has a spare room Sam, but she lives in Suffolk. (she tried to make it light)

Sam: Too far, too far. Jill, Elaine, I really do need your help.

Jill: We know you do and you have our help.

Sam: I know it sounds bad, I feel bad, I need to get better.

Elaine: Why can't you do that in your own house?

Sam: I will do eventually but I need you two to help me out. I really do feel bad. I need your places so I can go to sleep. I really feel bad. I can't say a lot, perhaps somewhere to sleep tonight.

Elaine: Yeah ok Sam (Sammy lies down again)

Sam: Sorry I'm like this Elaine, sorry. sorry.

Elaine: Do you want a nice cup of tea, Sam?

Sam: No, I need to get out of this place; I need you two to help me.

Elaine: Have you seen Kelly?

Sam: No, I wouldn't mind seeing Kelly.

Elaine: So you would like to see her? Well you will tomorrow.

Sam: Good.

Elaine: See that's something to look forward to, isn't it?

Sam: I feel really bad, really bad.

Elaine: Alright love, you're in the right place if you don't feel good, aren't you?

Sam: Help me help me. I do feel rough. I really need to go.

Jill: Where would you like to go, Sam?

Sam: Somewhere, where I can have a sleep tonight.

Jill: But you have somewhere.

Sam: Somewhere else to sleep.

Elaine: What about Howard Avenue?

Sam: No I need to come with you tonight to look after me.

Elaine: Because you don't feel good? Don't you think Melissa can look after you?

Sam: She will do later on, but she doesn't know what I'm like at the moment.

Elaine: Why, she's not stupid is she?

Sam: She doesn't know I'm like this.

Elaine: But she sees you Sammy.

Sam: No ... she doesn't know I'm like I am, honestly. She doesn't know. I need you two badly, quite badly.

Jill: Why don't you tell Melissa?

Sam: No, don't tell Melissa anything. I'll stay with you. Tell her later. I need you for the next couple of weeks, please bring round some stuff I'm sorry I sound like this.

Jill: But you've had all these nurses to look after you for the last few months.

Sam: But I haven't spoken to them. I need you two badly. Sorry just a couple of weeks. Sorry, I sound like this but it's the way I feel.

Elaine: you may have a touch of flu. Have you got a headache?

Sam: I'm groggy.

Elaine: He needs to get out really.

Sam: I need you two to start with, to get me right. Take me home tonight, somewhere to sleep tonight. I'm sorry I sound like this.

Elaine: But you were okay this morning you were watching the snow.

Sam: But I didn't feel right.

Elaine: What, when you got your news?

Sam: I didn't get any news like that, (astute, Elaine thought) I really do need your help, honestly, the two of you.

Sam: I've got to rely on you two otherwise I am going to go right down the pan.

Elaine: You won't go down the pan, we'll make sure Sammy. You're worried, aren't you?

Sam: I am.

Elaine: But what are you worried about?

Sam: It's the way I feel all over.

Elaine: And you don't feel you're going to be looked after properly?

Sam: I can't help anyone else.

Elaine: No you need help, don't you?

Sam: I want you two, you help me out.

256

Jill: We don't expect you to help us. We're here to help you.

Sam: I'm sorry to be like this, girls. I don't feel right.

Jill: Do you want me to ask the nurses if they can give you a couple of tablets?

Sam: Take me home with you.

Elaine: I don't think you're well enough to move Sam. I think you should stay in bed.

Sam: No

Elaine: I think you should.

Jill: Where would you like us to take you that would be fun?

Sam: One of your places. Go on Elaine, one of your places .Somewhere to sleep tonight.

Elaine: They won't let you, Sammy. They won't allow you.

You know I can take you out for a visit but today's not a good day with all that snow. You'd fall.

Jill: When you go home tomorrow, Elaine and I will still come and visit you and take you out.

Sam: Today I want someone to take me out.

Jill: Maybe another day and where would you like to go?

Sam: I've got to lie down. One of your places if you don't mind.

(Sam tries to leave the ward and they place him back in his seat).

Elaine: Are you feeling better now?

Sam: I want to go back to your place.

(a man comes up to Sammy and asked him if he's going home tomorrow)

Sam: I hope not.

Elaine: Why did you say I hope not?

Sam: Well it's a load of rubbish. It's nothing to do with him; it's you two I want.

Mother-in-law: He was just being kind.

Sam: I need you two so badly for the next week or two.

Elaine: What are we going to do there?

Sam: Sleeping I want.

Elaine: You've not been eating properly have you? You've lost weight, why?

Sam: I'm not hungry am I?

Jill: Are you not doing enough exercise?

Sam: No not enough, not in the last couple of days I haven't.

Jill: You have got to start eating daily; you've got to build your strength up.

Sam: I want to come to your two flats please Elaine, if you don't mind. Or I come to yours Jill?

Elaine: You don't like my dogs do you?

Sam: Yeah they're alright, they move a lot and lick me.

Elaine: That's because they like you.

Jill: One of them slept on you when you were a sleep on the sofa. Do you remember?

Sam: They can come and see me at Jill's.

Elaine: (laughs) you want me to bring them to Jill's house?

Jill: Listen, do you mind if I come to Howard Avenue when you're there?

Sam: Eventually.

Jill: I would like to see your nice garden; you have such a lovely garden.

Sam: Eventually, eventually, I need your help so much, honestly.

Elaine: When you go home to Howard Avenue, if you're not happy there, you must tell your helpers that you don't want to stay and you want to see your sisters and we will come and get you.

Sam: Make sure I'm at yours and Jill's. Show me you're flat. I'll sleep there tonight. I know it's funny. It sounds strange.

Elaine: Has Melissa been up to see you, love? Have you seen her over Christmas?

Sam: No, not for a couple of weeks now.

Elaine: Ah. That's a shame. You'll see her tomorrow.

Sam: No, she don't know how to look after me though.

Elaine: Well, she's a sensible lady.

Sam: You two have a spare bed. Let's go tonight.

Elaine: It will be nice to see Kelly, won't it?

Sam: Eventually, yeah. get me out of this place and take it from there. Ok, Elaine?

Mother-in-law: You don't like it here then?

Sam: No, sorry, it's childish, there are no principles here.

Elaine: What, nothing to do?

Mother-in-law: Do you put your television on?

Sam: Not at the moment, no.

Elaine: Have you not been watching the football?

Sam: No, not lately.

Elaine: Why not?

Mother-in-law: We have.

Elaine: You have got to get an interest Sammy.

Sam: There's the snow. I need help badly.

Jill: You're going to get help. Just relax, don't worry (he wanders off again) Elaine: Sit down, Sammy.

Sam: I need help.

Elaine: What are we going to do in the summer, Sam? Let's think about the summer. Do you think you'll be doing your gardening?

Sam: Next year, hopefully.

Jill: Get out in the garden, with all your flowers around you, and all the roses, like you used too. And guess who you will be able to see?   You're tortoise, Fred.

Elaine: Have you seen Larry at all?

Sam: Not for a while. I need you two so badly.

Elaine: When you're in bed here lying down, what are you thinking about?

Sam: Nothing really, things are just not happening in here.

Jill: You just lie there?

Sam: I need you to help me out.

Jill: Alright Sam.

Elaine: Do we have to tell Melissa what to do?

Sam: Yeah, you tell her.

Elaine: So she needs to be told what to do?

Sam: Yeah.

Elaine: But she'll be given all the expert help.

Sam: But she hasn't got it.

Elaine: No, but she will be given it, professional help.

Sam: No, I want you two.

Jill: Sammy, you're not worried are you?

Sam: Yeah I am a little bit worried.

Jill: Why, give me your reasons?

Sam: She just doesn't know me now.

Elaine: Come on Sam, what's worrying you?

Sam: It's my balance.

Elaine: Is your head spinning?

Sam: Yeah. I do need your help. I know it sounds a bit urgent, but you can help me.

Jill: Do you fancy going upstairs and getting a cold drink?

Sam: Only if you two want to.

Jill: Let's all go and have a nice cup of tea. (They make their way to the coffee shop) Elaine switches off the tape until they get there and then mentions – it's nice to have a change of scenery which starts Sammy off again.

Sam: Yes a change of scenery. But I need you two urgently.

Jill: Do you need anybody else urgently?

Sam: Not like you two, I really don't. Melissa doesn't know me like you two do. I need you two so bad, urgently. I will end up in a mental home eventually, unless I get one of you two to help me get away from here.

Elaine: Why will you end up in a mental home?

Sam: Because I'll get worse.

Elaine: What, when Melissa looks after you? But she'll make you better.

Sam: She won't do things for me.

Elaine: Yes she will, as you'll be there tomorrow. You're going home tomorrow.

Sam: Are we? That's good, go back to your places eh?

Elaine: You've only got to sleep here tonight, and tomorrow you'll be going.

Sam: I don't want to stay here, tomorrow, tonight.

261

Elaine: Why not? All your friends are here?

Sam: But that's it, I don't want that, I want to see one of your places tonight and I may see Melissa tomorrow. But maybe she doesn't want to see me.

Elaine: She does. She's expecting you home tomorrow.

Sam: Is she? I don't know what I'm going to do at home, mind you.

Jill: It will be nice for you, Sammy.

Sam: I can rely on you two, honestly.

Elaine: You can rely on Melissa.

Sam: and then eventually, Melissa. I need just a couple of days of this, as she doesn't know me as well as you two.

Elaine: You're her husband.

Sam: She doesn't know me like you two, honestly.

Elaine: Like your sisters.

Jill: Your flesh and blood.

Sam: Yeah (he gets a little teary) I don't know what Melissa is doing for the next couple of days.

Jill: Alright darling.

Sam: Back to your places next. I know it sounds a bit drastic but.

Elaine: Well, soon you're going to have your dinner. Then after dinner time you can go to sleep and in the morning..(Sam butts in quickly)

Sam: I'm going round to one of your place, aren't I?

Elaine laughs, (he was still on the ball)

Back on the ward the conversation went on in a similar vein with Sammy still protesting about not wanting to go home, although there did seem eventually some kind of acceptance.

Chapter 28 - Send him home.

Elaine was pleased she'd been able to tape her brother before he was sent home, although for sure, upsetting to listen to in the future.

His concerns not missed, he'd expressed himself clearly and adequately under such circumstances and Elaine could only imagine once again, what he might have accomplished if given the rehabilitation he'd deserved. Especially if receiving the love and support most people would have from their next of kin at the start.

But with the conversation still going round and round in circles, the sisters took Sammy back to his bed. He was relentless and the pleading was driving them mad. 'Please let me come and stay at yours,' he kept on saying, and they found this terribly upsetting as what could they do? And as it was only they who were there to console him as usual, they felt this was very unfair.

Obviously distressed, neither his wife nor a doctor came anywhere near - if only to explain and put his mind at ease. It was disgraceful.

With nothing more that they could do, they kissed their brother goodbye and left him there, reluctantly, not sure if they'd see him again. And they wondered how he was going to cope the next day and more importantly the rest of his life. As what chance did he have of improving with Melissa in charge?

Before they made their way home, Elaine had considered speaking to Janet Armstrong again but thought - what was the point. She'd got nowhere with her the day before and she didn't really have anything more to tell her, except to say how distressed he was yet again. And she was certain the recording wouldn't make any difference, as the nursing staff had heard him pleading too, surely they would have reported it. So the sisters decided it was probably best to put their grievances in writing yet again. Their meetings had proved useless in the past, it was better to write them down, at least then it was official. But Elaine did hope this new move to send him home hadn't been triggered by her letters. Still he couldn't stay there forever.

Elaine left the ward with tears in her eyes, while Jill still wanted answers and so went in search of one the more senior nurses, who'd, spent a lot of time with Sammy during his stay there. Sat in her office, she too was clearly upset, and very worried by the way this news had affected him, she said, pointing out he still needed proper care.

'It's a shame he's going home,' the nurse said, her eyes full of tears, 'only I'm not too sure he'll get the care he needs at home.'

Jill nodded knowingly. 'I know you're not supposed to comment on your patients and their family situation,' Jill said quietly, 'but do you think he's really ready to go home now?'

'I know for certain he isn't. He's very distressed at the moment, but there's nothing we can do. She says she loves him and needs to prove it to everyone and that's why she wants him home.'

Jill shook her head. 'But that's ridiculous. She hasn't even been anywhere near him lately. If she loved him, she would have shown it by now, surely!' and Jill started to cry.

'Yes we all know that,' the nurse said passing her a tissue, 'but there's nothing we can do. He's so upset and so are we … especially seeing him like this. We're all very attached to him here.'

'Is there nothing you can do at all?' Jill pleaded.

'We're not supposed to get involved. Our hands are tied I'm afraid … it's such a shame.'

'It's criminal! It's like the bloody Dark Ages not the twenty first flipping century,' Jill was incensed. 'What on earth is happening in this country, it seems like everyone's too afraid to speak out about the wrongs these days?'

Now feeling she'd let her brother down, Jill walked away that day wondering once more, if she'd see him again. As even though Melissa had said the sisters could visit, she knew this would be a problem.

Later that evening, Elaine received an unexpected telephone call from Mrs Nolan, Sammy's next door neighbour.

'I thought I'd better ring you,' she said, sounding slightly flustered. 'Only I bumped into Melissa yesterday on the bus. She made a bee line for me in fact, which is very unusual as she normally tries to ignore me, making out she hasn't seen me.'

'Really.' Elaine said, she was tired of Melissa's games now.

'Anyway, she couldn't wait to tell me Sammy was coming home. She said she has a wheelchair and crash helmet waiting for him and it's all been sorted out.'

265

'Yes, that's right; he's going home for good tomorrow. There was nothing we could do to stop it.'

'Well that's interesting, I asked her if it was for good and she said, "oh no, heaven forbid, just for a few days." I then asked what will happen to him after and she said "he'll probably go into a home, but I won't be going to see him there as I have no intentions of visiting."'

'The cow … I can't believe it…' Elaine was angry. 'But there's nothing we can do Mrs Nolan. They just won't believe what we tell them. We can only hope it all works out in the end and he'll be okay there.' And Mrs Nolan agreed, although they both knew that was highly unlikely.

Elaine was grateful for her call, but she now felt there was even more to worry about, her news confirming this. There seemed to be no solution to their brother's problems, especially when Melissa was involved. And thinking later about the call, she realised- no wonder Melissa said she could come to visit Sammy, as she had no intention of keeping him there, more than a few days ... 'The scheming cow,' she groaned.

The next day Sammy went home as planned. Social services had already told the sisters there'd be carers calling in everyday to check on him. They'd be helping Melissa wash and dress him and assist in his daily care. However they only hoped this care would be adequate.

In the meantime the sisters had to switch off, after all what could they do? But they found this very difficult, even though their consciences were clear. They'd helped their brother as much as they could; this was out of their hands now.

As promised, Lawrence paid Sammy a visit the very next evening, worried that perhaps he should have written that letter of objection sooner. Although it had happened all too quickly, there hadn't been time.

Lawrence walked into the sitting room where Sammy was laid out on the large printed sofa beside the door. The room in total darkness, except for a lamp that shone a bright light directly onto Sammy's face, appeared most strange.

'Hello, Sammy,' Larry said quietly, still taken aback by the lamp. 'How are you?' he said, touching his shoulder gently.

Sammy remained silent though as he lay in this weird, eerie room. His mind lost elsewhere again it seemed.

'Oh, don't worry about him. He's been like that all day ... hasn't said a word.' Melissa said dismissively, as she stood behind Lawrence. He could feel her breathe on his neck.

'What's with the light? Is it really necessary? He doesn't look very happy about it.'

'Well it's very good for him actually! I've read, an orange light is very calming and helps with the healing process. I thought he might benefit from having it ... that's right isn't it Sammy?' she said turning towards her husband, the sarcasm in the tone of her voice not missed on Lawrence. But she clearly wasn't expecting an answer.

Lawrence said nothing, but his face said it all – he thought she was definitely mad. Now incensed by her uncaring attitude and the lack of any understanding, he pulled her to one side. He wanted to clear something up and out of ear shot of Sammy.

'I hear Jill and Elaine came to see you regarding this guy, Steve?' he whispered, now stood in the hallway together.

'Yes, that's right! They had a right go at me,' her face was a picture of innocence. 'In fact Elaine even threatened to hit me… I was frightened to go out on my own for weeks after that!'

'So, is it true? Is he your boyfriend?'

'What, you must be joking!' she said starting to look flustered. 'He's a married man of sixty! He can't even get it up.'

Lawrence was embarrassed, his face turning red and didn't dare to comment. After all what could he say to that? And he quickly made his way back to his friend, who lay quiet and unresponsive still.

Lawrence took stock, as there stood beside Sammy in the lounge, was a large black Minor bird in a silver coloured cage, twittering loudly in his ear. Sammy seemed oblivious to its presence though and Lawrence looked on disapprovingly.

'I brought him that bird especially.' Melissa explained who'd followed him in. 'I thought it might keep him company,' and she tried to sound caring, although the cruelty in her voice was still present.

Lawrence poked his finger into the cage, inquisitive about its purpose. But the bird let out an almighty squawk that made Lawrence jump - Sammy didn't bat an eye lid. 'Bloody bird,' Lawrence protested.

Unable to get through to Sammy, Lawrence soon became frustrated. He knew his friend could do so much better and was upset by his inability to communicate. He knew this wasn't right.

Taking the focus off Sammy, Lawrence asked where Kelly had been keeping herself these days. He hadn't seen her for a while, he said.

'Oh, she's upstairs doing her homework,' she casually replied.

And Lawrence guessed upstairs was most probably where they spent most of their time together, just as they did before Sammy's accident - leaving him all alone in this strange gloomy room, with a shining light and bloody bird for company.

'Well, Melissa, the bird's very nice but I think he could do with some visitors ... only I know Elaine and Jill would love to come and see him.'

'You must be joking,' she screeched. 'Under no circumstances will Elaine be allowed in this house!'

'Oh, I see,' he replied. But this was probably just as well as he knew Elaine wouldn't be happy with this set up.

Now eager to leave, Lawrence checked on his friend again but still not happy with the situation he promised he'd call back soon.

Lawrence rang Elaine later that evening to tell her about his visit. He told her - he didn't believe the situation was suitable for someone recovering from major surgery.

But Elaine wasn't sure she felt interested anymore. The battle to save their brother had proved fruitless so many times; she no longer had the energy to fight. And should anything happen to him it wouldn't be on her conscience.

As far as she was concerned it was the social workers responsibility now; let's see how they get on.

Still concerned though, after all how could she not be, she asked, 'So how was he then?'

Lawrence who was still clearly baffled by his visit, tried to explain the strange atmosphere he'd found his friend in. Stressing how unhappy he was with the set up.

'Well, there's nothing I can do Larry. He's got carers going into see him each day apparently, surely they'll keep an eye on him ... but mind you, with Melissa about that won't be easy for them,' and she laughed in frustration.

'I didn't even see Kelly,' he said. 'She was upstairs doing her homework, supposedly. Although I had this feeling someone else was in the house.'

'Perhaps it was a friend,' Elaine said sarcastically; which was completely missed on Lawrence.

'I've got to say, Elaine, I'm not happy about this at all; he shouldn't be in that environment.'

'I would suggest you write that letter then. Explain what you've seen ... and then they'll have someone else on record complaining about his wife, other than his sisters. Only we've told them countless times how badly Melissa treats him. It would be good if someone else did the same.'

Lawrence promised to write the letter and Elaine hoped he kept his word. But now it seemed she had other things to worry about. After all she didn't know what was happening to her brother back in that house.

'By the way, I asked her about that Steve bloke,' Larry continued.

'Really' Elaine's said all ears now.

'Yeah… she said something about he was a 60 year old man and he couldn't get it up.'

'What! How would she know that anyway?'

'I also mentioned about you visiting Sammy, but she said she wouldn't allow you in the house, I'm afraid.'

'Oh don't worry about it, Larry. I wouldn't step foot in that house if you paid me. Mind you that's not what she told the social workers… another lie!'

'I just hope Sammy's alright.' Lawrence said, still concerned.

'Well, according to the next door neighbour, she doesn't intend to keep him there very long anyway.'

'I must admit, I really don't know why she decided to have him at home in the first place, she told me only recently she didn't want that. Well not until he'd been in a home and was much better she said. So I don't know what's changed her mind.'

'Well, something's forced her hand. I wonder if she found out about us contacting the Guardianship office. Maybe Janet or Sue told her.'

'I don't know. She didn't say.'

'Anyway, I would appreciate it Larry if you would write that letter. You never know it may help.' But somehow she guessed it was too late.

The care workers did their job as promised, according to Janet, coming in every day to attend to Sammy's needs, making sure he was properly cared for. And by all accounts, each day Melissa busied herself, fussing around him in front of these carers, which the sisters assumed was part of her act. Concerned though, it seems the carers had mentioned in their reports, their doubts about her mind set.

But the sisters suspected this was probably ignored. Yet Janet did let slip in another follow up phone call that the carers were still worried. And yet Melissa was saying, 'he'd settled in well,' of course more lies.

On Sammy's fourth morning at home though; Elaine woke up to a phone call from Janet who sounded rather sheepish, 'I'm afraid Sammy's been returned to the hospital Mrs Bowers.'

'Why, what's happened?' Had he been drinking from the bleach bottle again? She certainly wouldn't put that past Melissa, offering it to him as a drink; after all, she would have wanted him gone by now.

'He's been sent back as 'High Aggressive' I'm so sorry. He attacked his wife on the stairs apparently and Mrs Clayton told us, "There's no way he can stay there now with Kelly in the house."' Sue paused, she was probably waiting for Elaine to explode but she didn't have the energy or inclination, all she could think of - was what more could they do to poor Sammy?

'What!' she replied? 'That's ridiculous! Sammy hasn't even got the strength … and anyway he's never been aggressive to me or anyone else come to that… Where is he now?

'We had to place him in the psychiatric unit here, as there's nowhere else for him to go. … I'm sorry.' Janet seemed upset, and actually sounded remorseful - but then so she should, the bloody useless bitch!

Angry with the casual handling of her brother's problems, Elaine rang her sister to tell her the news, but Jill already knew.

Keen to find out if there'd been any permanent damage inflicted on their brother, the sisters made arrangements to meet up that afternoon in the reception area of his new ward. Incidentally, the same ward their father had been sent to after being in Melissa's clutches all those years ago.

Chapter 29 – Psychiatric ward

Later that afternoon the sisters met up on the reception area of Sammy's new ward, which still looked vaguely familiar, anxious to see him again.

Pacing the floor like expectant parents, they fretted over their brother's sanity, having been sent back as a high aggressive patient. Was this really happening to Sammy again? His life had been one drama after another, and they guessed this wasn't too dissimilar to the films Melissa liked to watch.

The sisters felt exasperated, although remorse and guilt played their part as well. But could they really have done anymore to stop them sending him home? They doubted it very much, and they worried now how they might find him.

When suddenly pushing his way through the clear, stiff plastic doors, came Sammy, like a cowboy coming to town, albeit a wobbly one. Confused and disorientated at finding himself on a different ward no doubt, he appeared visibly worried. Until he recognised his sisters and a smile touched his face, beaming from ear to ear.

The sisters were instantly relieved. Sammy seemed unharmed and apparently oblivious to the dramas he'd caused, reminding them of the day when their father arrived at Jill's place after fleeing Melissa's clutches. What a shame Sammy hadn't done the same, as he didn't deserve this. After all it should have been Melissa on this ward - not him. She was the mad one!

Pleased with his lucky find; Sammy looked expectantly towards his now bemused sisters. 'It's good to see you girls,' he said in a shaky but excitable voice, as he eagerly linked arms. 'Come on … let's go home.'

And that's when the pleading started.

Pleased with how well their brother seemed, his pleading still upset them, consistently asking, to take him home to theirs. Only how did they explain this time that they couldn't do that? He clearly thought they'd come to fetch him and save him from this hell hole.

Obviously disappointed when he realised this wasn't to be, his face quickly changed and he now wore an expressio that seemed to say – 'what do I have to do to convince them I need to get out of this place - don't they realise what it's like here.'

Yet Sammy had no option but to accept his fate and no doubt exasperated and at his wits end the pleading carried on. And there was nothing the sisters could do or say to console him. He didn't have a clue where he was and of course it didn't help that all the nurses on this ward were unfamiliar. This must have been his worst nightmare.

'Please, please let me come home with you, Elaine? … Let me come and lay on your sofa ... please.'

'I'm sorry, but you can't Sammy,' Elaine said holding her brother's hand.

Sammy looked disheartened – fed up with it all.

'Come on, you mustn't worry; the hospital will look after you. They will make sure you're okay,' and with that,

Elaine laughed inwardly, as she thought – that was a joke in its self. But what else could she tell him?

'So what happened, Sammy? Why have they sent you back here?' Elaine wanted to know the truth ... well at least a version of it, assuming he had one.

But Sammy just shrugged his shoulders, wearing his bewildered look again, which he always put on when questions were asked involving his wife. Which made the sisters think he was still protecting her, but why? They could only assume it was because his mind still retained his love for her, in spite of her ill treatment. Or just maybe, nothing had actually happened, all fabricated in some way in order to suit her plans. As no one knew how devious Melissa could be, they were sure. And they were certain she'd been up to her tricks again.

Placing their arms around their brother, relieved to have him back again, they tried to reassure him, which appeared to cheer him up for a little while. And they wondered then, if they'd ever know the truth.

Pleased by Sammy's apparent good spirits, disregarding the disappointed looks. But the sisters were disgusted by the way he was now dressed. As his clothing was still a miss mash of garments all thrown together from his old cupboard box. Yet he appeared unaware of his tatty clothing, which was probably just as well, as the red chenille jumper he was wearing was almost threadbare - with sleeves shrunk up to his elbows. And teamed with badly stained jog pants and cheap plastic trainers, Sammy looked a mess.

These were the least of his worries though and although looking like a scare crow rather than someone's other half, he didn't seem to care, still excited at seeing his sisters.

Concerned for Sammy and life going forward, the sisters felt it was important that the nurses on this new ward were made aware of all his family problems. As they didn't want them hearing only Melissa's version of events. Only they guessed from past experience information regarding his previous misdemeanours wouldn't be passed on by his old ward. So not trusting the hospital system, they thought perhaps it was up to them to bring them up to date. If only so they realised he wasn't a complete mental case, as Melissa liked to portray him.

Ready to put things straight, the sisters asked to see one of the senior carers working there that day, keen to explain - that although Sammy may appear psychologically damaged; that damage, they felt had been caused by his wife.

A little later, sat in a small office cubical, just off from the main ward, the sisters soon found themselves facing, a middle aged, buxom lady, with a round jolly face. Encouraged to speak their minds, the sisters explained between them, keeping it brief, exactly what Sammy had been through since his accident - while trying not to sound too vengeful. Giving this woman what they felt was a clear and concise picture of what life had been like for their brother.

'Please, please, you mustn't worry about anything. I know all about your brother.' the woman replied, her warm friendly smile reassuring them both. 'I will make it my priority to take special care of Sammy. I know he's been through some difficult times but I can assure you he will get all the love and care we can provide here. I will personally make sure of that,' and she looked at the sisters, with what seemed genuine concern in her eyes, before she carried on. 'It's very important that we now make Sammy feel safe and secure again. If you have any problems, please do not hesitate to come and see me.'

The woman sounded very concerned, her sympathetic words comforting to the sisters and they felt much happier having spoken to her. They felt at last they now had someone who'd look out for Sammy and who understood his case.

But little did they know they would never see or hear from this woman again. More empty promises and clearly more lies - so much for looking out for Sammy.

After the meeting with this 'soon to be illusive carer', the sisters, not having yet received a full explanation of why Sammy had been returned to hospital, went in search of Janet, still annoyed with the whole scenario. They wanted to know, why their brother had been labelled 'aggressive'. As they felt sure the hospital were hiding things - only this gentle man, crumbled and weak, was supposed to have attacked his wife. How could that be? It seemed ridiculous.

When they finally found Janet in another office, she was extremely unhelpful and wouldn't tell them very much, although she did say, 'it was obviously unsuitable for Sammy to live at home now.' The sisters, however, got the feeling she was avoiding other things and seemed overly cautious towards them; after all it was her departments' decision to send him there in the first place. Although of course they would never admit to that after the sisters had warned them.

Knowing Jill was still incommunicado with Melissa - off the Christmas list so to speak, after their last encounter. Elaine decided to ring Melissa herself later that evening. She wanted to find out exactly what happened on the day of the attack. She wanted answers now.

Setting aside her indifferences, Elaine dialled her number feeling she owed it to Sammy. She needed to know the truth, once and for all. Well at least a version of it and how better than from the horses' mouth and she switched on the louder speaker in order to tape the call.

'Hello, Melissa it's me, Elaine,' she said, feeling fairly brave, although she didn't say who was calling, it seems she didn't need to. Melissa said she'd recognised her voice straight away and rather than putting the phone down as Elaine thought she might, she replied with caution, 'shaken but not stirred'.

'I've just been into see Sammy... what on earth happened for him to end up on that awful ward?' she said, trying hard not to sound blameful. After all she wanted answers.

But Melissa was still shocked that Elaine had even called it seemed and taken unawares she replied, 'I know he's a state, isn't he?'

Elaine was flabbergasted, wondering why she'd even say such a thing and answered in his defence, 'Well, he's not that bad Melissa, thank God.' knowing full well she was talking about his appearance and not his mental state, which was rich coming from her, considering she'd provided his dreadful clothing.

'Didn't social services tell you what happened then?' Melissa asked, suspiciously

'Well, bits and pieces ... but they didn't actually say what went on.'

So Melissa launched into a tirade of excuses, a story which she appeared keen to offload. But given Elaine's call was unexpected, it didn't seem too well rehearsed. And she went to great lengths to explain just how agitated Sammy had become with one of the carers who called in each day to help wash and dress him. According to Melissa he had taken a dislike to this one particular woman, who just happened to be of a similar build to her, with the same coloured hair.

After waffling on for some time about Sammy's daily care, Melissa then admitted she'd placed a bolt on his bedroom door, locking him in of a night. 'In case he left his room and fell down the stairs,' she said. But once realising he'd been locked in, Sammy turned aggressive, according to Melissa, smashing their wedding photo against the bedroom wall and breaking the glass. Melissa seemed to think this was symbolic in some way, raising her voice to express it.

Eventually, after releasing him from his imprisonment, she said, Sammy went on to attack her on the stairs, pinning her to the floor, apparently, and she raised her voice again.

Melissa then claimed Sammy had mistaken her for the red haired carer he disliked so much; only he couldn't possibly dislike her - could he?

But Elaine knew perfectly well Sammy wasn't strong enough to pull Melissa down and how on earth did she expect him to react after finding himself locked in? After all the sisters knew she didn't want him there and they also knew he didn't want to be there. But more importantly, they knew she had no intention of keeping him there more than a few days. In their opinion this was just another part of her warped and wicked plan and now poor Sammy was in a psychiatric unit with 'high aggression' stamped all over his file. It just wasn't fair.

Not happy with Melissa's story, Elaine had no option but to accept it, as after all she hadn't actually witnessed it herself. However, she did decide to pass this one by Janet the following day.

'She placed a bolt on his door you know? Now how did she think he would react to that?'

The boyish-looking figure, not having shown any interest up till now, placed her papers to one side and gave Elaine her full attention.

'Well, she told me, she only did it for his safety,' she said a bit too abruptly. 'She was only concerned he might get hurt by falling down the stairs.'

Yeah, I bet, and Elaine wanted to know who put the bolt on the door anyway and ....oh she just happened to have one lying around. Elaine wasn't happy.

In fact Elaine wanted to scream, 'Never once has Sammy been aggressive with me, or any of the nursing staff on his ward.' And Elaine started to wonder if Melissa had someone with her in the bedroom next to his. Now that would upset him. Enough to make him want to smash their

281

wedding picture, that is. That's of course if any of it actually happened and she mentioned these concerns to Janet.

Janet raised her eyes, as if to say 'who knows' and she certainly didn't look as if she cared anymore.

'You know Sammy is a lovely man and a good natured person. He wouldn't hurt a fly,'

Janet didn't answer.

'Well, no, YOU wouldn't know. You haven't even tried to get to know him. He is just a name to you… you can ask any of the nursing staff how gentle he is. I just hope this hasn't set him back, he was doing so well!'

Elaine soon realised she was getting nowhere with this seemingly detached woman and stormed out of the office, dissatisfied with the lack of understanding shown.

How on earth did these people get these jobs she thought, and when they did, was it just a case of keeping their heads down and looking the other way in order to keep them? Elaine couldn't comprehend.

That evening, Elaine played back the recording of her conversation with Melissa and listened again in disbelief to her ramblings. She'd even told Elaine, 'they the sisters had done too good a job with Sammy over the last seven months and the hospital was only too happy to let them do so, while they continued to do nothing.' And although it hurt Elaine to agree, there may have been an element of truth in what she said.

Still going along with Melissa's analysis, Elaine had confessed, she was taking a step back, which was actually the truth. It had all started to get too much for her lately and she was fed up of being slapped in the face for simply caring. The only problem was - who else was going to do it, as sadly no one other than her sister seemed to care and Jill's time was usually limited.

At the end of the recording, Melissa repeated several times, 'Well at least you called Elaine,' which really annoyed her. And she switched off the tape, angry by this woman's attitude and especially her lies. Who did she think she was?

Elaine, who was still going through some difficult marriage problems of her own, thought perhaps she'd been concentrating on her brother too much again. She now felt she and her sister had done all they could to help him; perhaps it was time to take that step back after all. They should let the professionals take over. But that didn't look forthcoming.

So how could they possibly leave Sammy in this terrible situation? They could only hope this new ward would help him as it did their father. But that seemed highly unlikely with Sammy and they wondered if anyone was prepared to take care of him properly, providing the care he desperately needed.

As even after approaching a well-known charity for help that specialised in brain damage, the sisters were quickly told, this wouldn't be possible. And this made them think, had they already been put off by Melissa in some way, who'd always exaggerate her husband's poor health in order to make him look helpless. Or was it simply a case of everyone letting him down?

A few days later, Elaine went back to the hospital to see if her brother had settled in on his new ward and found him much changed. Placed in a large clinical room that he shared with another patient, Sammy lay on top of his steel framed bed, his mind faraway again.

Full of drugs, depressed and unable to communicate, Elaine felt for her brother, who was probably thinking - he'd been abandoned in this awful place. And who could blame him for that.

Elaine went in search of explanations and was eventually told, Sammy had turned aggressive again and the staff had no option but to calm him down with sedatives; hence his present state. But Elaine wondered if this was just a case of making life easier by keeping him restrained in this way, as nothing would surprise her now.

However, the very next day Elaine was shocked when she found a foreign looking gentleman sat beside his bedroom door, patiently observing the scene. He told Elaine; he'd been placed there for Sammy's safety, in case he tried to harm himself, especially as he was considered 'high risk' now.

'He needs twenty four hour surveillance,' the man said. Elaine couldn't comprehend. What had happened to her brother and in just a few days? What else could they do to him?

Confirming this place wasn't right for him either; she wondered where on earth he could go now. By rights he should be in rehabilitation but as that wasn't on offer, what were his options.

Jill had also visited Sammy earlier that day and she too had found him in much the same state. She told her sister later, that whilst she was there, the staff had told her; Sammy went missing again but had found him later, wandering around the hospital grounds. One other carer also said, Sammy had made his way back to his old ward, where Elaine guessed, he once felt loved and protected. But when finding his old nurse friends, whose face's he clearly recognised, in his eagerness to interact, he apparently became a nuisance. And when trying to get back to his new ward, he found himself lost.

The next day the very same thing happened again they said. But this time they found him asleep in one of the outside cafeterias, with his head resting on the table. They now had no option but to sedate him, to stop him from wandering again and hence why the guard at his door.

Yet it appeared many of the other patients were given a similar treatment, all doped up by the looks of things - but Sammy was the only one with a guard stood by. They said this was also because of his aggression but Elaine wondered if Sammy didn't like to be restrained in this way and probably only tried to resist them.

Which also made her wonder, if this restraining had more to do with Sammy leaving the hospital grounds rather than getting lost. As should he then cause an accident, this would leave the hospital liable, given he was in their care.

The sisters were not happy with their brother's situation but what could they do? They could only hope they could get him out quick.

A week or so later, the sisters were asked to attend a meeting with Sammy's new doctor, much to their surprise. But as they felt they were viewed as interfering busybodies, Elaine decided to ask Jackie, Lawrence's wife, to come along as an independent witness - given Lawrence worked full time.

Melissa was not present at this meeting however, which surprised the sisters. It was just the three ladies, the new lady doctor and her lady assistant.

The doctor, an attractive woman in her mid-thirties, told the now expectant woman sat in front her that she was concerned for Sammy and his present situation and was curious to know the start of his problems. Although she pointed out initially, just how well Sammy had progressed, considering his terrible injuries. She too, like the sisters felt he could achieve a lot more if put on the correct care plan.

At last ... hooray! Elaine thought someone who really cared, someone who understood his situation - a professional who looked further than their nose. In fact, she was the first doctor who had even bothered to speak to them.

'Do you actually believe it was an accident?' the doctor asked, throwing the question out to whoever wanted to answer.

Elaine stepped in immediately, 'Well, no, we don't,' confirming the doctor's thoughts it seemed, going by the expression on her face. 'We feel it may have been an attempted suicide, possibly coerced.'

'Who by ... his wife?'

'Well, yes, only she doesn't really care about him. She just makes the right noises to the right people. And she rarely goes to visit him, and actions speak louder than words, don't they!'

'I see,' she said, and the doctor made some notes.

'They were also going through some difficult marriage problems just before the accident,' Jackie interjected, adding to Elaine's statement.

'And he'd also been suffering on and off from high anxiety.' Jill chipped in. 'We were all very concerned, but we thought he was getting better.'

The ladies then explained in full, Sammy's strange story, telling her how he was taken onto the Tube and how what happened before hand, got suspiciously changed.

Surely everyone knew all this though; especially about Sammy's depression, although if Melissa chose not to part with this information, perhaps they didn't? Although knowing Melissa, she would have used that to her advantage.

After further discussions, the doctor finally admitted she didn't think this was the right place for their brother - he needed proper rehabilitation and she promised she'd look into this. 'A report would be typed up immediately on her findings,' she said.

The ladies were elated by this news and thought this could be a turning point for Sammy. This was more reminiscent to the type of care he received at Whitechapel hospital. And they left, feeling far more confident.

But little did they know they would never see that doctor or her assistant again and at a follow up meeting, Janet Armstrong said, 'She had left the hospital unexpectedly and for good.'

'How come... Elaine said, confused by her sudden disappearance, 'She said she would help us with Sammy's case and was typing up a report?'

'Well, she never handed in any report to us,' Janet said, smugly.

'But she agreed with us. She said, she didn't think it was an accident. Surely you can see that?'

'Well, we do have our doubts about what might have happened. But our hands are tied I'm afraid.'

There she'd admitted it at last, which made Elaine think - there was definitely some kind of cover up going on or something that they didn't want her to get involved in. This just didn't seem right and it certainly felt like another slap in the face for them, and especially for poor Sammy.

It had been nearly three weeks since their brother found himself on this dreadful ward but he was now allowed to leave his room as and when he pleased - no longer at risk, and a guard no longer required it seemed.

However, Sammy still looked heavily drugged and appeared more like a zombie than ever, and not dissimilar to some of the other patients. Poor Sammy didn't seem to know if he was coming or going and was clearly very depressed and extremely low.

This must have felt like his worst nightmare had come true. Especially after telling his sisters, not that long ago, during his recording - if sent back to his wife, he'd end up in a place like this. And oh boy was he right.

A month or so later, on one of her rushed visits, Elaine was horrified when she'd found her brother lying naked on top of his bed, having used it as a toilet, not able or wanting to move it seemed. She was told by another patient that no one had been near him all day. But this wasn't a care home after all. He shouldn't really be there.

In fact Elaine would often turn up to find she needed to clean her brother up in some way. His fingers normally covered in excrement. And sometimes she even had to clean the carpet around his bed, already stained from similar mishaps.

What on earth was going on she thought? What else could they do to him? The tablets were clearly not helping and each day she'd watch him deteriorate further.

All the work the sisters had put in, in trying to help him get better was now in jeopardy. They were not happy. Especially as Sammy was now back in incontinence pads. Although they assumed, this was to make it easier for the staff by not having to take him to the toilet. Consequently he'd now become doubly incontinent again.

So even though Elaine had vowed to take a step back, she realised she couldn't give up on Sammy and felt there was only one more option left open to them.

'I'm going to see if I can get an appointment to see the local MP in his Reigate surgery next week.' she said to Jill, over coffee. 'I'm not sure if he will be able to help, but I don't know what else we can do sis. Would you mind coming with me?'

Jill looked exhausted by Sammy's problems and who could really blame her, after all, it was one thing after another. And the family it seemed were unhappy with the strain it was putting on her. Plus the knock on affect on them no doubt. But Elaine hoped she'd continue to give her support, as she couldn't do this on her own and this could be their very last chance to help their brother.

'Of course I'll come,' she said. 'I'm disgusted with the way they've treated him. What's happened to Sammy is criminal, and as for the social workers, who are supposedly there to help us as well … they're clearly all a useless bunch of what's it's. They tell us what we want to hear and then do nothing about it!' And she wagged her finger vigorously, stressing her point. 'I think it's a good idea sis…. what have we got to lose.'

Chapter 30 - The Surgery.

Later that week, Elaine booked an appointment with their local MP to discuss Sammy's problems – while vowing not to get into any of the sinister goings on with regards to Melissa. Although she'd still make it perfectly clear, she wasn't helping with their brother's situation.

On the morning of the sisters meeting with Chris Gresham, MP Jill received an unexpected phone call.

'Hello, Mrs Jones. It's Janet here. I'm just ringing to let you know, Mrs Clayton was sent a list of nursing homes to look at for Sammy... she's had them sometime but as yet, we've not heard back from her.'

'How come you haven't told us this before?' Jill asked.

'Well it's up to Mrs Clayton to tell you really, but I thought perhaps you should know, put you in the picture so to speak ... I take it she's still checking them out. Perhaps you could chase her up, only we haven't been able to get hold of her.'

Jill switched off her mobile, nonplussed. 'Why ring today to tell us?' Jill said to Elaine, who was sitting next to her listening.

'Yes it's a bit of a coincidence I must say ... just before we're about to see our MP as well – it's strange she suddenly thinks to tell us things might be moving again; very convenient,' she surmised.

'No, this doesn't add up at all,' Jill said. 'They know they're in the wrong. They should have told us about this list before. And how long has she had it anyway. They're covering their useless backsides again I'm sure.'

'Yes, they must have known about our appointment today ... hence the phone call,' Elaine said.

'Do you think we should still go then?'

'Well, I am. It's pretty obvious Melissa's still holding things up.'

Sitting down later in the reception area of Mr Gresham's barren, makeshift office, the sisters waited nervously to air their views. They had never done anything like this before and felt unsettled.

It wasn't long before they were led into another room though and soon found themselves sat round a smart but well used office table, in the middle of yet another dull and dingy room, which appeared part of an old church building. The room, devoid of luxuries, no carpets or drapes, its function just to provide this service, smelt stuffy and stale.

Chris Gresham, who sat opposite, looked at the sisters attentively now, while they reminded themselves they had to tread carefully where Melissa was concerned - as who knew what she had planned for Sammy. And they needed this man's help urgently.

Mr Gresham, a tall, stately looking gentleman, looked at the ladies with a wise understanding in his steely grey eyes. Having studied their brother's case before hand no doubt, he appeared sympathetic.

Once formal introductions were over, Elaine then explained, slowly and carefully - Sammy's sad predicament, while making sure she didn't include any of Melissa's antics. After all she didn't want to sound vindictive. Especially when expressing her concerns and frustrations at her slow response when sorting out her husband's care. And explained they were particularly worried as he was declining rapidly on this present ward, which was driving them both to despair.

The sisters also decided to tell him, Sammy's wife could be finding it difficult dealing with her husband's problems. Suggesting, this was why she hadn't pushed for the right kind of help, perhaps not fully understanding her husband's needs or capabilities. Maybe too upset, she didn't realise what was best for him, as she saw no future for him anyway.

The sisters hoped this softer approach would convince Mr Gresham; they wanted nothing more than to help their brother. They needed assurances, that Sammy would get all the help he needed with the opportunity to improve, as their brother deserved that.

Chris Gresham sat back in his black Leather chair, pondering on their predicament. They guessed he'd experienced similar situations before and would be aware of most the procedures, but without Melissa's backing this was clearly a difficult case.

After delving deeper into their problems, it soon became apparent, Mr Gresham knew far more than he was actually letting on. It was clear to them he had made it his business to find out and hence the earlier call from Janet. So the sisters expressed again their concerns, fearful for their brother and his rapid decline. He needed to be moved and fast they said. While also pointing out, how important it was that Sammy should be recommended for rehabilitation, only it seemed there'd been no effort made in this direction. And told Mr Gresham, Sammy was capable of a lot more than the doctors or his wife even realised.

'Given Sammy's been knocked backwards, he has a lot of catching up to do and this needs to be sorted out quickly … before he slips any further.' Elaine said, and immediately felt better sharing her concerns, turning to Jill who backed her.

'I can see your problem, Mrs Bowers,' he said, in his well-polished voice, 'and I understand where you're coming from… but this is a difficult situation, although I do sympathise with you both,' and he looked towards the window, distant now.

There had never been a kind or friendly word spoken to either of the sisters before, and especially not from any of the professionals involved and this was refreshing to hear. In fact they had never actually had the opportunity to even talk to a professional, even though social services had promised them. No … there had been only one doctor who'd expressed her concerns and she had mysteriously disappeared.

Mr Gresham though clearly understood how anxious the sisters were and continued to reassure them, 'I suppose I could put in a good word for your brother in certain quarters,' he said softly. 'And possibly for rehabilitation at Claygate - but I can't promise you anything I'm afraid, only … if this isn't his wife wishes; there's nothing you or I can do.'

'But why wouldn't she want this?' Elaine said. 'She should want the best for her husband?'

'True Mrs Bowers, but unfortunately, what she says goes, she is his next of kin and that's the law.'

The sisters looked despondent. 'Surely this can't be right … the law's an ass then,' Elaine insisted, and Mr Gresham just smiled.

'Don't worry, ladies,' he said, obviously aware of their troubled expressions. 'I will do all I can to help your brother. Even though, it should really be his wife in this office discussing these problems with me.'

'Which speaks volumes,' Elaine insisted.

'So let's get this straight,' Jill said, butting in now, her brow wrinkled in confusion, 'no one is able to protect him from his wife because the law is on her side and there's nothing anyone can do?' Jill couldn't comprehend. 'It all seems so stupid,' she muttered.

Mr Gresham didn't respond but advised them both that the best solution maybe to go through the Guardianship Office to seek out power of attorney. Or even court protection for their brother, especially as they felt Mrs Clayton didn't have her husband's best interests at heart. But Elaine advised him, an application had already been submitted to which they were waiting a reply.

Depleted by the options left open, although pleased enough by Mr Gresham's positive words, although he clearly didn't want to raise their hopes, they kept their fingers crossed that help would soon come. As Mr Gresham had promised he'd make some further enquiries at the hospital regarding their brother's position. And the sisters thought it wouldn't hurt for social services to know that Sammy's case was being discussed elsewhere.

Later that afternoon, the sisters decided to pay Melissa another visit to see how she was coping with this latest list of homes. The list they hadn't even been told about until earlier that day.

Wanting answers, Jill knocked firmly on Melissa's front door. She was clearly not amused by the situation and she now meant business. But Melissa looked flustered by their presence and kept them on the doorstep, her arm across the doorway, blocking their way. And this made them wonder, if the boyfriend was there today.

'We understand you've been given a list of recommended homes for Sammy,' Jill said in a no nonsense manner and a matter of fact tone.

'Yes, that's right,' she replied, a look on her face that said, what business is it of yours.

'Can you tell us what's happening then? Only Sammy needs to get off that dreadful ward and quickly,' Jill said irate.

But Melissa looked agitated and replied begrudgingly, 'Please don't worry your-self Jill … I have it all in hand. In fact I'm sorting it out now...you've been very good, but I'm handling this myself.'

'But don't you realise how urgent this is? Elaine interjected, annoyed by her attitude too. Although she guessed she probably had no idea how urgent it was and did she really care, as Elaine understood she hadn't even been into see him on this new ward. And she doubted she had any intentions of doing so?

'Yes, that's all very well, but I haven't found anything suitable yet.'

'What would she know about suitability? She thinks he's a useless case anyway,' Elaine mumbled, under her breathe.

Not happy with Melissa's attitude and having heard enough of her pathetic excuses the sisters left in a rage, concerned more than ever with their brother being left in her clutches. She'd had no intentions of discussing the homes with them and there was no point in hanging around. She was in control as usual and it was all down to her. The sad thing was they could have helped her with the viewings, given she didn't drive. Still they suspected the boyfriend was doing this, or not, as the case maybe.

A few days later, Elaine received a letter from Mr Gresham, which read:

Dear Mrs Bowers,

Thank you for attending my surgery at the constituency office on Friday 14th February 1999.

I am sorry to hear about your brother's poor state of health and the difficult family circumstances you face. I have had an informal word with contacts in the local NHS, and it does appear that we will be constrained in what we can do by the fact that next of kin consent is needed before I can make representations. I am trying to get further information for you, but I fear that the legal route may be the only one open to you.

I will be back in touch with you shortly.

Best wishes

'But why should we have to go to court?' Elaine said to her sister when they next met, incensed by the letter. 'I'm not fighting for Sammy only because he's our brother. I'm just seeking justice for a fellow human being who's found himself in a terrible situation, thanks to the laws of this land it seems. Surely it should be social services fighting this, not us, given it's obvious to everyone what's been going on.' And she looked at Jill flabbergasted.

Jill nodded in agreement, acknowledging her words and Elaine carried on.

'I mean ... maybe this is why they've been keeping so quiet and ignoring Melissa's antics. They probably don't want the costs or the aggravations of a court battle themselves.'

'Or maybe they're covering something up?' Jill added.

But either way, Elaine wasn't happy. 'No, no, Jill, I will take this no further, I'm not prepared to go to court. I've got enough problems of my own and I haven't the money... I mean why don't you? You might even get legal aid as I'm sure Melissa will?'

Jill didn't answer, she too didn't want that problem it seemed and who could blame her. And Elaine wondered – was this how so many cases slip through net, left unchallenged because our legal system was so complex and up the preverbal wall, and it always came down to money in the end. Solicitors making their pots of gold out of other people's sad and desperate situations; our laws were a mess. Particularly as it now appears only the rich can afford to defend themselves or attack, as the case maybe.

The following few weeks were probably the worst for Sammy, only on two separate occasions, each sister had found their brother curled up stark naked at one end of a tatty settee, placed in the middle of the visitor's lounge. His feet dangling over the side, he laid there exposed to one and all. Oblivious and vulnerable and no doubt unaware of his bizarre actions, no one even bothered to cover him up. This place was unbelievable, and this made the sisters wonder how many times this had happened before. Only no one was reporting back to them and they doubted they were even reporting back to his wife, realising she didn't care.

Not only was this just unbelievably shocking, it was also sad to have their brother humiliated this way and with no one giving a damn. Especially when, all the sisters could do, was to badger Janet, his social worker further, to make her do something about it. To which a meeting would quickly be arranged, on the pretext of sorting things out and then cancelled at the last minute. While still promising he'd be accepted at Claygate and withdrawn at a later stage. The sisters' realised games were being played in order to placate them, and they found this upsetting. Although more upsetting for Sammy as they watched him each day deteriorate.

The sisters were eventually told, there were still arguments going on between the two different health authorities, over their brothers funding. It appeared neither body felt, they should be paying and this was causing the problem, delaying any hope of Sammy getting better or out of that place it seemed. They were at their wit's end.

Chapter 31 – Get him out

Still troubled about their brother's situation and his sanity, the sisters knew they needed to get him moved from this current ward and fast, concerned how he was coping. Which frustrated the sisters greatly particularly when all they could do was write more and more letters, having exhausted Janet's ear. But they needed to let everyone know now, what was actually happening to a patient in their care. Trusting then action would be taken and fast.

Letters were also sent to the Complaints department of the NHS Trust, pointing out, how their brother's condition was worsening and how fast he was going downhill. Also explaining how they'd found him on two separate occasions, exposed to one and all - they dread to think how many times this had happened. And mentally aware or not this wasn't acceptable.

They also stated in their letters, that the Psychiatric unit had actually come clean by admitting there was no benefit in their brother being there. 'A place in a more suitable environment should be found immediately,' they'd said.

Sadly though, not only having this nightmare to contend with, they had also found out funding was definitely not available for Sammy at Claygate. They were both disappointed, as they knew Sammy would have benefited greatly from going there. Instead he was slipping away from them fast. It just wasn't fair; would he ever be given a chance to get better?

The sisters knew it was vital now to get him off that ward and looked after properly. He needed somewhere more appropriate to recover - a more caring and loving environment. Even a nursing home would be more acceptable if they could move him there quickly - before further damage was done. The sisters agreed it was far more important at this moment to concentrate their efforts on getting Sammy moved; rehabilitation would have to follow later.

In the meantime Elaine kept Mr Gresham in the loop and copied him in on their letters. While he in turn appeared to be doing all he could within his boundaries, in the hope of obtaining help. Unfortunately, though, as he didn't have the backing of Sammy's next of kin he could only go so far, he said.

So the sisters continued to write more letters, sending them to social services, the head of Sammy's ward and his doctors - again pointing out his obvious deterioration and neglectful care.

After little response, the sisters then made it clear - if something wasn't done quickly they had no option but to contact the local papers. They were sure they would be interested in the fact they had a recording of their brother, who at that time could communicate quite easily. He could hardly talk now.

It was soon after this bombardment of letters that a meeting was eventually called. Noises had finally reached the right places and the gods and their ranks now appeared to be closing in – all protecting each other's useless backsides they guessed.

At the time of the meeting, Elaine's husband Mark, who was still working in Singapore, his job still safe for now, happened to be over in the U.K. And although not fully conversant with Sammy's case, Elaine asked if he would join them - his strong, forceful presence may make a difference, she hoped. The powers that be might perhaps be more willing to sit up and listen to a man, only action needed to be taken and fast. No more games, this had to be sorted out once and for all.

'But I'm not sure if I'm going to be of any use Elaine. I don't know enough about Sammy's case,' Mark complained.

'I know - but just the fact of having you there will help, I'm sure. Anyway I don't really expect you to say anything, unless you feel inclined. But if you think at any time, they're actually 'out of order', please, please, just step in; that's what we need.'

The world and his wife were at this meeting, with at least four doctors and their assistants in attendance. Also there was Janet Armstrong and her assistant, together with Melissa, Elaine, Jill and Mark, making quite some gathering. Elaine had to wonder how the hospital was functioning with so many medical staff attending. Although she wasn't really surprised, as she often wondered where the doctors were hiding - as they were never to be found on the wards.

The doctors, not only from different departments but some originally from different parts of the world, now sat opposite their enquirers - their arms tightly folded and their barriers up, they clearly meant business. And this was before they'd even started.

Ready to begin, Elaine, no longer embarrassed at having to speak out, took the initiative and waded in with her concerns about her brother, giving them the latest update on how she found him of late, besides expressing her concerns for his present mental state. But with little response, she then asked what their proposals were going forward, regarding Sammy's future care and his ongoing treatment, together with an approximate time scale. 'It's been almost five months since he was placed on this present ward; surely it's time to move him.'

The main consultant, heading Sammy's case, who appeared unperturbed by her frustrations, was the first to give his answer. 'I'm afraid it's all very experimental at the moment as we need to establish what's best for Sammy first. Only he's considered, a square peg in a round hole… we really don't know where to place him. The main problem being, he's still a relatively young man and most care homes are for the elderly. But we are monitoring him closely…. be assured we are doing all we can. Although we do feel, in view of his present condition he is probably in the best place at the moment.'

The doctor turned towards his colleagues, an arrogant look on his face. He clearly expected them to back him up and no one dared disagree.

Elaine was incensed by his answer, especially with Melissa sitting at her side nodding in agreement to every word he uttered. Her 'yes's' of confirmation grated in her ear, like a knife twisting deeper into the wound - the one she'd made in the first place and Elaine wanted to scream.

'Due to his original accident and subsequent operation, this has all been unavoidable,' another doctor said. 'After all, part of his brain has been removed and we don't know yet, the full extent of that damage.'

But the sisters had already heard this before and were not totally convinced this was true. As they knew for certain Sammy had been knocked backwards into this present state due to the treatment on this current ward and they guessed the doctors knew this too. They probably also knew, Sammy was capable of a lot more, even if Melissa didn't want to think so, and had to wonder, why they choose to ignore this? Was it a case of covering things up again?

'So, could I ask what plans you have in mind for Sammy's foreseeable future? Elaine asked, directing her question at the main doctor, already worried by the earlier sound of defeatism in his voice. 'Is it likely that Sammy will be allowed rehabilitation at a later stage?'

The doctor looked thoughtful, almost lost for words and looked expectantly at his colleague beside him. But no one appeared able to answer and the question though simple, got passed around the large gathering, as vacant looks spread across their faces. Even Janet Armstrong kept her head down; embarrassed by their silence, no doubt.

Confused at having to answer such a direct yet simple question it seemed, Mark became visibly angry, clearly frustrated by the lack of feeling and professionalism shown, shocked by their incompetence.

No longer able to contain himself, Mark leapt to his feet as he bellowed, 'This is a farce! This is unbelievable... I am just a layman here; I leave the difficult stuff to you lot, after all that's what you're trained and are very well paid for.'

Elaine, amazed but pleased by Mark's outburst, looked around the room at the expressions of unacknowledged bewilderment on their faces, as he continued to wade in.

'When someone asks a simple question, they at least expect an answer!' he shouted. 'Only we rely on you lot to give us those answers … all we want to know is, what you have planned for Sammy and as far as I can see, you're all unable to answer! Surely that's not difficult?'

Red with temper, Mark waved his hand dismissively towards Melissa who ood and arrrrd beside him, clearly surprised by his cutting remarks and his obvious blatant attack aimed at the doctors.

'Oh shut up, you have no idea,' he mumbled towards her, while he prepared to tackle them further.

When suddenly one of the junior doctors stood up, he looked concerned by Mark's outburst and tried to reassure him. 'We are sorting everything out Mr Bowers. It's all in hand at this very moment, I can assure you.'

At which point Elaine interrupted.

'But our brother is deteriorating each day while you lot try to sort things out. It just isn't good enough!'

The doctors looked at each other contentiously, as accusations started to fly back and forth between them all. When it quickly became apparent there'd been a great big cock-up somewhere along the line and things were being hidden, they suspected.

The principal, responsible for patient placements, Mr Afrieda, looked concerned by the rumpus caused, and ushered Mark and the sisters out of the room on the pretext of discussing homes. Although this may have been a ploy, either to save the doctors embarrassment, or to get them out of the way to defuse the issue. Yet he did suggest they should sue. The sisters however, had no wish to do so; after all, it would be of no benefit to poor Sammy. They just wanted him out of that place and fast.

Mr Afrieda, still flustered by the situation then told them - he would soon be meeting up with the owner of a very good care home close by. He would make it his business to get Sammy on their list.

'It may not be ideal but at least it will get him out of that ward quickly,' he said, appearing to be helpful.

And although this wasn't what they had wanted initially, as they believed he needed rehabilitation, they were nevertheless pleased with his plan. But the sisters had heard their promises before and decided not to raise their hopes again, not until they knew for sure. Yet why had it taken this outcry to get things moving?

After the meeting, Mark and the two sisters went together to see their brother, hoping to find him a little improved. But sadly, he appeared much the same, due mainly to the drugs he was being given, they suspected and remained unaware, they were there.

Needless to say, Sammy was taken off them the very next day, which they of course found suspicious and he was now allowed to venture down stairs to the games room. Here the sisters found him watching other patients playing a game of Poole. A game he'd once enjoyed with his father, many years ago. Stood now with a smile on his face, the sisters hoped he may be remembering better times.

****

The following day, after visiting their brother again, the sisters were asked if they would call in on Janet Armstrong, who seemed remarkably amenable this time.

'So what did you think of the meeting?' Janet asked, wearing a curious look, perhaps wondering what their intentions were now.

But the sisters were unimpressed by her lack of cooperation in the past and could feel nothing but contempt for this woman. Guessing she was probably worried and keen to pass the buck. Lay the blame at someone else's door just like everyone else.

'Well, we thought it was a farce actually,' Jill replied, in a matter of fact tone.

'Oh, I wouldn't say that,' Janet said, a little surprised, 'Hopefully things will start moving again… Mr Afrieda did say he would be looking at Broadlands Nursing Home, for Sammy. It's a beautiful place.'

'Does it have rehabilitation facilities and a physio department?' Elaine enquired, knowing she was pushing her luck but she guessed it was worth a try.

'Well, no, not rehab, but I believe they do have a physiotherapist there.'

'I suppose that's something,' Elaine muttered, unimpressed.

'Because you do know the main problem was caused by the two health authorities fighting over Sammy's funding? It became very difficult for us to arrange things.'

Janet was quick to get her explanation in and no doubt keen to distance herself from the blame.

'So, it was all down to money,' Jill said, looking at Janet wearily.

'It normally is, I'm afraid, and in the meantime he needed to be placed somewhere… and of course we knew going home wasn't an option, as it clearly didn't work.'

'No, it certainly didn't and you were warned!' Elaine stressed her point with a poignant look.

Janet lowered her eyes, embarrassed it seemed. But that decision hadn't really been down to her; it was Sue Walker who'd instigated that.

It appeared it had been a case of pass the buck all along and this had clearly suited Melissa, who'd agreed to all their plans, knowing they were stalling for time. While Sammy was the one suffering as usual, with Melissa not kicking up a fuss as a wife would normally do. And they got away with their time wasting, while Sammy continued to deteriorate.

'Anyway,' Janet said, quickly changing the subject, 'I called you here to get these papers signed. The Guardianship Office wants me to complete them,' and she pulled them out from her draw.

'I thought they were already dealt with?' Elaine said, thinking Janet had probably been sitting on them.

'No … they've only just sent them back for me to add my comments, but you need to sign and complete another part.'

'What a performance!' Elaine moaned as she signed the papers where indicated. 'Why do they make everything so complicated?' And she wondered if Mr Gresham had mentioned anything to Janet regarding the court of protection. Or could it be, now that the mud had been stirred Janet thought the papers should be dealt with, only it seemed a coincidence they should reappear now. The sisters didn't trust any of them.

A few days later Elaine decided to make another appointment to see Mr Gresham. It had been a few months since her last visit and she wanted to update him on their recent meeting, while Mark was still in the country. She could do with his support if needed, after all it had worked before – it may work again.

However, on the morning of their meeting with him, another coincidental phone call was made, to Elaine this time from Janet.

'Just to let you know Mrs Bowers, it's been confirmed that we've managed to obtain a place for Samuel in Broadlands Nursing Home.'

'That's great. When does he go?'

'They're taking him there this afternoon to see how he fits in, and as soon as a place becomes available, which happens quite often, as many of the residents are very old. He can then move in on a one year's probation period. After that he becomes permanent.'

Elaine put the phone down pleased with this news, although still apprehensive, only things didn't normally go right for Sammy. And she wondered if there was any point in going to see Mr Gresham.

'It seems funny how these things keep happening on the morning's we're due to see him,' she said to Mark over breakfast, 'it's a bit of a coincidence don't you think?'

'It is a bit strange, I must say... so are we still going?' Mark buttered his toast; he didn't appear bothered either way.

'I think we should, if only to explain the situation, make it official so to speak. Only I still don't trust them.'

Elaine and Mark arrived at Mr Gresham office dead on time and made their way towards the dull, uninviting office, keen to share their news. Only to be met by Mr Gresham himself standing in the doorway - a surprised-look on his face. It was obvious he wasn't expecting them.

'I thought your appointment was cancelled?' he said, looking at his watch.

'No?' Elaine replied.

'Right, I must have got that wrong then. Please come through. So how is your brother Samuel?' he said as they sat themselves down at his desk.

Elaine was impressed he'd remembered her brother's name and most of his problems no doubt, without even looking at his notes. And thought he probably also knew what they had come to tell him, but quickly updated him anyway, right up to the point of the telephone conversation with Janet that morning.

'Well, that's good news ... isn't it?' He didn't look too sure.

'Yes, and we just wanted to say thank you for all your help. Hopefully this should work out nicely for Sammy, although we would have preferred if he'd received rehabilitation, but at least he'll be off that awful ward at last.'

'Please don't thank me Mrs Bowers, I had nothing to do with it,' he said, insistently.

Mark held out his hand in a gesture of gratitude, 'Help or no help, thank you all the same,' and they left his shabby office, trusting that things were dealt with.

On the way out though, Mark whispered to Elaine, 'I actually think he could've done a lot more. After all if it hadn't been for me, Sammy would still be on that dreadful ward'

'True.' Which left them wondering why Mr Gresham had thought their meeting was cancelled, as nobody else should have been involved. Was it yet another coincidence? Still, at least Sammy was sorted out at last. That was all they could have hoped for.

It wasn't long after Sammy's initial visit to the home, he soon found himself safely ensconced in his own cosy room, in a part of a beautiful country manor called, Broadview. Where they hoped he'd be surrounded by loving and caring people, receiving all the help he deserved.

Chapter 32 – The home

'So what type of physiotherapy do you have here, Mr Chigwell?' Elaine asked the kind looking gentleman sat opposite her. The owner, in his late fifties, glanced at Elaine over his dark rimmed glasses as he pondered on her question. His wisely face, with its permanent smile, fascinated her. She was sure he was a man who'd stand up for this home should its quality dared be questioned.

'We don't have physiotherapy facilities here as such, Mrs Bowers, but we do have an exercise regime that's carried out each day.'

'That's good. So what does that involve?'

'Well, we throw balls to the patients, basically. This helps them with their co-ordination and reflex responses.' He tried to sound professional but Elaine wasn't convinced.

'Oh, I see ….and that's all you have?' She sounded disappointed; she'd been led to believe there was at least a physiotherapist there.

'Your brother has been through a lot this past year. It's going to take some time for him to settle in. Be assured, we will do all we can to help him. We look after our patients or, as we like to call them here, guests very well.'

Elaine turned towards the large Georgian window that looked out onto the beautiful countryside of Surrey and thought how lucky they were to have such a wonderful view. Perhaps she was worrying unnecessarily and her brother could be happy here. It did seem very nice.

Mr Chigwell, seemed aware of her unsettled feelings though, and continued to reassure her. 'You mustn't worry, Mrs Bowers. We know it can be very difficult for families but remember you can visit your brother whenever you like. Please just ring us if you have any further concerns.'

Elaine felt comforted by his kind words but left his office still uncertain if this was the right place for Sammy, although they certainly appeared to care.

Jill too had spoken to Mr Chigwell earlier that day after visiting Sammy in his new abode and told Elaine later, in a phone call that she was also concerned about the place. Yet she too had been delighted and pleasantly impressed by his surroundings and especially his bedroom, in fact the living area in general. But she'd had her reservations about his fellow inmates, finding them all quite odd.

'So what did you think of the place, Elaine?' she asked, sounding extremely unhappy.

'Jill, all I can say, is it's a lot better than where he was.'

'I know…but it's full of strange people, their all so old.'

'Well I don't really think that's fair, Jill. They're just people who've been very poorly and now need looking after … mainly people with Alzheimer's, stroke victims and probably with senile dementia and that happens to the elderly I'm afraid.'

'But he's too young to be there.' she protested. 'I had to run out; it was too upsetting to see him sitting there amongst them. I couldn't stop crying.'

Jill had always been the emotional one but Elaine understood her concerns.

'I know what you mean, sis,' she said, trying to be sympathetic. 'But let's just see how it goes. Give it a couple of weeks and we'll have a chat with the owner again, or maybe the head nurse. We can then find out what they intend to do about Sammy's rehabilitation and then hopefully we can get him out of there at a later stage.'

It was on Elaine's very next visit however, that she too became alarmed - her experience more than a little surreal. As on this particular afternoon, after first using codes to enter, and then making her way through a set of heavy wooden doors, which were preventing the residents from leaving. She then had to sign in the visitor's book, stating her name, who she was visiting, and the date and time of her visit. A signature also expected when exiting.

Pushing through yet another set of doors, she was suddenly hit full force by an overpowering smell of urine - accidents from the many incontinent residents who lived there, unable to help themselves or their bladders.

On entering this large reception area full of wonderful elegant paintings, an elderly lady fell to her knees, still holding onto her handbag, carefully over her arm. Elaine was bemused, particularly when she pleaded with Elaine to pull her back up.

Elaine later found out this was Jennifer who'd lived at the home for many years. She would sit in this particular area most days, performing this little party trick and usually with new visitors, unaware of her games.

Pulling her up, Elaine then made her way through to the lounge, hoping to find her brother. When a loud disturbing scream came from one of rooms close by, prompting her to hasten her pace, the pungent smell of urine still following.

As she approached yet another large, elegant, communal room, situated at the end of the corridor, she was met by a distraught looking woman who begged her for some money. She told Elaine, she wanted to go home to see her family and needed some coinage to make a call - desperate for them to fetch her. The poor woman was clearly distressed and Elaine hadn't a clue what to do.

But then she noticed in another larger adjoining room, where a small group of residents were sitting in a semi-circle, and facing a large television screen that no one appeared to be watching. Elaine made her way towards them, leaving the poor woman still waiting for change.

It was here she recognised her brother sitting in a large comfy armchair, now sat amongst them all and a smile touched her lips. His eyes tightly closed though and his posture defeated, Sammy looked lost again. While his companions who sat beside him constantly starred into space - as loud cries and continuous screaming undoubtedly deafened their ears.

Elaine approached her brother just as he opened his eyes. He didn't seem to recognise her at first, a glazed look still clouded over them.

'Are you okay, Sammy?' Elaine asked as she kissed him on his cheek.

'No,' he replied.

'What's the matter, is it your head again?' She reached out for his hand.

'Yeah,' he said.

'Is it still spinning?'

Sammy nodded slowly, answering 'yes' and immediately closed his eyes again. Poor Sammy she thought and Elaine's heart went out to him, while wondering if he was trying to blot out all that was happening around him. And who could blame him for that. So his eyes remained closed for most of her visit.

Feeling unsettled her-self, Elaine wondered what kind of place her brother had ended up in; now sat there amongst these unfortunate people. Although she realised these people needed looking after too and someone somewhere had to do it. But poor Sammy, he was really too young to be there. It was all very sad.

During the next month or so, the sisters kept their distance. Mr Chigwell had advised them it would be best for Sammy if they didn't come too often. 'He needs time to settle in and get adjusted,' he said. 'He needs to establish a routine and to start trusting the people around him in order to feel safe and secure again.'

Yet even after this allotted time, the sisters still found Sammy troubled and hardly ever speaking. In fact, he didn't want to talk at all at times and would often find him sitting with his head bowed down and lost in that other world again.

And Elaine wondered if he was trying to shut out the past, and possibly the future - besides what was happening around him. Perhaps now thinking, what on earth was he doing in this crazy place? In fact the sisters thought about this a lot – could this actually be his worst nightmare come true? After all, hadn't he predicted this outcome? And the sisters felt again, they'd let their brother down.

Elaine also realised why Jill found it so upsetting when she went to visit Sammy, as it wasn't just the poor people around him. It was watching them deteriorate day by day before their very eyes, until eventually they passed away, which happened all too often and sometimes very quickly. A wakeup call perhaps, but poor Sammy had found himself in the midst of it all. It certainly was an eye opener and very upsetting indeed, and not only for their brother.

Finding this all very sad, they realised many of the residents had probably endured terrible indignities before being placed there too. Some having to sell their house, to pay for their care and after looking after themselves for most of their lives, it just wasn't fair. While many had even suffered illnesses brought on by the stresses of modern life - worried where they'd end their days.

It appears there are lots of people suffering today from depression and increasingly amongst the young. How long would it be before these homes were filled with much younger people who just couldn't cope anymore? Yet why wasn't our government addressing this, as the demographics prove these figures were quickly changing. There was something very wrong with society today.

In spite of everything, Sammy was slowly but surely improving again and was already out of incontinence pads. The sisters were delighted. Although over time their visits had become less and less frequent as they both had their own lives to lead now, commitments and responsibility's restricting them. It was therefore inevitable, Sammy would find it harder to remember who they were whenever they came to visit. However, it didn't take him long to learn again, as long as he was in the mood. Yet when he did recognise their faces, his face would light up in response, hoping perhaps this time they had come to take him home.

On one of Elaine's earlier visits, she brought Sammy in a gift, a moving in present she called it - a soft, grey, fluffy, toy rabbit, which she told him she'd named Bruce. Noticing a tear in her brother's eye as he thanked her for his present, Elaine realised, Sammy had remembered his favourite pet. The one his family laughed at all those years ago. And she thought, if this was so, surely he could remember so much more?

Sammy had been in the home now for nearly three months and the sisters decided it was time to find out just how well he was settling in. So a meeting was arranged to see the head carer in charge that day; a woman in her mid-fifties and of mixed race.

Sat in front of them now, she appeared to show little interest in the ladies. In fact, she looked more akin to one of the patient's than the staff that actually worked there.

Her eyes heavy and tired and her clothing dishevelled when this woman eventually spoke, her Southern American drawl was almost inaudible, which made it difficult for the sisters to understand her; the patients would stand no chance.

'W..h..a..t.. c..a..n.. I.. do for you ladies?' she said in a dry dour voice, while barely lifting her eyes up from her desk.

318

'Well we'd like to know how our brother, Sammy, is doing,' Elaine said, thinking the situation quite laughable, the laugh being on them.

'As... well... as... can... be... expected,' she groaned. 'You must remember... it will take some time for Sammy to settle in, but... he is settling in very well.'

'Is he on any medication?' Elaine asked. 'Only he doesn't seem himself,' a desperate tone in her voice now. It seemed this woman wasn't going to offer any information voluntarily.

'Just a couple of tablets … they stop him from shaking, but nothing else.'

'So, no depression tablets then? Jill butted in. 'Because sometimes he seems doped up and very drowsy.'

'No, he isn't on anything else … you must remember he has been in a very bad accident!'

If she had added – why are you asking stupid questions, they wouldn't have been surprised and this coupled with her awful accent and uncaring attitude, made the sisters want to scream! They were clearly being a nuisance again, when all they wanted was to make sure their brother was being properly cared for.

Elaine didn't want to give into this woman's disinterest though and continued with her questioning.

'The thing is … he was so much better than this when he was in Reigate hospital. Well, before going into the psychiatric ward that is. So we know he's capable of a lot more.' Here we go again, she thought. How many times had she heard herself explaining this? She was beginning to sound like a broken record.

The woman eyed the sisters up and down, knowingly. It was obvious by her face she'd been told about them; no doubt warned - troublemakers she'd been told, and they watched her suspiciously sussing them out.

'Uhhhhh … yes,' she drawled. 'The thing is, no one knows what the brain will do long term. We'll have to wait and see what happens.' The sisters couldn't understand the rest of her strange appraisal and gave up on that line of questioning.

Then Jill asked her usual question, 'Has his wife been into see him lately?' She asked this whenever she went to visit Sammy – even when in the hospital.

'Oh, yes,' the woman said, and then nothing more. This made the sisters think perhaps she'd been told not to divulge anything concerning Melissa, particularly to them.

'That's funny,' Jill replied, 'because she hasn't signed in the visitor's book.'

'Well, I can assure you, she does come into see him,' and that's all she said. She had no intentions of discussing this.

Annoyed at being treated with contempt, like the interfering sisters again, they left feeling unhappy. Back to square one, the same old rubbish. But at least he was out of that 'Hell Hole'; this had to be better.

Sammy's bedroom was comfy and yet spacious by normal standards, in fact quite lovely on reflection and the sisters were at least delighted with that. Plus he also had the room to him-self, which was good, given some had to share.

Also Melissa had kindly brought in some Chinese ornaments to decorate his room, much to their surprise. Jill

320

said she recognised them from the bedroom in their house. It seemed Melissa had told the care staff, she was redecorating her bedroom and changing it from the oriental theme it was at present and didn't need the ornaments anymore. Typical she was slinging things out but still it made his room look homely. Especially with the fluffy toy rabbit that sat in the centre of his bed.

His room, now complete with an old television set Elaine had brought him in, and a few familiar pictures that sat at his bedside made it feel homely. But the sisters still wondered why there wasn't a picture of Melissa and Sammy together. Or one of Kelly, come to that. Although a photo did eventually appear of Sammy holding Kelly as a baby, to which one of the care workers, who'd known Sammy a while now, asked whose baby it was. As he didn't even know Sammy had a child.

The care worker was amazed when they told him it was his daughter, as he knew she hadn't been into visit at all, and he told the sisters; he thought this very strange and certainly uncaring.

Christmas was approaching fast and they were now preparing for their yearly festive party with entertainment laid on. The families of the residents were also invited, although not many could attend; all too busy with their own lives no doubt. However, Elaine was able to join them; she wanted it to be enjoyable for Sammy and hoped it would help him settle in.

Not really knowing what to expect though, it actually turned out to be a brilliant afternoon. The large elegant communal room was turned into a massive Santa's grotto -

decorated with tinsel, lights and sparkly decorations. And with a huge Christmas tree stood boldly in the corner of the room and countless festive cards displayed on the mantelpiece above the large marble fireplace - the focal point of the room, it all looked amazing.

With all the residents dressed in their fine Sunday bests, they balanced bright paper Christmas hats with difficulty on their heads. And teamed with necklaces of sparkling baubles and bright shinny beads, they waited expectantly for the show to begin as the atmosphere sizzled with excitement.

Then suddenly, when the music started to play, a glamorous and vivacious middle aged lady stepped proudly in the room.

With her hair in abundance on the top of her head and heavy makeup applied to thrill. Plus a twinkly outfit to dazzle them all – this didn't go unnoticed by Sammy, particularly when she wiggled in front of him in time to the tune.

Now in full flow, the woman started to sing some popular songs to her thrilled and titillated audience, as her energy filled the room. But although not the best vocalist in the world, she certainly still brought enjoyment to her audience as Elaine clapped her hands along with the songs, trying to encourage Sammy.

Strutting her stuff still, in front of them all she stopped beside Sammy once again; pointing a finger towards him, while starting to sing yet another favourite song …

'How I love you, how I love you, my dear old Sammy.'

Sammy unable to contain himself any longer whooped with laughter. Now clapping his hands in excitement and wearing a smile bigger than Elaine had ever seen before. She was pleased.

'Thank you, thank you, sis; this is so good,' no longer embarrassed by the attention this woman still gave him, as she ruffled up his hair - what little he had left now.

Elaine hadn't seen him looking so vibrant in a long time. She was glad she hadn't missed this, it made her realise just how happy Sammy could be.

Then she noticed Mr Chigwell looking over from the doorway, smiling too. And Elaine smiled back, so glad she was there with Sammy - perhaps she was worrying unnecessarily; maybe he could settle here.

Chapter 33 - Official Statements

Sammy was slowly but surely settling into the home. Although settling in with some of the residents did prove a problem. As sadly at times, Alzheimer suffers can turn aggressive and on several occasions Elaine noticed one or two of the residents with shiny black eyes, Sammy being one of them.

Around this time Elaine had also witnessed one of the younger male residentss' wandering about the home looking quite menacing. The older folk appeared to avoid him. It was only after his disappearance that the black eyes disappeared too, which confirmed he'd been responsible.

Putting asides this unpleasant episode, Sammy seemed content in his new little world, although it was still hard for the sisters to see him there. Knowing too, he hadn't yet reached the stage he'd got to, before being sent home. As he didn't even want to go out these days, refusing any trips to the seaside that the home provided at times. His confidence long gone it seemed.

It was around this time that the sisters received a follow up letter from the Guardianship Office. They wanted to know why the sisters felt their brother needed an independent panel of people to preside over his welfare.

Perplexed, Elaine responded by sending more copies of her previous complaints, together with a synopsis of what she felt was a clear concise picture of his wife's indifference towards her husband and his care. Explaining in full the sad details of what she felt was an obvious lack of understanding and remorseless neglect on her part. Confirming yet again, that she hardly went to visit, let alone provide for him properly; not the actions of a caring person with her husband's best interests at heart.

Elaine also pointed out; that although the home was providing good care for Sammy, any chance of him improving further was zero, as there were no facilities at all for rehab and even the physiotherapy was questionable. The sheer fact Melissa found this acceptable spoke volumes, she wrote.

Jill had also received a similar letter and wrote back in much the same vein, supporting her sisters' comments.

Soon after, the sisters each received a statement from Melissa's solicitor, via the Guardianship Office, in response to their letters - fighting off all allegations made. Elaine was surprised and also annoyed; particularly as this statement appeared full of more lies, still claiming her innocence to her obvious neglect.

On top of this Elaine still had her own problems to deal with, she didn't need more.

But going through the solicitor's pointers methodically, she made some notes, as she tried to comprehend Melissa's defensive remarks that were clearly untrue.

As it seemed Melissa strongly disagreed to Elaine's statement regarding her husband's accident, being otherwise. While also fighting off any claims that his present care home wasn't suitable. Stating that in her opinion Samuel's condition was unlikely to improve significantly and therefore felt he didn't warrant anywhere better.

With regards to Elaine's reference to her not having her husband's best interests at heart, at statement she had made, she regarded this as nothing more than malicious, stating that Elaine had taken an instant dislike to her since she married her brother. Which Elaine thought strange as it was always considered the other way round. She even stated, Elaine had once asked Samuel to choose between them! To which Elaine had to laugh.

She also objected to Elaine making reference to their marriage going through a difficult patch, although she did admit herself there'd been some problems - pointing out, one bone of contention between them was where they would live in the future. She claimed that Samuel had always wanted to move nearer to the coast to be closer to her mother, but this hadn't been possible while Kelly was at school. Which of course amazed the sisters, as they'd never heard about this before or neither his best friend Lawrence. And considering Sammy had fallen out with his mother-in-law they wondered how this could be.

With regards to her having always had full control over Samuel, a statement made by Elaine, she considered this ridiculous as he was a grown man and he could make his own decisions. Although she did admit she often took over the financial arrangements - like writing out cheques, because Samuel couldn't spell, she wrote, which was clearly another lie. And they wondered what she'd been up to with regards to these finances, as what were these cheques she'd been writing?

She also said the reason for his depression had been mainly due to Samuel losing his job. But added, he'd been looking forward to starting work at the LEB again, as they'd been searching for his type of expertise apparently, which again the sisters had never heard of. And they had to wonder if she was going for compensation in some way?

With regards to the day of the accident and the events that followed, Melissa explained that their trip to Wimbledon, was a fairly regular occurrence, either by tube or bus, even though the sister' had heard otherwise. But she then stated there was no reason to believe this was a problem - it was only a moment of inattention on Samuel's part that led him to lean over and be hit by the train. And Elaine had to wonder what happened to the mice, or even the lost ticket.

She also wrote, the incident was on London's transport CTV and there'd already been a police investigation. No one had suggested she had done anything criminal, negligent, irresponsible or otherwise culpable, only his sisters, she put.

She then went on to say, after the accident she wasn't able to talk and couldn't communicate to pass on the news of her husband's death, as she had thought initially he was. Therefore she had no idea who had given out this information to the family. If Samuel's sisters were concerned, she stated, why didn't they make contact?

Elaine couldn't believe what she was reading at this stage but continued on, furious with her silly statement that didn't make sense.

Regarding Melissa calling her husband a cabbage or brain dead, she seemed to believe, because he'd been in a

327

coma for over 3 months (which was also incorrect) it was not clear to her or anyone else what Samuel would be like when out of it.

Then covering herself regarding the state of her husband's appearance, and his disgusting clothing, she wrote - Sammy had lost 6 stone in weight, (which sounded excessive), and she had to buy him several sets of new clothing, which was proving difficult to keep clean only Samuel had a tendency to put tissues in his pockets, which made them look shabby after washing. She also hadn't realised doing his washing in the hospital was a problem and had thought it normal and was happy to let them do it. She then mentioned that some of his clothes had disappeared, probably stolen - which immediately made Elaine smile, remembering the jacket.

And with regards to the problem of the photographs, well lack of, even after countless requests to bring some in - Melissa stated that she actually had her own book of photos which she took in each time she visited, and this she said she did every other day. With reference to the photo of the man she'd had her arm around; she said this was her brother-in-law, her rock, who'd been helping her to sort things out.

Elaine couldn't believe the lies she was spewing, she knew this wasn't her brother-in-law, but the fibs just kept coming. Flabbergasted now, she read on in amusement.

She then claimed - when the sisters took Samuel back to visit his home; she was shocked when she saw him. Or would have been if she'd arrived at the hospital to find he wasn't there, she would surely have thought the worse.

The rest of the statement was a case of going over what happened to Sammy when he supposedly turned aggressive, after his experimental visit home went wrong. Stating that this was when he had to be placed in the psychiatric ward. She never said anything adverse about the way he was treated there. She did say however, that several meetings had been held with the professionals, of which the sisters were never excluded. Which wasn't in fact a lie but what she didn't say was all these meetings were subsequently cancelled.

She then went on to say, Samuel had been placed in Broadlands nursing home, because the other homes had not been suitable, given they were unsecure units. With Samuel having a tendency to wander the other's weren't considered safe. Broadlands, she said, was the much better option for the help Samuel needed and therefore sufficient for his requirements. Pointing out he was lucky to be alive considering the extent of his injuries.

In Melissa's opinion, he was getting all the help he needed that could reasonably be expected at Broadlands. He seems to have no memory of the accident and he eats and sleeps well in his own room. Samuel also joins in with the exercises' provided there. He has improved in the sense that he is no longer in a coma and is walking. Adding - there have been some physical improvements, but none in his mind and insisted he still didn't know her. While also adding, he is now doubly incontinent and wears incontinence pads at all times. He is always confused in his mind but considering he has suffered the removal of the front lobe on the right side of his brain, this is not surprising. Indeed he is lucky to be alive. The letter had clearly been formulated by her solicitor.

Elaine was dumfounded, she couldn't believe the extent of her lies. She was surely guilty of something. If anything, this only proved to her, everything she'd ever thought regarding Melissa was true. Any thoughts of any misunderstandings were now long gone. Jill also felt the same.

Elaine didn't have the money to spend on solicitors to make her reply, unlike Melissa it seemed. And anyway why should she, after all her actions were only to safeguard a vulnerable person, regardless he was her brother. Elaine actually felt this should really be down to the law of the land to protect Sammy. Or even social services, considering he was in their care. Or even perhaps his carers, or the nurses who also expressed their concerns but then did nothing about them! Consequently this left only the sisters again to deal with it all. So Elaine read through Melissa's statement carefully in order to make her reply.

Chapter 34 - Replies.

Elaine wasn't sure how to react to Melissa's blatant attack and was still incensed by her statement. She needed advice and someone to turn to, concerned by the whole scenario. But people had grown tired of the stories concerning her brother, although they'd never say. Yet their blank expressions and glazed over eyes, really said it all and who could blame them.

In fact the family all thought it unhealthy for the sisters to be so involved, especially Elaine, as she hadn't been treated kindly by Melissa or Sammy in the past.

In spite of this, Elaine wanted to help her brother as much as she could. She hated unfairness and especially lies. No, Melissa was evil as far as she was concerned and preferred if she had nothing to do with her. But in view of the official tone of this letter, Elaine had no option but to reply - responding as honestly as she could, under such circumstances. And so without any help, she responded accordingly.

Following the format of the solicitor's letter and all the issues raised, Elaine firstly pointed out, in answer to Melissa believing Broadlands Nursing home was more than adequate for Sammy – Elaine wrote, in her opinion, given it had no rehabilitation facilities, it was clearly not suitable, even though Melissa thought so, particularly as the physio offered consisted only of a big bouncing ball. Plus the staff didn't even have time to talk with Samuel, or help in his progress. And even though Melissa didn't feel anything else was required, contrary to her opinion, Samuel was capable of far more than she'd ever be prepared to believe.

In reply to the accusation made regarding Elaine disliking her – she happily admitted she had no feelings either way but did feel strongly about the way Melissa treated her brother, especially since the accident and questionably before. It was therefore only her brother she cared about and wanted the best for him.

She also gave her reasons as to why she questioned the accident as being one, explaining that many others had expressed their doubts too, the Metropolitan police and psychiatric doctor being just two of them. And given the two stories offered, for the lead up to the accident had not appeared plausible, this also made her reason the accident was definitely questionable, besides the many other factors that didn't add up.

With regards to them having marriage problems - Elaine only stated what others had told her, as she'd not been in contact with her brother for years.

She'd also heard that her brother had fallen out with his mother-in-law and it would therefore seem illogical to suggest he would want to move nearer. He now gets upset if his mother-in-law is even mentioned.

Elaine also questioned why, if they went regularly to Wimbledon by bus or tube, they'd forgotten this particular shop didn't carry clothing. She also understood Samuel hadn't been on a tube in over 20 years and therefore this wouldn't be considered a regular occurrence.

Elaine then explained she'd only found out about the accident from Samuel's best friend. Who was initially told he was dead by Samuel's work colleague. How he found out was anyone's guess, especially as Melissa couldn't speak. And why on earth would she ring Melissa anyway, particularly if she hadn't spoken to her in years – now thinking he was already dead?

Also, Elaine made it very clear Samuel was in Whitechapel hospital for less than a month, and not the 3 months Melissa stated. He came out of his coma around the time he was moved to Reigate. Perhaps if his wife had spent a little more time with him, she would have known this. Elaine also stated that in all of her visits to the hospital, not once had she or Jill bumped into her, so she clearly didn't visit too often. It seemed Melissa had told neighbours she didn't like hospitals anyway and only went there when asked to.

With regards to his soiled clothing, Elaine wrote she only knew about this particular problem concerning the washing because the ward nurses had complained to them. So it clearly was a problem, which Melissa chose to ignore, according to the nurses.

And with regards to Samuel turning aggressive, not once had he been aggressive with her or her sister, or to her knowledge, any one of the hospital staff before being sent home. To which they had to wonder why.

Elaine then went on to confess, she had in her possession the picture of the man Melissa said was her brother-in-law, stating that Samuel had accidently pulled it from the book and was now in her safe keeping. This she knew for a fact was not Sammy's brother-in-law! It was a picture of a Mr

Steven Brown, the man she calls her 'rock' an ex colleague of Samuels, who he'd apparently fallen out with. Why - she didn't know.

She was also very angry at Melissa's reference to Samuel being doubly incontinent, and wrote, he only became incontinent again when placed on the Psychiatric ward after his experimental trip home went wrong. He certainly wasn't incontinent before and understood he was already clean again thanks to the home.

Elaine actually believed Broadlands was a nice home but clearly not the right place for her brother going forward.

With regards to Samuel not knowing who his wife was though, Elaine also wrote, perhaps if she'd spent more time with him, he might actually do so. As he always remembered her and his other sister, and most of the pretty nurses that worked on his previous ward.

After twenty five years of marriage, as Melissa keeps pointing out, this I thought would be considered part of his long term memory. And given it's his short term memory supposedly the most affected - remembering his wife should therefore not be a problem.

Elaine was also concerned that there'd been no mention of Kelly visiting her father and wrote - it would be nice if this was to happen, as it could help her father with solving past memories, while perhaps helping him feel loved, rather than abandoned.

She also stated, perhaps in future, Mrs Clayton should sign in the visitor's book when entering and leaving Broadlands, just like everyone else - then her visits to see her husband wouldn't be queried.

In view of the aforementioned, Elaine clarified - it was obvious to her; Mrs Clayton should not have sole dealings of her husband's affairs. Suggesting in future an independent panel of people should be involved in any decision making concerning her brother, worried by his wife's intentions.

Elaine sent off her statement hoping this time someone may actually sit up and take note given it was a vulnerable man's life in question. And a similar response was also sent by Jill, with a copy of a letter from Sammy's good friend Lawrence, who hoped it, might help. His read:

Dear Jill,

I have read the accompanying statement from Melissa regarding Sammy and I am concerned there are a number of inaccuracies in the statement, which would give the wrong impression about Sammy's circumstances and state of mind.

I list below additional comments that I think are material to the case and which should be corrected for the record, i.e. I stress I do not intend to give personal opinion about Melissa or her intentions. My only concern is Sammy's future welfare.

I have never been able to understand why Melissa will not accept the actual facts about the 'accident'. I did initially accept that the cause of Sammy's injuries were due to an accident as she described. But I subsequently visited the scene of the 'accident' at Colliers Wood tube station and became doubtful whether it was in fact an 'accident'. This is because the alignment of the track into Colliers Wood from Morden is such that it is impossible not to be aware of an oncoming train well before it enters the station.

My doubts were confirmed later whilst watching a television programme on 23rd March 1999. The programme describes a male tube driver who had been off sick for some months, due to trauma after having some-one attempt suicide under his train at Colliers Wood tube station. The facts he then described of the accident, including the date and how the man ended up severely injured on the platform are such that it can only be Sammy, the man who attempted the suicide. I keep a diary of events and did in fact keep a copy of the description of the programme as published in the newspaper.

It is news to me that Sammy was considering a return to work in the Electricity Industry. He had lost all confidence in his ability to do such work; in any case he would not have wanted the 'aggro'.

Similarly I never heard him express a wish to move to the coast. Melissa's parents and sister live near the area in question and whilst he had a soft spot for her father, Sammy could not stand to be anywhere near to his mother-in-law or her sister.

The statement made by Melissa also contradicts Sammy's normal actions. It was a very regular event for Melissa to go shopping daily; on her own. It was a very rare event for both Sammy and Melissa to go shopping together. After retirement Sammy NEVER used public transport of any kind.

I found out about Sammy's 'death' from a phone call on the Friday morning from the owner of the shop where Sammy worked part-time. He told me he had received a phone call from Melissa to say that Sammy was dead. I was naturally in great shock and it was I that phoned Sammy's younger sister, Elaine, to find out more. To my shock she was unaware of Sammy's 'demise'. I subsequently received a phone call from Elaine early the next day; who found out that Sammy had been airlifted to The Royal London Hospital, Whitechapel and was on a life support machine. I immediately went to the hospital to see Sammy, and whilst I was there by coincidence Melissa arrived at the hospital, also to visit Sammy.

Sammy recovered from his coma whilst in the 'Royal London'. I later received a phone call from his older sister Jill to say that he had opened his eyes and was awake. When I visited him on the 20th June, I made a note he 'was breathing unaided, moving his legs and one arm and he opened his eyes.

Whilst at Reigate Sammy was never in 'Intensive Care'. He did start off in the High Dependency Unit and was moved from the HDU to a General Ward.

Melissa's 'rock' was also a Mr Steven Brown who used to be a colleague of Sammy's at the London Electricity Board. They fell out some years earlier as Sammy felt 'used' after Sammy did some driving for him. Mr Brown came on the scene whilst Sammy was in hospital and he was doing odd jobs around the house for her she told me. The last time I had contact with Melissa, was when I visited Sammy at home, after being sent there by the hospital in January 1999.

On that day, I was horrified at what I saw and how Melissa was treating Sammy. When I phoned the social worker to complain, I was informed that Sammy was already back and in the psychiatric ward at Reigate.

337

I consider Broadlands to be completely unsuitable for Sammy. He is amongst elderly people the great majority of who are either senile or suffering from dementia. Sammy immediately recognises me and my wife, Jackie every time we visit and he greets us by our individual names. He has indicated to me that he hates being in Broadlands and wants nothing to do with the patients, none of whom he has anything in common with. Sammy is 'incontinent' only because it suits the hospital authorities. Whilst he was in Reigate General, I took him myself to the toilet and waited outside whilst he 'went about his business' He was perfectly able to look after himself without any help. I did make an entry in my diary when I visited Sammy in the psychiatric ward when the patient in the adjoining bed complained to me that they had allowed Sammy's 'incontinence' to develop and would leave him all day to fend for himself.

Sammy is able to tell the time without any assistance. Indeed, when I asked Sammy to tell me the time from the clock on the main living room wall in Broadlands, he read the time precisely i.e. '3.21' rather than the more usual 'twenty past three')

The thought that Sammy may spend the rest of his years in a place such as Broadlands fills me with a great sense of fear and foreboding. I strongly believe that Sammy is very aware of his predicament and as a consequence is becoming deeply depressed and withdrawn.

I am quite alarmed that Melissa suggests that she is content with Sammy being there. I know that if my spouse was in such a place, at Sammy's age, physical condition and mental capacity, I would move heaven and earth to have my spouse moved from such a depressing and unsuitable place. The fact that Melissa finds Broadlands acceptable, speaks volumes about her lack of interest, sensitivity and conscience about Sammy being incarcerated in such a place. I am also concerned about the obvious inaccuracies in her statement and her possible future intentions.

For those reasons alone, I wish you and Elaine every success with your application to become jointly involved with Sammy's future affairs.

A month or so later, Elaine received a reply from the Guardianship Office:

RE MR SAMUEL CLAYTON.
I have been advised by the Court that it has received no evidence to indicate that there has been any financial misuse of Sammy's funds by his wife. As the Court's jurisdiction is limited to the financial affairs of a patient, it has been agreed that the application should not proceed.

If you have any remaining concerns about the patient's placement, welfare or health matters these should be referred to his medical advisers and/or the Social Services.

I have written a similar letter to Mrs Jones.

The sisters were gobsmacked. In all their dealings with the C.A.B, Social Services and their M.P - Mr Gresham, had anyone ever explained the Guardianship Office was solely about financial matters? Mr Gresham had spoken about the Court of Protection, but he never explained this wasn't covered in this procedure. And where in their conversations had they ever mentioned money?

Was it that in all probability when families argued it was normally over finances and it had been assumed this to be the same? The sisters had made it perfectly clear they were only concerned for Sammy's welfare, worried that his wife hadn't his best interests.

In fact, in their opinion, they were sure Melissa hadn't wanted him around for a long time and had probably been thinking of leaving him before this all happened. Although, they knew there was no way she would divorce him now, especially as the alternative was to be left with only half his assets. No, she wanted everything it seemed, and she wouldn't have been happy otherwise.

'I don't know, sis, it didn't happen like this for Perry Mason. Where is he when you need him?' Elaine's sense of humour was the only thing keeping her sane. No, they had done all they could to help him and all they could do this time was laugh in frustration.

As for contacting Social Services about other concerns, they'd already done this and a long time ago. In fact, almost from the very start of Sammy's problems when he arrived in Reigate hospital - passing them on all relevant information, as and when it came to them. But as usual it was clearly ignored or thought to be irrelevant, which made them wonder again if there may be a cover up of some sort.

All the sisters could do now was let this horrible episode go; they both had their own lives to live after all. Melissa had won again. They could only hope someday she would get her comeuppance.

The sisters were tired of it all now and none of this was going to make their brother any better. The only thing likely to do that was rehabilitation and that didn't seem forthcoming. Melissa saw no point. And they wondered if their brother would ever get help.

Chapter 35 - Coming to terms.

Over the next few months, Sammy started to put on weight with all the good food he was eating at the home. He'd always loved his food and seemed to be in his element just lately. Although this weight gain may have been caused by the food he'd been stealing off the plates of the other 'not so aware residents' when eating together in the dining room. The staff said, 'in order to stop the thieving, they had to keep a close eye on him and feed him separately at times.'

However, in spite of this Sammy got on well with most of the staff and never failed to make them laugh with his great sense of fun. Except when he felt low of course and then he wouldn't talk. And when he was like this and the sisters went to visit, they often found him sat quietly alone. Although their visits weren't so regular these days, they found it too depressing, especially for Jill. She once told her sister, 'I often feel, it would have been kinder if Sammy had actually died. After all, you couldn't call this living.'

Lawrence and his wife, still visited Sammy occasionally though, but they weren't happy with the home. They said it was unsuitable for their dear friend and seeing him there would sometimes upset them, particularly Lawrence. In fact he once told the sisters, Sammy was no longer the man he'd once known and loved. He wasn't the same person sitting there and was always overly concerned that this wasn't the right place for his dear friend.

Lawrence also told the sisters - Sammy would sometimes make out he didn't recognise him and he thought perhaps he was punishing him for actually leaving him there. As he always remembered Jackie, his wife, and would chat away happily to her. And this he found upsetting. The friend he'd confided in for so many years, since they were children in fact, was now lost, he said.

However, the sisters continued to visit their brother whenever they could, regardless what mood he was in. And sometimes they'd just chat about silly things, if only to get a response. While other times they'd just sit and hold hands, as Sammy remained silent.

And every now and again, the sisters would pop into the office to enquire after his progress. To be fobbed off time after time with 'He's fine and not to worry. He's going to be okay,' and normally in the same patronising tone. Although Jill always insisted on asking - 'had his wife been into see him,' only to be told as usual, 'yes she has', and then nothing else. It seemed Melissa was still being protected.

On one occasion, another head nurse told them, 'Melissa came in regularly to give them money for Samuel's incidentals, and each time she would leave them with a substantial amount.'

Elaine wanted to laugh and thought, didn't they realise this was so she didn't have to go there too often? Melissa wasn't interested in Sammy. Surely they knew that by now.

****

343

On Sammy's birthdays though, it seemed, Melissa often turned up with a silly balloon, although not always on the day and sometimes not at all. But when she did, she'd usually attach it to the back of his chair, with the words 'birthday boy' written right across it. This of course made Sammy look silly but thankfully he wasn't aware – well according to the carers he wasn't.

On Sammy's 60th birthday, Jill and her husband had gone along together to visit him, to help celebrate his special day. Jill was gobsmacked though when they unexpectedly bumped into Melissa, especially when they heard her voice booming across the room - as if from a long lost friend.

Excited to see them apparently, Melissa shouted out, 'Jill, Jill, hello… It's so lovely to see you,' flicking her long red hair off from her shoulders with a gesture of frivolity.

Jill stared in amazement and shocked by her embarrassing performance, she could only manage a nod; not wanting to feed into her fantasies or play-acting any more.

'I'm so glad I bumped into you,' Melissa carried on, clearly unperturbed by Jill's silence. 'What do you think of him then?' she said, as she looked in Sammy's direction, a disgusted expression on her face. Jill was incensed by her actions; she hadn't even said a word to Sammy and wondered how she could be so cruel. Was she really that insensitive to her husband's feelings?

'What do you mean?' Jill answered, still shocked by her insults. 'Sammy's doing fine!'

Melissa laughed. 'He doesn't even know who I am.'

Sammy looked away, clearly aware of her remarks and kept his head down, especially when she fussed around him, placing the obligatory balloon behind his chair.

Carried away with her normal fabricated stories, Melissa told Jill, 'I'm very busy these days and don't have time to visit too often.'

But Jill didn't want to know and carried on talking to Sammy. She wasn't interested in Melissa or her presence and especially her lies and tried to ignore her.

Yet Melissa, who appeared unruffled by the rebuff, immediately started talking to another visitor who sat close by. Jill noticed the man listening intently as she told him her story and thought how easily she took people in.

A few minutes later though, Jill realised Melissa had disappeared, leaving in a hurry without even a goodbye to her husband. Or her long lost friends from just minutes before. Although the visitor she'd been talking too looked thoughtful.

Eventually, the man walked over to Jill, still worried it seemed, and whispered discreetly in her ear, 'I feel so sorry for his wife; it must be very difficult for her, I don't know how she's coping,' his face was a picture of pity.

Jill was angry, and unable to answer. She felt this said it all. Melissa had been spinning her yarns again and people were still falling for them - while this poor man, her brother, whose life she had helped destroy, still couldn't get the help he deserved. Who felt sorry for him?

'So, why did she shoot off so quickly without saying goodbye then?' Elaine asked her sister, as they chatted on the telephone later.

345

'I don't know. One minute she was there, and then the next she was gone.'

'Well do you think perhaps the boyfriend was waiting outside? After all, she doesn't drive and it's a long way to go to stay only minutes. Maybe she was frightened you might offer her a lift or possibly bump into him outside!'

'I never thought of that, Miss Marple ... yes, you could be right. But it was very sad, as she didn't even talk to Sammy when she was there.'

'But I thought she never did.'

Still incensed by Melissa's actions, on her next visit Jill went and chatted to the carers, which she often did when she visited, to see what they knew. And she'd often inquire about his wife's visits. She was once told in confidence by one of the more regular carers, that sometimes when Melissa came in to pay Sammy's bills, she'd run up to her husband and get him all excited and then run out again, leaving him confused and unsettled. Exactly what she did when Sammy was in hospital.

But if by chance she did stay a while, she would only sit and stare at Sammy and not say a word. Showing little emotion and making no physical contact at all, which all looked really creepy, well according to the carer.

Thankfully, though his wife's visits were very rare and when Jill put her usual question to the staff; 'Has his wife been into see him?' they normally told her 'no!'

On one occasion, however, when Jill had asked after her brother, another carer told her, 'This isn't the right place for him; he could be doing so much better in a more suitable establishment,' and she then placed her finger up to her lips, as if it were a secret. No doubt afraid to speak out, in case they lost their job, which only added fuel to the fire for Jill, knowing her brother was stuck there. And although the sisters were fairly happy with the home and its staffing, they didn't want Sammy just vegetating there. They wanted him to get better.

It had taken sometime for Sammy to settle into Broadlands but they were now beginning to see some improvements again. So the sisters decided they were ready for another meeting, but with his doctor this time. Maybe he could finally get him the important rehabilitation they felt their brother deserved and needed. After all, even a prisoner gets rehabilitated.

Making their appointment proved easier than they thought, returning within the week to see the doctor - a handsome man on reflection, the aging process only adding to his charms.

After introducing themselves, Jill asked the doctor how Sammy was progressing.

'I must say, we're all very pleased with him here,' he said, wearing a smile the sisters found charming. 'He's actually settling in very well, considering how poorly he was when first arriving here and especially after coping with his initial operation. In fact on reflection, he's doing extremely well … I know we've had a few mishaps in the past, but there's been nothing too upsetting I'm pleased to say… no,' he said again, 'he's doing remarkably well.'

'I see. Well that's good then,' Elaine replied with caution. She didn't want to send out the wrong signals this time; they weren't there to cause trouble.

'Actually, that's why we wanted to see you. We did hope Sammy might be receiving rehabilitation by now? Especially, as he's doing so much better... I know you don't have the facilities here, but is there any chance, he could still get rehab somewhere else?' Elaine was hopeful.

The doctor thought carefully, his demeanour more formal as he looked through Sammy's files.

'Well ... sometimes we are able to send a few of our patients out to a nearby centre once or twice a week, so they're taught certain life skills. If you like, I could send them a letter to see if they'll assess him for their programme.'

'Oh that would be great!' the sisters said together, surprised by his quick suggestion.

'Okay. I'll write to them today and hopefully we should have an answer back within a month or two,' and smiling at the sisters he shook their hands, 'So happy to have helped,' he said.

'That was easy,' Elaine whispered as they left his room. 'Just goes to show ... if Melissa had been playing her part, she could have done so much more for Sammy.'

'Ermmm, I see what you mean.'

The sisters waited the two months as suggested by the doctor. But not having received any news they arranged yet another meeting.

This time, though, they were stuck with the Southern American drawler who sat them both down in the office, while she proceeded to look for Sammy's notes.

'Arrrr, yess... Here ... Weee ... arrre. Let ... meee ... see ... emmmm... It says here ... in answer to Samuel's recent assessment … we do not feel Mr Clayton is up to the requirements set out for our programme.'

'Yet another waste of time!' Jill groaned as they left the office despondent again. 'But the doctor must have thought he was good enough to have even written the letter in the first place,' Jill continued, outside. 'When will Sammy get his break Elaine? It's always bad news!'

'Well we've done all we can, Jill. I don't think we could've tried any harder, I really do feel we should just give up. We seem to be getting nowhere as usual.'

Jill nodded in agreement. 'Bit it's not fair on poor Sammy and that cow is getting away with everything! She should be the one in here trying to help him, not us.'

'It will all come back to haunt her Jill, don't worry.'

A year had long passed and Sammy was now a permanent resident in the home. During this time though, Elaine had decided to spend more time abroad with her son, which was always her intention after splitting from her husband a while back now. And as Jill still lived some distance from the home and was finding it hard to visit so often, this became a problem when trying to keep an eye on Sammy. But what could they do?

So life went on as best it could for the sisters and their brother. At least they knew Sammy was being well cared for now, even though the home lacked proper stimulation.

On Elaine's visits back to England though, she always looked forward to seeing her brother and was usually amazed by Sammy's good humour and sense of fun. Although his progress seemed slow still. But they always had a laugh and joke together whenever she saw him and normally end up giggling about silly things.

Sometimes though, he'd become confused when visiting and Elaine often had to explain who they were to each other but he always found this amusing. So every five minutes Sammy would ask the same question, as if it were a game. 'Who are you?' he'd say, which, he'd repeat again and again and normally in the same cheeky tone - while displaying a smile that was almost toothless these days.

These little name games would carry on for ages, but just lately whenever Jill got mentioned, he couldn't quite comprehend. It seemed somewhere along the line Sammy had muddled her up with Melissa, and he would insist Jill was his wife, who had died in a car accident, together with their daughter Kelly. At which point Sammy pretended to look sad, dropping his bottom lip. And although this was a crazy made up story of his, it was a story Sammy stuck to every time they played this name game. Which always amazed Elaine, given this was part of his short term memory.

'No, no,' Elaine would always correct him, 'Jill is your sister and Melissa's your wife. Your daughter's called Kelly and they're both still alive.'

He'd then accept Jill as his sister, but showed no sign of remembering or acknowledging his wife, or daughter, come to that, which she thought was very strange. And whenever Jill went to visit, he'd always remember that she was his sister.

Elaine often wondered about this made up story and could only surmise – if Jill had always looked out for Sammy, especially when young, perhaps he saw her more as a wife figure and someone who actually cared. Or maybe he just wanted to forget Melissa, inventing this made up story in order to wipe her from his mind and who could blame him for that.

But, if his memory was supposedly as bad as they said, especially his short term memory, then how did he always remember this recently made up story whenever they went to visit.

Perhaps this was his way of protecting his sanity. As although certified as brain damaged, it seemed he'd clearly found ways to cope. He was and is an amazing man, trapped in a prison of his own.

Chapter 36 – Life carries on

A few years had passed since Sammy entered the home and he was now what they called, 'institutionalised', which of course was understandable - becoming more like the people around him.

In spite of this, the sisters noticed he was starting to improve again; taking a keener interest in things in general and particularly the television placed in the lounge. The sisters would often find him listening to the news, or sometimes watching comedies. He particularly liked programmes on nature, and of course his beloved footie - and they saw this as a big step forward for their brother.

They had also noticed, his speech was improving too, although at first it sounded like gibberish. Which was probably due to a lack of communication, as his speech would quickly improve as they happily chatted away with him - becoming more fluid and certainly much clearer in what he had to say.

These were all good signs, the sister thought but they had been a long time coming. But at least he was back to the stage he'd reached before being sent home on that experimental visit that went wrong, almost five years ago now - a visit which clearly proved a disaster.

The sisters later discovered this improvement had mainly been due to a change in the management within the home. The owner had taken on a younger fresher group of people who it seemed, took a greater interest in their residents' and their progress. They took the time to talk to Sammy and his counterparts and it showed.

Just by helping to stimulate his mind, they had achieved many improvements, which pleased the sisters no end, as this was what they had hoped for, from the start. Think how much better he'd have been if this had happened sooner.

However, the doctors now insisted - due to the amount of time passed since his initial operation it was far too late for him to be given rehabilitation. They felt Sammy's brain had settled at a certain level and would therefore be difficult to kick-start again. But the sisters disagreed - as simply by monitoring his progress during their visit, they'd notice a quick improvement.

Fitting in with the others around him though, Sammy no longer ventured very far and still wouldn't participate in any trips out. But he'd made a couple of friends there and Sammy appeared happy to remain with them, safe in their little world.

One of his friends was a strange little man called Derek, who always stayed close to Sammy. He'd lived at the home far longer their brother – a weedy man who looked much older than Sammy, his beady eyes and bony body, tight and tense with nerves. And whenever Jill went to visit; Derek always made a bee line for her, which normally annoyed her, she said. As his persistent 'emmmmings as he looked her up and down, 'emmmm' as he crossed and uncrossed his legs, standing up, sitting down, constantly fidgeting, irritated her. As he was always looking for something, but what it was, no one ever knew. Yet he'd taken a liking to

Sammy, following him around wherever he went – which of course wasn't far.

His other friend Bob was a little plump man, around the same age as Sammy. He was new to the home and appeared like any other, although not dissimilar to the autistic character in the film 'Rain man' - with rosy glowing cheeks and a twinkle in his eye.

It seemed he too had become fond of their brother and often told the sisters and whoever else he felt should know, 'what a nice man Sammy was.'

Clearly embarrassed by his friend's compliments though, Sammy would only laugh, snorting out his protests, followed by a 'Nooooooo'.

Although Sammy's laughter at himself was equally matched by his laughter at others, as Elaine would often tell him just for a laugh that she called her husband, 'Mark the monkey'. To which Sammy quickly responded by making squeaky noises and funny monkey movements underneath his arms.

His childlike humour was endearing, which appeared to amuse them all and this made the sisters think - how could anyone be unkind to this sweet gentle man that he'd clearly become?

So it would appear, this strange trio of friends now represented life in the home for Sammy as they were often seen together passing the time of day. While probably watching others come and go, although sadly, not always back to their families. And no one really understood if these three realised the implications when others seemed to vanish. As how awful would that be if they did?

Yet no one knew for sure what life had in store for them, as who could have dreamt Sammy would end up in a place like this, at the young age he was. As far as the sisters were concerned, somewhere along the line a crime had been committed. After all, their brother had done nothing wrong but to love a certain woman too much. How cruel can life be.

Especially with that person punishing him further , by keeping his daughter away, even after he'd provided for her all her young life – it just didn't seem fair. And this woman, who he'd almost lost his life for had more or less abandoned him. How can that be?

It seemed this innocent man, of only sixty years of age now, had been swept under the carpet like the rest of them there - a square peg in a round hole with nowhere to go.

This was such a shame though, as the sisters had done all they could to help him. But sadly all their efforts had failed against the politics and bureaucracy involved in dealing with the various authorities, who ultimately had the power to decide their brother's fate.

In the meantime, Elaine was happy living abroad with her son but she still missed her visits to her brother, although Jill kept her up dated.

While she lived abroad, Elaine always looked forward to watching her favourite debate programme, aired from the UK each day. On one particular morning a topic came up that caught her interest. 'Have you ever killed someone in an accident?' This was referring mainly to car accidents but it was left open for the viewers to phone in with their own experiences.

355

The host of course treated the subject delicately, discussing the topic with strict sensitivity. Aware it could offend or even upset his audience.

So Elaine listened intently to the calls; always interested in others, eager to share their stories and points of view – when a man phoned in called Chris who worked on the Tube lines in London.

'I've worked for the underground for roughly five years,' he said sounding slightly nervous, 'and on one of my earlier trips out as a driver, a man jumped out in front of my train.'

Elaine realised straight away, this caller could possibly be connected to her brother's case, as the dates and circumstances given matched.

'There was nothing I could do...' he continued. 'I was so shocked. It really upset me. In fact I've never been the same since, suffering on and off with depression. I really do think this is a selfish act ... as it's certainly ruined my life. I will never be able to forget it'

The host was of course sympathetic, as the caller still sounded upset, although slightly angry.

Realising this man was more than likely the person who'd driven the train that hit her poor brother, Elaine wasn't happy by his conclusions. Firstly because her brother wasn't dead, so therefore he hadn't actually killed anyone and secondly, and more importantly, he didn't show any sympathy for his victim or their family. And Elaine had to wonder if this was because people could only see how things affected them in this me, me world we live in today.

Elaine also wondered why it was that it was never taken into account who or what drove these people to it, the story behind their troubles. After all it was an irrational act by a person not thinking rationally.

Of course, Elaine, also sympathised with the driver, as she realised things were never that simple and guessed we were all affected in different ways. And she then wondered how it would affect her, if a similar situation should happen. Yet she still marvelled at the chances of having heard this man call in on her favourite daily programme – oh the wonders of synchronicity.

It was only a week or two later, still in Spain; Elaine was about to take her dogs out for a run, and would normally drive them to an area not far from her home. A friend, who was visiting at the time offered to come a long and help her with the older dog, who was suffering with dementia.

So packing everyone into the car, Elaine placed her seat belt around her, knowing her friend who happened to be a Ship's Captain, would certainly insist. Although she didn't normally do so, as she wasn't travelling far.

Slowly pulling away from her driveway she turned onto the main road. Still in second gear and going into third, Elaine suddenly noticed a car turning the blind bend up a head and speeding towards her.

Not panicking just yet, expecting the car to straighten up, Elaine pointed out to her friend, 'Look at that car in front of us … it's on our side of the road!'

The next thing she remembered her friend was waking her up, having been knocked unconscious. Her head resting against the air bag, which blew out on impact, Elaine felt lucky to be alive. While the dogs still safe in the back, looked extremely unhappy, no doubt shaken by the sudden collision and probably not getting their walk.

Her friend, who'd been trained for such emergencies, ran up to the blind bend up ahead to stop further traffic from driving into the carnage they couldn't yet see.

While a young woman, who happened to be a nurse, staying in one of the villas close by, ran over to the wreckage, concerned. She told Elaine later, when she saw her body slumped against the wheel she thought she was dead.

But thankfully, still very much alive - unfortunately the young man, who'd lost control of his car, had sadly lost his life. He hadn't been wearing his seatbelt.

Pulling herself together, Elaine discovered she was virtually unharmed, with only a few bruises to contend with, as she waited for the ambulance to arrive.

In shock though, Elaine thought about the programme she'd recently watched, where they had discussed such situations. Baffled by the strange coincidence, Elaine wondered again in amazement at yet another weird synchronicity.

But what did this all mean she wondered? Had she actually asked for this? After all, she'd now got her answer. And rather than feeling sorry for her-self as many might have done, Elaine could only feel sadness for the man who'd lost his life, and his grieving family. How could she be angry?

Elaine also realised she had been protected in many ways that day, which she also found comforting. As not only had she been travelling with a Captain, trained for such events, when normally travelling alone. She'd also put her seat belt on, when often she wouldn't, especially for such a short journey. What more could she have asked for but a nurse who came to her aid - who just happened to be on holiday in a villa close by. Furthermore, the emergency services were brilliant, taking her straight to hospital where she was completely checked out. She certainly had her guardian angel looking after her that day.

Chapter 37 - Laughter in the home.

Now that Sammy had started to improve again, whenever the sisters went to visit, conversations were far more interesting – now able to talk about other things besides his beloved football.

Although, when they reminisced about their childhoods together, Elaine would often remember the funny arguments he and their father had when he would tease Sammy about his team.

So with a cheeky smile Elaine would often ask her brother, 'So, who are your favourite football team?' knowing full well what his answer would be - teasing him like their father had.

But to her surprise, on one occasion, he didn't answer as she thought he would – and told her it was Chelsea instead, which was the team their father supported. And with Sammy looking so much like him these days and even sounding like him too, Elaine had to wonder - was it her father sitting there now - had he come back to help him live through this nightmare - as that wouldn't surprise her at all.

Putting these strange thoughts aside, Elaine happily corrected her brother. Telling him, 'I thought it was Man United,' to which Sammy eagerly agreed.

Pleased that things were improving, unfortunately they'd reached that stage again where conversations with Sammy wouldn't last too long before the pleading started up –

asking the sisters to take him home once more. They thought he'd given up on this request some years ago but ever since this improved state, it started again, to their horror.

This as usual upset them, and one day Elaine explained light-heartedly - he wouldn't be as well looked after at her place as he was in this home and neither would the food be as good or the cleaning so pristine.

Elaine even suggested, she might like to move there herself, although just for a few days she said. Which made Sammy laugh, replying, 'Yeah - that would be good Elaine.'

Fed up though with these requests to go home, Elaine asked, 'so what would you do all-day Sammy if you came back home with me?'

To which he replied, and with a serious face, 'Sod all, as usual.'

Elaine roared with laughter, surprised by his quick response. While thinking, he still had a good sense of humour.

Unfortunately though, it wouldn't be long before the pleading would start again, 'Home, home, home with you, home' he just kept repeating. Elaine, now exasperated by this constant request, then told him - he sounded like ET, and pointed her finger towards the ceiling, crying 'Home'.

Sammy laughed, obviously amused, but this still didn't stop the pleading.

'I told you Sammy, now what did I say?'

'Sod all,' he said again, and she laughed even harder this time, even though she knew she shouldn't.

Over time, Elaine often found herself in cahoots with her brother, just like mischievous children and they'd often end up laughing about the people around them, but always in good taste. And sometimes out of devilment she'd ask him, if he had a girlfriend at the home. But clearly shocked at such a thought, his eyes wide with amazement, he'd quickly protest, expressing his indifference - supported by a 'nooooo.'

Well, at least he wasn't saying he was married anymore, which was interesting.

On another occasion when visiting her brother, an elderly woman in a long grey tweed skirt and brogues, her hair pulled back in a neat tidy bun, leaped across the room in front of them singing a song.

'I'm lazy; I'm crazy, look at me.' She sung.

Elaine now amused, looked at her brother and quietly laughed.

'She's very nice,' Sammy whispered, placing his finger up to his lips, 'but she's very ugly,' and then he pulled a funny face.

Elaine laughed again, not sure she should and said to the strange woman, now staring at them both. 'Sammy has his eyes closed so he can't look at you,' to which Sammy promptly closed them, realising he should.

The strange woman paused for a moment, deep in thought. And then replied, 'Very sensible,' and she leapt back out the room.

Elaine felt she'd become part of a scene from 'One flew over the cuckoo's nest' and found this quite amusing. Especially when on that very same visit, an elderly gentleman came into the room, dragging behind him, by her hand, a sweet little old lady, seemingly unaware of their actions. To find only minutes later, after leaving the room with the bemused looking lady, the man had come back again, dragging yet another victim behind him – while mumbling incoherently in her ear.

'Sammy!' Elaine exclaimed, surprised at such goings on, 'he's got another woman in tow, what is he up to?'

Sammy burst out laughing, as did she, pleased to be sharing this insane world he lived in with him. Yet, although amused, Elaine's heart went out to them all - the residents, the carers and the families left helpless, their dilemmas all very sad.

'Home, home, come on, let's go home,' Sammy started up again, grabbing her hand to go. Exasperated, Elaine looked at Sammy in despair - what else could she say to stop this.

'Home, home, come on, let me go home, go home with you and Adam to your home.' Elaine was dumb-struck. Adam was her first husband and she hadn't even mentioned him on this particular visit. Although he had been into see Sammy a little while back, as she knew he felt sorry for him. But Elaine was amazed her brother had remembered. And it made her wonder, why Sammy still couldn't remember his wife.

Elaine, who had been separated from her husband Mark for some time now, would often discuss Sammy's situation with Adam. After all he was in Elaine's life at the time Sammy's troubles first started - when Melissa had flirted with his friends on their wedding day. And not forgetting the Christmas day when she passed them both on the stairs, without a word of greeting. They knew then she was going

363

to be trouble but they never guessed things would end up like this.

'He needs a nice woman,' Adam once said. 'Someone who would be happy to take care of him'

'Yeah,' Elaine replied, 'A nice Filipino lady, or a Thai lady maybe. Perhaps we could order him one,' and she laughed.

'If he could get a divorce from that cow, I'm sure with his money, he would have no problems finding someone nice to help him get better.'

Elaine smiled as she thought about her brother. 'Yes, that would be good, but that's not going to happen in a million years. Melissa would never divorce him now. She would lose half his pension and half the house.'

One day, keeping Sammy well off the subject of wanting to go home, Elaine asked, mischievously, 'So … who is your best friend in here Sammy? Is it the man with the two women he keeps pulling around? He seems very nice.'

'Nooooo.' Sammy said, looking confused, obviously trying to remember. And to her surprise, after much deliberation, Sammy then stated, 'No. Larry's my best friend.'

Elaine was taken completely unawares, 'Oh that's nice Sammy shall I tell him that? He'll be so pleased.'

But Sammy replied, 'No. It's all in the past now … it's all history,' and a sad look appeared in his eyes.

Elaine was flabbergasted; shocked by his answer. His memory was definitely better than anyone thought. But not being qualified in this area, how would she really know if this was good; although she guessed he was doing much better than they cared to admit. And he'd definitely benefit from expert help.

But as this had never been forthcoming, Sammy appeared to accept his fate and that his life had changed for good. This was his destiny. His only chance of escape was through his sisters and as Sammy started the pleading again, Elaine thought, who could really blame him? Only if he truly understood what was happening around him, as the sisters suspected he did, it must've been difficult coming to terms with his terrible situation.

The sisters had always known, this wasn't the right place for their brother and they also knew many others felt the same. As over time different people had openly remarked, 'Sammy should be somewhere different receiving better help,' but alas it was never the right people.

On one of Jill's later visits to the home, a volunteer helper told her, 'I often come to talk to the residents here. I try to amuse them in some way, making their lives a little more bearable.'

Jill smiled but didn't comment.

'Is Sammy your brother?' the lady then asked.

'Yes,' Jill replied cautiously.

'I hope you don't mind but I've been reading your brothers' notes … it's very sad what's happened to him,' and she looked at Jill knowingly, as if sharing a secret.

Jill was surprised however, that this stranger had been allowed to know more about her brother and his medical history than she'd ever been permitted. It just didn't seem right and it was very upsetting for Jill.

'Yes, it is very sad,' she said, begrudgingly, not knowing if this woman who'd openly admitted she'd read his notes, had read the correct version, or the version Sammy's wife had offered them. And she didn't feel inclined to discuss it. After all she didn't want everything raked up again and she certainly didn't want to listen to any sympathy, other than for her brother, as she suspected there might be.

On one of Elaine's later visits, she was confronted by a new senior carer, working at the home, who told her he'd taken a particular interest in Sammy. This made a nice change she thought - they approaching her about her brother.

The carer, a pleasant man, with oriental features and a well-defined face looked at Elaine knowingly. 'Are you Sammy's sister?' the man enquired.

Elaine nodded curiously, wondering why he'd asked.

'Your brother, he very well liked here you know? We all have soft spot for him, although I know we shouldn't have favourites, but he is very funny man, he make us all laugh.'

Elaine nodded. A smile on her face now, as she looked cautiously at this enquiring man, 'Yes, he is a lovely man,' she agreed.

'His wife, she rarely comes to visit.' He probed.

'Does she not?' she said standoffish. She'd aired her views in the past, regarding Melissa and she like her sister certainly didn't want them brought up again.

'No,' he continued, 'she too busy.'

Elaine smiled in amusement but didn't respond.

'She's a hairdresser she tell me and her daughter an air stewardess for B.A. Her mother, she say, she travels lots, she doesn't have time to visit her father,' and he looked at

Elaine curiously, a crinkled concern on his forehead, as he waited her reply.

But Elaine didn't feel inclined to answer, although eventually she did. 'I don't think that's quite true, do you?' not wanting to stir things up again.

'No, I not think so... I understand she may have psychological problems,' which sounded like a question. He clearly wanted confirmation.

Elaine just responded with a smile though. But she could see he understood her. Which made her wonder how this man had managed to suss her out so quickly, yet social services had supposedly not, still allowing her to make decisions on her husband's life. This can't be right?

Troubled still by Sammy's situation it seemed, the carer insisted he would keep an eye on her brother while he worked there. But he too disappeared soon after.

It certainly appeared, they were finally realising Melissa was not the dutiful wife she'd tried to portray and was probably now aware of her obvious lack of commitment. Yet this had been a long time coming.

It seemed hopping for Sammy's clothes were also left for the staff to sort out these days, the staff told the sisters. Especially now they realised Melisa's visits were few and far between. But as her willingness to part with cash for things like clothing, it must have been difficult to collect the money. Although going by her past record, it was probably best she wasn't involved in his wardrobe choice, as the sisters had been fed up with him looking like a scarecrow. And with an almost toothless smile as well these days, it was obvious she didn't spend money on dentistry.

Although it would certainly be interesting to see how he coped with dentures in the future. As coping with only a few teeth had been bad enough apparently, having almost chocked to death on several occasions, unable to chew his food.

In fact, one Christmas day, the home actually had to send him to hospital after choking on his dinner. The sisters never found out about this until many months after, which of course annoyed them both.

Yet even with all these problems, Melissa still didn't feel inclined to sort his teeth out. Even though she was still living quite comfortably on his LEB pension of £250 per week - and clearly determined not to spend it on her husband.

Sammy had lived at the home now for almost seven years and thankfully appeared much happier these days. Although sometimes they still found him distant and often wondered what he was thinking. On one particular day when in one of these quieter moods, a new Carer at the home approached Elaine, while she sat beside Sammy trying to make conversation. He was a foreign looking gentleman, who seemed very pleasant but was insistent on conversing with her.

'Hi, my name's Maraud,' he said warmly, exposing a huge toothy smile. 'I just wanted to say what a lovely man your brother is,' and he nodded in Sammy's direction.

'That's nice of you to say.' Elaine replied lost for words, especially as Sammy wasn't responding. 'Yes, he can be lovely at times,' and she turned towards her brother smiling. But Sammy was still unresponsive.

'He sometimes has problems in the middle of the night,' Maurad continued. 'This is often when he needs to go to the toilet…only I have to help him, like I do the others. It's my job after all. But he doesn't stop apologising for having to disturb me and of course I tell him, that's what I'm here for Sam.'

Elaine smiled, not sure what to say.

'I know I get paid for doing this job,' he said, 'but when your lovely brother tells me I'm such a good man, it makes me feel this job is all worthwhile. And that means a lot to me.'

Maurad smiled again, leaning over and grabbing her brother's hand. But Sammy appeared oblivious to his actions and what he'd said, although he smiled back nonetheless.

'Yes that is nice,' Elaine replied, laughing to herself, only her brother had told her the very same thing and it did make you feel good, appreciated by someone in this sometimes ungrateful world.

A month or so after this incident, Elaine went back to see her brother but took a friend with her this time, who Sammy had never met before. It was always better if there were two or more visitors as it was easier to have a laugh and Sammy liked to laugh - and he also liked her friend it seemed. As when they ventured upstairs to his bedroom, on the pretext of showing her, his nice cosy room, Sammy automatically climbed into bed and waited for the friend to join him - a twinkle in his eye now. Her friend laughed.

On another visit with the same friend, just after her brother's birthday, who at this time was sixty two, they discovered Melissa hadn't been into see him at all. Although Elaine believed he hadn't missed the obligatory balloon. In fact he appeared in good form, and wouldn't stop talking, especially to her friend, but never about his wife.

Yet when pushed to do so, he would still insist his wife was called Jill, who had died in an accident. Elaine couldn't understand why he persisted with this made up story and from some time ago now. And this made her wonder if Melissa may have told him a version of this story herself? As that wouldn't surprise her at all, hoping perhaps she wouldn't exist in his mind anymore. Confuse him.

'No, no,' Elaine insisted, 'Jill's not your wife, she's your sister and so am I. Your wife's called Melissa and she's still alive.'

On that note her friend then showed Sammy 'the elbow gesture' followed by a strange disgruntled noise, which made them all laugh. Realising this amused him; they continued to repeat this game, again and again whenever he insisted Jill was his wife or at the mere mention of Melissa's name. By the look on Sammy's face he knew the connotations and what was suggested. He was definitely not stupid and very much aware.

Still laughing at their silly game, Elaine ran upstairs to Sammy's bedroom wanting to place his birthday present on his bed. When she noticed a new photograph sat on his mantelpiece. Elaine put on her glasses to have a closer look - not recognising the person in the picture. On further inspection, it turned out to be a picture of a pretty young lady dressed in a smart stewardess's uniform with a large beaming smile. Elaine chuckled to herself as she thought surely not. Was Melissa trying to make out this was Kelly? Elaine had already heard she was huge these days and knew you had to be over twenty one to join B.A anyway, which Kelly, was definitely not.

Who was she trying to fool? Was this for the benefit of the staff to substantiate her lies and explain her daughter's absence? This was amusing but worrying.

Wanting to share, Elaine called her friend up to have a look, who immediately took the back off the frame, only to expose a magazine cut out, placed there to mislead.

'See what she's like,' Elaine said to her friend who didn't really know Melissa, although she had a good idea it seemed. 'She's a scheming cow. You never know what she's planning next. It's all those bloody television programmes she watches. She lives in some sort of fantasy world, always has done.'

Elaine was seriously troubled, as Melissa might be capable of anything knowing the stunts she'd pulled already and that's just going by her past record. In desperation who knew what she could do? As Elaine was sure Melissa would be tired of her present situation by now, keen to move on with her life no doubt.

'The problem is … if you say she's not signing in at reception, she could come in and do anything to your brother and no one would know she's even been here … unaware of her presence!' her friend was clearly concerned for this lovely man she'd only recently met.

'Well, my brother-in-law has already told them about her not signing in,' Elaine said annoyed. 'He's pointed this out on several occasions. Do you think I should say something?'

'Well, I would. At least then if something should happen, god forbid, you've done all you can to prevent it.'

Agreeing with her friend, Elaine went to look for the senior carer working on shift that day. Finally catching up with a young Chinese girl who said she was in charge, the ladies tried to explain the presence of the photograph in Sammy's room. Stating, it was definitely not of his daughter, while expressing their concerns at the deceit.

'Oh, dear, that often happens I'm afraid' she said. 'Their photos get muddled up at times and end up in the wrong rooms. Just like the residents do sometimes - they get confused and end up in the wrong beds too,' and she smiled in amusement.

'No, no, you don't understand,' Elaine protested. 'His wife's trying to make out the photo is of their daughter. She's told your staff the daughter's too busy to visit because she's an air stewardess. That is in fact a lie.'

'Oh I see. That's not nice, having a strange photo sitting there.'

Elaine looked at her friend exasperated; had she grasped her meaning?

'This is the sort of person she is I'm afraid. I do feel she should sign in the book like we all do, after all, who knows what could happen.' Elaine tried to emphasise her last point, hoping this apparently naive woman would eventually understand.

'Yes I see what you mean. … I will talk to her next time she's here, please rest assured we always know when Sammy's wife comes to visit… we always make a note.'

Elaine wasn't so sure about that though. Still she had told them her concerns and she felt a lot happier, although she wasn't convinced anything would be done, but at least Melissa will know they were still on her case. That's of course, if they even bother to tell her.

Chapter 38 - Forgotten

Over time it became obvious Sammy had started to vegetate in the home, as nothing they talked about lately ever appeared to encourage him. It seemed he had lost all hope and each day was just like another. The sisters despaired but would could they do, nothing they did helped. They could only hope he was happy in his own little world and at least no longer in danger.

But the sisters had hoped others might be visiting him more often, yet it didn't look that way- forgotten by many already no doubt.

Still in touch with friends from Sammy's neighbourhood, Elaine occasionally received reports on Melissa's fleeting appearances in the area. As she was still seen doing her usual walk along to the shops apparently. Although these friends had pointed out, the shopping trolley had been exchanged just recently for a suitcase on wheels.

Her daughter though, was not seen so often, apparently still massive by all accounts and looking more like a man than ever before. And it made the sisters wonder what may be happening with her. As this strange duet not considered unusual by social services, were still seen on occasions, openly displaying their affections - while Sammy remained trapped in the home. It just wasn't fair.

Sometimes when Elaine went to visit her friends in the area, she'd drive past her brother's old house out of curiosity. And often noted it looked in need of repair, the front garden now full of weeds. And it certainly didn't look lived in, the curtains always closed.

On another evening, when driving by her brother's house, Elaine noticed a brand new van parked right outside, advertising a new electrical firm. Someone had recently set themselves up it seemed and Elaine had to wonder who that was. Had someone come into some money?

Out of curiosity though, Elaine wrote down the number advertised on the side of the van, intending to call it later but of course she never did. What was the point? Even if she did have evidence of collusion, what difference would it make? The sisters had never been listened to before, why would they now.

Ringing Jill later to discuss her find, she too felt it served no purpose; although it did make them wonder what could be happening between them. And finding themselves back on the subject of Sammy, they soon found themselves reminiscing again - mulling over old stories that ultimately led to their brother's incarceration.

'You know what Jill, this would make a bloody good book ... although would anyone ever believe us?'

'Well, no one has before, why would they now?' Jill replied.

'True,' but then the idea had been implanted.

Another story got back to the sisters, involving the neighbours who backed onto their brother's garden - a nice couple, who'd lived there longer than Sammy, and had always got on with him. But recently they'd decided to pull down the very large shed at the bottom of their garden, which hid them from view.

In the past they often chatted with Sammy when he worked above the shed, cutting back the overhanging branches. Yet they'd never spoken to Melissa before, given she never ventured out in the garden much.

The two gardens now exposed appeared one day two ladies trying to cut back their overgrown lawn.

'Hello, are you Melissa?' The neighbour's husband shouted as he tried to fix his fence. Although he'd asked this same question, years before – when he too had been trying to cut back the overhanging branches, a job once left for Sammy. But the woman had denied it and said, 'I've only recently moved here and I don't know who Melissa is.'

This time, however, the woman with the bright red hair said, 'No, I'm not Melissa, but we rent from her and have done for nearly five years.'

The wife, of the man enquiring, who happened to also be a friend of Elaine's, already had a description of Melissa, and was sure these two women were her and her daughter. So in order to confirm her suspicions, she rang another neighbour who lived close by. She said she'd come and check, as this friend definitely knew what Melissa looked like and came straightaway.

'Yes, yes, that's her and her daughter,' she confirmed, nonplussed by her denial.

'Well, she's saying she's not and that she's renting the place from Melissa.'

'I wonder why? Perhaps she's trying to pull some sort of scam. She's very strange, isn't she? In fact, Elaine thinks she's got mental problems,' and they laughed as they peeped at them through the net curtains, while Melissa strutted her stuff, trying to cut back the long grass that clearly hadn't been touched in ages.

'How long do you think she'll be doing that for?' the neighbour, asked her friend.

'As long as it takes your husband to finish off fixing that fence, she definitely hasn't changed,' she grinned.

When this story got back to Elaine, she thought perhaps, Melissa hadn't wanted to talk about her previous life, although she'd probably forgotten already, together with Sammy she guessed. But she still had to wonder where her 'rock' was. After all why wasn't he cutting the grass?

Elaine's thoughts then turned to the rose bush, which hopefully still stood amongst the overgrowth at the back of the house. And of course she immediately thought of her mother, wondering what on earth she would make of it all. As she was sure only her mother would know the real truth still.

On one of her more recent visits to see her brother, Elaine found him yet again, deep in thought; his face long and distant. Not knowing what to talk about in order to cheer him up, Elaine pulled from her handbag an old family photograph that she often carried about. She gave it to Sammy to look at. Gazing at the photo, he clearly recognised his sisters as young girls and immediately started to laugh. But when Elaine pointed out he was standing in the background; he became distant and thoughtful once more.

Trying to cheer him up again, Elaine started to sing a song. But not blessed with a wonderful voice, she didn't have to try too hard to make him laugh. And so struggling pathetically with the words to 'Danny Boy' but replacing Danny with Sammy, he finished off the song quite easily.

'And I thought you were the one with a memory problem,' she said laughing herself, and pleased he was cheerful again. But scratching her head for something else to amuse him she suddenly remembered the little blue angel she also carried in her bag.

Showing it to her brother, Sammy keenly eyed the pretty object, while she explained; she kept it for her protection.

'Would you like to touch my angel, Sammy?' she asked, as she held it out to him.

'Yeah,' he replied, as the shiny transparent glass of the ornament reflected in his eyes and another idea came to her, as she passed it over to him.

'Why don't you make a wish Sammy,' she said, wondering what he'd say.

Yet without hesitation, Sammy closed his eyes as he thought about his wish - holding tightly onto the angel.

He stayed like this for a while before he slowly opened his eyes again, and Elaine saw her brother as the young man she once knew and loved, innocent and free of worries. Where had he been all this time?

'What did you wish for, Sammy?' she asked, having no idea what he'd say.

And to her surprise, he said, 'Good health,' as he passed her back the angel.

Elaine couldn't believe his reply and with tears in her eyes, she placed the little angel back safely in her bag and ran up stairs to his bedroom. She was speechless, only she'd often wondered if he might have wished he was dead. Poor Sammy, when would it be his turn for good news?

Checking Sammy's room - making sure things were just as they should be. Elaine found the room as usual, clean, neat and tidy with 'Bruce' the toy rabbit placed on the bed, which all looked warm and cosy. Nothing appeared to have changed, his wardrobe still full of clothing, most of which hadn't been worn.

So all seemed well in Sammy's word, until she noticed it sitting by his bedside - the picture she had told them about, warned them about in fact, laying there face down next to the picture of mum and dad.

At this point Elaine wanted to scream. What else could they do to him? Would they only listen, when it's too late?

But still, if Sammy thought the picture was of his daughter, in her smart airline uniform, what harm could it possibly do? Perhaps it was nice for him to think his daughter was doing well, even if she didn't come to visit.

It was difficult to know what was best for Sammy these days and so they would still occasionally push for rehab but that seemed well off the agenda now. Even though Elaine thought the new staff working there might have been interested, given they were keen to help their residents improve.

So one day she decided to take in the recording of her brother from years ago - trying to prove to them, how much better he'd once been. But they still wouldn't take it further, although the doctor did admit how coherent he was at that time. But it seemed nothing would convince them to help him further.

The recording was considered insufficient and the sisters were dismissed as usual but then it was probably too late to help their brother anyway. He was too institutionalised now, just like the rest of them there. And Elaine left the home that day, wondering what on earth would become of her brother, left in that home to do what? They could only hope he remained safe in his own little bubble, protected from everyone else.

Yet, although not the real world, neither was the world he found himself in for many years before it seemed. And all Elaine could do now was shake her head in disbelief at the sad way his life had turned out.

Poor Sammy still ensconced in his prison today - although thankfully hidden and more importantly, protected from the cruel uncaring world outside. A world that had treated him badly and a society that didn't seem to care – now pushed to one side to grow old alone and to vegetate amongst the many ...   they quickly began to realise, their poor unfortunate brother, was SOON to be FORGOTTEN by many.

This was to be the last chapter of this book but sadly Sammy unexpectedly died exactly one week after these last words were written. Please read on.

Chapter 39 - Sudden death.

The helicopter hovered over-head as it came into land, its frantic whirling sounds causing havoc on the ground. Mr Chigwell who had been working in the garden that afternoon ran over to the large propelling machine, baffled by its presence - its turbulence forcing him backwards as it came to a halt.

'Paramedics!' the man shouted out, trying to be heard over the groans of the propeller's, now slowing down. 'You have a patient … just suffered a heart attack?'

Mr Chigwell looked confused.

'It's Sammy, Mr Chigwell,' a carer close by shouted. 'We called the ambulance out … he didn't look good,' and she asked them to hurry. But Mr Chigwell was shocked. Sammy was fine that morning, what had happened since?

Pulling himself together he quickly shouted back 'Yes, first floor,' and he pointed to Sammy's window. 'This lady will show you the way'.

The men ran off in the direction indicated, stretcher in hand as they followed the rotund woman who was struggling to lead the way – the unexpected drama disrupting the sombre atmosphere in the home.

On reaching Sammy's room, the shocked and bewildered onlookers quickly stepped aside

'Is he dead?' a carer dared to ask.

But the paramedics ignored her, as they immediately felt for their victim's pulse; only a pasty look had already spread across Sammy's face. Mr Chigwell, having followed the men to the room, looked on, gobsmacked still.

'He's barely alive,' the medic said, quietly to his partner. 'Let's get him out of here quick!'

Leaving fairly swiftly, they left their astonished audience behind, still watching in silence as they carried him away, no doubt hoping they weren't too late to save this poor man's life.

It wasn't long after the helicopter took off that the police arrived in full force, much to everyone's amazement. And while official statements were taken, Sammy's room was cordoned off. Mr Chigwell said he'd never witnessed or experienced anything like this before. Not in this home or anywhere else and was baffled.

'Have you managed to get hold of his wife yet, Mr Chigwell?' said a serious looking policeman stood in his office later.

'No, she's not answering her phone I'm afraid. We've been trying her land line number, every five minutes, as her mobile appears to be switched off - we've sent several text messages asking her to call. Hopefully, when she reads them, she'll ring straight back... let's hope that's sooner than later.' Mr Chigwell looked harassed and opened the window to let in some air.

'Perhaps we should send an officer round to the house,' the policeman suggested. 'But, I suppose she could be away? Mind you if she was, surely she'd let you know?'

'Well, not necessarily,' he muttered lowering his eyes, knowing full well she'd never report her whereabouts to him; she could never understand why she had to. 'Do you think we should inform his older sister?' Mr Chigwell asked, concerned Sammy may die with no-one at his side.

'No, we shouldn't really, not until we've contacted his wife.'

'Oh that's a shame ... so do we know how Sammy's doing?' he asked wiping his forehead with a clean hanky, hoping there wasn't bad news.

'No we don't I'm afraid. I will chase that up now,' and picking up his radio phone the policeman contacted his station.

Two days later; a call was finally received from Melissa, unflustered by the urgency of their texts it seemed. Maybe she had expected some minor mishap, or just perhaps the news she should have, all those years ago. After all, this had been a long time coming, what difference would a few days make?

'Mrs Clayton...at last,' Mr Chigwell stuttered, as he struggled to tell her the news - as even though a regular occurrence in his field of employment; it never got any easier especially when concerning someone he particularly liked. 'We've been trying to get hold of you for ages, I'm afraid we have some sad news... I'm sorry to tell you ... but Sammy passed away on Friday, late afternoon. We think he may have suffered a heart attack whilst in the shower.'

Melissa never said a word.

'We're very sorry for your loss, Mrs Clayton.'

But Melissa remained silent, no doubt taking stock of his words, so Mr Chigwell carried on regardless,

'Unfortunately he died on the way to the hospital. I know they did all they could to save him... anyway, the police are investigating it now. Hopefully we'll be able to tell you more, later, especially after the post mortem's been done. Are you still there, Mrs Clayton?' now worried by her silence.

'Yes, yes, that's terrible,' she replied. 'You said the police are investigating – why is that?'

'I'm not sure Mrs Clayton. I know they've spoken to all the staff here and I understand they may want to talk to you too.'

'But why ... I wasn't there!'

'I have no idea. I'm sure it's normal procedure. I can only say once again how sorry we all are. He will be sorely missed by us all.'

Melissa mumbled her acceptances and sounded keen to get off the phone.

'Would you like us to inform Sammy's older sister, Mrs Clayton? She doesn't know yet.'

'Yes, you'd better,' she clearly didn't want the inconvenience.

'It will also be necessary for you to come in and collect his things later, once the police are finished that is. At the moment no-one is allowed in his room.'

Mr Chigwell, now eager to get off the phone himself, promised to keep her informed and immediately rang Sammy's sister, Jill, knowing she'd certainly be upset by this news. The news she couldn't be told about earlier, which all seemed so ridiculous to him.

Later that afternoon Jill arrived home from shopping to be told by her husband that Mr Chigwell had rung to give them the sad news regarding Sammy's sudden death.

Jill was of course shocked but wondered why this all sounded familiar, like a dream repeating itself? Hadn't she been down this path before?

'I'm afraid he died on Friday, on his way to the hospital,' her husband placed his arm around her and gave her a hug. She cried.

It had been almost eight years to the day she'd heard those very same words. But was it for real this time? Or would she find out later he was still alive, and her head began to whirl with the shock of it all while she tried to comprehend the unexpected news.

Friday, she thought. All this time and she hadn't known. How could this be? Holding her hands up to her head, she thought of her poor brother, he was only sixty two, how could this have happened?

Once calming down, Jill rang her sister in Spain, clearly reluctant to give her the news.

Shocked at first, Elaine said she felt only numbness as the terrible news sunk in. 'Those words 'Sammy is dead,' we had heard them before I know but is his time now finally over? Jill didn't know what to say.

'How ... why?' Elaine was confused. 'He was fine the last time I saw him - well, nothing life threatening that was!' And she like her sister couldn't comprehend. Although she thought his death had been timely she told Jill , and said, she marvelled at the fact it had only been a week since she'd written the last words in the book she'd at last decided to write. 'Perhaps he has given me a final ending? '

It was also Elaine's birthday the following week and that made it exactly eight years to the day that Sammy's nightmare really started.

'My God, Jill, I can't believe it … it's so sad… but I'm not being horrible; it's probably a blessing in disguise,' and Jill had to agree.

'Yes, I think it's the best thing that could have happened; poor Sammy, at last he finally got his break,' Jill groaned. 'After all he didn't really have a life? He could have been in that home for another twenty years, just vegetating there; a prisoner in his own mind with no-one really caring, except you and I of course.'

And Elaine too agreed as she appeared to reflect over the awful life he had led.

Elaine made her arrangements to fly over to England later that week and was keen to know the details of her brother's funeral. Jill said she would find out, even if it did mean contacting Melissa again. It needed to be done and Jill was just pleased Elaine could make it over - Melissa though would be very surprised to see her at the funeral.

Later that evening, sipping at a much needed glass of wine, Jill had to wonder why the police had got so involved in her brother's death and why Melissa just happened to disappear that particular weekend – and not forgetting his post-mortem. Was this all normal?

But as Jill tried to get her head around the strange turn of events, the phone beside her suddenly rang making her jump. Jill picked it up quickly, not expecting it to be Melissa.

'Hello, Jill,' she said sweetly on the other end. 'I expect you've heard the news by now?'

Jill recognised her voice immediately 'Yes, it's very sad,' she said, as she struggled to even be civil to this woman now. Although she knew she had to, in order to find out what was happening with Sammy's send off.

'They couldn't get hold of me that weekend,' she stated, 'only Kelly and I were in Scotland, staying with my sister. She lives there now you see. I've been so busy lately, it's been hard to find the time to visit Sammy, but I went to see him the Saturday before. Because you know I'm a mobile hairdresser now.'

Jill smiled as she thought of the suitcase on wheels that she'd been seen about with lately and thought perhaps she used this for her hairdressing, given she didn't drive. But then of course, was any of it true.

'Because you know Kelly's pregnant now?' she suddenly announced.

'Really,' Jill said secretly amused, guessing it was probably yet another of her lies.

'The father is Scottish and she's expecting twins; over seven months she is.' And she then twittered on about babies, much to Jill's annoyance.

Here we go again, she thought, not once had she mentioned the sad loss of her husband. And Jill's head began to spin again with the twaddle she had no option but to listen to.

'It's funny you know, Jill... we had it all planned. Kelly and I were going to take the twins into see Sammy once they were born. We were going to place each one, on each of his knees and then take a photo of them all together. He would have liked that.'

As if she cared. This woman was sick. If Jill could have got hold of her there and then, she would have quite happily strangled her. After all this was ridiculous, Kelly had never been anywhere near her father the whole time he was in the home and Jill doubted she'd visit with babies in tow. That's if she was even pregnant.

Jill made a few noises of encouragement just to push her along as Melissa appeared on a roll - wanting to spill the beans. She was definitely happy about something. You wouldn't have thought her husband had just died!

'Yes, it's all very exciting at the moment ... only Kelly's thinking of getting married in Scotland as well next year. We had hoped you and Sammy would have walked her down the aisle.'

Jill wanted to laugh. As if she wanted her involved in Kelly's wedding or Sammy come to that. She was unbelievable and doubted Kelly would ever get married anyway let alone have babies, considering how reclusive she had apparently become and butch.

Starting to lose her patience, Jill cut the conversation short, even though Melissa was still in full flow. 'Do we know what's happening about Sammy's funeral yet?'

'No... apparently the police want to interview me first, but I can't think why. I was nowhere near him, after all'.

'I think that's normal, Melissa. They did say they wanted to talk to me too - only they need a character profile on him it seems,' (although that never did happen).

'Apparently, they've cordoned off his room too.' Melissa said, all excited. 'I would love to go and see it, wouldn't you? See where it all happened.'

'No, not really,' Jill was convinced this woman was nuts.

'Because you know I lost my mother last month as well. It's been a very upsetting time for me.'

'So, what are you doing about Sammy's funeral?' Jill interrupted again, not wanting to talk about Melissa or her family. Suspecting they were lies anyway.

'I'm thinking of a burial.'

Jill was impressed. 'A burial? Who will be coming? Will that guy that Sammy worked with, be there?'

'Oh, that bastard!' she said.

'What do you mean, bastard?' Jill replied quickly, realising she'd dropped a clanger.

'No, no I didn't mean that… poor sod… yes… he died you know. Wham, bang, wallop, dropped down dead; died of a heart attack.'

Jill wanted to laugh. She'd clearly been caught out. But who had she been talking about, was it her rock, or John from the Aquarian shop, which incidentally had closed down a couple of years before. Still, whoever it was, they'd probably worked out by now - she wasn't right in the head.

Keen to get off the phone Melissa promised she'd keep her up dated, while Jill couldn't wait to tell her sister all the news.

Elaine was amazed by these unexpected revelations and thought it sounded like Melissa had been dumped and who could blame them. She also doubted that Kelly was pregnant and felt this maybe an excuse for her being so large - should she make an appearance at the funeral that is. Although Elaine also doubted it would even come to that and thought it more likely that it would be announced – Kelly had gone into labour that day, excusing her and her mother from attending the funeral. As Elaine was sure his funeral was the last place Melissa wanted to be or her daughter and was prepared to put a bet on that. Still, whatever, she was sure it was going to be an interesting day.

With the coroners not having yet issued their brother's death certificate, the sisters still didn't know when the funeral would take place. But not wanting to check with Melissa, Jill rang the home to see if they'd received any news.

'We understand it's going to be a cremation now,' Mr Chigwell said. 'Let me just check that … yes, that's right. She's booked it for Monday the 29th May, 9am, at Reigate Crematorium.

God, that's an early slot, Jill thought. The day after Elaine's birthday too, that's weird. And surprise, surprise a cremation after all.

Jill had also heard, the church Melissa had in mind for Sammy's burial, was in fact a Catholic one which Sammy was not – but she guessed this was yet another lie Couldn't she even get his religion right?

'Mind you the death certificate hasn't been issued yet' Mr Chigwell continued. 'So I don't know how she's managed to book it already.'

Jill didn't know either but thanked Mr Chigwell for his help, asking him to keep her informed - given Melissa hadn't even bothered to call her back. Although that was fine with as she didn't really want contact with her anymore, if she could help it. Only she didn't want her thinking she was gullible enough to believe all her lies and made up stories. And she promised herself she would put her straight in the end.

Elaine arrived in the U.K still upset by the news of her brother. Only on her arrival back she normally went to visit him. But decided to call in at the home anyway; wanting to express her gratitude to the people who'd cared for him for nearly seven years.

Driving into the now familiar grounds, Elaine marvelled at the beautiful scenery that surrounded this lovely elegant building. As she watched with interest, the wild baby rabbits hoping freely around in fields now scattered with buttercups. Under different circumstances this place would be idyllic but it surely wasn't appreciated by the residents there.

Sat opposite Mr Chigwell a short while later, having first spoken to Sammy's regular carers. Mr Chigwell expressed his regrets yet again - for the loss of her brother. And although originally startled by Sammy's sudden death he said, he'd now come to terms with what had happened. But he still didn't understand the police's involvement and was surprised by their enquiries. 'I have never before experienced such procedures in this home or any other and I still wonder why it was needed in your brother's case.'

Elaine too was flummoxed, although she did wonder if it may have been her doubts for his safety in the past that could have alerted them. Perhaps her warnings had triggered something off.

Mr Chigwell then went on to explain to Elaine what happened on the day of Sammy's death.

'Having demolished a large slice of cake with his afternoon tea,' he said, 'he then stole another from someone else's plate ... this wasn't unusual for Sammy, especially if he wasn't being watched,' he paused as he then moved some papers from the top of his desk and placed them in his draw below, before he continued. 'After gobbling down both slices, it seemed he'd made a terrible mess - having only a few teeth left to chew with now. So his carer suggested he took an early shower, and with his mouth completely empty, he made his way up to his bedroom, keen to get cleaned up for bed.'

Elaine listened carefully, now thinking, Mr Chigwell's summary sounded well-rehearsed, ensuring they took no blame she guessed.

'It was while in the shower Sammy suddenly placed his hands up to his chest, indicating pain,' he said. 'While at the same time bringing up all the cake he'd just eaten. They now believe it may not have been a heart attack that killed him, but asphyxiation caused from the vomit. Either way, after their enquiries, it's not being considered suspicious.'

'So, why do you think the police were so involved?' Elaine asked.

'I have no idea.'

'So had his wife been into see him that day?' She dared to ask. 'Only she indicated to my sister she may have been.'

'No she hasn't been in for a while. We couldn't even get hold of her that day... in fact not until the Monday,' and he showed Elaine the texts, as if that proved anything.

Yet the fact they couldn't get hold of her for nearly three days, was enough to make Elaine even more suspicious, but, then again, she never did trust Melissa.

Elaine had always been worried something like this would happen, especially with Melissa not signing in the book when she entered. Still, if the police were investigating his death, surely they'd find out if anything untoward had happen - wouldn't they?

Elaine, now wanting to change the subject and talk about her brother personally, told Mr Chigwell, how on one of her last visits and conversations with him that he'd actually remembered Lawrence was his best friend. 'How marvellous was that?' she said.

But Mr Chigwell looked surprised by this and Elaine thought to herself; surely to god they knew just how capable Sammy was. But guessing that Melissa always told them - he didn't know who she was, as he always pretended not to, Mr Chigwell probably thought he didn't, although he should have known different by then.

Keen to clear away Sammy's things it seemed. Mr Chigwell asked Elaine if there was anything she wanted from his belongings that had already been placed in another room. Only to discover the items she'd asked for - a few of his photographs, which were originally hers anyway, had also been requested by Melissa. Although she suspected, it may have been the photo of the air stewardess that Melissa was keen to get hold of. And Elaine realised she should have taken it the day she discovered it was fake.

However, Mr Chigwell promised he would try to retrieve the ones she had in mind, if it was at all possible.

As it drew closer to Sammy's funeral, the sisters were starting to feel anxious, as it hadn't yet been confirmed. It seemed they were still waiting on the death certificate according to Mr Chigwell. But as they needed to order flowers, the sisters were obviously keen to know when it would be.

'I've tried ringing the funeral directors,' Jill said on the phone to her sister, 'but they told me they weren't allowed to say if a death certificate had been issued or not, evidently this information is only privy to his next of kin.'

'Oh no, here we go again. This bloody law, it's ridiculous!' Elaine groaned.

'However, I did try the crematorium afterwards,' Jill continued, 'and they said she could make a preliminary booking without the death certificate, but as yet they hadn't had confirmation … but they're assuming it will still go ahead. But who knows'.

The following day, Sammy's interment was finally given the go-ahead, even though they apparently still didn't have the certificate. It seemed it was just a formality anyway. Although Mr Chigwell did confirm, he actually died from asphyxiation and not a heart attack as first suspected. But it seemed his body had finally been released.

Chapter 40 - The Funeral.

The day of the funeral was very hot; in fact it was the hottest day on record for May in three hundred years. Needless to say, black was not the ideal colour to wear.

It was also the day after Elaine's birthday and had it not fallen on a Sunday this particular year, in all probability his funeral would have been on that day, which was strange given the accident happened on her birthday too.

The early start had also proved a problem, only most of the mourners who'd come to pay their respects, had travelled a fair distance. While also having to cope with the Monday morning commuters as they fought their way to work, which was always difficult but especially in that heat.

Lawrence and his wife Jackie had been the first to arrive at the crematorium, keen to give their friend the send off, they felt he deserved, they said

The sisters hadn't seen them for some time though and thought at first they'd appeared distant. But after exchanging condolences, they seemed more relaxed, worried perhaps, about emotions spilling over, due to Sammy's unexpected death. Although they too agreed, it had been a blessing in the end.

Lawrence, while waiting for the others to arrive, had already taken a note of the running order for the services that day and pointed out to the sisters, after Sammy's slot, there was in fact a gap of nearly two hours before the next. It seemed the 9 am start hadn't really been necessary.

'So, you mean she picked this time on purpose?' Jill groaned having travelled a distance herself that morning, and was clearly angry by yet another of Melissa's dirty tricks.

'Have a look for yourself.' Lawrence said. 'The running order is up on the board just inside.'

'What do you expect? She's a cow,' Elaine interrupted. 'She knew we all had to travel a long way this morning, and she wasn't going to make it easy. She was probably hoping no one would turn up!'

'Or perhaps it was cheaper,' Jill said.

Elaine also exasperated by Melissa's games turned in disbelief towards her ex-husband, Adam. There not only to support her, but to show his respects to Sammy. As Adam had always been fond of him and even went to visit him on the odd occasion. And he was more than aware of what Melissa was capable of, having seen it himself in the past. So he wasn't surprised by her actions, he said.

A small crowd had now started to gather around the pretty chapel, all sweltering from the heat of the early sun. It appeared however, most of those that made the effort that morning, were from Sammy's immediate family, of which sadly there were only a few. There seemed none from Melissa's side at all - as far as the sisters could tell.

But as promised, two carers from the home turned up, although they kept themselves to themselves. Their focus transfixed on the pretty flowers that lay on the ground outside, no doubt having been told, to stay out of any complicated family disputes.

Then she arrived, dressed head to toe in black. Wearing a fitted black jacket tightly belted at the waist, together with tight black trousers tucked into black knee high boots. And with her cap partially hiding her face, the image she had hoped for, had surely been achieved. But, oh boy, must she have been hot!

Yet still managing to look cool, it was clear, her slim frail body had started to show the signs of age, as she walked towards the small waiting crowd, a lonely solitary figure. But tired of her performances, the small crowd of mourners on seeing her coming, dispersed like clockwork, all going in directions different from hers.

Elaine, not even wanting to acknowledge this strange woman, immediately turned her back. As she knew Melissa wanted nothing more than to steal the show as the grieving black widow. While the last thing Elaine wanted to hear was how upset Melissa was about losing her husband, when she certainly knew different.

All alone, Melissa made her way into the tiny chapel and sat at the front, rocking herself backwards and forwards. While Jill, went in search of the vicar. She wanted to ask if it was possible to give a reading in memory of her brother, only to be told she had to ask his wife's permission first.

Spotting her sat at the front of the chapel, Melissa appeared terribly distraught. But Jill didn't feel inclined to offer comfort, knowing how she'd treated her brother in the past. After all, what did she expect?

'So, where's Kelly then?' Jill asked.

'Oh Jill you're never guess, she went into labour at 6am this morning. My sisters with her now, but I'm really worried. Whoppers they are; big ones… whoppers!'

'Really,' Jill replied, not amused by her story and certainly not interested in more of her lies. She hadn't even mentioned her husband or his passing on this sad day.

'Actually Melissa, I just wanted to ask permission to do a reading for Sammy.' She didn't want to talk about babies anymore, especially not today particularly, as she doubted if they even existed. Melissa didn't appear interested in her reading though and Jill took her vagueness as a yes, convinced, more than ever, Melissa was completely mad and had never cared about her brother at all.

However, Elaine laughed, when she heard the news about Kelly, believing she could have written the script. 'So no surprises there then. I should have had that bet after all, although I suppose Melissa has turned up.'

Standing close by was Lawrence and his wife who were listening with interest to their banter, amazed by their conversation. 'So isn't she pregnant, then?' Lawrence asked.

'I doubt it very much.' Jill replied.

Elaine couldn't believe it. After all this time, they were still being suckered in. But then why shouldn't they believe her? They were decent people; they didn't expect other's to lie about such things.

'Just take whatever Melissa says with a big pinch of salt,' Elaine suggested, and then quickly changed the subject.

With Sammy's service about to start, the small gathering began to assemble into the tiny chapel where Melissa was still seated in the front pew, a lonely pathetic figure - all on her own. Although the lady vicar, who was holding the service did join her briefly, placing her arm around her as she sat by her side.

The sisters glanced at each other knowingly. She was at it again, playing her little games they guessed. Or were they being unfair? Perhaps she did have some feelings after all, only she did look vulnerable sat all alone, still rocking back and forth. Maybe she did miss Sammy.

Elaine placed herself towards the back of the chapel staying close to her ex-husband. She felt her presence was best kept low key as her feelings regarding Melissa were well known and she didn't want confrontations.

The Vicar then started the service by paying her respects to the bereaved, while Elaine kept an eye on Melissa, who showed no interest sat at the front. Although at the mere mention of Sammy's parting, she did suddenly start to shake. Elaine was not convinced by this sudden drama though and couldn't believe her eyes, knowing how little she really cared. Surely she didn't think we'd fall for this. And any feelings of compassion quickly disappeared.

The vicar then announced that Kelly his daughter had gone into labour that morning and of course couldn't be there. Her empathies were clearly honest and certainly sincere as she told those there assembled the news. And Elaine had to wonder what the vicar would think if she really knew the truth. After all, had Melissa actually got a person of 'The Clothe' to lie in church? It was truly unbelievable.

Jill then gave her short eulogy, which was all very nice and then handed back to the vicar, who continued on with the sermon, speaking warmly of Sammy's life. Describing to the small gathering, the type of person he once was - his loves and dislikes and funny things. Although there was talk of strange things too, which didn't seem connected to Sammy and this totally confused the sisters. And by the end of her deliverance, everyone seemed confused, wondering who the hell she was talking about. Had she got the right bloke? But of course they should have known - there was only one person who'd given this information and she was full of lies.

It was when the vicar mentioned Sammy's time in the home and his wife's devotion to him there, that it seemed the carers in attendance could contain themselves no longer, as loud laughter could be heard from the back.

This was ridiculous; it was a farce. How could she do this to Sammy, tainting his memory like this? Still, at least Jill's reading had saved the day.

Closing the sermon, the vicar went on to say, how Sammy would be missed by everyone, especially his wife, Melissa, Kelly his daughter and his sister, Jill.

Elaine immediately picked up on the fact she'd been missed out but chose to ignore it. It was only words after all. But Adam started grumbling and Elaine had to tell him to shush, placing a finger up to her lips. Five minutes later though, the vicar repeated this again and no doubt realising it wasn't a mistake, Lawrence shouted out.

'I'm sorry, but Sammy has another sister; she's seated over there,' and he pointed in Elaine's direction.

Embarrassed at being looked at, as all eyes were now on her, well except for Melissa's of course; Elaine wanted to disappear.

'I'm so sorry, I didn't realise Sammy had another sister,' the vicar said out loud, as she looked over the top of her glasses and down at Elaine.

'That's okay, don't worry,' she replied. 'Sammy knows I'm here, that's all that matters.' And Elaine had to wonder, where these words had come from, while she marvelled at the gift Melissa had handed on a plate. After all she couldn't hide this deliberate nastiness and Elaine smiled to herself as she looked up towards the pretty stained glass windows, with the sun shining through. 'Thank you,' she said quietly.

The vicar smiled at Elaine as she closed Sammy's service, which still seemed unconnected, as was the strange and bizarre music choice that Melissa had selected. One of which sounded almost satanic. Although another made Jill cry, which was the song called 'He's not heavy he's my brother', by the Hollies, only this was also her father's favourite song.

Elaine, not amused by the whole event, turned towards Adam and whispered, 'I know what we'll be playing when Melissa passes on,' and she laughed.

'Oh what's that then?' he asked.

'Ding dong the witch is dead,', and they both burst out laughing.

After the coffin disappeared behind the curtain and the service had finished, everyone stood outside, now talking about the unrecognisable choice of words and the strange music selection. When the vicar approached Elaine wanting

401

to apologise again - explaining that Melissa hadn't told her Sammy had two sisters. 'But she was rather fraught at the time,' she said, as if that excused her.

'I'm sure she was,' Elaine replied, the sarcasm in her voice hopefully not missed and she chose to take it no further. What was the point? Sammy was gone and Melissa had shown herself for what she really was. It was a gift.

Melissa then tried to make her getaway. Away from the hate that she no doubt felt surrounded her. Anyway, she had her grandchildren waiting for her somewhere, didn't she? And a cab she'd apparently booked earlier, suddenly turned up, right on queue. Melissa didn't want to waste anymore of her valuable time with them it seemed.

Picking up the floral cross, which had adorned her husband's coffin only minutes earlier, she placed it in the boot of the cab, obviously to take home with her. Jill, then seizing her opportunity to say her piece, ran over to Melissa and grabbed her arm – after all this could be her last chance to speak to her and Elaine close by listened

'I'm taking the cross home with me Jill, so I can place it in the garden by your mother's rose bush; which incidentally is where I intend to place Sammy's ashes too, I thought he would like that.' But Melissa sounded nervous and clearly thought she'd been caught out taking the cross away, and looked embarrassed by her actions.

'Yes, I'm sure,' Jill said, still wanting to say her bit, but Melissa carried on unperturbed.

'Because you know I will never sell that house Jill, not with your mother's ashes there,' and as she got into the cab eager to leave, Jill placed her hand on her shoulder. Melissa, who probably thought she'd fooled her again, took hold of Jill's hand and looked her in the eye - as Jill finally got to say her piece.

'Well Melissa it's taken you eight years, but you've got what you wanted at last.'

But Melissa didn't bat an eyelid. It seemed Jill's comment went straight over her head, although the vicar at her side certainly must have heard it.

Still ignoring Jill's remark, Melissa made a sign for the driver to leave; keen to make her escape, while Jill made her way back to the group who were listening intently close by.

'So, no invites back to her place, then,' Elaine laughed.

'Doesn't look like it, sis,'

'She seems to have got away with everything again,' Elaine said complaining once again and she could only hope she'd get her comeuppance in the end and soon.

'Maybe she'll be made to pay back some of that tax payers money spent on Sammy's care.' Elaine said disgruntled. 'As no doubt she'll be selling that house now, especially after she said she wouldn't.'

'I don't understand how she's managed to get away with not paying towards his keep anyway,' Jill replied, 'or is that why she didn't want Sammy in rehabilitation. Mental care is a different set up I've heard.'

'Well she's getting plenty of money from Sammy's pension. I wouldn't mind some of that,' Elaine added. 'I think she could at least have contributed something, as I don't think she's even been living in that house.'

'Yes, I agree … and then at least that would be some kind of comeuppance,' Jill replied, 'although I would like to be there to see it, just for poor Sammy's sake.'

'Well... they do say 'what goes round comes around' Aunty',' Jill's daughter Tessa, butted in, having overheard their conversation. She was eager to get home now she said. She was putting on a spread.

But Tessa's comment had made Elaine think back to the day she'd sent her brother that letter, when she'd tried to warn him about his wife, which was just after their father had tried to take his life. In fact she remembered she'd written those very same words. So perhaps Karma will pay back again, as it certainly had for Sammy.

Given Tessa lived the closest to the crematorium, arrangements had been made for everyone to meet up at her house, to enjoy a drink or two, on behalf of Sammy and his sudden departure. He was at last at peace and that was definitely worth celebrating.

So, slowly one by one they started to leave the sombre scene - the final act of Sammy's sad passing.

'Did you notice the wig Melissa was wearing, Aunty?' Tessa said laughing as they started to walk away. 'It was actually attached to her hat!'

'I thought her hair looked rather thick. I can't believe she wore it in this heat,' and Elaine laughed at the thought, keen to move on from the heavy mood of the day.

Making their way towards their cars Elaine began to reflect over her brother's sad life again and rightly so, agonised over the archaic laws of the country.

'It seems to me, the laws of this land are set up mainly to protect the perpetrator.' Elaine moaned again, turning towards her sister for acknowledgement. 'It's ridiculous that the next of kin has the only and final say.'

'Yes you're right, sis … all this would never have happened if she hadn't been in control at all times. With the law always backing her up, we never stood a chance. We pointed out ages ago, she was the main problem.'

'And we all know they knew she wasn't right in the head … so you do have to question …whose really to blame for Sammy's demise?' Elaine was angry. 'I mean, not even one nurse or carer would speak out… too frightened to lose their jobs I suspect. And that can't be right.'

Jill looked thoughtful. 'Yes it does seem ludicrous.'

'Oh well, he's out of it now,' Tessa said, interrupting again, and placing her arm around her mother, she suggested they should go.

Leaving fairly swiftly they were quickly followed by the few left behind – consisting mainly of immediate family plus a few close friends.

Back at Tessa's house they all sat and chatted, going over once more their fond memories of Sammy. And after a few comforting words and some much needed nibbles, they all lifted up their glasses and drank to his memory. To which they all agreed, 'although forgotten by many, he would never be forgotten by those who truly cared,' a final ending to Sammy's sad story.

Epilogue

Melissa got out of the cab relieved to be home at last. The home she'd spent most of her time in over the last, six to seven years. Removing the flowers from the boot of the car, she placed the cross on the garage floor and took the yellow roses out one by one ready to place in a vase.

'No point in wasting them,' she groaned, making her way through the back door and into the kitchen.

'Hello, love, I'm home,' she shouted. 'Do you fancy a cuppa? … I'm really parched.'

'No thanks,' a voice called back from the lounge, the noise from the television heard in the back ground.

Taking off her hat and jacket, Melissa put on the kettle and waited for it to boil – now deep in thought.

Drained by the heavy heat of the day, in more ways than one, she poured the boiling water into the cups, pleased she'd completed her last performance as the grief stricken wife. Sammy could be put to rest and forgotten about at last.

Hot and exhausted Melissa struggled to take off her boots.

'Give me a hand with these love,' she shouted. 'I'm really quite tired.'

Kelly got up from the settee in order to help her mother. The settee she'd been attached to for most of the morning and a place she spent most of her time in it seemed.

Struggling to pull off her mother's boots, she never once mentioned her father; perhaps not even knowing the cremation had happened that day.

'Have you heard from Granny or Aunty Julie this morning?' Melissa asked pushing her long red hair away from her face. 'They said they might come to visit us later this week.'

'No,' Kelly replied, 'but Steve rang … he's going to be home late this evening.'

Kelly turned her attention back on the programme she'd been watching in the lounge earlier and Melissa decided to join her. Sat down beside her deep in thought again, she sipped at her tea.

'Remind me tomorrow to ring the estate agent, love; it will be interesting to see how much we can get for our old house. It might even be nice to buy a little holiday place right near Granny. The fresh sea air will do us both good.'

Kelly nodded in agreement, probably not daring to contradict her mother and anyway it appeared the programme she was watching was far more interesting.

Remembering the flowers she'd left on the garage floor, Melissa quickly got up to retrieve them. On opening the door, she was hit full force by the heavy heat within this closed area - like a furnace sucking her in. And she scrunched up her nose at the sweet sickly stench that now filled the garage.

Then she noticed the flowers lying there, now turned a putrid brown – the foliage decayed and withered. While the crumpled leaves shed like tears lay scattered untidily around.

Not happy, she picked them up and placed the mess in the bin.

'That didn't last long,' she moaned, 'and it was expensive too,' and she gagged at the smell which still lingered.

Making her way back to the lounge, Melissa sat down next to her daughter feeling relaxed at last and not having to act any longer.

'So is there anything good on the television this afternoon Kelly; any films worth watching?'

Kelly's eyes remained fixed on the screen as she passed her mother the TV guide, knowing full well she'd want full control, no doubt and she never said a word.

Melissa cast her eyes down the long list of programmes and suddenly started to laugh, as she read out loud 'Unsolved crimes'. 'I think we should watch that later,' and she snuggled up close to her daughter who kept very quiet.

Six months later, unbeknown to the family, Melissa placed the house on the market, the house which had once been Sammy's lovely home. The house she said she would never sell and the house where their mother's ashes still hopefully lay and supposedly their brothers; if they were ever picked up.

When the news of the sale eventually got back to the sisters, although not via Melissa, they were certainly not shocked by her decision to sell yet definitely curious. And they eagerly searched the website, 'Right move' keen to see how the house was now looking. If the rumours were true,

Melissa had let it go ever since Sammy's accident, rarely having lived there they'd heard.

But as she and her daughter were still seen about, the sisters thought she must be living close by. And suspected she'd moved in with her rock, although it was never confirmed.

Like a trip down memory lane, the sisters scrutinised the photos in front of them looking for clues. And noticed the garden, which had once been kept immaculate was completely overgrown. While the place where their mother's Rose bush stood was now covered in a mass of weeds.

On scanning the rooms by way of a virtual tour, the sisters were amazed that the property appeared devoid of most of its furniture and was therefore obvious Melissa wasn't living there. As in the main bedroom, which Melissa once said, she'd changed from its oriental decor; was now completely empty. Except for one solitary picture of a Chinese lady that hung in the centre of the wall, which still smiled sweetly at them. A picture that once looked down on a married couple as they lay in their bed below - a moment in time 'soon forgotten' and becoming a distant memory.

Elaine then realised, Melissa must have moved out around the same time Sammy moved into the home all those years ago. When she'd adorned his room with the disregarded Chinese figures, which the sisters had thought at the time was an unusually kind gesture for her.

Could this woman really be as calculating as she appeared? Or was she just plain evil? The sisters would always wonder.

Still seen occasionally in the area, they were often spotted walking hand in hand - but never with any babies in tow.

Although it was confirmed during a telephone conversation between Jill and Melissa shortly after their brother's cremation, that Kelly had given birth to a girl and a boy, giving them both names and birth weights.

Yet their names could have been Twiddle Dee and Twiddle Dumb for all Jill cared, as she guessed she was still being lied to. And even though certainly curious, she didn't want to listen to her twaddle anymore - before she'd had no option.

Wrapped up in her stories however, Melissa still carried on regardless as she continued to tell Jill ...

'Kelly's moving to Scotland tomorrow to be with her new boyfriend.' she said all excited.

'Oh that's nice,' Jill replied, the sarcasm hopefully not missed. And she realised this was probably mentioned just in case she suggested a visit to see the new babies.

'I promise to send you some photographs,' she said but of course they never came. And Jill hasn't heard from Melissa or her daughter since then, which didn't surprise her at all.

A couple of years on, Melissa often get's seen around the local area. Her daughter not so often though. The sisters had often wondered what happened to her - perhaps she was in Scotland after all but they doubted it very much.

Yet on the odd occasion, when Kelly was spotted, out and about, it was said she resembled, a little old lady - frumpy, dowdy and very overweight and sporting a short, curly perm - a slightly darker colour than her mothers. In fact she looked more like Melissa's mother, than the young twenty three years old that she was now. And the sisters had to wonder -was this what Melissa had wanted?

Concerned for Kelly, the sisters would often wonder what else they could have done to help this young lady she'd now become? Who just like her father they suspected, had been trapped and systematically conditioned over the years. As sadly, mental cruelty, if indeed it was, is hard to detect at times, although can be just as destroying. Yet who will be there to set her free?

Thinking back though, Elaine also had to wonder who really was to blame for Kelly's situation. As she remembered all too clearly what Sue, the social worker had said to her, all those years ago – "You cannot save everyone, Mrs Bowers". She would never forget those words. Was this young girl's life really not worth saving? Apparently not it seemed and the sisters often thought, what may have become of her now, still under the control of her mother? Let's hope she really was in Scotland.

It was a shame they couldn't have helped her more though, but without the backing of social services, there was nothing they could have done for this young lady - who could be their brother's child, their niece. And they could only console themselves with the fact, she probably knew no different. But was she really happy to take her father's place - subservient to her mother?

It was shortly after the news of the house sale; the sisters heard rumours, of a man playing darts in one of the local pubs, bragging that Kelly was his daughter. It would seem the man in question, looked just like Melissa's rock; the man she'd turned to all those years ago and further back they guessed and this didn't surprise the sisters. But what could they do?

As time went by and Melissa became a distant memory, the sisters would sometimes think, perhaps they'd been wrong to judge her – perhaps they'd possibly misunderstood her and unintentionally read her wrong. After all, no one in Reigate had picked up on her strange behaviour. Or had they, they wondered?

Elaine however, could never really believe she was the innocent party, as she was more than certain her actions were those of a psychopath. Or even someone just plain 'evil'?

So let's leave that for society to decide, or those that set up the systems or even those that make up the laws? For the sisters were more than sure they'd all been complicit in some way, in the death of their dear brother.

It was on the day new people moved into what was once Sammy's lovely home, Elaine lost a diamond from her mother's ring. The ring she'd worn every day for over twenty five years – in fact ever since her mother died.

Confused and yet amazed by this strange synchronistic event and its possible symbolic meaning, Elaine began to wonder -

Maybe it was time to move on now ... perhaps even time to forget, now that their poor brother Sammy would surely become, a man SOON FORGOTTEN.'

THE END.

Authors note.

Several years after this story ended, Elaine went to visit a Medium. She would often go from time to time, whenever she fancied a reading. On her visit, the Medium who knew nothing of her brother or his death, told Elaine that he was there with them now and had come with a message.

Elaine was intrigued as the Medium then told her, 'He wants to tell you he is ashamed.'

She had no idea why he felt this way though, as he had suffered greatly, himself. But then she remembered the letter she'd sent him all those years ago when their father had tried to take his life. She had told him then that he should be ashamed for the way he'd treated their father. She never did get a reply, until today.

Elaine, amazed by this sudden reveal, smiled knowingly, finding comfort in the fact he was still around her today. But perhaps he could now move on.

Printed in Great Britain
by Amazon